# voXpop

## The New Generation X Speaks

# voXpop

## The New Generation X Speaks

*Jayne Miller*

*Virgin*

First published in Great Britain in 1995 by
Virgin Books
an imprint of Virgin Publishing Ltd
332 Ladbroke Grove
London W10 5AH

ISBN 0 86369 784 4

Typeset by TW Typesetting, Plymouth, Devon
Printed and bound in Great Britain by
Cox & Wyman Ltd, Reading, Berks

# Contents

'It makes you realise how unfriendly, how uncaring, cities
are. No caged animal is a happy animal.'
'You get used to cold baths or filling them up with the
kettle.'

'Are skinheads thugs? You get nutters in all youth cults, aggro often comes with the territory.'

'The crop, boots and braces are what make us famous. It's a working-class uniform.'

'The likes of Shabba Ranks are nothing compared to the originals, but at least the music is getting a play.'

'We're not louts now.'

'We're a conservative lot on the whole.'

'I've got long blonde hair and so has my friend Judy, but we ride our own bikes.'

'I am an Essex boy – I've got the old Essex mentality – anywhere, any place, any time!'

'Where I come from, and probably where most people come from, the bulk of the trouble is caused by women.'

'A lot of girls like the rough look.'

'I don't call myself a teenybopper, but Mark is gorgeous! It's his fault, he shouldn't have a body like that.'

'There's not much to do at home – local pub, friends' houses, so it's worth saving up for this [Glastonbury].'

'Honey tastes nicer than chemicals.'

'I've got lots of lovely lingerie, I spend a lot on it, over £1000 last year.'

'My father goes in and gets them for me – I can't go into a newsagent and pick up *Penthouse*!'

'What do I think about Aids? That's a bit heavy, isn't it?'

'MPs are so out of touch with everything else that's going on in the real world, how could they be in touch with the nation's sexual preferences?'

'I worked on the switchboard of a rent boy agency. You know, people phone up for a boy, say the type they are looking for.'

For Marley and Alby

# Introduction

Thirty years ago a book called *Generation X* canvassed the views of a cross-section of the newly christened teenagers and twentysomethings of the sixties about their attitudes and lifestyles – their music, jobs, aspirations and views on politics, God, sex and life in Britain. This is the nineties version – a collection of comments and conversations from Britain's current crop of 18–25-year-olds.

When *Generation X* was published it was a crucial changing era for the interviewees – coming affluence, more varied education and job prospects and their own youth market gave a naïve glow of expectancy to their comments.

The term 'Generation X' was hijacked by American writer Douglas Coupland for the title of his first novel in 1992. Rather ironically, it has now become a commonly-used label for the slacker generation of the US, that is, those born between the late 1960s and late 1970s. However, it's very likely that Coupland gained the inspiration for his title from Billy Idol's punk band of the same name – itself inspired by the original book of 1964 which was compiled by Charles Hamblett and Jane Deverson.

And so to the nineties. Thatcher's children – for most have grown up under her leadership, never witnessing life under Labour – are they really lazy, self-centred and convinced that society owes them a living? Times have changed significantly in the last 30 years, more school-leavers can expect to go on to further education and training, but what can they expect at the end of it? The unemployed of the nineties aren't just those who didn't pay attention at school, as their sixties counterparts were warned, but highly qualified and sussed young people.

Many of them are disenchanted, some are disenfranchised but increasingly they're doing something positive to help themselves, in spite of, not because of, what society has to offer and often without back-up or support from the system. DIY Culture is a phrase that comes up and applies time and time again.

Music in 1964 was bluebeat, Mod, Mersey beat and rock and roll, with references to Mods and Rockers and the Junction Boys scattered throughout the original *Generation X*. Pop-pickers were just starting to swing. Now we've a richer music and youth cult network, with a plethora of styles of music and dress. Grunge, Goth, hippy, reggae, dance, hip hop, pop and indie fans, ravers, crusties and queens make an appearance. Mods and rockers never die, they're here but many defy categorisation ... like the scooterist who's into raves. The right to be an individual is a strong motivating force, and here's a collection of them. Read their stories.

Pizza deliveries, working in McDonald's and hours spent on Sonic the Hedgehog; fanzines, comics, Aids, peace camps, travellers and car hijacking – these were never mentioned in the *Generation X* of 1964 ... and the racial mix is entirely different. Drugs and crime are still around but the allegiance has altered. What else has changed?

The willing talkers featured here come from all walks of life and all areas. Some chatted with me face to face and some on the phone. They weren't given a list of questions survey-style, rather a chance to tell their 'story' or rant about what they felt was important to them, so there's no uniformity to the conversations. Hence the chapter listing is loose. Political issues, music preferences and social comments fall within each section, so the chapters are a kind of rough guide to lifestyle!

Most people were happy about having their identities revealed, though about 20 per cent preferred a pseudonym so they felt happier discussing their lives, problems and attitudes frankly without fear of reprisal, but the ages and occupations are correct.

I haven't commented on anyone's viewpoints at all, nor altered their comments in any way, and editing has been minimal to allow the reader to get a clearer picture of the individual. There are many lengthy discourses punctuated by a few sound-bites – as in the sections on Sex, Politics and Religion, where pertinent comments from people featured elsewhere in the book have been collected together for the reader's convenience.

At times, looking at the collection of conversations, it's hard not to feel saddened by the lack of opportunity and hardships faced by so many talented young people. But few of them come across as depressed, lethargic and embittered. Some are refreshingly original in their approaches and style, revealing a sparkle and humour that makes you laugh out loud (well, they made me smile), some people seem to possess a droll sense of fun that makes even hard-bitten cynics look at life afresh. For the most part they share a common bond, the will to find a way through. And I'm sure that included here are some people who will be talents of the future – in music, art, dance, film or whatever their walk of life. You'll spot them – not by huge egos jumping off the pages, but by a fighting spirit; a biting determination to succeed.

Again and again I was struck by people's willingness to chat openly and lucidly about themselves and their attitudes – with no bribes! Though I have to admit that occasionally when I approached people in the street, pub or shop, I was told to 'go away' – or words to that effect. But then, their comments aren't preserved for posterity. This isn't intended to be a survey of viewpoints of all 16–25-year-olds in Britain, just a glimpse at the lifestyles and concerns of a wide and varied cross-section and a reflection of Britain in the early nineties. The newspaper cuttings help put the comments in historical context. And hopefully people will be able to use *VoXpop* as a valid and interesting comparison with youth in another 30 years' time.

I would like to say thank you to everyone who gave their time and chatted openly with me.

# 1 School Shorts – Education

Nationwide, only 11 per cent of university undergraduates (including those of the former polytechnics) and 19 per cent (excluding them) were educated at public schools, according to the Department for Education.

A spokeswoman for the National Union of Students recently expressed concern about this. 'The expansion of higher education is still targeted at the upper-middle classes,' she said. 'Public school students get a lot more encouragement to apply for top universities.' (*Guardian*)

Ministers have always argued that they are providing enough cash for the universities to meet their target of one in three of the 18–21 age group entering higher education by the year 2000, compared with one in eight in 1979.

But the public spending crisis, and the signs that demand for university places will outstrip forecasts, has prompted a rethink.

Students and their families have been paying towards maintenance costs for years, but all tuition has been free since the mid-1970s. (*Guardian*)

School-leavers are now so badly educated and sloppily dressed that two of the country's biggest store chains are looking for older people to fill job vacancies.

Both Dixons and John Lewis are thinking seriously about only recruiting people in their early twenties, claiming many 16-year-olds cannot spell and have no idea how to dress for an interview. (*Daily Express*)

Trendy teachers were blamed yesterday for turning out a generation of dunces who cannot find Britain on a map.

A shock survey showed one in ten 17-year-olds could not pin-point their country. (*Sun*)

## James, 18, schoolboy, Bradford

I'm in my last year of A levels, which is not a pleasant time. I'm doing English, German, French and a philosophy

5

AS level which is half an A level. Myself and the group of friends I have here feel a general dislike for school. It would probably apply to any school just as much as here. We feel we're treated like children. Perhaps that's slightly unfair, but some of the common rules and regulations forced on us just shouldn't be necessary for 18-year-olds.

In your last two years at school, you don't have to wear the regular uniform, but you do have to wear a tie and sports jacket, which isn't exactly your own everyday clothing. We have to come in for registration every morning then go to religious assembly. Even if we do make more of an effort to put our ideas across, nothing we do or have to say is taken seriously. There are no meetings between teachers and sixth form to discuss changes or that sort of thing. It's difficult to get rules changed, it's established tradition.

We are not allowed to smoke at all on the premises – anywhere. We don't have a common room at all, and you're only allowed out of school during the lunch-break. You can find places to smoke if you have to, but it's not allowed! You can see why a lot of 16–18-year-olds go to sixth form college. I kept wondering whether I should have gone to one. But, staying on at school does have benefits. Sixth form college is all about self-motivation and I'm devoid of that really, and the school forces you to do work!

There's also a tradition at this school of applying to Oxford or Cambridge. Plenty of people go on to one or the other, and people who don't consider Oxford or Cambridge as the be all and end all are frowned upon. Originally I intended to apply for Cambridge and then decided not to. I was looked down on – by teachers and certain people in the school, they think you've let yourself down.

I suppose I will stick it out, stay at school for the last few months as I'm not sure what else I could do if I left, and then I'll go to university – follow the path laid out for me by my teachers and parents. I can choose my own degree at least. Throughout school it's taken as read that you'll go to university. It's only over the past few months that I've realised there are other options, but you get the impression that the school would regard you as a failure if you didn't. I've come to realise that that's not the case – you're not a failure; it's your choice.

Even so, I will go, if I pass my exams, mostly for my parents. I am quite scared of my parents. They are very lenient and good to me – probably because they don't know everything I get up to. I do respect them to a degree. I bet all people of my age say this, but I don't think they know best. I don't think they understand the youth of to-day – it sounds a hackneyed phrase but it's true! They take a dim view of certain things young people do that they don't know anything about.

Certainly, if they asked me what I thought about drugs, I'd pretend to them that I'm as anti-drugs as they are, but I'm not at all, it's just that I know if they thought I ad-vocated the use of them, they'd think I was taking them and curtail my freedom. Life wouldn't be worth living then. I'm totally financially dependent on them, so they could stop me doing things by taking money away. They are very good financially. They give me money every week, and I've got a bank account with quite a lot of money in it, some of which is my savings, but a lot of it they have put in for me, and I draw on that regularly, if I want clothes and stuff. I'm not interested in saving, I'll wait until I'm older.

They don't tell me what I can and can't do. They frown on me if I go out during week nights, but as it's close to my exams and I've got an awful lot of work to do, I wouldn't go out during the week anyway. But last term I did. There was a certain amount of resistance but they wouldn't stop me. There's only a certain amount they could do to stop me – I've got my own car, etc. I go to Manchester a lot, which my mum doesn't like.

They think it's a good thing for me to go to university away from home, to get my independence. I'm definitely looking forward to it, mostly for not having to be in the position I am now of having to lie a lot to them. When I'm no longer financially dependent on them, they won't be able to have control over me in the same way or over my spending.

I spend most of my money on socialising – going to raves. I don't spend as much on clothes as many of my friends. We've all got various looks, some typical rave, some more clubby gear. Some of my friends spend a fortune on designer labels like Paul Smith shirts. I'm not into labels, I wear things like older Adidas T-shirts and Adidas Gazelle trainers. Leeds, which isn't far from Bradford, has some quite good places, plenty of variety. Occasionally I'll go on a spree, but it's shopping once in a while, not every week.

I lie about my social life. If I said I was going to a night-club in Manchester it's different than saying I'm going to a rave. If I said I was going to a rave they'd say 'you're not going any more'. They presuppose all sorts of things about them that they don't about clubs, mostly to do with drugs. They've not been, so they don't know the full picture. You could get drugs at a night-club too, but it happens to a greater degree at a rave. So I don't say I go to raves – they would stop me – just by taking the money away, and that would be it.

I lie a lot. I don't want to, but they wouldn't understand. Most stuff I do is illegal. The raves are legal ones – the one I go to most Saturdays only goes on until 3 a.m.; it's more what I do. I take a lot of Ecstasy for someone at my school. I've taken a few other things too, whiz (amphetamines) and dope. That's illegal – but as far as I can see the grounds for marijuana, at least, being illegal are ridiculous, it's far less harmful than drinking. I think Ecstasy and amphetamines – all drugs – should be legal, because I feel everyone has the right to take what they want to. It would cut down on the purified and mixed E going around if there was some control on it, and cut down on the drug-related offences.

I consider them a perfectly fine form of recreation. Unlike alcohol there's no third-party effect. I wouldn't beat anyone up. People I know who drink get into fights and vandalism. There's never any trouble at raves, the majority of people are happy and friendly, there's a great feeling, unlike at certain pubs and clubs.

Manchester has still got a really good rave scene, it's a really good place to go out, very mixed crowd and great DJs. There's no alcohol at the one I go to regularly so there's no age limit, mostly people are 16 to mid-20s though there are some in their 30s and 40s! It's a tenner to get into and although you don't buy alcohol, soft drinks and water are very expensive – compared to what you'd pay in a shop.

Drugs are very popular there. I almost always get Es from someone I know. I'm not so worried about whiz, I get that off anybody. I know it's stupid, but I wouldn't risk it with Es. Even so, I know the stuff in the Es I take isn't always MDMA because the effect varies so much; often it's like a tranquilliser.

Apart from raves, I don't go out a lot. Occasionally I'll go to the pub, but not often; I'm not a big fan of drinking.

I used to go and see bands, but not any more. I like dance music and rave now, not hardcore, mostly garage and progressive. I listen to some stuff from the sixties, I'm quite into the Beatles. Before I became a raver I used to be a sixties revivalist. I've only been into rave about seven months. I have been in a band in the past, with some schoolfriends, and when I was into that scene, I used to think rave was laughable. Until I went to one! The very first one I went to, I got turned on to it. The atmosphere is so good, the music and the dancing. I really enjoy dancing. Now going to see bands just isn't enjoyable.

There aren't that many modern bands I like. I like Primal Scream – though they're dance and St Etienne and The Stone Roses are a great band, they're the best band and I hope they come back and continue to make music as good as their first album. A lot of the indie music is really awful, really, really bad, it's unpleasant. So I suppose I don't buy many records!

I'm not worried about moving away from my friends and the rave scene here, I'm more apprehensive about making new friends. The friends I have now I consider to be very good ones so I'm sure we'll stay in touch, and as they're mostly at school with me, they're all moving away to different universities themselves. I'm going to Nottingham which is supposed to have a good club scene, and apparently everyone gets into clubs when they grow out of raves!

I'm studying sociology, though I've no idea what I want to be, which is quite a problem. Ideally something that will give me a good lifestyle! I'd like to be a writer, but I appreciate you can't just leave university, write a book and make a fortune. Not that I'm materialistic, I just want a good standard of life. Really, I think that by the time I leave university, marijuana will be legalised and I can start up a little café and do something with that!

## Clara Barnes-Gutteridge, 15, Stirling

I'm studying for O levels at the moment – English, maths, physics, chemistry, French, German, art and history; then it will be A levels. Scotland still has that system. I want to go to university as I want to work in psychology. It will definitely not be in Stirling! I want to move away, I hate it here.

My parents won't stop me going to university or living in another part of the country, though they will miss me. I'll never come back to Stirling – apart from to see my parents! Maybe I don't like the place as I've grown up here. It's a nice place if you're a tourist, but it's too small to live in, though there are a lot of people who just don't want to move . . . There are loads of people who grow up here and go to Stirling High, leave, stay here and then send their kids to Stirling High. It's depressing.

I much prefer London to Stirling, it's a dull life here. I'm not saying that because I imagine London's a great place – I go there a lot more than most people who don't live there; my aunt and other family live in London, so I stay regularly. There's such a wide range of things to do, whereas Stirling has one town centre, it's so small there's not much there and if you don't want to see particular people, you know you can't avoid them so you don't go out. It's just so small and narrow in outlook too.

There are pubs, clubs and stuff, as far as places for us to go, but it's just that it's so narrow-minded. I'm quite grungy – and my friends are mostly like that as well, a lot of them don't go to my school so we meet up on the weekends. I've got purple and pink hair at the front and a few of my friends have different hairstyles but as none of them are at my school, there I'm a 'weirdo'. It's only a hairstyle! I don't think the teachers care about looks. Teachers think I'm eccentric. If I ramble on about politics or morals, they think if they don't question me, I'll shut up! I'm not given to rambling on all the time, it's just that I do have a viewpoint about most things, and if people discuss it, then I'm keen to join in. People think I'm strange because of that. Why should it be unusual for people my age to have a point of view? It's just that I'm not as apathetic as a lot of people.

A lot of my schoolfriends never listen to the news and don't care whether they vote. I find I'm probably being too judgemental about people. If they aren't interested and don't know what's happening, I wouldn't be as well disposed to them. Having said that, I'm not at all judgemental about looks. I have a rule whereby I try not to be particularly biased about people just because I wear weird clothes . . . it doesn't affect the way I see them.

Music's important to me; I buy a lot of records – usually going to Glasgow to get them. I'm more into indie music and stuff, though I have friends who like rave and they go to a few rave clubs. There are still a lot of raves around here, though there are hassles and you often have to travel to Edinburgh and Glasgow. One club I go to quite regularly has a rock night, which is more heavy metal; my friends go there so I'll go along too, even though I prefer the frenzy of indie music. Round here it's more pubs that have indie nights rather than proper clubs, they put on different nights to attract different crowds. I'm not into music enough to be in a band, though I have a lot of friends who are in bands. Well, they say they are, but they never practise and no one plays anything! One of them plays bass so they form a band – it's like that! It's not really a hotbed of talent – there are a few up and coming bands in Stirling, but they won't get anywhere!

I read a lot – not the so-called teenage novels by people like Stephen King; I've never read anything by him. I prefer proper adult novels, classics, like George Orwell's *1984* and *Catcher in the Rye*.

There is a lot of violence in some parts of Stirling: there's a tough area, with a few murders lately, and there is trouble on one big council estate. It's like anywhere, there are areas that you wouldn't go to at night. There are people who hang around and if someone looks different they'll get battered. One of my friends got a black eye because he went to one of the dodgy areas and looked different, it's just casuals who do it. Quite a lot of my friends have been chased by the casuals who just pick on 'hippies', as they call them.

I'm not opposed to the countryside – I wouldn't mind living in the countryside near a big city, and I'd like to travel and see more of the world, hopefully when I'm at university, in the holidays, making use of those student discounts and travel cards.

I rely on my parents for money at the moment. I don't have a Saturday job – I babysit occasionally, but that's all. I worked in a chip shop once but it was horrible, all weird people coming in, and the smell! I stuck it out one night, and that was the training night, when they teach you how to wrap chips . . .

Unemployment is high here, but then unemployment is a problem everywhere. I don't really know any unemployed people – but most of my peer group haven't got there yet; my parents have a few friends who are. Even though I know unemployment's a problem and a large percentage of university graduates won't get work – especially the kind of work they want to do – I'm still going to university. I think I might as well do it, for myself, and there's even less choice of jobs if you haven't been. Without a degree, you end up doing a job you don't want to do.

## Mukrash, 19, Canterbury

I can't go out any more. I'm grounded, since I came in at 5 o'clock in the morning. I know I ruined it for myself. I'm at King's College studying chemistry. I was in digs for the first year, but I spent all my allowance and time, going out, drinking and having a good time. Now I'm living back at home with my parents in Kent and have to travel to London to college. I'm working hard at the moment – I flunked my exams the first year and had to retake them. Now if I don't work hard, they'll stop me continuing with the course. I don't mind being back at home, it makes a change, you get into a routine, it's a bit boring but it's cheaper and everything's done for you. Living away from home – everything gets to you, you can keep going out, but you have all the washing, cleaning and stuff to do!

My parents don't have a set career pattern for me, though they expect me to get a good job and do well. They've worked hard and spent a lot of money, and they expect me to work hard too. They'll always give me money for studying – but not for socialising. I'm hoping to do research, scientific research, though I wouldn't mind working in industry, they pay better there!

## Anraj, 19, Gravesend

I study economics at a college in Gravesend. It's funny, the English students sit on one side, the Indians on the other, it's like a half-way split. And if an Indian sits on the English side, they call him a coconut – black on the outside and white inside! They do mix, but they're just taking the mickey out of each other. It's friendly really. I don't have a Saturday job, I have no source of income except for my parents. I go out a bit, I still go to the day-time gigs and some evening ones – they're the proper ones for those living away from home! They're a good laugh, I get pissed! Whoops – well, let's say everyone goes home a bit merry . . . happy. Indian girls aren't allowed to drink, though a lot of them do. It's like everything. Parents don't know, they go home and go to sleep. They're all secret, you find out by word of mouth. A DJ or Gravesend person organises it, if it gets out, the parents go round and have a go, complain they're leading their son or daughter astray! So it's all word of mouth. Seriously, they've been round to my mate's house. They could stop them, stop the DJ. So rumours go round the group of people who go to it.

## Jonathan, 18, Bradford

I'm still at school doing A levels in Russian, French, maths and maths with further maths. I want to do Russian at university. We've got a broad-minded Russian teacher, he covers anything we need to know about the social, economic and political set-up. He took 20 of us to Moscow and Leningrad and we got to visit a school. They really resent Westerners there; the fact that we seem to have a lot more material things, they weren't very friendly! Eating was a problem, though I think I had a better deal as a vegetarian, though they tend to stick meat even in vegetable soups, but at least I didn't get the chunks of fat.

I've had offers for the School of Slavonic Studies in London, and I've done the entrance exam for Oxford, though I feel I've done badly in it. The school more or less expects you to take the exam to get in, they're interested in getting as many people in as possible, for their reputation. But at least if I went, I'd go to St Anne's College which is the least public school of the Oxford colleges, it's more like a normal university.

Sixty or so pupils apply. To a certain extent I think that's bad because it's arrogance to think that more people from just one school will go. For a lot of people, it's their automatic choice, but there is a pressure to go to Oxford or Cambridge. I don't know which one I'd really prefer –

Oxford might be useful for contacts and meeting people, but being in London is a more exciting prospect. Neither of the two colleges, St Anne's at Oxford or the Slavonic School, are campus places, so you won't have so many students around and it's hard to develop outside interests. I don't want to be at Christchurch or one of the other famous colleges – all intellectually stimulating places, posh architecture and posh people. Though I'd enjoy St Anne's, I think the Slavonic School seems more interesting. It seems to offer better subjects, not just the language. I'd like to do Russian plus Polish/Ukrainian ... and I'm really into literature.

I don't have that much time to read other stuff outside of my course work and related books ... I've got a massive stack of old *NME*s to go through and loads of books to catch up on!

Apart from my reading, my social life has suffered, though I never really went out during the week and as I work in a pizza fast food place on Sundays, doing an eight-hour shift, it only really leaves Friday and Saturday night.

If I go out, I like to see bands. I respect the Velvet Underground, though Lou Reed is changing. I usually go to Leeds as that offers a better selection than Bradford, and I always plan to go to Reading Festival – though I've never made it there yet.

Leeds is really quite hip. I'm prepared to travel as far as Leeds, I go to underground stuff. I can't drive yet so I have to get a lift or go by train. Russian music isn't an option, they all idolise Iron Maiden – it's metallic and if there's a gig by anyone from outside Moscow, about two million people rush to see it and that's bands I wouldn't find very exciting if I was a Russian. They are into New Wave and punk but it's not the same as here ...

I mostly shop in Leeds, there are lots of Goth shops and record shops and good second-hand stockists. Leeds has strong connections with certain Goth bands like Sisters of Mercy, Andrew Eldridge and The Mission, so I suppose the influence is there. I usually wear darkish clothes, I like black, especially velvet jackets. I don't go in for the complete Goth and I'm not grunge. I used to be a Goth and people who don't know me in the pub might think I was grunge but I'm not. You don't dress up·to be grunge – it defeats the object really!

I get a clothing allowance of £34 a month for my own clothes and we have to wear a uniform of sorts to school: dark trousers, school tie, velvet jacket – that's my bit. I'd wear a uniform anyway, people take the piss if you dress differently.

I used to be in a band with a guy at school . . . I still sing in a band. We're called Pseudopod. I like it because when you write it down it's almost symmetrical. We've played a few gigs, not masses, but it's tailed off while the A levels are approaching. We've played two university venues, a cellar bar plus a seated hall with 500 capacity. We've not exactly made a fortune – we got about £15 each for supporting Kinky Machine one time. It's very unlikely that I'd follow a music career, we're crap! Well, that's not fair. We're a three-piece, the drummer's got a deal, the bassist is going to Oxford, so I don't think there's a future. It's hard to find mainstream parallels for Pseudopod – a mixture of slow Nick Drake songs and fast Sonic Youth. Nick Drake songs are all folky – mandolins and obscure instruments. I suppose everyone says this, but we are not like any other band.

I sing, except that I can't, it adds to the punk element. We have songs with cute words about holding hands and eating ice cream but they're not harmonious. It's kind of jingly jangly with parts of Sonic Youth. We've had a bit of a following and been written about in a fanzine – *The Blaze* – so our fan base is really acquaintances and people who read the fanzine.

I wear jeans and T-shirts, going for grunge, hand-painted not printed band T-shirts. It would be quite nice to have a girl in the band – if I knew any girls who played guitar. It's a matter of friends that form bands rather than forming bands and friendships later. I couldn't be in a band with people I didn't know. There's always massive strops and at least if you were friends first you could cope with it. I'm quite egotistical, too.

16

Of other bands, I think Suede are quite interesting. I know they don't seem revolutionary, but I think they're like The Smiths were in the eighties. I know Smiths fans might not agree but people my age never saw The Smiths and so they do seem quite extreme. I think they went to the USA too early, they should have stayed and consolidated with a few more Top Ten hits first. There's a Bristol band called Flying Saucer Attack who I like – they're not exactly mainstream, they are new.

My parents think the band's a bit frivolous, but they wouldn't stop me. They don't try to influence me about what I do. Choosing Russian was an entirely personal decision. I'm looking forward to going to university, though most of my worries relate to it.

John Major introducing that pay-back grant system is a real burden to the students, it will put off a lot of students from going on to further education, but it's not helping the finances of the grant-giving bodies either. If you take out the money from the local body, you are supposed to pay it back later, but they are losing money because they are waiting for the money to be repaid, especially as so many students have to go on the dole after they've finished university.

I want to be a Russian teacher or do a post-grad – I'd like to get an MA, and then get a job . . .

### Becky, 17, jewellery student, Kent

They let you in here with five GCSEs. I only just got in by the skin of my teeth. It's supposed to be the equivalent of an A level college.

I like tribal-style jewellery from different cultures, modernising it. The sort of thing that would sell at festivals. I usually go to Glastonbury and Reading but I couldn't afford to go to Glastonbury this year – it was too expensive. At the moment we're getting together some work for our diploma show, it's supposed to be the work we've done over the past two years, but we're behind, as we pissed about over the first year.

17

When I leave here I'm going to do a BA, probably at Central St Martin's or Epsom. The college is supposed to sort it out for you, but friends tell me that they try to get you to stay on here and do the HND course in jewellery, a bit like schools prefer you to stay on to do A levels. Though in my case I never had the option, I was told I wasn't allowed to stay on in the sixth form.

I don't think you need an art background to make jewellery, but it does help; you have got to be able to draw, especially if you want to get on to a BA course. A B-Tec is equivalent to two or three A levels. We study jewellery, history of art, art in practice and computer studies – a wide range of stuff.

I wouldn't like to do an apprenticeship because the companies who offer them are usually middle of the road and boring. I'd like to get more qualifications at college first.

## Shelley, 17, jewellery student, Bromley, Kent

You can't really say how different the students work is, as we get briefs on what we're going to do, make a pendant or brooch. They're really into traditional, fine jewellery, it's got to be fine, not contemporary. Our teacher always thinks our ideas are too difficult! But I'd prefer to do more contemporary stuff. Bracelets usually have to be a certain size and in silver, quite boring, but I suppose we're learning the basics.

If I have to, I'll stay on and do an HND here, then go and do an apprenticeship with a jewellery company. I'd rather leave after the two-year course. Basically I want to move to London, I'll get some trade magazines, see what companies I like the look of and blag my way in. I want to work. I've done a lot since I've been here, but I've not much to show. I think I'll learn far more on an apprenticeship. The basic problem with all practical classes is that even if you learn something small, you have to wait for a day or so for the next process, because there are so many people in the class and the teacher has to get round to you all and show you each stage, when you're working on your own projects. Sometimes he'll do the connecting jobs for you, rather than show you, because it's quicker; I'd rather learn everything.

We are the youngest here, us two, both 17. We both live at home. I wouldn't get a grant to live down here in outside accommodation, as I live too close.

## Stuart, 24, MA in computer animation, Middlesex University

I did a fine arts BA in Newcastle-upon-Tyne. I've lived all over the place, in Scotland, the Midlands. I have no base, though my parents are in the Midlands now. After finishing my degree I went through a post-degree trauma, doing bits and bobs and waiting for something to come up! I had vague ambitions about being an artist and tried selling my art – mostly print-making and photographing computer-generated images. I didn't make much money. It was time to direct my skills, and I thought I'd try to do something more commercial – so I applied for the MA in computer animation. There are three or four colleges that do computer animation courses, but Middlesex includes three months' work experience and study abroad. It's organised with colleges in Spain, France and Holland. The course is made up of four blocks of three months. The first three months were spent studying in London, then Holland for three months, while the Dutch students came here, then the next three months were spent on a work placement, wherever you can get it. It's been different year to year with some students spending time in France and Spain or Holland – this year there were great administration hassles and we didn't have much choice about the country we would study in. The communication wasn't there. It's because of this that London's going to drop out next year, which is a bit of a shame for others who like the idea of the course.

I had work experience in Brussels. We fixed it up off our own backs; some students worked in Paris, some Holland, some came back to London. I don't speak Dutch! It's easy to get by in Holland and Brussels as English is the third language, so many people speak at least a little.

The money is vaguely adequate. It doesn't cover your living expenses though. You have to find your own living accommodation in London, though they helped out in Holland. Four of us studied in Holland – three males, one female – the whole course only caters for six students at a time. But it's not always male-dominated, the first couple of years it ran, it was mostly female. Apart from the student ratio, it's a very intensive course, three months is just enough time to find your feet and learn the system, so you have to squash in as many hours as possible. We work from about 10 a.m. to 8 p.m.

Workwise, ideally I'd like to start up on my own with staff! It is a growing field and there is a lot of potential, I wouldn't mind working in research or commercial animation on the production side. There are plenty of companies who use it – computer games, advertising agencies, or research for a games company. Then there's image-processing, making paintings look like they're painted by Picasso. That's a growing field, they sell better than if you sit down and create something of your own. I'm happy to stay in London as that seems to have the option of jobs, but if I have to move out or go abroad, I will. I like the idea of living in London – more companies, more galleries, pubs and life, but I'm living on the edge of London so it's not as if it's convenient to get to the galleries! Newcastle and Glasgow have a good choice of jobs too.

I rent a room in a house with just one bloke who's a school teacher so it's not bad. Social life isn't wonderful. I'm working long hours and being out in Winchmore Hill everyone's trying to get home after college. There was far more organised at Newcastle, when I did my BA, but that had a campus and a university environment. They also put on a good degree show for us at the end of the BA – Jools Holland came. This college isn't very political compared to Newcastle, but then I'm in a smaller group and we're all concentrating on what we're doing.

## Jamie, 21, computer animation, Middlesex University

I was born in Dover, lived in Seaford on the Sussex coast – a very dull town near Brighton full of old men in their 70s, and came here via Northern Ireland . . . I did my BA at Ulster – basically it was the only university that accepted me! It was the last on the list; I went through in alphabetical order.

I wasn't too worried about going to Northern Ireland. I thought if things were as bad as they were painted, then the place couldn't support a population. Like New York . . . if it was really as violent as you hear, then people wouldn't live there.

College was great and after finishing my degree I became a technician there, then taught video for a while. I studied sculpture and video and used video for my final degree show which no one else there had done, so they offered me the job. I met a guy at the Belfast Film Workshop who shot films for Channel 4 and started doing bits for them, and I started doing freelance camerawork, filming news coverage for Ulster Television.

It was a good time to be over there, with plenty of opportunities as the European Commission were giving grants to help fund community businesses. A land of opportunity in some ways! I got work helping make videos for a co-op set up by a member of the Communist Party, making films about the community! A strange organisation. Great experience and very experimental, though I didn't earn much money. I was working for Protestants and Catholics – making pop videos for groups with both Catholics and Protestants. I was the only person who did the camera work there, but I wasn't trained.

Things are changing now in this field. Now technological developments mean companies don't demand so much skill from technicians. If you're working on a feature film, less importance is placed on your role – the lighting and filming side – more money is pumped into post-production. They are more likely to get any old video footage and improve on it . . . It's very capital-intensive.

I prefer to make the camera-work look good and get skilled lighting technicians so there isn't so much post-production work, but I thought that by learning to create computer images I'd have the complete means of production – which is why I went to do the MA in computer animation. With computer graphics you've got the skills at your fingertips – literally.

You can create your own world on computer, and it's more active on a computer than on video. The two complement each other, combining video footage with 3-D animation.

Coming here – to Middlesex Poly and Winchmore Hill – was more of a culture shock than going to Ulster. That was a shock itself. Imagine going from sleepy Seaford. Its population has quadrupled over the past ten years, but it's full of young families or old people. The young families who were moved there didn't mix with the locals and it's a bit like a ghost town, plus it's very Conservative – it's had the same Tory MP since the year dot.

When I lived there I used to see lots of 20-year-olds with new car phones and flash cars. To go from there to the abject poverty of Ulster was a complete change, but they had a brilliant social life and everyone mixed well at college. It's easy to get to know people in Ulster, it's far more open.

I'm not itching to go back to Ulster, though it's not as bad as people make out. I'm very suspicious of the news coverage as it's all so one-sided, which you see when you live there – and that comes from someone who helped provide news footage! I distrust all media coverage – .even when I lived there, unless it was something I'd seen for myself. I can't deny it if I see it. But it's got a great feeling over there.

Middlesex is appalling by comparison. I live in Southgate – that part of London is awful. There are a couple of bars. You're not really in London, you have to go to the West End, but it's the other side of the Tube network. I don't mind right now. I'm not drinking much anyway at the moment! I drank too much in Holland over the past three months. I've just returned from six months there, three months studying at a college there, and three months on a work placement in Amsterdam. I worked for a weird company run by a guy who used to run the Dutch ICA, publishing art books and doing the tail end animation of ads.

Freelance seems to be the way we're moving here. Work is definitely sporadic or part-time. But that's essential in a way if you're working on computer, spending ten hours a day on the screen – it's not good for your health to do it over long stretches of time. Lots of people are getting the ability/means to create their own media for artwork and to a professional standard, so it's an interesting time. I definitely want to work where the weather is better. I'm not joking. Weather is very important. People have so much more energy when the weather is good, and they go on later into the evening. This affects your social life too.

In London, I'm sitting in a pub, it's dark at 6 p.m. and there's crap on TV. It's sad, isn't it! If I was in Spain, I could be out eating *al fresco* watching a sunset over a sea! But London is the European centre for post-production computer graphics, and the standards are very high here.

It's tragic that the course I'm doing is closing down over here, because it's very good, and one of the growth areas in Britain, so there should actually be jobs for students! But it's all political. The Spanish and French swapped *en masse* so we had to go to Holland, I'd loved to have gone to Spain. The college is understaffed chronically and there's not enough equipment, but it all boils down to financial difficulties – they have to cover service debts so there's no money to re-equip.

Also the introduction of career development loans means the goal posts have moved slightly for students. If you've got to pay for your course, and are getting in debt for it, then you expect a higher standard and more equipment, you have the right to be annoyed if the course and schedule doesn't meet your expectations. In a way it should give students power. Most of the MA students got funding, but 18 of the 20 of the computing in design course students had to have a career development loan – it cost seven grand to do the course, they've got that hanging over their heads as they start looking for work.

## Roz, 20, union official, Kent Institute of Art and Design

We look after people's welfare and the social side. We had a cut-back in funds and had to spread it thinly, mostly we organise dances. Last year we used to have a few bands at college – there were college members in bands, and we provided places for them to play.

I've been here a couple of years. I did a B-Tec in spatial awareness and I'm now studying for my architecture degree. Although it takes up a lot of my time, I follow my college work as well as doing the union work. All of the union officials are on courses.

The college is changing at the moment, its taking on three-year degree courses for the first time, so we'll attract different students. That's why the college has agreed to have a bar, we've bought the pub over the road. That will become the student bar and a place for events, plus as it's a hotel it will serve as a kind of hall of residence as well. The students will have to show identity cards to get in.

Most of the students here aren't very political – although there has been a form going round to stop VAT on books. That's usually as far as it goes. And here as a union, our role is working with the system to help change and get better conditions and facilities for the students. I suppose we're lucky because the lecturers are quite happy about us. We have a newsletter, but that's usually telling of events and what's going on.

There aren't political campaigns or anything, and the lecturers don't give us orders or ask the union to report to them before making decisions. There aren't any teacher-student mandates in issues like date rape and so on. I don't think there has ever been any trouble at the college, not in my time, though there have been rapes in the fields. The area does have its problems. The staff are more concerned about the welfare and safety of the students.

And now the college is trying to compete with universities, so they're working hard with us, as if we fail, they fail, so it's a good time to be here.

A lot of the students go to London at the weekend for events, clubs, raves – we like the ones on the noticeboard! We've got a party we've put on as a kind of start-of-term event.

Outside of college, I work in a bar in the evenings, with Nicol who's also on my course and a union official. A part-time job's essential if you want money to go out. As far as they go, my job's fine.

There are three main types of customer – squaddies, the Friday suited lot out to let their hair down, and students. Apart from that, most of the customers are on the dole! It's a good place to work, it's a young bar.

The worst aspect is that the bar has a camera on the staff – it should be nice to think they're watching in case you get hassled – which we do sometimes – so they can come and help, but no, it's there to make sure we're not doing anything wrong. It's not very pleasant that they can't trust you. But I think it's common practice in bars. I'd prefer to be working there than be using it. Sometimes, friends will come in for an evening and you'll think wouldn't it be nice to just sit and chat and drink with them, but at the end of the evening when you're still clear-headed, you're glad you're on the other side, especially because you get £20 for the night.

## Lisa, 18, Chigwell, Essex

I'm studying photography, I'm hoping to be a commercial photographer. I did a B-Tec at Southend College, and I'm now doing a diploma. After that I'll work as an assistant to a photographer whose work I like. I've got my own camera, you may as well learn with the one you use at home. I take it out and about. I've photographed bands playing. Sometimes I approach the press office for a press photographer's pass, tell them it's for a project and they're usually OK. It depends. I got a pass to see All About Eve and took photographs there. It was at the Marquee, London, so there wasn't great vision, but it was good experience. I'm building up a portfolio. I studied with my best friend and she came to college with me here. We've both moved into local rooms, the college helps to find them, though our landlady wants to put up the rent. I work on Saturdays in a baker's, to get some money, otherwise it's a grant.

My mates in Essex are really into role-playing. We all choose characters and have to dress and act the part, develop the characters totally. I've got some ace characters, one of my favourites is the Red Wizard. She's seventies rather than medieval, and wears a red halter-neck dress, she's a bit vain. That's just her character, haughty, you have to keep to it. We have to find suitable locations, and climb over the walls, like one time it was a local castle. They know you're there, but we don't ask them, they turn a blind eye because we're not doing any harm. We do it at night. You have to be careful, though. One night, while role-playing, we met some people on LSD just wandering round the grounds. They wandered up to my friend who was a wolf, with a latex wolf beard. We had to get away from them.

You find out about role-playing from games' shops. Groups of role-players meet up through putting ads in the shops, you can get really into it. It's about scoring points awarded by the Dungeon Master, and we've all become good friends.

I always go back to Essex at weekends. I like going out there, my friends are there, and boyfriend. He plays Brit Ball, he's quarter-back in the youth team. He was spotted in a field throwing a ball to his mates and someone approached him! Honest, it happened like that.

## Louise, 21, jewellery HND student, Kent Institute of Art and Design

I'm planning my life out. I'm 21 now, I finish this course when I'm 22. I'll work solidly for three years in a jeweller's to get some experience, and then I'll go back to full-time education again. I'll work in London definitely, though Canterbury is a very good area too. Canterbury is very with it, it's near Dover so it has good European trading links. In England, you've got to be very smart, and know where the market is to sell anything.

I'd also like to live in Spain, France or Italy for a few years so I learn a language. I'd have to jump in at the deep end, but that's the best way. I don't have a language despite the fact that I come from Tobago which is Spanish-based. My parents live in Tobago, and I was born there. My father's Trinidadian Spanish, my mum's English.

I like to be in a different culture, I love talking to different people, it helps you develop. I want to include everything in my life. I'll probably live in Europe until I'm about 28.

I'll go back home in my late twenties. I'd like to settle down there, marry a West Indian! Tobago is such a nice place to live. It's very quiet and laidback, and by that time, I will have gone through my wild years, my living years . . . You can't go wild there. It's too small and everyone knows you! It's only about 32 miles by 7, so it's like living in a village – people gossip. It's a nice idea to mellow out in Tobago.

You can't go wild in Chatham either. I can't stand it. I don't go out very much at all. I travel all the time. I'm always in London, I go up for the weekends. There are museums, music, things going on, just looking at people inspires me. There's nothing in Chatham. It's only because of the students that Chatham is lively. It's depressing when there aren't any students around. When I came here a week before the beginning of the term, I had to have a spliff and put my shades on to get me through! People in Chatham are completely different, it's vicious. I feel safer in London I have friends in Golders Green, it's lovely, a Jewish area.

I've moved around a lot. I went to a boarding school in Ashford, Kent, from the age of ten, then did a foundation course at Canterbury. This is a two-year jewellery course. I've got one more year here. I'm an overseas student and the fees are very expensive. That's why I had to choose a two-year course, I was limited in my choice to do courses that were just two years as they were cheaper than degree courses which are three years or longer, so that narrowed my options.

The college teaching is very manufacture-based, very commercial, mass production jewellery, like Ratners, H. Samuel, not what I would choose to do. After my foundation course in Canterbury I was buzzing, full of ideas and I thought I'd found myself. I was on a different wavelength and coming from Tobago which is full of shells, stones and natural materials, to come here and have to do very geometric and modern work, completely threw me; it took me a year to adjust so I feel I wasted the first year.

After jewellery, I want to do glass blowing, and get into new fields to expand and develop the skills I've learned already. I'd like to study fashion and textiles, photography and do an English literature course ... even if I've got to do night courses, I'd dearly love to study them. Personally I feel that everyone should carry on doing some studying, even if they're working, education should never stop. I've done stained glass at adult education already. I want to do lathe work, and combine the skills. By learning lots of things you keep your mind open.

Every three months I pack up and go to Tobago. You do get tired of living on the hop, but I have been very lucky because I've travelled. I took a year off to travel before I came here. After A levels and my foundation course, I went away for a whole year. I helped my dad in the office in Tobago and saved some money, then travelled up the Caribbean, did the Grenadines in a day, went on a catamaran, went to Grenada, Dominica, Barbados – just my boyfriend and I. It was so expensive, we could only spend a month in the West Indies, but it was great.

Apart from going up the islands, I've been to the States, Canada, Denmark, Paris. They weren't all holidays: I used to play a lot of hockey and I went to Canada on a tour. I know I'm lucky – and I can go home to Tobago for holidays.

I don't work at all here, so I rely on my parents for all my money, but after this I'm on my own. My dad gave me two cartons of West Indian cigarettes and a bottle of rum as I was leaving at the end of the summer holidays and I thought 'I love you, dad'. I rang him last night, I'd had such a lovely day in London, I was buzzing and I rang a Tobago friend who's studying in Bristol and she's having a whale of a time, and I thought of them.

My dad's coming to my graduation. I have made my mum jewellery – a pearl necklace and I am going to make my dad a letter-opener as he's a businessman and it will be something he'll use every day. He's into sailing, so it'll have a wave effect or something to reflect the sea. I sail a tiny boat.

My boyfriend and I broke up last Sunday, he rang up and said F off. Well . . . he said, 'Do you mind if we're just friends?' We used to go out a while back, then split up for a year and saw each other again, we'd both matured and grown up. But it didn't work. He's studying law in London and has a very tough course, studying until 10 p.m. in the library every night. He thinks my course is very lax. I'm so glad I'm an artist and very happy to be doing something I like, and that I can switch on and off whenever I like, not having to do this from 9–5. I want to be able to switch between skills like architecture, pottery, ceramics.

I am lucky I'm sharing a house with a fine artist – a dope-head – a girl who's doing fashion and architecture. We'll be drinking red wine and spliffing up and we'll be getting stoned and mixing ideas. I'll be designing her dresses and getting new ideas and trying architecture. I designed a bed a couple of nights ago. The ideas are seeping into me.

Our house is very cheap and bills are included, and it's near to the cinema, pub and Tesco's . . . so it's a perfect location, although it's up a hill! I've just done up my room, painted it cream and got a hammock, candles, futon, shelves and plants, and lots of shells. I've created my own little world in there to get out of Chatham. This area is so depressing, it doesn't help creativity. If you compare a jeweller in London and a jeweller here, they have so many more ideas and lots going on to get inspiration.

My friend and I try to go somewhere different in Kent every weekend. Staying in one place puts a blinker on your ideas and your imagination, even the teachers are suffocating.

Actually I'm happy at college as I've finally got through to my teacher, he's a very nice guy but has to teach the straight methods. I wanted to work with sea urchins and inlay opals, he's like freaking out, 'No, that won't sell', he's always got his eyes on manufacturing. He gets a pencil out and draws his design over yours.

I'd rather fail the course and have a happy show at the end of the year.

I'd love to create one-off pieces. When I qualify I'll definitely be self-employed; I can't work for anyone else. I've been brought up in a family business. Trust no one, you can always do things better yourself. And I don't want to limit the things I make. If I have an idea for a belt, I'd like to have contacts to sell it, or a dress; I want to be flexible, creative and into so many different aspects. A painting, card design, recipes, interior decoration. Why should everything be so limited?

Both my sister and brother work for my dad. My father expects me to work for him, in the end. Part-time, so I'm not pressurised, but he does need the help, a family business will only survive with family. But his work has helped influence me. I feel that if you work somewhere like McDonald's you end up throwing your cheeseburger across the counter, but work for yourself then you put more into it.

Tobago has influenced me a lot. Musically, I'm narrow-minded because I know reggae, dub, West Indian and Spanish-influenced music. Although everything we get in Tobago is pirated, videos of TV and concerts taped at Sunsplash or at concerts in Trinidad. I like ragga here, I hear that and I'm off dancing, but it's losing the effect and meaning of reggae as it's commercialising it.

## Mandy, 23, textile design student, Rochester, Kent

I don't want to stay in this area when I'm qualified, though I was born in Rochester. I've travelled but I haven't found the right place – I've lived in Belgium, and travelled over Europe – I've lived all over the place – but I've come back to Rochester, Strood, Chatham . . . There's nothing to hold me here, only friends. Workwise, I want to work in theatre design and the better options are in London.

I'm doing textiles. It isn't quite what I wanted to do, but it's working towards it. I have only just started this year, in the second year I'll get to look at prospectuses to see where I can do theatre design – somewhere in London, hopefully, or Leeds. It would be good to check out stage sets, since that's what I want to do. I've been to the London Opera House, but I can't afford to go to lots of plays.

I didn't come straight from school. Before I worked as a social worker but I left as I got ill through work. It's very stressful. I was off work for a while through it, then I went into doing a market stall in Rochester and other markets, I did it with a friend. Back in the summer I was working on the stalls, I'd do a couple of flea markets a week, sell what I had then go to loads of jumble sales, collect loads of stuff and present it well. You can sell anything if you present it well!

## Janet, 22, fashion student, Essex

I come from a normal family background in Essex. I left school at 16 and went to work at Nat West. I stayed there for four years, I was working in Unit Trusts, then I went on to a merchant bank. I didn't think about what I wanted to do, it was more of a decision that the family needed money. My brother was at Oxford and my dad supported him, then he became ill and had to give up his job. My sister had had a baby and I was the only one who could go out to work. I wasn't very academic, the only subject I liked and was good at was art and everyone told me you can't make a career from art, so when I was offered an interview at Nat West at a careers evening at school, I accepted.

I was living at home, then when my brother left Oxford and wanted to move into a flat in London, I joined him. We got a flat in Bethnal Green. Once free of the family, I realised that it wasn't my choice, I wasn't really happy in the bank. I know people would say I was mad, I had a job, was earning a decent salary and I would have to give that up and live on nothing. But I wanted a career change. I was interested in fashion and art and chose a varied course so I could find the particular area that suits me. The course I'm doing covers fashion styling, hairstyling, costume, make-up, the whole visual side of fashion. It's very creative and enjoyable.

Up until recently I was hoping that once I got my diploma, this summer, I'd get a job, but I've realised that won't be easy so I'm going on to do a course at the London College of Fashion – following one of the elements of this course and going back to something I really wanted to do as a 12-year-old – beauty therapy.

Hopefully, I should get a grant for that. Up until now I haven't been entitled to one. I've had to pay my own way totally. The course is several hundred then you've got to find your rent, travel and living expenses, plus course books and equipment. It's been tough. I'm in so much debt and it will be more by the time I get out of college that you wonder if it's worth it, but you're working towards getting a job. A career change isn't a good enough reason to warrant getting a grant or financial help if you leave a job. I can understand the authority's point of view in that I gave up a perfectly good job to go to college to study a totally different subject, but it wasn't out of laziness or a desire to go on income support. It wasn't an easy decision to make and I gave it up because I wasn't happy. The course will help me get another job, a job that I want to do.

There were also health reasons that prompted me to leave the bank. I was suffering from the viral syndrome

ME. It was recognised by my doctor that the work didn't suit me; it was high-powered and stressful, which some people thrive on and like, that's fine, but my heart wasn't in it and it made me feel bogged down.

It was nothing to do with the people. They were a nice enough bunch, I made many friends in the bank and still see them, especially from the merchant bank when just ten of us worked together. But they aren't the same sort of people as me. Most of them do seem to have the same character, they're quite materialistic, into clothes, neat with matching shoes, that sort of thing. I've never complied, even when I worked in the City, I'd look different from the norm. But, I don't fit in totally in college either, I'm not as wacky as some people, I look different from the people in college in the same way I didn't conform in the bank! I'm in the middle!

I'm living with my sister at the moment, but I hope to move to London again soon and then I'll be able to get bar work and work in a club Fridays and Saturdays to help financially.

## Justina, 23, student/single parent, East Sussex

It's a strange time for me now. I've just gone back to college, I'm re-evaluating my life. Since I had my daughter – I had her when I was really young (20), I've just been doing shop work, jobs that paid OK but allowed me part-time work or flexible hours to get to and from the nursery where Katie was. But she recently got a full-time place and I thought I'd go back into doing what I did before I had her. I was a PA, which was brilliant fun, and much more interesting than the work I've done since. But things have really changed in that market over the past few years. You used to get a job by looking good, having a nice personality and smile, and being able to type with a good telephone manner. Now it's all word processing skills! So, I've gone back to college to learn them.

I've always wanted to work and be independent, though I have had income support and do now I'm at college and a single parent. Probably the best help I get as a single parent is Katie's nursery place, which I know I'm lucky to get. So many other people I know with children pay £30 a day for a place privately because council nursery places are like gold dust. But I wasn't always a single parent, my boyfriend and I split up when Katie was one, it was hard but for the best. We were too young, we were only staying together for her, but she gets a better deal from having one doting parent. I take her everywhere that other children go, probably out a lot more, swimming, dance classes, toddler gymnastics! Her grandparents live far too far away to see very often (Wales), so I don't have help from them and they're missing out on her development. She still sees her dad whenever he wants to take her out and he looks after her one evening a week when I go to the gym to do weight training – I've got to stay fit and look good to get a job!

I really like the fact that I've got older. It's much better than when I was 18 or 19, you know your mind far more and know where you're going, you don't feel lost in the sea. I really see it at college when the school-leavers are wasting time or doing as little work as they have to – I'm doing the work for me.

I'd really like to have another child, to meet someone else and have a family, but how do you meet someone when you already have a child? Apart from at college and in a work situation, I don't really get out, and who would want to take on board someone else's child? Katie comes first.

# 2 Career Opportunities?

More than 1,500 people applied for a dozen £9,000-a-year jobs in Birmingham – as traffic wardens. (*Sun*)

Thousands of black Londoners will face continued unemployment even if the most optimistic government forecasts about the end of the recession are right.

New research reveals that even when the jobs market is good, blacks in London are two or three times more likely to be unemployed than whites. (*Time Out*)

Nearly one in four youngsters wants National Service brought back both for men AND women, a poll found.

More than half of 16 to 24-year-olds backed our role in the Gulf War, says the Gallup survey. Only 18 per cent support Government defence cuts. (*Sun*)

National Union of Mineworkers' officials are defying their leader, Arthur Scargill, by backing private initiatives to rescue mothballed pits. Leading a growing rank-and-file rebellion, they are threatening to split the union.

Some senior members openly admit that the battle to save the nationalised coal industry is all but lost, leaving Mr Scargill increasingly isolated.

NUM membership has declined from 250,000 to 25,000 in 11 years and 130,000 miners have lost their jobs. (*Observer*)

Yuppies are back – but this time they are being careful with their six-figure salaries, City experts revealed yesterday.

The 90s Yuppies are very different from the red-braced 80s versions who took out massive mortgages and ran Porsches, only to be sacked in the recession.

Many are being enticed back to their old jobs with 'golden hellos' worth a year's salary and bonuses which could double £100,000-a-year pay cheques. (*Sun*)

## Roberta, 24, trainee doctor, London

It's depressing working in the British health service. I've spent my work experience in the Casualty department of a

London hospital. It was on the outskirts, so it wasn't usually cases of life or death, it was very busy but not the dramas you see in the television series. Mostly it was people who wanted to talk to someone and didn't have anyone else. Especially at night. They'd come in complaining of something, you'd examine them thoroughly, chat and discover there was nothing wrong – physically. Then there are the people who didn't believe their GP and came for a second opinion, especially parents with young children, worrying. There should be somewhere for these people to go for help – but Casualty is not the place.

The tragic thing about working in the health service is that most of the illnesses are caused by poverty, and that's something we can do nothing about. That's something the Government should be addressing. Instead they are making it harder. Cutting back on beds and hospitals in London when they are already stretched beyond their capacity, and cutting back on funding. If we can't cope with the current level of funding, what's the point in reducing it? Does that make sense? It's amazing, when you go to a hospital in a rural area, you can see empty beds and you're looking around for the people who should be there! In London, that never happens, the waiting lists are endless. Having said that, I'd rather work in London than the country, I like the variety and the pace. It's probably just as well, because I'm black and many of my tutors have advised me that I'd be better off staying in London; I wouldn't get jobs if I went for them in a rural area. There are prejudices there.

The worst thing is that the Government seem to be looking more and more at the American model – and their health system has to be one of the worst in the world, grossly unfair, they are not attempting to find a system that will work. And that doesn't just apply to hospitals, it's the same with GPs. It's not a happy profession to work in. We need to help poor people to raise their standards of living. That would do more to help prevent most of the current health problems than anything else.

## Andy Musson, 25, miner, Thoresby Pit, Nottingham

I was in the last draft of young people into the mines. It's a youthful profession (in that the average age of a miner is 32, at some mines the average age is 26) and a dying one. They won't be taking any more young people on.

I became a miner at 18. It was just before the strike ended, the pits in Notts took on a lot of young people thinking that the striking miners were all going to get sacked. I wasn't a strike-breaker. I'm broad left – I've supported Labour since I was 15, and been a member of the Labour party. I went up to the picket line official and showed him the letter offering me a job and he said take it – it was just two weeks before the strike ended.

There was a lot of bad feeling in the pits at the time. My father scabbed. We never saw eye to eye over that – we never share political views. But the sad thing is that the strike-breakers and miners who were against the union then, now see what Arthur Scargill was going on about. My best mate down the mine scabbed at the time. He was made redundant last Friday, we were chatting and he said: 'Scargill was right, wasn't he? He were right.' It's too late now.

So many miners say the same thing now – Arthur Scargill did that and that for us and should have had that vote. Lots of miners are now coming round to it. The same people who in '84–'85 were anti-Scargill, realise now that he were right – 99.8 per cent who were anti-Scargill then, are saying he was right, now. But they didn't see it at the time.

I love the pit, you can't explain it. It's steeped in history and there's a great feeling down there ... Mining wasn't my first job. When I left school, I went to the careers office and they were all for those YTS schemes, which I don't like as they sound like slave labour to me. Kids do a full-time job for £27.50 a week, and they never get offered a full-time job when the scheme's finished. It's just there to massage the unemployment figures. So when he offered me a YTS place with Trent Buses I turned it down. I'd rather be on supplementary benefit, so I'd be a figure, stop the Government hiding the true numbers of the unemployed. Then he phoned and said he'd found me a job for £45 a week walking a sandwich board around Nottingham. I told him what he could do with it.

Luckily I got work with a building contractor. I worked there until I went down the pit. My father was pleased that I was going into the mines – it's a tradition, like, but he took redundancy in 1985.

We all think about redundancy all the time, I live in fear every day that there won't be a job for me tomorrow, and Thoresby is the biggest producing pit in the country, but that doesn't mean anything. I got made redundant once already. I worked in another colliery before this one, but I was lucky because I had a choice to come here.

British Coal are offering many young people money to get out of the game, so they leave the coal industry with £10,000 and up to £20,000 in their pockets, which seems a lot to them, but in 12–24 months it's all gone, and there's no other work. In one sense working and living in a city there are a few more jobs on offer. If I worked in North Notts, the Mansfield rate of unemployment is a lot higher, it's absolutely unbelievable, a lot of the lads who left the pit four years ago still haven't got a job.

There's not a cat in hell's hope of any more young people in the mines now. It's not going to be a career choice any more. And competition for jobs at the pits used to be very fierce. I remember there was a notice on the gates of school saying they were looking for young miners. I went down to the pit, and took friends along with me – 3500 Notts lads turned up for those interviews that Tuesday and Friday. Usually, if you've got family in the mines it helps.

It's a multi-racial mix around here, but most miners in my pit are white. It wasn't like that at Gedling. We used to call it the League of Nations, there were white, black, Hungarian miners, Poles, even an African tribal chief! I suppose it was because it was just 2½ miles from the city centre. I suppose there is a bit of racial tension in the pits, you hear comments, though they are mostly meant in jest – or so they say.

I can't honestly say there's other work for us all round here, and for those young people who would traditionally have gone into the mines. I was National Youth Officer for the NUM for a year in 1991 and I'm used to keeping an eye out on other jobs and conditions for the young ones. I only stood for a year. I could have stood again, but it's a lot of work, because it was alongside my own work down the pits and it cost me my marriage. I'm divorced now. I'm back with my mum, and I stay with other friends. 'No fixed abode' is the offical term, as there just aren't enough council flats for everyone. My four-year-old daughter lives at home with my ex-wife, most of my money goes on my daughter.

The estate where I'm living is a typical poverty-stricken, run-down council estate.

Having said that, Bestworth Park has got its good points. It's got a great community feeling. Despite the loan sharks and drugs. I'm lucky, I've got a job, so it doesn't involve me, but you can see it and hear it. There's always a lively social scene where there are protection rackets happening.

I'm out every night. I play pool three nights a week, and I'm in the quiz team at the local pub one night. That's the friendly side of the community. I can go into the local any night and I'll know someone there, even if there are only two or three people in it.

I do a lot of sport – mostly squash and football occasionally, and rugby union. It's important to take care of yourself to work down the mines. I'm definitely physical. You can lose 10–12 lbs in a shift, that's very common, because you work in such high temperatures – you're 1½ miles at least inside the mine and working physically hard. Most of us work in our underwear. Seriously. Boots, gloves of course, shin guards, hats and vest and underpants. A great sight.

I love it down the pits. There's such a great atmosphere, all the blokes look after each other's backs. Down there we're all really close. I work with blokes from the UDM, the breakaway union, but you don't care when you're in the pit, you all look out for each other. I'm on regular shifts at the moment, which is six in the morning to a quarter past one. You're down the pit all that time, though you have a 20-minute snack time. Personally, I can't eat at all when I'm down there, it makes me feel ill. I chew tobacco and drink pints of water. But that's just me, most miners take food down with them. I have my dinner when I come up. You're aware of the risks and dangers, which is why you watch for each other, but that doesn't put me off. I practically broke my back in an accident in Gedling mine when a roof collapsed on me. If it wasn't for another miner who pulled me clear, I would be a cripple. As it was, the bone at the base of my spine came away and then shot back into position. I know I was lucky.

### Nadia, 22, trainee teacher, Cardiff

I've always wanted to be a teacher. You know, inspired by the great ones I had and vowing to do better than the worst – so many alienated the kids. But it is hard going. I've had two lots of teaching practice so far and one was with 12–13-year-olds who are very cocky. Because you're young, they either think, 'She'll be a pushover', or they try and get you on their side. It's funny to watch them work. Younger kids really like young teachers, it's all 'Miss, can I help' . . .

The other big disappointment is that at the moment in the current set-up you don't get the time and the leaway you imagine you'll have. There are millions of novel things you plan to do, to make subjects more interesting and appealing and help the children achieve the best of their ability. And when you know there are problems with some of them and you want to help them, to make them want to learn and realise that they are as clever as the rest, that they have got it within them too, but there simply isn't time. So much now is geared to getting on with the national curriculum as it stands, there's so much in it that you have to cover in a set amount of time, that there are precious little resources, energy or time left to do things that help the individual personalities within your class. That's the problem of the British system, it's geared to the majority – the very good ones in a way are left to their own devices and those who are slightly slower just miss out altogether.

We argue about this at college all the time, but it's not the teachers' faults or down to the head-teacher's policy, it's the fault of the system – having to keep proving to parents you are covering the national curriculum because that's all they've heard about and what they are told to expect from a school, and you need to keep them on your side, and having to meet targets, get test results and show the outside world that you are doing exactly what other schools are doing. That's fine in theory but it's too rigid and time-consuming. Kids are individuals and each responds to a different approach. It's like school reports, if you've seen one lately, it's all 'has covered this and that', 'so and so has learnt about the world in geography'. What happened to the reports geared to telling parents exactly what that pupil is good at and their special problems? That's because it's drummed into teachers to show they're covering course work and also lack of time to elaborate on anything else.

So why am I going into it? You have to change things from inside. It's like individual schools. If parents who can afford to pay for their child's education all take their kids away from the local state school, then imagine the morale at the deserted school, of teachers, children and the parents. If they're going because the school isn't totally satisfactory, then they should stay and fight, because the more parents who support a school or involve themselves and help, the better it will be.

## Bobita, 22, shop assistant and voluntary worker, Medway Towns

My husband hates it here. In India he trained to be a lawyer, but the qualifications aren't recognised in Britain. He's

41

learnt English, but still finds the language a problem, getting through more exams would be so much harder for him here. He can't do the work he wants to do, can't earn the money he would be able to earn as a lawyer, so he feels there's no future for him.

His standard of living in India is so much better than here. His dad is a top magistrate, with bodyguards and a huge house full of servants. I don't feel tempted by that. I really don't want to go and live there. All I'd do is stay with the mothers and women and children, families gather together there. I wouldn't have any freedom. I wouldn't be able to work, I'd have nothing to do during the day . . . He has two more years to finish off his studies and qualify to join the top rank of the legal profession in India, they have to do it within a set time limit and so he will have to go back soon, if he goes. If he went back to qualify, he wouldn't want to return to Britain afterwards because he wouldn't get such a high standard of job here. He intends to go back, but that's a bone of contention between us. I want to stay here and be a policewoman.

## Roddy, 21, unemployed, Clapton, East London

I'm a single parent. I've a three-year-old daughter. She's great. I have her half the week exactly, we share her care fairly. I pick her up from nursery on Tuesdays and Thursdays and she stays the night. I like taking her out. I take her to the park, Clissold or Victoria Park and play games, chat to the mums with kids. Her mother and I get on fine now, but we just couldn't get on when we were together. It's better as it is. I haven't got a girl right now. But I'm always looking!

Her mother's working. I'm between jobs right now, as they say. I used to work in a factory in Dalston – in ladies' lingerie. But they laid me off. It happens a lot in that business. Then I started a market stall – in lingerie. I did it with a mate but he lost interest. It's cold and horrible on wet days, but I think you can make a lot of money from it. Get the lingo right, charm the ladies. I'm trying to save up and learn to drive now. That's my next big plan, then I can handle the stall on my own.

Most days I sort myself at home in the mornings, get organised, then I'm back on the streets. I'd get bored at home. I spend most days hanging out with my mates.

## Kirk, 24, aspiring artist, DJ, self-confessed bum, Manchester

To be honest, I've never applied for a job. I've never actually looked for work since leaving university. At the moment, I'm very happy as I am. There's plenty to fill my time, I never get bored. I had this same conversation with my flatmate last night, and admitted that you could lock me in a padded cell and I wouldn't feel bored. I could just sit and stare at the walls for hours on end.

I came to Manchester to go to university from a sleepy village and stayed. I've nothing better to do! My flatmate and most of my best friends all went to the same college – part of the old boy scene. None of us got jobs when we left, we didn't want to.

A lot of my friends who I've been hanging around with for the past few years seem to be drifting into employment or doing other courses. I suppose we could do with a life-style break. That isn't prompting me to do anything myself. I don't mind being the only one around, doing nothing. I like staying at home. I go out most nights – it depends on the money situation – and rarely see the mornings. I could spend the time doing art, I do bits. But that's not what I do all day. I'm not at all disciplined. I'm a terrible slob of a man. I sit and doodle and draw or read, listen to techno. I'm not purely into techno, though that's what I tended to play when I DJed. I still do a bit of DJing, though not so much now. I play hard techno and the clubs that are doing best in Manchester are into piano-y sort of dancing. So that's not such a source of money as it was. I still organise the occasional club night.

How could I afford to get a good collection of records to DJ? Well, it is difficult. Housing benefit and income support is about £60–£70 a week, and then selling dope is pretty lucrative. A lot of the money I have made from that has gone into buying records. My busiest time for dealing was over the last two years, when I wasn't a student, though most of the contacts came from the student network. The people above me in the chain were students, the person above them could have been a dodgy bugger, but the people I met weren't your hardened criminals.

I started dealing because I was smoking pot and had to buy it for myself, and then I was offered free pot by selling it to others. Then you realise if you can do that, you may as well buy and sell more and make money on a larger scale. I don't do hard drugs, I don't hang around Moss Side, the poor area. It's more the student connection.

I've given up the buying and selling now, because I got tired of dealing with dickheads, and being ripped off. You come into contact with some horrible people when you deal. Not necessarily the people you buy stuff off, but people who want supplies. They come round your home, or you meet up. I don't hang around on street corners. Good God, no! But, you have to make yourself available to people you wouldn't normally bother with. I didn't just sell to friends, just various idiots, quite a large crowd. Most are too nauseating to contact, which is why I've given up.

My flatmate got a bit paranoid about being caught dealing, but it never bothered me. It wasn't fear that signalled the end. In a place where you can get shot for fly-posting, dealing dope is nothing! I've only ever dealt in cannabis, though such large amounts as I had would never be mistaken for personal use!

I was attracted to Manchester because of the social life, and that's what's keeping me here. I was never interested in going to London, it's too big and sprawling. Manchester's a large place, but I tend to stay within a small area, living, going out – we don't have to venture very far.

I did an academic degree, but I'm good at art and that's what I can see myself doing, eventually. I don't know how

I ended up on the course I was on: wrong advice? I just messed up! I might do an MA in art somewhere, that's a possibility. I've got these ideas that maybe one day I could earn a living by writing a book, or drawing and painting. Something that doesn't involve years of graft at a nine-to-five job. But now I'm quite happy just to carry on as I am. I've had two, nearly three years of play since leaving university.

# 3 DIY Culture – Film

## Danny, 25, South London

I'm a classic case, I've come to realise through talking to other film-makers. I did my film degree – a three-year degree in film and video at Farnham, Surrey – and from there wanted a job in the film industry. But, like so many others, I found having a film degree gets you nowhere. So having tried all the avenues I could, I went back to the bottom of the pile and took a job as a runner with a post-production video company hoping to work my way up. I wanted to be a video editor. After two years I'd worked my way up to a tape operator. It would have taken me several more years to get near what I wanted to do, so I left. I realised, as did many other people in the company, that it wasn't film-making, it was button-pushing. No one was enjoying it – just button-pushing for clients who treated you like shit.

I became a freelance film-maker. That's what I am. I do get work – music promos and bits and pieces like a commission for a documentary for an art collective, and I do my own projects, but generally there isn't a lot of work around and I sign on, then sign off when the work comes in.

My own projects involve making films for around £10 on a reel of Super 8 – everything above that is a luxury! Super 8 is getting more recognition. It's popular in music promos, as it gives that edge effect, and with students, as it's the cheapest form of filming, more than 16 mm. I prefer Super 8 to 16 mm anyway, as there are no restrictions, you can just shoot and if something gets messed up, you haven't wasted £100. It's far more relaxed.

It would have been all too depressing if I hadn't got involved with Exploding Cinema – a loose collective of dissatisfied film-makers. It was formed two-and-a-half years ago at an art squat – CoolTan – in Brixton. There was a notice on the wall one week suggesting film-makers got together and suddenly about eight film-makers turned up for a meeting and I met other people who were pissed off with the industry and the funding system for films. I've spent a whole year trying to get funding from the London Film Makers' Co-op for a project and got refused and knew that I'd be resigned to a life of filling in forms while my work gathered dust in the files if I waited for recognised funding. A lot of people had similar experiences, and had no outlet for their work. It's frustrating, all that creative talent going to waste. So we decided to hold open screenings of our work.

It grew from showings in the kitchen to other regular venues. We're now on our fifth venue – Union Tavern in Camberwell – where we hold fortnightly screenings showing films to about 300 people at a time. We show anything, the idea being that Exploding Cinema doesn't censor anything or say whether it is good or bad, it's a platform for young film-makers to show their films, and we are trying to promote Super 8 as a viable film form.

Not all our membership – which has grown to about 25 – are film-makers, some are in post-production, some are performers and some are just interested in films. And the audience is very mixed, we want to make films accessible to everyone. We have a populist approach to film-making – we want to show that you don't have to be educated to a certain degree to watch films and be able to understand them. You don't have to be part of an art clique.

Last summer we held an all-nighter at Brockwell Lido. It's an empty swimming pool in Brixton which had been taken over by squatters and we did a huge show there for five or six thousand people. It was legal in that we told the police we were doing it and they came along to check there was no illegal stuff, but we support the whole squat culture – we started off in a squat, and many of us have had to live in squats.

We got big publicity and interest from that and made a

couple of thousand which we used to buy new projectors and equipment. None of us get paid – all the money made goes into the group.

The films we show aren't political – they aren't any particular category. We've shown footage of the poll tax riots, gay life or drugs, which are political in a sense, but many of the films are fun – they can't be categorised or stereotyped. If people are prepared to stand up in front of 300 or so people and defend their film, that's fine. I don't know what would happen if we had to deal with a Nazi propaganda film – we'd have to have a strong debate about that – but they would have to watch the film with the audience and stand up at the end.

We take the atmosphere away from the usual cinema feel, we have an MC, music and live performances. There's usually three live acts – stand-up comics, bands – though the emphasis is on films, so there are visuals behind them or as part of the act. And then there are the films. People don't stay quiet for them – we don't want them to; we want them to tell us what they think. If they don't like it they say so. Many get booed – usually if they are too long – anything over 30 minutes! People have low attention spans. I don't mind if my films get booed – it's better if I learn about what people like or not. And usually the film-maker stands up at the end of the film and talks about it. We've got a Vaudeville approach to film showing, not at all art-house.

We don't get Barry Norman coming along to screenings, though on that note there is a production company in Brighton who are formatting a low-budget short film review television programme – as in films that cost around £10–£20,000 to make. They're going to get established film-makers to review the films. It could be interesting – getting Alan Parker to comment on a low-budget short, and so on. It may open up the whole debate, though it depends on the films they pick and the way it goes really. It could just end up with more avant garde films.

There is a difference between avant garde films and the underground films we show. Avant garde is an art ghetto.

Underground films were going along nicely in the sixties, when there were places where low-budget films were shown to whoever wanted to watch them. The places got hijacked by the art élite, saying this is the way low-budget underground films should be, and so pushed a lot of people away. That's the problem, it's put people off seeing a low-budget film because they think it will be an experimental piece that they won't understand. Underground films are populist low-budget films that everyone can watch – they are not just for the élite.

The shorts we show are varied – a home movie next to one that may have got funding and cost £50,000 to make. It encourages people to go away and make films themselves. Some of them have never had film training. Just because I spent years training, it doesn't bother me if someone can make a film without any experience, or if they have access to expensive equipment that I don't – good for them.

The whole film industry in Britain is so messed up. There tends to be three camps: the established film industry who make feature films, adverts and promos with large budgets; funded films – made by people who rely on the BFI (British Film Institute) for funding to make their films; and then there are those film-makers who can't get funding because it's a closed shop and their films don't fall into the set ideals of the BFI and other fund-making bodies.

There's a whole fund of film-makers who are fed up with applying for grants and not getting them. Even the music promo work is drying up as the music industry is increasingly contracting certain companies all the time, and the indie bands who used to want low-budget videos are being squeezed so they don't have anything to spend. At least their ideas are not just gathering dust; we'll show them.

Another film-maker, Donal, and I are making a film, *The Last Hour of Elvis Presley*, it's got drug references and will be a bit trashy, but we think it will be good; there's no way we'll get funding in this country. The BFI and all funding bodies fund similar films each time. But we're going to make it anyway, on a smaller budget, and show it at the Exploding Cinema – it will reach some people.

In fact we're networking like crazy. We're doing a show in Manchester – there's a group up there. Someone came down to see us and took the idea back, that's what we want to do, get loads of groups going all round the country. We did a show in Dublin last year – we've got a strong Irish contingent in the group. We're doing a screening in Glasgow and Brighton and hopefully in Europe. We just want to give encouragement to young film-makers everywhere.

Our membership is a real mix, it's 50–50 male and female and we're getting more black people. Sadly, film-making is still the domain of the white middle-class and we want to get away from that. We have had some very promising film-makers showing work who you know should really get recognition. Some have. Like one guy, Andrew Cotting – his films are brilliant. We showed an early film a couple of years ago and knew he deserved a wide audience. His films are hard to describe, idiosyncratic and very stylish. He's got Channel 4 funding now. We showed a Richard Stanley film which he shot in Afghanistan and couldn't get it shown elsewhere, so at least it reached the Lido audience – a few thousand.

Obviously if I was given funding or a huge budget I'd be happy to make a film, but I'm just as happy working on my own projects. I prefer working under my own steam, with no restrictions. The Exploding Cinema has approached the Arts Council. We don't have a very good relationship with them – we go to their screenings and hand out fliers, because they've got a funding conspiracy. We get everyone in the group to fill out forms and apply for funding, then if anyone got it, we'd share out the money. So instead of one person having £20,000, 20 people get £1000! The Arts Council don't like that!

I don't know how it can change. Sadly there are many people in the industry who have a vested interest in keeping the establishment status quo, we can only do our little bit. At least the London Film Makers' Co-op have bucked up their ideas. It's sad because the talent is there in Britain, but there is no money. An injection of money is definitely needed, but it's not going to happen. In America if you want to make a feature film, there's a system of building a way up, but here you're banging your head against a brick wall for years and still getting nowhere. It's soul-destroying.

## Iffy, 22, Wandsworth, South London

I'm working for London Underground right now – but I'm spending all my free time working on a film script and writing poetry. The script I'm writing is for a competition run by the National Film School. If they like my idea they'll give me a bit of funding and I'll be able to make the film this summer. Then I go to university in the autumn.

I've written my first collection of poems. It's not been published yet, but I've had a cover and illustrations designed for it, so it's a finished product. I wanted something to give me an edge when I approached publishers, this way it's ready to go. Plus I didn't want someone telling me, 'We're going to present it like this', and missing the point. The artists I used drew subliminal drawings which explain the poems and give you something to think about.

The poetry started almost by mistake. I was working on the outline for a book about the turmoil in South Africa, the apartheid and hate turning to civil war, with the central character getting caught up in it all. I wanted to write a poem to start and finish the book. When I started writing I thought 'I like this poetry business' and kept on at it, leaving the book! I've gone back to the book since, the outline's there.

I find it easy to write poetry. I listen to a lot of black music and always have lyrics going around my head. I think about certain issues, why people act the way they do, the way the world's going. People have an attitude here – to push things away until tomorrow, but it never comes. They never deal with anything. That's the kind of thing I write about. I have considered putting the poems to music, but I'm not really musical myself and it's very hard for anything to materialise here. You need contacts and money, and you have to push and push for quite some time and still get nowhere.

Though I haven't had anything published, my poems did help to get me on a film course with Halfway Production House. It was a project funded by Wandsworth Youth Development – which has sadly mostly been disbanded now, though Halfway Production House itself is still going. The Wandsworth Development Trust funded it, and since we worked in 16 mm film, which is very expensive, it meant they paid for most of the costs, otherwise it wouldn't have been possible. It gave myself and other unemployed young people chance to learn about and make films. Four films made by Halfway students were screened at the Clapham Picture House, and people in the industry were invited. They try and show you everything about film-making – camera, lights, sound, directing, scriptwriting, assisting, which is good. Eight of us co-wrote, co-directed, shared the camera work and so on, of the films. Out of everything, I like writing the best.

Although the films we made were short comedies, they were just a vehicle to teach us the basics. All of us used to sit around discussing issues and the films we'd like to make. We all felt strongly about the type of films we wanted to make, the issues we wanted to cover. One girl there has since made a documentary on battered wives. She feels as strongly about those women and their problems as I do about crime.

The LA riots happened while I was there and we'd all talk about that. There are similarities here to what's happening there. It's frightening and people don't want to think about it, but it's true. And that's why they should look at the LA riots and what caused them. Should you protest? The people in South Central had been protesting for years, and nothing was done in all that time. And, I know the LA riots caused deaths and damage to the area which has still not been repaired, and I don't want to sound flippant, but at least people took notice of them, far more than the talking that had been going on for years with their voices not being heard.

It is a shame that it's their shops and run-down area that's damaged, when they lived in a poverty-stricken area anyway. But then at the same time, look at some of those in Hollywood Boulevard, who have worked their way up to get what they want. Is it their fault? The sad thing is that the riots were just a rumble, it hasn't even started yet . . .

People criticised Spike Lee for his movie, *Do The Right Thing*, which highlighted the problems, when he's middle-class, he doesn't come from a ghetto with no money, but he showed he was in touch with what was happening. What he depicted, the types of frustrations the people felt and the reactions, was all true.

I feel if someone shows the lives exactly and how people feel and what will happen, then if it comes to pass, it shouldn't be criticised, it shows whether or not the problems have been dealt with.

I want to make good films like Spike Lee. Not about violence, but films that show I'm in touch with the types of issues and thinking about the trends and what's happening every day. But, more importantly, I want to make films about black people. Movies that put black people in main roles, like Wesley Snipes. In his latest movie, it's not that he's black, he's a cop. I want to showcase black people, the harmonies, all the facets, not just the sides we've seen in *Jungle Fever*, *Boyz 'n the Hood*, etc. I want to show that having lots of black characters is normal, put lots of black men in the police force, and that sort of thing!

The script I'm doing now is *Ride Through The Black Side*, it's more or less shot from inside a cab. That's the other thing I want to do, develop a style that people will recognise as mine. Like Martin Scorsese, who has a distinct camera style, so you know it's him. He uses the same head of camera every time to establish his style. I want to leave a hallmark on my work.

The film starts off in South Central LA. I want to film people on the streets, everyday happenings from the inside of a cab – using some characters but some real life people too – then I'm coming back to London and doing a similar thing here, going round the streets, showing what's happening. I'm going to film in King's Cross, Brixton and Broadwater Farm. I want to show that the same stuff is happening here. I want outsiders to realise that the responsibility belongs to everyone, we've all got to go half-way. It hasn't even started yet.

If all goes well, I'll film the short this summer. I will go to South Central to shoot – that's why I'm working hard now to get the money to go and to get the camera. I've got family living outside so I can stay with them and go into the area, do some work and shoot the film. It shouldn't take more than three or four days' filming if all goes well, it depends on the weather and what happens. I needn't find actors over there because a lot will be freestyle, raw action from the streets, and I won't have much money to spend on that part. I'll finish it off back here.

There isn't going to be a lot of dialogue. I'm going to read a poem prior to the movie and at the end, something that sums it up or reflects on the ideas in the film, but isn't too explanatory, and I'll collect some newspaper cuttings to show what's happening here. Murders, not so much racial problems as things like car-hijacking. That's something foreign to us, but it's happening here now. When did it start here? It's not necessary. I want people to see for themselves the similarities between the areas – I don't want to have to put the points blatantly, I'd rather they thought for themselves.

I pray it's not too indie. I don't want it just to reach the few who are probably aware of the issues anyway, I want everyone to see what I'm saying. That's one of the things that really makes me angry, the way films are shown in this country, only a few films get shown nationwide. People aren't encouraged to see a wide variety of films or think for themselves about what they want to see.

Hopefully, when I get into the industry, if I ever become a voice to be reckoned with and have people come to me for comments on film and related topics, I'd voice my opinions on how wrong the system is, and how so many films that are made never get shown to a wide audience. If a film is made it should be shown and give the public a chance to say whether they liked it or not, rather than having everything decided for them.

I want to make good-quality stuff and I want to show that I'm in touch, but at the same time I want to make my living from it. Why can't the two go together? I want to make good films that will be enjoyed, I don't want to make that nasty Schwarzenegger stuff you watch on the screen, have a good laugh about and forget. I want people to watch my films and think about them, and a couple of weeks later to still be thinking about them.

The script I've written on my own, but if I manage to secure funding, I'll involve friends for the camerawork, etc. I've also taken the best paid odd job I can find to try and save up some money – I work at a London Underground station. The way I see it is, I've been waiting about two years to get to go to university, and I can either sit and wait and do nothing or keep working. I work on my projects in the spare time I have and I've taken so many odd jobs – at least six in that time, to earn myself some money so I can save up to make a film. At least I haven't wasted that time. And the jobs are a great source of characters – I've worked in Burger King, in Häagen-Dazs, a video rental place, a shoe shop and so on. Working at the video shop was eye-opening, everyone felt so passionately about the videos they hired; if they didn't like them, they'd complain with a passion! It's good for me, because I want my films to be seen. What's the point of making a statement if no one hears it? If people don't sit up and pay attention, I may as well keep all my thoughts to myself and not bother.

I want my films to be entertaining. I don't want to force the issues of racism down their throat, I want it to be subtle, to let people think about it for themselves. Take those rappers like Ice Cube and Ice T, etc. They're very loud, very aggressive. That's fine, and it works for some people. But there are others who hear it and think, 'That's heavy, I'm out of here.' There has to be different ways of reaching people.

Others from my video course have gone on to college already. It was a great place for meeting people who felt the same way as you do. We've got a pool of creative talent that we'll call upon when any of us get to make a film. I definitely know the two people I want to work on the cameras for me.

I had thought that doing that six-month course would be enough – that making a film would be easy. I'd just write a script, send it to Warner Brothers and earn a million. Now I know differently! I've applied to go to college in September 1994 – hopefully the National Film School, but I've applied to others too.

I've had to wait so long to qualify for a grant, because although I was born and brought up in Britain, I went to Nigeria for five years – the formulative years of 14–19 – for education reasons, and came back two-and-a-half years ago. It was a kind of tradition thing, there's nothing wrong with the standard education here – it's the same, O and A levels – it was the cultural education. My mum wanted me and my brothers and sister to know about our history and learn about Nigeria, where the family comes from. The standard of living there is so much better and people far more friendlier. At that time, I liked the UK a great deal and thought I'd be missing out on my friends and everything happening here, but it was an interesting experience.

My mother and the rest of my family joined me out there and my mum has stayed there, but when I left school I returned to London as did my sister and the older of my brothers. (My father died when I was young.)

I also learned Tae Kwondo there, as my cousin's a champion. It's good to have some form of self-defence, since I'm tiny, but it's better training for the mind. My cousin taught me to be aware of what's around me, but never let it influence me too much. If people are richer or more popular, don't fret, just keep working, take your time and get there at your own pace.

The interesting thing about coming back is you do notice the decline in the country, standards of living, for ordinary people, especially in my area – South London. And you can see how what's happened in America will happen here eventually. In Nigeria, I could see it even more closely, many of the people at my school were American and the country mirrors the USA. It's got the same political system and the idea of states and the same lifestyle, the way there are very rich areas with complete luxury like Hollywood, and right next to them such poor slums. You can imagine the kids in the squalid little hut looking across the road at the guy in the rich house thinking why has he got such a lot and I have got nothing? Then you can understand why they go and deal in drugs, thinking it will be a quick way to get the riches they deserve too. How do you explain all that to a kid? We're a step away from that too.

Every time I go outside the area where I live, out of the country and especially America, they say, 'Where are you from?' and you say 'South London', they give you respect. They say I want to be on your side, not against you. But hey, I can't fight, even if I wanted to. I'm tiny, but the area and its associations rub off.

Of current successful directors I like Martin Scorsese. *Goodfellas* is one of the best films ever made. Trying camera tricks like he did by shooting one continuous length of film for a long time, rather than cutting angles, is great, but it's hard to do well. You have to be careful with camera tricks. As a director your ideas and vision have to be conveyed to the audience. If they are just your vision, there's no point doing it. You've got to give your audience a tad bit of a chance to get into it.

## Johnny, 19, animation and computer graphics student, Sheffield

Films are very important. I detest watching animation – even though I study it! There have been no decent films for the past five or six years. None of the mainstream films. No general films appealing to a wide audience about cities and the people who live in them. *Boyz 'n the Hood* was appalling.

I'd read these reports on the horrific lives of the youth of South Central LA and then I saw this saccharine view, it lacked the edge. The only film I've seen lately that was worthy was *The Making of Apocalypse Now* as it mirrored what was happening. In *Boyz 'n the Hood* they should have got their hands dirty and filmed it like it was, and let us get to see some real reactions.

The main problem with films is the dialogue. There are very few people capable of writing good scripts – or books. There are few good authors about.

Our culture is very visual. Even if you eavesdrop on real conversations, most of what is said is inane and not worthy of a wide audience. I'd love to make films but I'm limited by my skills – I'd make a very good cameraman but not the lighting or sound – and by finance – I've not enough money!

### Saz, 23, trainee camera assistant, Hull

Things are going very well this month; I've had a lot of work. I've been working as a clapper-loader and focus-puller on films. I want to work on feature films, doing camera and lighting, but at the moment I'm gaining experience and contacts. I've been doing volunteer work at the National Film School in Beaconsfield, helping out when they've needed crew, even doing a bit of sparking.

I'm also working with a theatre company, who are staging *Hamlet*, as a lighting operator. It's in London at the moment, but goes on tour in April so I'll go on tour with them, for at least some of the venues and I'll actually get paid for that!

I don't often get paid, since it is mostly volunteer work. I have been paid on a couple of projects like pop promos where there's a bit more of a budget, and sometimes I'll get expenses – travelling, etc. – but basically I'm doing it to get experience. It's the only way; everybody does it. Volunteering is the only way to learn and to get in. I'll try and get to work on films that will teach me something or be interesting projects. I helped out with the DOP – director of photography – recently for a Kodak competition commercial, and some of my footage got used which was nice. And I've done camera assisting with a cameraman who's a high-speed technician shooting an underwater scene for a BBC natural history programme at Crawley swimming pool. The idea is that if you help someone out voluntarily and they're pleased with your work, they might think of you when they get paid work. I know some people wouldn't be prepared to work for nothing but that's what you have to do in this industry. And then, I'm used to not having a lot.

I used to be a hairdresser and make-up artist and there was not much money in that. I produced shows at places like The Hippodrome and The Limelight, but I felt I didn't want to do it for ever. At 21, I decided to get the A level I needed to do a history of art degree course. I started the degree in Stoke-on-Trent but it didn't work out. I'd done an A level in film studies and I knew that's what I wanted to be involved in. So I came back, did a short course in 16 mm film to learn the basics and now basically I volunteer myself.

I don't feel used working without being paid. It depends who you work for; most of the films I've worked on are for people who are doing it on a shoestring and you know they can't afford to pay you, and because I'm not fully trained, you could say they are taking a risk with me. Some people have been a clapper-loader for 20 years. I want to be a really good camera assistant, and I'll pick up as many tips as possible along the way.

I don't just want to work on other people's films. I'm currently working on a script and I'll try to get sponsorship to make the film myself. If it comes off, I'll get a crew together. I know a lot of people who would be willing to work on a film with me because it would allow them to get experience in the area they want to learn. Also, I can afford to be experimental. I've nothing to lose. Even if the film bombs, I'll have learnt something from it. It's the camera and lights, the technical side I'm interested in, not producing, though I'll probably co-direct. It's not like I've got to speed through the project, I've got a lot of time, so I can iron out the creases first. I can take my time and enjoy it. I've talked to people about the idea and it's been well received, I know it's got an audience there.

In the industry at the moment everyone is struggling for work, although it's picked up a little lately. I have to accept that as part of the industry I want to go into, and I know it's one that's accused of being male-dominated. I've never come up against a problem being female though I've discovered that it's only over the past four years that women have been 'allowed' to get in there. Now people are proud of women getting there so they have a fairer chance of getting the jobs. I have found I have to be more pushy than I am by nature, or just confident.

I'm getting more choosy about the voluntary work I'll do. It's camera assisting I'm interested in and there is only so much you can learn as a clapper-loader on a film school shoot. Sometimes I'll still do it, if it's a 35 mm film then I'll load for that, or a very interesting 16 mm film, but if it's more of the same 16 mm work, I've done a lot of it and I'm not getting paid, you can only do so much. I'd prefer to opt for work doing focus-pulling. Obviously paid work is a different matter, but when it's voluntary work and you're doing it for experience, you have to decide what training you're getting out of it. You are trying to progress.

There's a Job Fit scheme, a two-year industry-based training which I'm hoping to do. You do everything from running and work up, pointing out which department you want to get into and they'll try and fit you in. You get a basic wage for that, which at least keeps you together. I'm on the dole right now, so that's the only thing keeping me together. On some projects you're really out of pocket, if you have to travel across London every day and so on. The theatre project where I'm doing lighting operating I have to fund myself while it's in London with no expenses, not even travelling. When it tours, I'll get paid. But I'm building up a good CV. I've also done work experience at companies learning camera maintenance and they were happy with my work. That's what I do, build up contacts and experience.

I could use my make-up and hairdressing skills, but to be honest it doesn't interest me anymore, and the place where I'm living I couldn't have people round. I haven't really got time anyway, I'm busy running around trying to find work and getting from A to B to see people. The National Film School's in Beaconsfield and that means a journey across town – though there's a daily bus service to it. I've even moved to be closer to a drop off point – that's how much the film bug has affected my life!

I go round seeing production teams who are doing work I'm interested in, or if I see commercials to be shot or low-budget films, I'll jump in and ask, 'Can I focus-pull or load?' Though since I've been helping out I often get calls asking if I want to work now. The college is for producers, directors, camera operators and directors of photography, so they all need crews – focus-pullers, boom operators, loaders – they can't do everything. It's mostly post-grad stuff and I usually work with four directors of photography. They're graduating now and I think they're really talented, they'll do well. It's the DOPs who crew the camera side, not usually the producers, so hopefully they'll remember me when they get paid work. Besides, they're very helpful and if I have a technical problem in my own projects, they'd help me out. The wrap parties at the end of shoots are always fun – and you can make contacts that way.

But you're only as good as your last job. If you do make a hash of something, you'll never be asked back, your reputation rests on your work. In a way it's not a bad system. It doesn't all rest on who you know – your skill really matters. I know people whose fathers are DOPs and that doesn't guarantee them work, which wasn't the case in hairdressing.

It can be frustrating, like at Christmas I had three offers of work, so I turned down everything else for January to do them and one by one they rang saying the budget had fallen and the project wasn't going ahead. It happens all the time.

I've always been into film. In my A level I covered French New Wave and African film so I'm open to influences. I'm European-minded. But while I'd love to go to

France, the industry there is very tight and so it's hard to get into it. Socially, I go to see films a lot, I always have done, always. I love French, Japanese, British and classical Hollywood – Hitchcock and stuff. There's a lot of talent here – look at Merchant Ivory and new talent coming out of New Zealand, like Jane Campion's *The Piano*. The last film I saw was *The Conformist* – and that's from the sixties – that's a style of film I'd like to do. I'd love to be experimental in film-making. I think Hollywood rips off some of the independent ideas. Having said that, I'll go and see Spielberg's *Schindler's List* because of the camera and lighting techniques.

It is a struggle to get to do what you want to do when you're not earning, but I have done quite a lot of the things I wanted to do in the past. I took a year off and travelled Europe and that sort of thing. And, it's almost natural for me not to have money! That's a sad thing to say, but I did a YTS scheme getting about £27 a week while training to do hair and make-up and had to take three jobs at the same time, bar waiting and stuff like that, to keep a roof over my head, while studying. So this hasn't come as a big shock to me. I've even worked in cinemas to keep myself together. I know I'm going to have to keep on struggling for a couple of years until I get somewhere.

I'm 24 in two weeks' time. It's a good age to be – you're old enough to be taken seriously, but not too old to learn. I've always been not quite happy with what I was doing. Now, even after a couple of bad days, I've never felt like giving up. It's always fun to work, and meet new people. I've met lots of good friends. I've never done a job in an office – I don't think I ever could. I've never felt I don't want to go in tomorrow – I really love the work.

### John, 20, one-time horror movie fan, Upminster, Essex

My brother Darren and I write and produce a film fanzine ... called *Invasion of the Sad Man-eating Mushrooms* ...

Well, why not? I must say that our principal interest in doing the fanzine now lies more in actually putting the 'zine together than the subject matter itself! Before *Invasion* came along, three years ago, our main interest was playing the rather dull pastime of postal role-playing games. We even produced four issues of a 'zine called *The Voice* based on it, then we grew up and graduated to movies!

To be honest, before we got all creative, we were really out to make a fast buck, but to our dismay we discovered that fandom doesn't work that way. We soon got another kind of reward – satisfaction! Once we got *Invasion* together and out there, and once it was selling, we found we were pleased that people were taking an interest and reading something we'd produced. We put it together at home and sell it by post and through movie shops and other outlets.

As the issues passed, the pace picked up and the readership increased. There are a lot of horror fans out there. Before long we had a regular band of contributors and *Invasion* became an instrument for horror fans to write about what they liked and disliked. We even sent out a questionnaire with number four so the readers could shape the future of the fanzine. It really became a team effort (as our lengthy credits will testify), Darren and I are merely along for the ride. The first issue was out in September 91, with another in December 91, then four the next year.

We're now working on the *Invasion* book. It's nearly finished and should be off to the printers in January (this year). It's 200 pages long, made up of four issues of material – issues 5, 8, 9 and 10, due out February. It WILL knock the socks off the opposition and no mistake.

We both had an interest in horror films from an early age. Mine stemmed from some genre books my brother was given in the early seventies. I never actually saw many of the films concerned, I just liked to flick through the pages, fascinated by the odd images. When I was finally allowed to stay up and see a horror movie for the first time, I totally cacked my slacks (metaphorically, *not* physically)! Being older and braver, Darren got to see all the films I could only read about. As the few Hammer flicks I did cower through gave me nightmares, I avoided watching anything frightening until my mid to late teens.

When you delve into the wealth of films available in this genre, you'll find that 99.9 per cent of them are absolutely fucking awful. How people can sit through (let alone enjoy) the majority of films we feature is beyond me. Low production values, abysmal acting, poor editing, high body counts, OTT splatter scenes . . . all of these are the bane of horror cinema. It would seem that everyone is missing the point – generating fright. Not even the so called Italian 'maestros' (like Dario Argento) with their fluid camera work and lavish sets can achieve it. This is why I only admire a few horror films, those that actually finish the job they set out to do – scaring me!

But there are some that do it. Without a doubt, on a first viewing (on your own!) the ones that have you chewing your fingernails to the bone are *The Exorcist*, *Exorcist III*, *Salem's Lot*, *The Omen*, *Jacob's Ladder* and *The Evil Dead*. Though for pure entertainment value, you'll also have to sit through *Evil Dead II*, *Flesh for Frankenstein* and *A Clockwork Orange*. I have to admit, I prefer reading about horror films than watching them.

These days we're more general film fans, not much horror to be found among our top movies. Darren's all-time favourites include *Cool Hand Luke* and *Top Gun*! I love *Dead Men Don't Wear Plaid* (Steve Martin) and *Blade Runner*, *Enter the Dragon*, *Back to the Future* . . . and a whole host of other mainstream movies. Until someone produces another genuinely atmospheric film, I'd prefer to watch *Red Dwarf* than some lame arse splatter pic. Make our own films? Naaaaaw! But we do have contributors who make camcorder horrors which we review in the 'zine.

Most of our readers correspond regularly. A fair amount of them write just to find out what progress is being made with the issue in production. Many are contributors, chucking ideas for material and chit chat at us. Then there are those we've met and got to know through pub meets and the like – we organise meetings, usually in central London pubs, and publicise them in the fanzine, or to those who write to us. Anyone interested turns up. They're a friendly bunch, mainly film buffs, normal folk who like meeting people and having a laugh. I've only ever had one crack-pot hassle me through the post, and another guy who seemed nice as pie in his letters, but turned out to be a paranoid piss-head who alienated everyone at a pub meet.

I don't think we're very sad men – we're more cynical than sad.

# **4** Art Nineties-style

## Faisal, 23, artist/barber, Harlesden

All my work reflects life, culture, what I see around. I
didn't start off like that and I never intended to do hairdressing. I did a degree at St Martin's doing printmaking,
creating images and screen-printing them. While at St Martin's I did an exchange to America at Massachusetts
College of Art in Boston, and it was there that I found out
about my history and background. I hadn't learnt anything
about black history and culture before and I met all these
black people who were very conscious of themselves and
their roots and I felt left out. I began to take an interest
and took all that on board. It started being reflected in my
work.

And, while there I really needed a haircut. I kept going
up to all these black people in the street and asking for a
barber. I got pointed to one in Boston and when I came
out it didn't look like my hair had been touched at all. My
friend at college, who was sharing my dormitory said: 'I'll
cut your hair,' and he did. I used to watch him getting
ready to go out and he'd cut his hair – he wore a pony tail,
and shaped it all in. Then he'd do mine, before we went
out for the night. When I got back home, I started doing
my own! That's how I learnt hairdressing.

I've been working in a barber's on Saturdays while doing
my degree as a form of income. And then all the while I
was doing my MA at the Royal College of Art. I really
enjoyed it; it became a focus, a resource centre. I got to see
patterns and shapes in the hair and the styles on the heads
and started documenting them. I took pictures of the
people who went in to get haircuts, and the barber's and
my college work began to intermingle. I kind of saw it as

a temporary installation – I'd be in the studio all week and then in the barber's on Saturday, sometimes until midnight with people waiting for their hair to be cut. It's kind of a basic art deco barber's but the vibe is very lively, ragga/soul.

I took the photos of the haircuts, blew them up and screen-printed them on to steel sheets. They were shown in an exhibition at the 198 Gallery in Brixton. They even put a barber's chair in the space. That received some attention, through it I was asked to do a BBC documentary on barbers, and it's sparked off other interest.

I get a lot of pleasure from working in the barber's. I do it for an extra day a week now as I've left college, and need money to keep me working on my art. My lifestyle has changed meeting all those different people. The people that come in are full of street hype, their time is short – they live on the moment, and they know about fashion and music. When you meet these people you become respected by them because as a barber you can make or break them depending on how you sculpt their hair. It's important to them and many come to get their hair cut just before going to a club, so they trust you. You bring them a lot of joy. It is mostly male but I have cut women's hair, a few girls are willing to wait around in a male-dominated environment.

I'm a fine artist, but I use the camera as source material, it shows the moment that I took the picture. I then print it, putting the image on cement, steel tiles or whatever I want to do with it. It could be used for interiors – in fact, I'm trying to do something with Birmingham council's Living Art in the Environment project on that front.

I've done a couple of book covers – like one for Boxtree who saw the barber work and asked to have a word cut into a head and printed, and although my work's not strictly photographic, I got an exhibition at the Photographer's Gallery recently. Some pieces from that exhibition are going into the Art 94 show.

My work acts as a mirror on what is going on here. I live in Harlesden which is similar to Brixton and I make my work reflect where I live. I was criticised over my last work – that it was violent because it showed people with weapons, but I was just showing an image. And I didn't choose that image. I took photographs of a group, friends of mine, called Scientists of Sound – they're rappers. They are very intelligent guys, with a great knowledge of African history which they portray in their lyrics. They create images with words, and I create images in pigment, steel, glass . . .

I took them in a studio and took about 12 pictures of each one, which I blew up and printed. I asked each of them to choose an image to represent themselves – all of them chose the image of holding a weapon. I don't know why that is, whether it was making a statement about fighting restrictions, being in this culture or fighting against record company censoring, but each one wanted a gun, so that's why the pictures had weapons.

My next work involves black men and white men and women. I've got about 30 'models' – friends, ordinary people – to contact for it. Some of the shots will be taken in a studio, as I can control it, but I'll probably take pictures outside, on the streets too. I try to stop it being too artificial by playing music and getting the vibe going while I'm taking the pictures. Keep the energy there.

It was strange, at the end of my MA, my degree show did nothing, while some students sold all their work or got thousands of pounds in sponsorship. I thought, 'I'm leaving, I'm a dead man, I'll have to sit at home and look at the walls, my friends will say, "yes you're an artist, doing nothing with no money".' But it all started after I left.

Hopefully I'm going to have something in Harlem – as the director of the Harlem Cultural Center saw my exhibition at the 198 Gallery, they came along because it was called *From Nigger to Nubian* . . . and wanted to take some pieces over to Harlem to show. In 95 I'm having work in an exhibition in New York provisionally titled *British Artists of Colour* and I've got an exhibition at the Netherlands Photo Institute in Rotterdam opening at the end of October 1994, plus I've got some things happening here.

I'm keeping up the barber's – I do two days a week, since leaving college, to get money to finance my art. It's great, for me the barber's is going back to basics – the college and my fine art is an esoteric life, on a different plane, working on a visual level. When I get back to Harlesden, I can't communicate it all, it's like tripping. I have to be bilingual. At the barber's I have to know what's happening on the street, in my culture, in music. It makes life very rich.

## Mark Sinclair ('Prime'), 23, artist, South London

I was into art at a very young age. I did art O level, but that was as far as my formal training goes. I got the rest through practice. I'm a freelance graphic artist but I'm also really into street art – graffiti. I got into that when I was about 15. I started writing, and my stuff was seen around. You develop a name. There's a lot of artistic merit and skill involved there which isn't always recognised. I think there's nothing wrong with aerosol as a medium. It's hard to use and it takes a long time to get control of the can – it's an artistic skill.

I have had exhibitions at galleries. I had one at The Bedford Hill Art Gallery in November, and again a few years back, and at The Tabernacle and The Association of Illustrators gallery in the West End.

When you're writing on walls, Tubes or whatever, you develop tags, and other writers recognise your work and look out for it. I've always wanted people to recognise my work from the beginning. You get to know where to do your writing if you're really into it. If you do it a lot and you really get involved, especially if you go by Tube, you can choose places where your work will really get noticed.

I suppose I got a kind of notoriety in the early years, then I moved on and started doing bigger pieces, more intricate works – larger works with characters, colour effects and shades, they are all on walls. I suppose it is frustrating if you do a large piece on a wall and you put a lot of time and effort into it and then it disappears, gets removed or someone else does something, or the building goes, but most writers know it's a temporary thing and so they record their work by taking photographs of it. At least I've got the photographs to keep and show.

Back in the old days, there used to be a lot more people into it, especially around 1986. It started to hit this country in 1984–5 and by 1989 it had become really large. It died down after that as the old school of people went on to other things. Now there's a kind of revival, a few new young ones are doing it. They notice stuff about, read about what went on and want to do stuff themselves. There's one good 16-year-old boy who's really promising; I work with him sometimes.

I still do writing – graffiti – but it's usually legal sites, or at least sites where you don't get bothered. In the past, I have been half-way through things a few times and had to run away!

In 1986–7 I got my first show at the Bedford Hill Art Gallery – a gallery inside a squatted building in Wandsworth which has become recognised. We approached Ron, the guy who runs it, and he was keen because we were really young and still at school. We got funding that time, which was good considering how young we were. The show we did before Christmas was with one of my partners – we hadn't done anything for a while. Most of the stuff in the show we did especially for it – you don't build up a collection like other artists!

Obviously most of the pieces you do, you can't sell, but you can make prints and posters of them from the photographs. I'm getting more into that, doing posters of my recent murals.

I haven't done a lot with the local council, there's a lack of funding everywhere which curtails artistic work, but I have spoken to a number of councils and approached Wandsworth about a large project to brighten up the area. I wanted to use themes covering various places in the area, which are run-down and in need of something. My partner's going to be doing something along those lines.

I don't teach or anything like that, though I know of one writer who does it with a youth group. I wouldn't mind getting involved with a youth project, if it came up, because it's a way of encouraging young people to take an interest in art, when they're not the sort to go to galleries. People need more encouragement to experiment and find their own art form.

I got really into the history of writing, I was really serious about it. I wanted people to know about graffiti, and consider its value, even if it's only temporary. I went to America where it originated and looked at some of the street art there, around New York and places.

The terminology all comes from American street art. Being a writer involves everything, from someone who just does tags to someone who does major murals. It's an art form in itself – I call myself an artist. You get inspiration and ideas from seeing other art, but you don't want to copy. It's just not done. I get my ideas from various sources. I developed my own personal style of lettering, merging two graphic styles of writing and drawing in characters and background.

It sounds as though it might link up with my work as a graphic artist, but the two are usually kept quite separate. I did work with someone who went through the training and picked up a lot from him, but I've had no training in it myself, you just practise and build up a portfolio. I've been approached by quite a few people for commissions. I get work now and again, it's not too bad considering the climate. I've got a few jobs on now. The area I want to explore is record sleeves, doing logos for record labels. I have been approached to do that. Normally you get a brief and work to that, unlike my street art which is all my creating. They are separate styles, though in some of my graphic work I've been able to incorporate street influence. You have to be adaptable, not everyone's from that stance, not everyone admires it! I'm also getting more into doing T-shirts. I've been doing them but they're mostly airbrushed, one-off designs, and I want to get into doing prints, which are quicker to do and easier to sell.

At the moment, my partner and I are doing a backdrop for an event, that's another new thing for us, club interiors. Hopefully it will push us forward a bit, though I have done a large commission before for a George Michael party, to launch one of his albums. They wanted a huge street scene which we did in a film studio. Again none of this is permanent, it all comes off in a few days! It is a shame, but I'm used to it.

A few of my old works are still around. I had a commission for an outside party in Latimer Road once, that mural stayed up for years. I don't really travel round to see my old works, to see if they're still there – I just look at the photos. It is sad that street artists never get a collection together that will be valuable when you're old ... but that's the way it is.

I'm satisfied with how my life has gone; I don't regret not having gone to art school ... but it's not too late, and if I ever feel I want to go, that I could benefit in some way, then I'll enrol.

## Jason Brooks, 25, artist, London

A lot of the art world takes itself too seriously. I wanted to break down the prejudices that exist. I bring a touch of wit into my work. I like wit more than humour, humour can be stupid, but wit is missing in a lot of art work.

I spend my whole time painting in the studio, there's always an exhibition that I'm working for, or several. I like to keep busy working towards others, then if it comes to nothing, I just continue getting on with the next piece.

I've always been told that I was good at art, but when I was at school it was a toss up whether it would be art or sport. I used to be very good at tennis and played national tennis while at school, but I realised I wasn't really good enough to make it to the very top – the material side is as important as the natural ability. I didn't just want to be a tennis player so I opted for art.

I'm a bit schizophrenic in that each piece of my work is

different from the rest. I paint in different styles and different guises. Some people even think my work is created by a different person. I used to experiment with different styles and art forms, but as my grandfather used to say, I'd be good at them all, but master of none – it's clichéd but true, so, as people had always said I was better at painting, I painted from that point on. I did my MA in painting and at Cheltenham I studied painting.

When I was at college my art interests were somewhat different from my present artwork. I come from a middle-class background, and went to normal comprehensive schools, did a foundation at Cheltenham, then did a year at Goldsmiths but I had health problems – exhaustion, due to living it up too much – so I switched to Rotherham in South Yorkshire. I stayed there for three years – it was like going to a retirement home where it's so quiet you can sit and discover your identity, then went on to do an MA at Chelsea.

I did an MA in painting – I did all this stuff about commodity values. When I was at Cheltenham in the late eighties, everything was very work and business orientated, and everyone was into commodity values. We were all being taught that artists were as important as their work. So I pushed myself along with my work. I networked like mad and got known, everyone else was doing it a bit. It was and still is important for me for my work to be seen, to communicate. Even if it's only to one person, my work has got to say something.

I was young and naïve then, but I was able to talk about my work and have all the answers there. At Goldsmiths, the lecturers were trying to make students into overnight superstars, and that ethos infiltrated into my work. I wanted to be up there too! I still do!

I am aware of the fact that if you rise to stardom quickly, you can disappear even quicker; I'd rather stay up there, so I'm taking my time.

While I was doing my MA at Chelsea I worked on lots of shows that had little to do with my course work. I am a deadline junkie, I like working to something. I was working to the little shows and doing my course work. I was in the position where people were asking me whether working for all those shows was worthwhile, but I regard nothing as a mistake.

I finished a painting two weeks ago for an art fair, three days before the show was about to happen, then I have another one in a week's time and I'm working on something else that has come about via an exhibition I was involved with. A lot of an artist's success is due to contacts. It works in a mysterious way, just as in any business it helps if you get your company known. Some people hide away and work alone, but my work has to be shown. It was definitely important for me to do my MA in London to get to know the network! But I did it with humour, the whole work ethos translated into my work – my work is all about commodity values. I took this thing about artists and commodity values and started working with bar codes.

I appropriated other artists' work, using ideas from several artists on one work to show there's no original idea, people borrow, but it's not undermining their work.

I've been doing some shows which aren't in galleries but alternative spaces. I've been commissioned to paint a picture on Victoria Station over five days. Three artists are going to paint at three main stations, the idea being that hopefully the commuters will offer suggestions, even those who've never shown an interest in art before. I've got to do the painting from start to finish, so it will be a quick work. I haven't a clue how it will turn out. It will probably be made into a poster to stick up at the station.

I am a bit of an exhibitionist, and it will be good publicity, but I may fall flat on my face as I'll be thinking and working on the spot. I don't usually paint in public in front of an audience, but I think I'll turn myself off. It depends on what happens. It's a very short time to do a complete painting.

I work pretty quickly as artists go. I've created paintings over 14 days in galleries for exhibitions, but this time there will be people approaching all the time ... Who knows what I'll produce over five days? I doubt if it will be along the lines of the work I'm doing at the moment. I'm into S&M paintings. It's very relevant for the moment. My work is very ideas-orientated. I like there to be an equilibrium of idea and painting. If a painting has no content in terms of ideas it gives you less to think about.

I had a show before Christmas – a mask show. I showed a large bondage work – a mask party – at a gallery in Soho. I don't know exactly why I started doing S&M work. Ideas are always kicking around, adding up until they suddenly gather momentum. I'm influenced by what I see around and my personal life. I have been to a few Skin Two clubs. I'd been bobbing the ideas around first, then I went to the clubs. Being there gave me more images when I started painting other work.

When you do S&M or any other work with even a vague sexual overtone you'll get some sort of criticism. As I said I'm a bit schizophrenic. I'm always in two minds about things. We're living in that period when everything you say, you can say, 'Ah, but . . .' after it. I share the same belief as many that there should be no racism, no sexism, though my S&M work usually has women as central to it – but then women in an S&M situation are dominant. It depends which way you look at it.

I'm not sure who buys my work – my S&M work – or any other of my paintings. I do have a few collectors who buy my work generally and I've sold a lot to the States. On a day to day basis, I'm always working on several things, I switch working between them, depending on how I feel. So even when I'm making S&M paintings I have some other things on the go which have nothing to do with that theme. Some I need to make quickly and some take more time. If people were to see my work, they'd probably think a different artist had done the different paintings, because of the content and the same style. I've got many ideas running through my head – why should I have to paint in a particular style? I don't want to just do work in a repetitive way. You can always tell it was my work – through the name tag on the side!

Having a recognisable style doesn't bother me, though it

can be a problem in this country as people want to deposit you in a drawer. People here have a problem with artists whose work is varied, but in other countries like Germany, an artist's work can be very diverse and that becomes their style in itself – their work is eclectic.

I'm self-motivated. I think about the work I'm going to do while I'm in bed – the motor's already running. I'll play music while I'm painting – I like all music, country and western, The Orb, ambience and jazz. I've borrowed images from music – it all goes in. I don't stay in my studio and cut myself off. Communication is important, all this thing about isolated artists working alone is crap, we need to blow away a lot of myths about art.

When you're a young student artist, you might think living in a garret and starving for your art is wonderful, but get real! Having said that, I am very poor – because all my money goes back into my work! It's true, I might occasionally think, yes it would be nice to retire to the South of France or settle down and have kids, but that's way off in the future. I've got to be among artists and people because that's the sort of work I do.

I have been influenced by other artists – David Salle, Kenny Scharf and Martin Kippenberger – it's their style and attitude. Lots of my work comes from them. I was selected for the *BT New Contemporaries* exhibition 1993/94 which shows in galleries around the country, and the painting in that stems from a David Salle painting. Mine presents several different images (Elvis, a hog, a statue of a black sportsman and a bust). Salle never had Elvis in his picture, I put in Elvis to subvert the meaning of Salle's painting.

Salle's painting is about not having any meaning. In art speak it's about denying meaning, a theme of the late 80s and 90s that painting can have no meaning at all. Salle put pictures together that didn't go together. The pictures I put together don't go together, but on the other hand they do have a tenuous link. By putting Elvis in, we relate to Elvis. It's a fat Elvis, I like to think of it as a sad Elvis, and the painting deals with impotence and sexuality . . .

# 5 Comic Characters

Comics marts are crowded with people five years either side of their 18th birthday, predominantly male, but not exclusively white. And people don't go to comics marts just to buy new and second-hand comics; most comics buyers are adolescent males, a group noted for social bonding . . .

The rise of independent comics has meant even more fight scenes, but has also produced interesting, adult work, much of it, Yummy Fur, for example, or Todd McKeever's work, idiosyncratic enough to have its own fans.

Dave McKean, who paints the covers for Sandman and draws his own independent strip, Cages, produces work so beautiful that it has a small fine arts following unprecedented in comics. (*Evening Standard*)

## Peter Pavement, 23, Sheffield

I was sleeping on a friend's floor in Balham when I first got into comics. I found some lying around his place and that was it. I'd been studying architecture in Cardiff, suffering from terminal boredom. I did technical drawing there but it wasn't drawing as a way of expressing yourself; the influences were very much design, not drawing for the sake of it.

In 1990, I took a year off and went to India for a while and then Australia. I was getting shaky in architecture and asked to be let off for the remainder of the year to get it together. I never did get myself together again for the course! I did do some work in architecture in Australia, some drawings as a technician – it's really being the office skivvy.

I got my nickname while I was in Australia. I was doing pavement drawing for money, drawing scenes and bits on the streets in a tourist spot in Sydney and people used to say, 'Hey, hello Pavement . . .' It stuck. It is a bit sad that I couldn't carry the pavements home and keep them in my collection, but I think I'd have left them behind somehow. I took photos of them. I've got reels of films showing my artwork on pavements, some were quite colourful – copies of Tibetan demons I'd come across on my travels and Hindu gods. I drew them because they were strong images, not for some pseudo spiritual reason.

When I started up the 'zine I called it *The Pavement*. The first one came out in February 92, and then it became *Pavement Pizza*, but I kept getting linked to the group (Pavement), so I've just changed the name to *Ground Level*. I started doing the 'zine with a guy called Chris Tappenden. He still does a lot for the 'zine, all the stuff about Ed – a head who lives in a fishbowl – and The Bright Eyed Crazies – two dudes. He's doing a whole comic of his own stuff right now. Chris is really into it as a consumer – he's got lots of comic books and he knows which people are good. I knew him from Cardiff. We used to do jam strips in pubs – when we'd go round and meet in the pub and just do a panel. It was fun and got a lot of ideas off the ground. Chris still lives in Cardiff and sells copies of *Ground Level* down there! He's the Cardiff rep!

*Ground Level* has got strips, cartoons, rants and an interview, plus reviews of other 'zines I've been sent. I don't have that many characters. Peter Pavement features a lot – that's me – otherwise I don't like my characters to look too realistic. The others are strange-looking, they're not defined – and that's not because I can't draw. I can, so there!

I do have other contributors. A lot of people send stuff to me, some I approach because I like the strips I've seen of theirs. In the current 48-page issue, we've got ten contributors.

The 'zine is big on autobiographical content. It was like a game when I started. I amazed myself, will I do it or not, but I'm never short of ideas to put in it, what's going on around comes into it. It's the biggest mystery for me – if I write about my life for a day, no audience is going to buy the stuff, but they do . . . it must hit somewhere.

I suppose a lot of people are getting into doing their own 'zines these days. The small press is growing, one of the reasons is that it's quite cheap – you can print up 1000 that look reasonably good for about £300. I've got a colour cover and it's kind of glossy paper and the current one's elongated, so it stands out. I like to make it look a bit different.

I printed 500 of my first issue of *The Pavement* and it sold out. People seemed to like it – I don't know who! I have met a few of the people who buy it. I've sold from stalls at the Small Press Book Fair and the Anarchist Book Fair and a UK comics conference and I've set up stalls at gigs, so I'll see who buys it then. But generally, it's sold through independent bookshops. A lot of shops will only take five copies at a time, more when those are sold, which isn't many – though there's a shop in Brighton which is a powerhouse of the small press which takes 15 copies. It was because it was so difficult to get proper distribution – and I knew all the other people who sent their own comics to me must be finding it just as hard to sell theirs – that I set up my distribution side, Slab O' Concrete. I just get together a lot of other 'zines and take a selection along when I see shops now. It looks better for us all, and when it comes to mail order, people usually buy more than one. It's easier if they write to the same address. And that way you don't get tons of cheques for £1!

With other comic writers, there's a general swing for everyone to have a crack at doing a 'zine and swap what they are selling for your products. That's the way it works. There's a lot going on in the small press and indie publishing, but more was happening on the comic front in the eighties. Now *Deadline* is the only 'mainstream' comic to have kept going, and the latest issue is rubbish. It has its moments.

There are small press 'zines aimed at the art audience. They're a latent lot. There are people who used to do music fanzines and have generalised, there's such a big age range and variety. There are ones that have grown around the hippie festival front that are well crustie, some are good and cynical. There's *Girl Frenzy* run by Erica Smith who's in her late 20s and runs a 'zine by women – for a general audience, lots of women with attitude, and that was started before the Riot Grrrl thing. There are lots of interesting ones – and some dire ones too, with the quality of strips being a bit dodgy. But most of the small press stuff, I feel, is from people who have got a good attitude. It's like capitalism is out of fashion – they are not making huge magazines, selling to WH Smith's (who wouldn't take 'zines anyway) and having content dictated by advertising. They're using their talents for themselves.

There's not much about music in *Ground Level*, that's a kind of policy, though I have contacts as I used to promote bands and gigs when I lived in Cardiff, and lots of my friends work in the music industry. I do interviews each issue, usually with other comic writers or book writers, but I only want to interview people whose stuff I like – like Hunt Emerson and the writer Martin Miller (Lux The Poet, Milk Sulphate and Alby Starvation). I'm running out already! And some people I like I get to contribute for me – interviewing them would be incestuous! I love doing the interviews the most out of everything in the comic – I can talk rubbish forever! As I'm a fan of the people I'm talking to, it's easy to do. Sometimes if you approach people, they give you a good response because you're part of the small press, but sometimes, especially if I've approached an established publisher to contact a writer or something, they're a bit suspicious. I'd like to explore other fields, like books, cartoons and films because there is a cross-over.

I have a kind of theme each month, like the current one is the general work-slackers scene, and the next is TV. It kind of pulls it together. Most of the strips are short – I don't like doing four- or five-page strips – would anyone read them? Doing a 'zine isn't structured. I have deadlines for the printers, but that's about it.

I use an old lap-top to do some cut and paste jobs and basic word processing, but I don't want my comic to look like a lot of 'zines that are produced purely on a word processor and have that same format. They're handy, but you can go too far. What should be disparate ideas end up with a general Apple Mac identity. That's the problem with word processors, they help everyone have the means to production in a way, but they uniform design. You see it in the mainstream press particularly, it's all safe clean lines.

I have a kind of vision of making a living from this! But then that would have to be from publishing *Ground Level* and other people's work in reasonable quantities, and I don't want to become that mercenary. Besides, I've got used to having no money for ever. It's tempting to splash out – take out all the savings from the 'zine as I go along – but then I wouldn't be able to put the next issue out, so it all goes back. I have enough to pay rent now – I get housing benefit because I'm on the dole. Most writers of comics and fanzines are on the dole. That's how they have the time to do it. Most are creating fanzines as something to do, for fun.

It would be good to bring different media together, not just comics and fanzines, but music and animation, independent pictures, to have someone to help the distribution of them all – there is a certain amount of cross-over. For instance, promoting gigs through comics and so on. I've done film animation evening classes, I thought it would be a nice idea to do Peter Pavement in film. It hasn't happened!

I have been to comic conventions and meetings of like minds, but they tend to be a bit cliquey and art-house, more than the people who are actually doing their 'zines around the country . . .

I'm thinking of doing a resource guide, collecting stuff from all over the UK and doing a mail-out to people keeping them involved in what's happening on the small press front.

I have done a few strips and covers for other people, but most contributors don't pay – you can tell from the general feel of the editorial that they can't afford to pay, so it's just a way of getting noticed rather than making money! *Deadline* has picked up on people known through the small press. I'm sure some people do treat doing fanzines and small press comics as a way to showcase their work, but apart from other small presses there aren't the magazines to pick up on new talent. Though some of the youthful style media are picking up on a few of them.

When I went on my travels, I kept a book of drawings showing wherever I went, which I've stored away. I'm now doing a series of comic travelogues, autobiographical comics showing my trips abroad. Apart from India and Australia, I've been to Pakistan, China, Nepal on my own.

My father's emigrated to Dallas, so I've been over for visits, and went to Austin, Texas (where the film *Slackers* was made). I wrote hundreds of letters to the 'zine and comic world in the States – it's like opening a can of worms there. The small press scene is at fever pitch in America, people produce perfect bound books and put out just a few hundred of them, as well as comics and 'zines. And Montreal has a cool comic scene.

I've got a lot of creative friends, and a lot are in the music industry, but it was only Chris and me who were into comics.

Sheffield is a good city, it's quite a young place with a lot to do compared to other places. I've lived all over the place, even spent a while in a squat in Hackney. There's a great climbing scene here and a huge indoor sports centre with a climbing wall. You get people who do it for a living – those jobs where people are too scared to climb the outside of high buildings for whatever reason, and loads of people just climb all day. It comes in handy when you've got to leave a squat in a hurry via a top window!

## Carol Swain, comic writer, Camden

I've been into comics since I first discovered *Escape*, about 1987. It was that basically and an ICA workshop on writing comics and I started drawing and writing my own, printing them in my own comic 'zine . . . *Way Out Strips*. I started self-publishing in 1988. I have been to art school, though I don't think it matters if you can draw or not.

Most of my strips are based on real people – I base a lot on people I know, and people I've met. Real incidents and conversations spark things off, though I don't use them immediately. I leave a long gap, so they probably don't remember, or recognise themselves! A lot of the people I don't see any more, like old school friends. That's who I've been featuring a lot lately, and some bits of myself. I know a lot of comic writers who base a lot of their work on themselves, it's a kind of autobiography, but I can't do that. A lot of people write that way (personally), it's good, I've used myself in a few strips, though I tend not to. I always have the characters and story line in mind before I start on the pictures.

It started out of interest, but it is what I do for a living – yes, I do make a living from it, though not vast amounts. You have to work at it. I have been on the dole, but I went on the Enterprise Allowance Scheme – a sort of start-up scheme which paid you a small sum (£40) every week for a year. They've now cut the scheme to six months which is ridiculous – how do you set up a business that is going to be successful in six months? I took along four self-published – photocopied – *Way Out Strips*, and wrote a business plan to get on the EAS Scheme and I had to do a cash flow chart. That's guesswork, really.

Apart from *Way Out Strips*, I've contributed strips for other fanzines and comics. Mostly abroad, in America and Canada, though I've done some bits for *Deadline*, which is a mainstream comic. America has a great line in comics, but not here. *Deadline* is the only one of its type now. There used to be *Heartbreak Hotel* but that folded a few years back. That didn't pay though – it had a share-out scheme, which is a nice idea, but if you don't make any profits, there's nothing to share out. *Deadline* got a new editor who had worked in France (another place with a lively comic scene) and was clued up on the small presses and started looking for individual talents. He's approached a few people through the independent press, like me. He got my address through a comic!

It is strange that *Deadline* is the only one of its nature, but other people have tried. One of the mainstreams tried to set up another indie-style comic recently, but because it was a regular publishing house, they only gave it a couple of issues before deciding to cut their losses. That's hardly long enough to develop a new title.

If you do work for other comiczines, you usually don't get paid, though it's a good way of getting your work or your own comics known. I never thought about payment at first and normal comics never ran the right sort of strips. I was just doing it because I liked doing it.

Apart from selling my comics in Britain, I signed a publishing deal with a small press company in Canada, Tragedy Strikes. Sadly, it did, the company folded in a year. But they were the leading lights out there, starting up links and showing good taste the whole way through. Now they are distributed in Canada – Quebec – and America by Fantagraphics. I don't know why there are so many independent publishers in Canada. Printing is really cheap, so anyone can have a go at putting out stuff. There's a thriving scene and market because they don't have high publishing costs. And then there's the content – if you're self-publishing, you're physically in control of your stuff – that's the basic attraction. We don't see as many foreign fanzines as we should because Customs and Excise seize a lot of the stuff! Some are deemed obscene publications or whatever. There are a lot that are obscene – the writers just try to outdo each other!

I don't think about who my readers are – that's the difference between mainstream and small press. The mainstream comics are market-led – they're directed at adolescent males. I write for anybody who likes it! I do get letters back – so I can tell a little bit about some of them. In some areas they come in growing numbers. It's hard to work out who buys them. Shops take about five at a time – maybe more later on – and if they sell, come back for more. There's no particular image of a buyer or area where they sell brilliantly!

I suppose I've got a recognisable style, if you know my work, but I don't strive to have it that way. I suppose there's a lot of grainy art! I try to go for comic quality – in the drawing and language.

I hope my characters aren't right-on. I hate political correctness in comic characters, I like them to be more personal. They look like the people I see – style-wise, too.

I live near Camden Town and the clothes my characters wear and their looks reflect the people I see. There's no real deliberate attempt to make them look like anything. It is a bit of a male scene, though there's an outfit called *Girl Frenzy* run by Erica Smith who I've just done an interview with, and Carol Bennett's *Fanny* newsletter/comic titles. I keep my eye out for other independent stuff, I always check out the small press on the shelf in shops and people send me stuff.

I have a low print-run – about 500 on the fourth issue. You can't print thousands if you don't know how well it will sell, and be left with loads! I'll have more printed and better quality now I've struck a publishing deal with the Canadian company. I have to put out six in a year and a half, so at least I know I'll be keeping it up for the next 18 months!

I'd have never have made a living as an artist – it's too difficult to sell even a few paintings. Although I've just had some of my drawings for *Way Out* in a cartoonists' exhibition in South London – most of the pieces were editorial cartoons showing in a gallery. Normal jobs? I've tried child-minding and worked in a shop years ago.

I've also had work commissioned for Japan, it's an anthology of French and European artists. It's strange writing for Japanese comics as they have so many cultural rules you have to follow – you are sent a huge list – and they read from the back to the front, so you have to draw that way. I've been asked to do another strip – with no speech bubbles!

## Bear Hackenbush, 22, *Bugs and Drugs*, Bristol

I started *Bugs and Drugs* 'zine through boredom. I used to be into skateboarding a few years back and decided to write a fanzine about that – *Skate Muties and the Fifth Dimension*. It was all about skateboarding and punk, just full of crap! It lasted nine issues, but by the time it got to the eighth, I was sick of skateboarding, that was just a fad, and there's a limit to the amount you can extract from a piece of wood with wheels. We'd started doing it from an office, with other magazines like *Metal Hammer*, and spent most of our time answering letters, sitting behind a desk. So we knocked it on the head. A publisher offered us money to develop a magazine, but he went off before it came to anything, so we decided to do our own 'zine. I was writing bits and pieces and doing some illustrations and graphic design for *NME* and Bristol's *Time Out*, but never really as a profession.

*Bugs and Drugs* is produced at home, we do everything from thinking up ideas, writing and illustrations, to the stapling and selling. It's mostly me and my brother, Dino, though we live in a house of seven and so friends and girlfriends join in with cartoons or ideas, and we have other contributions. A lot of people who did bits for *Skate Muties* do similar stuff without the skateboards! It's a big mix. We all add what we want to add, though my brother always draws the character assassinations – a series of cards building up through each issue showing hippies, crusties, skinheads and so on.

We do get a lot sent in but it's usually too obscene to use. A lot of 'zines are rude – obscenity's used as a kind of humour, but it's not always funny. It's not grown-up enough! We're obscene, but not for the sake of it; we're cross at people's stupidity. We just seem to have developed an irreverent style, having a poke at everyone. We put in things that make me and my brother laugh – that's the yardstick, we don't think about who's going to read it, but it seems to have struck a chord with others. We printed 8000 of the third issue and we've had to reprint issue one, three times – so that sold about 5000.

I suppose there are a lot of readers aged 25–30, but I'd say the majority were 18–20; metally and indie kids buy it. We sell it at gigs – it always goes well at indie gigs, like the Manic Street Preachers and The Levellers and at festivals. It also sells through indie record shops and a few other places. We've got three main distributors in Britain and it's exported to America through Tower Records.

We fly-post – my brother and I – sticking up posters for

clubs and gigs; I'm living off the black economy! It means we get into a lot of clubs for free and we can sell our 'zines, usually about 100 a night, and I DJ as well as fly-post – every Friday night, a sort of indie/Rage Against the Machine mix. It all helps. My brother has another sideline – he helps demolish old chapels, selling on the useful bits from deconsecrated churches, like stained glass. Neither of us have ever had a real job since we left school, though my brother's had a few schemes. I left at 16 with no exams. I've done a few YOPs and we did a self-employment scheme for a year with *Skate Muties*. My brother was really good at art at school, and I liked art, but I didn't do it. We both draw stuff for *Bugs and Drugs*, though my drawings are matchstick men; my brother draws matchstick men in 3-D. I haven't progressed beyond two dimensions.

*Bugs and Drugs* isn't full-time. We do it when we want to, when it fits in. There are usually six-week bursts of intense activity, followed by nothing, though there are always letters to answer and phone calls to make to distributors. We don't have any set time for bringing each one out. Issue four is going to come out about March. In the summer we don't do much at all, we go to the festivals basically.

There are tons of 'zines around. Some are good, a lot of them are awful. My pet hate is those writers who draw themselves into a strip – and so many of them do it! We're not going to do that! We review a selection each issue, and forget the rest, though we have slagged some off, but we've no authority to, especially as they are all doing it for nothing. Very few people make any money from it.

We might by the time it gets to issue six! Everything we earn goes straight back into the fanzine. We've just put up the price to 75p. It was 50p up until now, but some distributors take a cut of 60 per cent. It will probably be 95p by issue six. The *Bugs and Drugs* T-shirts we do sell well. We see lots of people in them around Bristol, because we sell them at gigs and in shops here. I always want to go up and say 'I did that', but it embarrasses them! We try and get them in other shops, but a lot of shops are reluctant to sell them so cheaply. We undercut ourselves!

We have had interest and publicity. We were voted *Melody Maker*'s Number One fanzine, and *Deadline* have asked us to do two pages each month for them, which starts this January (94). We're used to deadlines from our stint on *Skateboard* and *Metal Hammer* magazines, so that's easy. I don't think it means the start of big things for us, we don't have any real strong characters to be taken up, not like Tank Girl, it's just matchstick characters, but I think our character assassination cards would do really well if we could find someone to put them out, and do it in packs of 80. We've already come up with 80 ideas for characters, so we know the complete set already, we just want someone to put them out.

They are people you see around! Going out gives you material, it's easy to come up with ideas, we knock about with things at home, our girlfriends come up with ideas, and two girls do a couple of bits for us, who are totally bonkers.

It's the girls who come up with the rudest stuff – a lot of the obscene speech bubbles. We're not sexist, just sexy! And the worst letters we get are from girls, all mixed up with drugs. We're really not into drugs, we don't even smoke dope, sadly we're just beer boys. We just spent three months coming up with a name and I saw it somewhere and liked it, my brother thought it was crap, so I said I'm doing it on my own, I was fed up with looking. It's only a name, it's like The Police, the group, you don't associate them with police as in crime. It's also got some great connotations and we can drop in pill graphics and bug graphics, like ants on acid, all over. We can't even blame the contents on drugs, though it could be the after-effects in the system. We were into things when we were young kids of 14–15, but that was more solvent abuse and scrumpy!

### Tom Binns, 23, funny person, London

I started off on the wireless – on BBC Radio 4 and 5. I did everything, it was news, serious stuff, though I always got the 'tits and bums' stories. I had a hot hits section and played 10 hits, then they told me no more jokes and said I wasn't in the entertainment business, which I found very strange! So that was it, I went. I'm currently negotiating a job with Kingston FM – which used to be Thames Television. They've got a new radio franchise, and hopefully I'll be doing a presenting slot for them, from the studios at Teddington Lock.

I do most alternative comedy clubs around London as a stand-up comic – and travel round the country doing universities. How I got in was by turning up one night to ask to do the 'try out' slot. A lot of clubs do it, usually you go on for five minutes and if you're good you'll be invited back for longer. But that night one of the acts hadn't turned up so I went on for 20 minutes! That was my first job, but I went down well. I've been back there compèring for the shows.

Not all comics can compère as you have to have material that gets individual quick laughs, rather than stuff that builds on itself. Because you have a few minutes between acts, by the time you come back for your next slot, the audience will have forgotten what you did last.

I have enough material to do long slots – I've got 40 minutes of stuff that I can use broken down, some fits two minutes, some 30–40 seconds, and they're on individual subjects. It's loosely structured, not completely mapped out so I can bring in anything the audience does and re-arrange the patter to suit the moment. For instance, if I've a joke about Liverpool and I get heckled by someone with a Liverpudlian accent, I'll bring that joke in. I love hecklers, I really do, they can bring your set to a higher level. They know you're responding to them, not just following a routine, and they respect you more. It allows you to be far more funny and get more laughs than you could just saying everything as planned. The audience appreciates that.

I do get more and more work as I go along; I haven't hit a plateau yet, there are new things happening around, new clubs opening, it's an exciting time in the comedy world. It seems to be a growing area of entertainment.

Alternative comedy has been marketed very well on TV and when you open the Sunday supplements there's always a piece on Jack Dee, Eddie Izzard or even Danny Baker and Chris Evans – who are funny blokes in their own right.

There are far fewer females on the circuit – though there are famous female comics like Jo Brand, who's got a radio show. There are about four or five top female comics on the whole – that's not many, is it? One of the funniest is Mandy Knight who's really good – and there are a few bad ones around. There are far more female promoters than comics on the circuit. I don't know why that should be. There's a great female promoter at the Meccano Club, Islington. You do get the feeling that female comics get booked as the token female, so it is a bit of a disadvantage, but then alternative comedy is still very much white, middle-class and male – there are hundreds of us – and you have to be quite intelligent, that's important!

The audience is usually pretty much made up of graduates and *Guardian* readers! I don't touch it! Though a lot of alternative comics base their material on news stories, and guess what they read?

I don't do topical stories like that, I take the mickey out of old-style comedians, like Bernie Clifton, Keith Harris, Jim Davidson. Most comics go fo anxieties that their social group has got. Because it's different, I do get a good response.

I work on new material all the time. There's a new material night at The Market Tavern, an Islington venue, when comics get to try out their new stuff. You have five minutes to test the waters. A lot of top comics go there. I always try my new stuff out there, and we take it in turns to compère. It's like a co-op, none of us get paid – all the money taken goes towards something like a big Christmas party for comedians, though we were thinking of getting a greyhound, a comedy dog. I suppose it's a club for comics as much as for the general public!

I don't change my stuff all the time. I generally have set pieces which I do – some people quite enjoy knowing some of your material if they follow you from venue to venue.

It's like going to see Status Quo at a concert several times – you know all the words. I'll change bits as I'm going along.

A lot of comics are getting on telly at the moment. It's not always the best circuit comics who get the TV and radio jobs. There are some much better comedians out there than those who've come through lately, but a lot of their stuff is unsuitable, either blue or just works better in a club atmosphere.

I had a try-out for a pretty big breakfast programme recently, but didn't get it! I do a lot of ads – if you've seen the man in the Coca-Cola ad that pulls a funny face – that's me. I belong to an agency that specialises in actors and comics who do ads and I get quite a lot of work, if someone wants a funny face or voice, and I've done improvisation for the camera for commercial breaks. That's really where I earn my money. You don't make a living from doing the London circuit – there's no money in it, but it's a showcase, I suppose that's the main reason. I do the university circuit too and I've been booked for the Radio 1 tour with Newman and Baddiel going round universities like Newcastle and Birmingham. That's got a backer so there'll be money in it. That's bread and butter, but ads offer a lot more. I might be cheapening myself but I've got to eat!

Because I take the mickey out of those top old comedians who do residencies at the Pier in Blackpool I thought it would be a crack to do a show there. It was a bit strange doing the place that's the butt of my jokes but I thought rather than tone down the show and compromise my sketches, I'd still continue to take the mickey out of the likes of Les Dawson and Jim Bowen; it was a bit risky because the audience love those guys. But I got all sorts of good offers for the summer season! Now I have a unique dilemma in comedy – do I do the Edinburgh fringe or Blackpool summer season? Do I lose money in Edinburgh or earn £5000 in Blackpool?! Edinburgh's street cred and a showcase, but there'll be money and Phyllis with her blue rinse in Blackpool!

91

I really enjoy doing Edinburgh, though it's crazy, there's too much going on. If you park your car for more than half an hour someone's turned it into a venue. It's the only place you can catch a show before breakfast.

I don't mind doing slots first thing in the morning. If I get the radio job, I'm after the breakfast show. I'd still do the clubs in the evening. The idea is that I do the clubs, stay up all night, do the breakfast show, then sleep. I'm used to it – when I worked in radio news I did the breakfast shows, then read the evening news.

Most comedians are a bit older, late 20s, early 30s, but that's because most of them are graduates and by the time they come out of university and establish themselves on the circuit they're pushing 27! I didn't go to university. I was living in Sheffield when I got work with the Beeb. I dropped my A levels to do that and stayed there until they said no more jokes! I got fed up and thought I'd go to university then – financial accounting in Sussex. I lasted one term. I thought I'd do that while I built up contacts on the London circuit. It took me three weeks to get bookings and that was it.

I suppose you're a bit older when you get the nerve together to go out there too – and you need experience to talk about. If you're going to do those life experience gags, you've got to have had a bit of a life! It also helps if the audience are a bit older and intelligent, or they don't get the jokes. I've been at one university and introduced one of the top alternative comics, who goes down really well on the circuit, but the audience was too young and well, thick – and they booed him. He'd just played the Albert Hall to 3800 people and they'd loved him!

Alternative comics have a bit of a uniform too – everyone's white, middle-class and wearing jeans and a jacket. I've been toying with the idea of having a comedy jacket. I thought I should break from the norm and go in for a loud plaid jacket and bow tie, like those comedians I rib. It could be more trouble than it's worth, either people will think 'that's a crap suit' and suspect I'm wearing it for real, or it'll work wonders and mean I'll have to go on wearing it for years. I've created a monster, I'm becoming like those men I've been taking the mickey out of for years. I want to be Bob Monkhouse.

# 6 DIY Culture – Dance

## Mariana Sutherland, 23, dancer and co-founder of the Longer Lasting Lightbulb Company

I've got a formal dance background. When I was younger I went to a local dance school, then I did O level dance at college directly after school and did a foundation course at Lewisham College in ballet, jazz and contemporary dance, doing A level dance at the same time. After that I went to the London Contemporary Dance School for three years.

When I left college there was no work. I went abroad for a while looking for work – to Belgium, France, Holland and Germany. But although there was a lot more happening there on the contemporary dance scene, it was in the same state as Britain. I went to one audition in Belgium, but there were 350 dancers auditioning for one place. Not good.

I came back to Britain and didn't do anything for a while, except a few open dance classes. I was funding myself. Some friends from college had gone on a government training scheme and were choreographing a musical, and the woman who directed there suggested that we get our own company together, since there were no opportunities for us to join an established one. Eight of us did that – and the Longer Lasting Lightbulb Company was formed.

We were all from the London Contemporary Dance, various combinations of friends. I'm the oldest at 23, the others range from 20. We don't have a grant but we went on a government training scheme, so we got income support plus £10 extra a week, a place to rehearse and an office to work from. I was given a six-month term on the scheme but the others ranged from three months to a year. We also got a little help from a business training scheme.

Apart from dancing we have to do the accounts, book venues – everything. We all have a go in different areas. I'm in charge of publicity and contacts with stationers. We use recycled paper, and we have a stationery company who gives us recycled paper and photocopying for free, which is a great bonus.

That's the big thing about the dance company, everything we do concerns environmental awareness. It's not just something to make us different, it matters to us. We don't just want to use the idea to get attention, we want to help make others more aware through our work. We've all become more aware of everything going on through setting up the company.

All our policies concern the environment – our sets and costumes are made from what we have around, things we have at home, things we borrow from shops and other people, and bits we find in skips. We've collected loads of crisp packets, cleaned them, turned them inside out and made them into a cloak. We don't do it to be different or strange, we want to actively support these issues.

We performed for the Walk for the Whales rally and at the Green Festival. We've done quite a few festivals. This year we're doing Glastonbury hopefully and the Kingston Green Fair. We also opened the National Anti-Vivisection Society weekend event in April 1994.

Apart from performing at events, lending support to campaigns and issues we believe in, we're spreading local awareness of the environment. Our offices are in a community centre and we've encouraged everyone else in the centre to take an interest in recycling. We get them all to buy from the local green stationery shop which has also meant low cost for us.

Since we've been together we've performed at 16 different venues over the last eight months. They've ranged from festivals to Birmingham College where we did a workshop and performance, and Thamesdown Dance Studios which was another performance/workshop, and we've just performed in *Resolution!*, a showcase for new dance talent at The Place in King's Cross. We got some bad press from

*The Stage* for that! But it wasn't full of hard evidence or any constructive criticism, in fact it wasn't really criticism.

The piece we performed was reflective, showing how people through the media are made aware of their body, and forced to hate their own body shape. We wanted to show people they don't have to be ashamed of their individual body, they should look in the mirror carefully at themselves to find their own image rather than looking in magazines for one. The woman in *The Stage* said what the piece was about, then wrote: 'Some of the company should look at themselves carefully if they want to continue dancing' . . . meaning that some of us aren't skinny. We don't have a direct policy to take dancers who aren't thin, it's just the way it worked, the eight of us who wanted to start up the company. Does it matter what our shapes are if we dance? We're not biased.

We were at the Barbican Dance Week, and our stall looked very different from the rest with recycled paper and no glossy brochures or masses of photographs. Many of our photographs tend to be photocopied and enhanced, so we looked very different to the images presented by the others. Basically, there are so many people involved in ballet and the commercial side of dance who are anorexic and look the same.

We're quite interested in having good, interesting sets and costumes, it's not purely dance, being skinny and technical skills. We do come up against a lot of criticism because of this from the established ballet scene, but then we get a good response from the audience. It's like at The Place – *The Stage* may not have enjoyed our work but there was a lively buzz from the audience and it was practically a full house. We actually made a little bit from it!

That's what we're about. We're not geared to ballet critics who write for people who enjoy ballet, we want to get out to the average person, perhaps people who haven't thought of dance before, and in other ways to get people to think about their lives in terms of recycling and just to be aware of the environment.

That's why it will be good if we do get to Glastonbury,

because it's not a place associated with dance. Many of the festivals we've done haven't been dance venues, and other plans include getting a wider audience, like we're doing something with ELO mix. The music we used has tended to be electronic music – though unfortunately not live, it's been difficult to set up facilities for both a band and ourselves. We're doing a music video this weekend and we've just done a piece for a television game show, so we're getting known in different areas.

Personally, I've found that by doing the company I have learned so much more than in anything I've ever done before, about choreography and dance, about growing up and about the environment. Ambitions-wise, we'd like to get people informed on environmental issues. It's so broad. We keep the group in touch. Regularly one of us goes to find out about what's happening about different policies, going to anti-vivisection, recycling and anti-fur groups, then we'll come back and tell the group. It all comes into what we do, the energy from it goes into the choreography.

We all get involved in choreography. Currently we've got five main pieces which were choreographed by different people in the group.

We are fighting against the attitudes of people who are in the established dance scene. But it's also attitudes of a lot of people. We're totally unfunded and all on income support. So many of my friends who are in other jobs earn a lot of money and keep saying, 'When are you getting a proper job that you get paid for?' They resent the fact that I'm on income support. I have to keep telling them that I work far harder than any of them, it's just that I don't get paid for what I do! It's not like selling a computer for a living. Of course we'd like to get paid, but in doing so we don't want to exploit others. When people get money it often seems to become a problem. It would be nice to earn just enough money so we don't have to worry about the next bill, to be able to cover our costs and perhaps have a little extra to be comfortable.

We've been trying to get sponsorship, but the kind of companies who care about the environment and related issues aren't the companies who have money! We approached a green paperback company and our local stationery shop and asked them to set up stalls at The Place when we did our performance. The stationers probably got more out of it because they introduced themselves to people and said what they were about. We try to support them in return for their support of us. It's kind of an exchange. Probably we're going to do better from the small local environmentally-friendly companies.

I do like other performers. You can't blank out the rest just because they do things differently to you. Personally, I like young companies with a lot of energy. I think energy matters more than experience and technical perfection; I'd rather they had life. I've seen great dancers in the fourth year at Lewisham College and at The London Contemporary Dance School, and they don't have to be contemporary dancers. I've seen a great Spanish dancer who's really enjoyable to watch.

We can't practise every day. We're trying to pull ourselves together now we've been together for our first eight months because we've let the dancing go a bit as there has been so much else to do. We have three classes a week and we rehearse in the afternoons on a general level. This weekend we're doing the music video and most of our performances are at the weekends, so we often work lengthy hours.

We're lucky that we have been given a lot of support from the theatre that the girls in the previous musical project were involved with and people we were with at college, so they're helping spread the word, but we've had to make a lot of effort to get ourselves known.

We've stayed pretty constant as we've always managed to get performances, workshops and festivals. It should get easier as we go along as you need to book a lot of venues in advance and it's through performing that you get known, though financially it's difficult when you fund yourself.

Dance is a growing area. If you take Lewisham, where I went, they're expanding their dance programme and they organise 20 schools a year all round the country. You can see interest in dance is growing, but what will all those dancers do when they leave?

## Sean Gaffney, 19, dancer/choreographer, London

For me, this year has been amazing, it's really taken off. I'm doing fashion choreography. My partner Gareth Griffiths, who I met at The Place dance school, and myself are setting up a business later this year, but we've been involved in a lot of shows so far. It started off with a small fashion show for Bart's rag week, for which we did fashion choreography and danced. From that we got a job offer and then more, so we've been to Liverpool, Nottingham and Leicester, choreographing fashion shows.

I was at The Place (King's Cross) until two terms ago ... it's strange how the people in my year have all gone their separate ways. I was there for two years – it's very contemporary-based, covering ballet and contemporary dance, which is fine if you want to stay in contemporary. Gareth has stayed on and another friend, Arthur Pita, who was in my year is one of the rising stars in the contemporary dance world – but I've gone commercial! I wanted to get into jazz, so I left to do another year at a different dance school (the London Studios Centre). For commercial dance you need a wider sphere to be able to take and use as many different styles as possible. You have to have energy and variety, it adds to the choreography on the catwalk. I want to incorporate dance into fashion. I create a whole concept, with a theme and carry it through to the end. The shows last about 50 minutes.

Once we decided, Gareth and I, to go commercial we had to find out more about what was going on, who the other commercial dancer/choreographers are in the same field and who's getting work – and why they're getting it. Jacob Marley is one of the main dancers. Now I'm freelance, I'm pitching for the same kind of work as he is and

I'm straight out of school. He's really clever, he's started up his own agency so he's got at least 100 dancers on his books who he can call on when he gets a booking. Say for instance he was asked to tour abroad with The Pet Shop Boys, he'd have all these dancers at his fingertips, rather than having to track them down, and they can all get on with their own projects that don't involve him in the meantime.

I'm doing a show at Central St Martin's which might be at The Limelight and then another in Liverpool – both are next month, so it will mean two shows to get together in a short space of time. We perform at all sorts of venues. Last night I was doing a show at the London College of Fashion. I teach there – that came about through the Bart's show too. I was asked to choreograph a fashion show there, which I did with Arthur and my partner, and through that they asked me to teach their catwalk models how to move on stage. It's still mostly female models there, but they've got four male models at the moment. It was a great show last night with over 1200 in the audience.

What we did was to get a couple of dancers and three tracks and choreographed a slot, then took the dancers there and worked in the models. The music we use depends on the clothes and the dancers, and the feel of the evening. I like to do something different, to add spice to the show. Ideally it would be great to see the clothes first and get to work alongside the designer and the person who's creating the music, but that's not always possible. I rarely get to see the clothes first. I recently did a show in Liverpool and I didn't get to see the clothes until the day of the show. I'd worked out the choreography and music, and when I got there, a lot of adjustments had to be made because they couldn't move the way I'd planned in the clothes they were wearing! Ideally it should be a big collaboration.

Gareth and I have absolutely completely different styles which is great, and he excels on the engineering side, while I'm better at creativity. This means we're a perfect combination. Outside of our partnership too, we're different. I love dancing in clubs, that's when I can really get to do my thing. Last night after the show I was off dancing at a club, whereas Gareth's not a clubby person. That's good, because that's when we get our time apart – we work so closely together, having brainstorming sessions, that we need the occasional break!

I'm getting quite a few contacts, people like The Changing Room/Ally Cappellino and Paul Smith who I've worked with and the photographers who take pictures for us. They all help to spread the word, and we video all our events. People are beginning to show an interest in us.

The main thing is getting your name and your work known. So far we've been offered a lot of work, it's just happened. The other exciting thing for me is being in a position to show the talent of new dancers who need work. I have a rota of friends from school who are good dancers and if I need dancers for a show, I know who to call on. It's good to be able to give them work and money. I still dance myself and so does Gareth, that's still important. I love dancing, so I'll choreograph myself a slot. I'm still taking classes and practising. A lot of the work goes on well into the evenings and weekends, especially while I was at school – The Place won't allow you to work while you are there and you don't get time off for rehearsals. They're not commercially-minded, which for me is an unrealistic approach because you are training to work.

Although in a way it's a big difference, working while you're still at dance school where you know you've always got a space at college to hire to practise in for free, but I'm confident that we can go it alone. You've got to decide where you are going to take what you have taken from college. I've got contemporary skills and I'm glad of them. I've taken the skills I've acquired and I'm doing something, though by the end of the year I might think, 'Mmm, there's something missing!'

There's also a lot of paperwork to do. Gareth and I have business meetings now! That's the difference between commercial and contemporary dance. Commercial gives you more scope, you're not dancing as part of a production, you oversee the lot, it's your baby and you carry it through and there are a lot of aspects to it. Initially I did think that the commercial side would offer more financial rewards than staying in the contemporary scene, which was another attraction, but now I feel the advantage is the scope. That's my personal feeling. And I am the sort of person who gets easily bored. There's obviously more responsibility, it's a whole project, not just dancing, and I like having that artistic input.

Apart from fashion shows we do music videos and events. I've just finished dancing in *Sweet Charity* at the Royalty and I've danced with Kylie Minogue. That was also off my own back. I saw an ad in the paper, got an audition and danced at Wembley Arena with her support dance group, Nomad. I was just 18 at the time. It was really amazing to get to work with professional choreographers while at college, you pick up such a lot from them. At college you can learn technique and how to dance, but the real learning comes from experience.

I never intended to be a dancer – I was dancing in a one-off production while at school, having had no training or thoughts of being a dancer, and I got offered a place at the London Contemporary Dance School. That set me thinking about dance and it snowballed from there!

It does happen that you get spotted dancing somewhere! Independently of my partnership, I've been offered work in Germany with a company later this year, which would mean going back to that side of things. That's an option, and I would do it, depending on how it fitted in with our business. I like to keep my options open.

# **7** DIY Culture – Design

### Joie, 26, anti-fashion designer, Epping Forest, Essex

Designing just happened. I never trained to be a designer or considered it as a career. I studied photography and fine art at college (Goldsmith's, South London).

I got into doing car boots to get rid of my old clothes and make some money. I had stuff by Viv Westwood and Jean Paul Gaultier. A friend told me I was mad selling those at a car boot, and suggested Camden Market. I couldn't see the point of a stall of just my old clothes. Instead I put together outfits – a top, trousers, hat, accessories – the whole lot. I took a photograph of the outfit then put it in a box, hanging the photo on the lid to show what was inside, and called them Pandora's Box. The bit I loved was arranging and taking pictures of the clothes because I was really into photography. I didn't sell them at Camden, but through Bond in Soho. They went well, and got quite a bit of publicity, in *Elle* and *The Face*. But your old clothes don't go on forever . . . I got a sewing machine for my 21st birthday. That must have been the turning point!

The first things I made were feathered bras and knickers and pompom bras with knitted knickers which were really popular with shops like Sign Of The Times in Kensington Market. Everything had to be very basic because I couldn't do anything technical. I'd never been taught to sew or pattern-cut. But I think a lot of it is logical. Like anything, you have to work it out practically; if you want to achieve a particular effect, you cut the shapes you want. It's instinctive. In a way, it's not a bad thing not to have done a conventional sewing course, because it makes you broader-minded or at least think differently, though there have been times when I've been impatient because I can't work something out. I'm lucky now because I have a samplist to help if I want to do complicated things.

It's brilliant here. I work from home – my parents' farm, near Epping Forest (Essex) – and have found local people to work for me when I need them, like machinists. They're all much older than me and I have to tell them what to do! For next summer I'm doing cream and black embroidered gypsy stuff and I've got a really nice lady in her 60s to do the embroidery for me, and through her I found the factory that does Vivienne Westwood's embroidery – right here in Essex! So fashion isn't based in London! I wouldn't like to move into Central London, it's good having the space, even if I know people around here wouldn't wear my clothes! The stuff is too outrageous for Essex.

The thing I lack most by not having been through college and the design circles is contacts and backing, I've had to find out everything on my own. Then there are the materials and suppliers. If you go to fashion college they give you advice on buying materials and how to sell. On the other hand, my fine art background and the years I was obsessed with photography and painting give me other areas of inspiration and influences.

Likewise, I don't get involved with things like The London Show because I've never really known how, but I am right now getting together some clothes for *The Clothes Show Live* (December), which will go on a stall run by No Photos. I'm just putting in my tartan and mohair stuff – bits and bobs I can get together quickly. It's a lot of organising. I seem to spend most of my time organising now, and I'd like to put a lot more time aside for designing which is what I like doing.

I was doing lots of mohair and punky tartan in June and July and it's become really popular now, so I've just brought it back again. And, last summer I was doing georgette clothes, and georgette is everywhere now. I used it because it was floaty and feminine and gave a feel of what I wanted, I didn't think about a trend or anything. Now everyone's into it, so I can bring back some of those old designs again.

It's just as bad being too far ahead with an idea. Last Christmas I was making clothes with safety pins and that's what's around now, so they'd sell better. This Christmas I've done lots of pink clothes, because people like to wear pink at Christmas – I think! And no one else is doing it.

I've seen my stuff copied by established designers and one particular guy got his assistant to borrow a dress of mine, then one very similar by him was featured in *Vogue* . . . it makes you bitter and twisted! I must concentrate on getting someone to do press for me. Lack of time really holds you back. Like I've been approached by a couple of stylists for clothes for Kylie Minogue and Björk. I said no. I would have loved Björk to wear my clothes, but I just didn't have time to organise it.

I don't know anyone in the fashion world, apart from at Red or Dead. They were really helpful. If I had a problem, I'd ring them up . . . in fact, my friend who worked there has just become my partner. He deals with finding stockists and approaching people round the country. I don't have time for everything any more. I've got 10 outlets now – mostly in big cities like Glasgow, Manchester and Liverpool. My brother sells stuff for me at the weekends at Camden . . . so I did eventually get the stall there!

I've never felt the urge to go along and watch who buys my clothes, nor how they look in the shops – it would probably depress me, shatter the illusion of them being hung and worn the way I had in mind! I don't really know who wears my clothes. They are all designed for females, but you get boys in them.

I like my designs to be pretty but naughty. The image is a lovely fluffy baby doll and stockings . . . a bit fifties sex kitten, I suppose. I've often seen people wearing my clothes when I'm at a club. The first time, I ran up to the guy and said, 'I made that!' because I was so shocked! I still want to scream and jump up and down when I see them on people, though other designers tell me you stop feeling like that after a while! Clubs are great because you do get an idea of what people wear, or will wear, though generally ideas just come to me. I go to clubs mostly because I really enjoy dancing.

Most of my friends are in film/art and that area. I've never had a fashion show but a friend, Fiona, who runs a club in Mayfair asked me to put on a show at a party at her club. Leigh Bowery was doing a piece and there was lots going on. We painted backdrops and there was a grand piano, thick hangings everywhere and a massive banquet. It got very sexual with models stripping and rubbing food over each other. It was strange because, when I chose the models, they seemed quite shy. I had them wearing tailored coats which when they turned round were backless, with pink bowler hats, and I wanted the models to improvise rather than have a structured set and they kept saying they couldn't do anything outrageous, so I said, 'Just sit on the chests and look posh.'

Then when they came to it they were over the top. The finale was a spectacular food fight. It was wild but I kept looking at the specially made shoes which were ruined and wondering whether it was worth it! I didn't get much publicity because it was a club, not a show ... but it was videoed. It was fun and I suppose it was the kind of event that anyone there will always remember.

Am I destined to be a cult designer? I don't do 50 of the same design. I like the fact that there are only a few of each design – or do I?! But I'd never do hundreds and thousands, I'm not likely to sell through the likes of Top Shop. I do small runs and a few one-offs. I do want to expand, especially as I've now established out-work, but you lose a lot of money. I wasn't in it for money initially, but I do want to be able to earn more to put into different areas. Not just fashion. I've got lots of projects – like my own magazine. All of those around seem to feature the same old clothes, same styles and designers, the black and white and the distressed look; and photography too, there is so much you can do in a photo ... No I haven't lost my interest in photography and film. I spend any spare time seeing films, like *The Piano*. I don't wear my own designs. It's sad, but you get bored if you've been working on them all the time, and I'd get embarrassed if someone asked if I'd made it! Do I sound like a workaholic?

## Trina, 23, market stall-holder, South London

I've run a weekend stall off and on for four years. I started off just helping out on a friend's stall selling clothes on Saturdays and Sundays, but I got hardly any money. Through talking to him I found out where he was getting his supplies and stuff, and I could see from standing there each week what was selling, so I thought I'd earn more doing it myself.

I've changed my stock over the years. At first I started making my own clothes, just running up hats. Felt and velvet floppy hats were doing well two years ago, and anything plain and black sells well – it still will! It's surprising how little clothes have changed really over the years. I'm even getting the micro-minis back out of the store cupboard. I never really had any sewing experience – I'd run up a few things for myself and followed a Very Easy Vogue pattern! That's not true of all the stall-holders – a lot of the people I talk to here have been to fashion college for years and this is their only outlet. For the past year, I've been selling a mixture of new stuff I run up and original seventies clothing, which has been the best money-spinner so far. Everyone's been into it, some surprising people, and some of the clothes are so hideous I think, 'I'll never sell that' – but they love it. Patchwork loon pants, tasteless wide-collared shirts, even boring plain clothes. I get clothes from jumble sales, second-hand shops, old warehouse stock – anywhere, especially over the past 12 months. Now I have people who look out for bits for me in different parts of the country so I waste less time touring round. I do travel a lot – seaside towns, sleepy country villages. I used to visit Scotland a lot for second-hand clothes though I did have a friend who lived there. You make the most of holidays and weekends away. Friends always know to say

'There's a great second-hand shop, market or whatever' if they want me to go away with them! When those embroidered bags and hats from Thailand were popular I took a long holiday with an empty suitcase! I'm serious – when you work for yourself you spend all your time working and thinking about the business. It's dreadful. You feel guilty if you take time off for a swim or sauna or something. Being self-employed is very unhealthy!

Is it worth it? I couldn't work for anyone else again, I don't think. The pressures are hard, there's a lot to organise and you have to stand in the market all day long on Saturday and Sunday so you don't feel like going out on the weekend. To some people I'm just a shop girl – and that's what you feel like usually, waiting for someone to buy, but then if it wasn't my stall, I wouldn't spend so long watching anxiously for the thieves. A lot of stock goes missing every week, you have to keep your eyes peeled all the time. Financially, I have made a lot recently (a lot being a few hundred pounds), but then there are months when it's very slow and you worry whether you're overpriced, if it's time to completely change your stock and whether you're wasting your time.

There are definitely some parts of the year when I couldn't live on the market takings alone – I still claim dole. I know I wouldn't always be entitled to it but many weeks I am, and the way the system is, it's all or nothing, you can't say, 'OK I took £25 today, that's all the money I have for the week, help me out please.' The dole just about covers the rental of a pitch at the market – and then you need to pay for stock, your travel and something to eat while you're there.

I'm not exactly a wealthy entrepreneur. I live with my boyfriend in a council flat in a grotty estate in South London. Most of the money I make goes back into buying stock. We rarely eat out or even have a take-away pizza. But, it stops me losing my brain cells and it makes me think that I'm doing something constructive which might help towards the future. If I ever built the business up to a good extent, and opened a shop, which I'd like to do, I'd come off the dole, but I need it right now.

Market traders get a bad press. Not many earn a fortune as customers imagine, though I'm sure some earn a lot more than me. For me it's getting out of the flat, not staying in hanging around in the vain hope of a chance of working for someone else.

# 8 Rhythm Generation

Mud, dogs and Englishmen. Bands, booze and drugs. An outdoor festival of contemporary performing arts. The weirdness capital of Britain. 'Glastonbury', as it is generally known, has been summarised and satirised to death; and yet it lives on. After 24 years and 23 festivals, it is now a fixture on the cultural calendar, a scruffy relative of Wimbledon, say, or – scruffier still – of Glyndebourne.

It feels strangely familiar to many who have never even spent three days amid the rolling fields around Worthy Farm, near the village of Pilton in Somerset. Jokes about Glastonbury's on-site toilet arrangements are heard by people who have never had the opportunity to sit in one of the 600 fragrance-free, green plastic structures in question. Like the famous and ancient vale of Avalon, which hosts it every year just after the summer solstice, the Glastonbury festival has now passed into the folklore. (*Sunday Times*)

Ecstasy is as emblematic of the rave scene as LSD was of the peace and love era. There are estimated to be as many as a million uses per week, mostly among the under-25s. Between one and five million people are now believed to have used Ecstasy. (*Guardian*)

An increasing number of teenage girls, some as young as 13 years old, are abusing dangerous drugs, often in the form of innocent household items such as hairsprays and deodorants.

A report based on a study of over 300 teenagers in the north west reveals that young girls are also increasingly using illegal dance drugs like Ecstasy and LSD – which have in the past been more often associated with young men. (*Big Issue*)

**David Gill, 25, editor of fanzine, *The Herb Garden*, Leeds**

Manchester is a city that's a victim of its own success. With the gangs and so on, the clubs and even the Olympics bid, everyone's trying to cash in on it. I don't tend to go out much in Manchester any more. There's still the Hacienda, on a rare mid-week night. It's not the place to go on a Friday night. There are a lot of moody people giving off bad vibes. You could end up with a group of people standing round you, making threatening noises.

One of the best nights out is Paradise Factory. It's a gay night but there's a lot of cross-over, and the monthly Flesh nights.

That isn't so in Leeds. It's OK for a homophobic centre. Leeds is good despite its restrictions. Lack of venues – for music, not just clubbing. There's only the Town and Country, with little more than student bands going on. We've strict licensing laws and there's no bar scene. There's no coffee bar culture.

There doesn't seem to be many one-off events by enterprising entrepreneurs anymore. It's more organised events now, it's lost the rave tag, and 'events' now happen in large mansion houses. The scene's gone up-market and left other people behind, very expensive and run by big money-making organisations like Fantasize and Universe.

They play pop music. Dance has become a massive popular culture. Now it's all about money-making, merchandising and selling T-shirts. The raves as they were have gone.

The problem is if people can't stop it, they commercialise it. Cash in on it and popularise the culture. It happened with punk, it will always happen.

You read a lot about research into rave culture. That makes me laugh. That's one of the reasons I do the mag (*The Herb Garden*), to show it like it is. Marketing types see the hype and advertise in the magazines. They see that they can get an audience of 16–25-year-olds. I've seen the rate cards for *Mix Mag*. They call us the Rhythm Generation! We spend X amount on records and X amount on clothes. What it fails to mention is the Rhythm Generation spend most of their money on Class A drugs. It's all a big lie.

Only the underground magazines tell the truth. It's corporate people who run *The Face* and *i.D.* OK, I've got the first 20–30 issues of *The Face*. It used to be brilliant. The people on those mags don't go out any more, they go corporate and they're under the thumb of the board. They have to make money.

Blag culture . . . that's another story. I don't have to pay to get in any more; I'm on the guest list! Everyone wants to blag their way in. If you had to pay to get into clubs, you couldn't afford to go out very often. Many dance clubs started off very cheap. Now it can be very expensive to go out. Drinking's back in vogue again because the drugs are so poor, and clubs are charging £2.50 for a can of Red Stripe. People hardly go out mid-week up here.

I worked in America for a time. Everyone had a job – nothing special, brickies, plumbers, but everyone could afford to go out. People here only go out once a week – at the weekends. People stay home and watch TV in the evenings, because they can't afford to go out. It means there's not a lot of choice of things to do. People don't run club nights during the week, they wait until it all happens on Saturday when people go out.

Kids can spend around £200 a weekend on drugs, beer, getting into clubs, travelling to others if nothing's happening. It's a lot of money for a night out.

Most mags take the piss out of raving. Raving is something the younger kids do. Clubs are for the older crowd. There's a kind of snobbery there. Clubs here have fascist door policies and you have to dress up to get in, so young kids can't get in, they have to go to raves.

The radio doesn't reflect the dance scene at all. Londoners don't appreciate Kiss FM, or that they've got a station that plays dance music all the time. We haven't got that here in Leeds. We've got Dream FM, a pirate station. It's good now that it's on at the weekends. It used to broadcast during the week and there'd be a lot of 'Respect going out to . . .' Now it's got a few quality DJs.

A good radio programme would be better than a dance television series. I'm not interested in watching people dance in clubs . . . That's why television programmes on dance/clubs are boring. Who wants to watch other people dance? I don't go to see bands – there are no good bands in Leeds or Manchester.

Scam culture is another label to stick on us. No one's a postman or a plumber any more. Everyone's booking DJs, putting out records – working on the edge of a black economy. They're not proper jobs. There aren't proper jobs for them. It's soul-destroying. At least they're doing something, though in a way it's part of 'Maggie's mentality' (Thatcher!). It's the only positive side of the eighties – that 'get off your arses' idea, but they're all working outside the boundaries of the law. Not quite how she intended. Lots of them are signing on while earning money to afford to go out. But they've no training, no education. They're having to do everything for themselves with no support or back up.

*The Herb Garden* is a full-time thing, though I don't make much from it! I write most of it, apart from anything with journalistic integrity. I write the bits in between, observations. Stories are sent in, anything related to dance culture. In the issue I'm working on, one of my contributors, Dean Cavanagh, is doing a piece on Death Disco in Happy Valley. It's a look at how old-age pensioners are dying at afternoon tea dances from heart attacks and so on – a kind of getting back at the reports of kids dying at clubs from taking drugs.

I'm not a journalist. I'm a frustrated creative. I worked in advertising – not the creative side, more print production. I dropped out – well, that's the wrong word. Seven years is a long time to spend in that world. Advertising and the record industry are full of people trying to get one up on everyone else.

### Mark, 23, Global Grooves, Birmingham

I'll borrow a quote from a great man, Alistair Cooke, who died last year. He said: 'Love whatever you do for a living and try to fall in love with your future.' I think that's a great motto for life. It's not easy because the need for money gets in the way. But that's pretty much what we're doing. We run clubs and our record shop-café because we enjoy it. We're having a first birthday party in a bar this weekend – we run a club on Saturdays and one on Thursdays in a club space.

The scene's not dead ... People in London may say so, but people who live in London should try travelling out of London before they announce what's dead ... It's very much alive. People are really into dance here. It's really getting going here ...

Recently it went through a period of being down ... No, it's always been gradually getting noticed with people travelling from other parts of the country to the area to go to clubs and all-nighters. Sometimes the hype that accompanies it can destroy it, but we won't let it.

The crown of the clubbing capital of Great Britain has been on every head so far, so perhaps it's going to rest on Birmingham since it's got here at last. It's taken a while. Who gives it the crown? Inevitably the media, but it starts off with the punters, finding the good clubs and going there. The people that go to our clubs come half from the town and half from all over the city. It's a good mix.

I've been into the scene for years. I went to Majorca in 88 and discovered acid house. It was just a holiday, nothing was really happening here at the time, then I went back in 1989 and got into it again, and I met Piers who was there by accident like myself.

Back here, I went to clubs in Manchester. Clubs were starting over here and people like DJ Sasha were on the scene. We started doing parties and in 1990 started a club, Eden, on a Wednesday night in Manchester. It had a cult following more than anything and only lasted two or three months. It had Sasha as a resident DJ ... I hate to say I helped establish his name, but it didn't hurt him! He's doing very well for himself. Sasha is still a good friend. He doesn't play at our clubs any more as he has commitments which prevent him from DJing, but he drops in when he's around and sometimes DJs at our parties. We ran two last year in stately homes. People kept on at us to put something on at a big venue – so we had one in a big castle.

We play just dance music at the club, not even any hardcore, and we promote it in the record shop, where we sell dance records! We also have our own label and are about to put out our fourth release, a record by Punchinella. We get sent tons of demo tapes; we encourage bands ... All dance stuff too.

There was a stage when people weren't into the dance scene, all the locals looked like indie, pop and grunge fans, but luckily the new crop of students are into dance music. That's important for Birmingham. There are three universities in Birmingham: they are the sort of people who go out to clubs and buy records.

## Piers, 24, Global Grooves, Birmingham

It's my life, running the club and shop. It's a small scene, the dance scene. When you know people, you see the same faces in London and here ... I'm often in London, I was there last Wednesday and Saturday, going to clubs and stuff.

It's great, making money for doing what I want to do. That's the way it should be. Part of this business is knowing what's happening, going to different places seeing what people are doing. That's what I'd be doing anyway.

I was in Chester a year ago running a different club, and didn't do much, but since moving to Birmingham and opening Global Grooves, I go out more, as Birmingham is more central and it's easy to get to London. I meet more people and all sorts of people. I talk to those on *Mix Mag* and stuff – I'm rent a gob.

Why Chester? I lived with my mum in North Wales. When I moved there I was appalled at the lack of clubs. Someone had to set one up. I got to know the local record shop and plugged them into it – running a club – so when I left for Birmingham, Chester wasn't left with nothing! Otherwise it was big club promoters, large venues, nothing fun.

When I met Mark we decided to open a record shop –
a very unique record shop with a café-bar and a gallery.
We run exhibitions too. The stuff's from local young artists. We've had one recent exhibition with work from
*Jockey*, a Manchester fanzine, and we've had photos taken
at clubs, work from young clubby artists – everything related to the dance world. We don't get reviews in
Birmingham art mags – they're not interested in our kind
of art; we're not high-brow enough.

The shop is a meeting place. We've also got a record
label – though we got our fingers burnt with the very first
release – we got sued by Sony for unlawful copying! It took
us a while to put another record out, but we've got our
fourth release coming soon.

We thought the shop would be a good way of promoting
the club. That's what the main focus was – the club. Even
the artwork reflects this. There's a girl who works here, left
college and couldn't get a job, but she does her own art, so
we'll show her stuff. It gives people a place to show their
work.

We make an effort with the decor of the club. The club
interior is fun. We had a Happy Hearts Party with hearts
everywhere and heart-shaped sweets everywhere; we try to
have a theme party occasionally. Another was a cowboy
night with a Wild West theme and lots of people came in
Wild West hats.

The club is called Fun – and it lives up to its name. We
came to the conclusion that the whole dance scene was
taking itself too seriously in an attempt to disassociate
itself from the rave scene. It was all going back into little
clubs and people looking very serious, so we wanted to
start a club where you could have fun.

People do like to dress up, but we don't have a dress-up
policy, in fact 'dress-undress' is what we used to say on the
flyers. It doesn't matter what clothes you're into, but if you
like to dress yourself up, that's fine too, it's an attitude. It's
great if you come in mad clothes or underwear.

I don't want it to be like one of those clubs attracting
people who are into the clothes shit. I'm very clothes-

conscious but I don't care about labels and what other people wear. I want people to lighten up.

Birmingham is really hot now; it's got to be the only city that has two really good clubs on a Saturday night and three all-nighters, which are strictly speaking illegal. The best one is run by CREAM which is totally underground. We've had links with them in the past.

We get on really well with the people who run the alternative Birmingham clubs and all-nighters. When we moved to Birmingham we probably annoyed different club promoters, but we get on all right with most now. We advertise flyers for different club promoters in the shop at Global Grooves. We see it as promoting the city, showing what it's got going for it, and helping to keep it going. It's good for us if it's really happening. I think Birmingham's got a far friendlier club scene than London. After our stately homes bash last year we're planning three this year on the bank holidays – so watch out for those!

We've all been going out for so long, the promoters now are people I remember from going out in their fluorescent shorts and trainers five years ago at warehouse parties. They didn't want to leave the scene, so they're running their own. They've got the same attitude.

I didn't want to leave the scene. It's pretty hard to get up on the days when you've been out all night . . . that's why it's good to have a job that fits in!

I was 18 in 1988 – the first Summer of Love. I was holding down a good job selling advertising. I had a Porsche and was quite well off at the time. Then I went out, doing stuff and getting off my tree, that was in that first real summer. By January 1989 I'd been sacked! The two things just didn't go together. There are a lot of disillusioned late-eighties yuppies.

For a while I sold hooded tops I made myself with awful kitsch slogans like 'Raves – Peace not police' across them. I'd be embarrassed to be seen near one now but, at the time, they did very well; there was no one else selling hooded tops near me at the time. Six months on, the big designers were featuring them in their fashion shows and every Asian textile company was making hooded tops. I went out of business, with huge debts at 19.

I had to go off and sort myself out after that! I met Mark on my travels. At one time, while Mark was running his club, Eden, he was planning a club trip out to Tenerife and sent me out for two weeks to set up the accommodation. That was in May. I stayed until January! It was great except I kept wondering what I was missing on the club scene here.

When you're going out and about all the time from the record shop to the club and then to friends' clubs in London, you forget about the real, or perhaps the unreal, world that still exists. I went out to an opening night for a club in Birmingham that I wouldn't normally go to, and people were still dancing round their handbags. Really! The sort of Shaggers night-club crowd. I'd forgotten about those sort of people. It's because we can go for so long without coming into contact with anyone outside of our social group. I can go 24 hours a day, seven days a week without seeing someone who's not into dance or clubbing. Those people at that night-club, ugh . . . It was horrible – dolly birds and drunken blokes.

We're lucky because we can have fun and work! It's taken over my life totally. We've made no real money from the shop because it's all ploughed back in. We pay ourselves a small wage, but we really established it as a contact for the street. We wanted a way to come across and target people for the club. We meet the people at clubs, but they're already in the know. Where else? There's no street level to a club, but a café-bar and gallery plus a record shop is perfect; people come in who haven't been to the club or who are unconnected with the scene.

It looked a perfect way to promote the club, so I stopped running my club in Chester, and Mark gave up Eden and we set up Global Grooves together . . . and Fun began.

I don't listen to the radio. We've got awful radio stations, all the legal ones are mainstream and the pirate ones are reggae-based, so there's no dance. We sell and play strictly dance, with mellow moments. Most of the young radio stations and magazines concentrate on indie/grunge, no one bothers with dance apart from the fanzines like *The Herb Garden* and *Jockey*, and the dance mag *Mix Mag*, but if you look at dance it's been consistently successful and popular for six years or so – and it lasts as well. You just can't beat the love of it. When you go to a club and hear a record from 1987–88 you still love it and can get on the floor and dance to it. And people hearing the records for the first time, who are just getting into dance, still think it's something; you can see 17- and 18-year-olds reacting as you did at a similar age. A lot of records are still based on those records of five years ago.

We have a very strict door policy. We have a 6-foot transvestite in stiletto-heeled boots – who stands 7 feet tall in full drag. He stands on the door and tells people they can't come in. It's not a snobbish thing, it's not down to looks, it's attitude. There are people who we recognise as trouble-makers who wouldn't make the club a better place if they came in. You have to select carefully. I don't know any club who doesn't. It's not just dress, or you'd get those people who look good and want to be seen out, standing at the bar, holding their Evian and looking good. That's not what we're about. We want people who'll have a good time, not just ape at everyone.

Besides, the latest accessory is a bottle of Becks . . . Alcohol is definitely back. Having a licence is important. Recently a big new club started up and the organisers put lots of effort into it, finding a huge hall with air conditioning, water and sound system, but no alcohol licence . . . it ran out of steam after two weeks. No one's really into drugs in the way they were any more. It's probably because they can't get them and if they do they're of a questionable nature, so why bother? Our club is a bit older – 19 to late 20s, maybe 30s, whereas it used to be 17–21-year-olds. I suppose we change when we get a bit older, we know what we want, though I have to say I'm still experimenting with life now, having a good time.

I'm happy running the club and shop and hope that will keep going for a while. We're also starting to write a book.

We bought a computer the other day and started bashing it out, it's going to be based on the lives of people we've met and come across, but completely fictional, showing the lives of people within the scene. No one in the scene has written a book yet, and similar types of stories that have appeared in the past were never really sussed, if you think of things like *Absolute Beginners* and *Quadrophenia*. Mark's got a talent for writing – very comical – so that's our next venture.

## Sharma, 22, Birmingham

Birmingham's the hip town at the moment on the clubbing front. It gets passed about. It was Manchester in 89, Notts in 90 and Leeds in 92 . . . Since then, Birmingham's taken off, we've had so many new clubs – and life goes on well beyond 2 a.m.! We've got at least three regular all-nighters. Tin Tin, a gay club; Wobble for the dressy brigade and CREAM (standing for Choose Right Easy and Mellow), finishing at 10 a.m. But it's not just dance, there's all sorts. There's a hot-bed of rubber and leather fans who get it together midweek at the Doggy Club. I've got lots of PVC, and my mate makes me clothes out of car roof vinyl. I like going to lots of different places because the crowds and atmospheres are really different. I don't like to limit myself.

## Jamie, 21, student, London and Belfast

People in Britain have a very ignorant perception of Ulster. There's the other side to the violence. There's an incredible social life. Great pubs – I used to frequent the Lavery – very hip at the time, which was popular with the in-crowd and 80-year-old bums. A great mix.

And the rave scene happened while I was over there. Protestants and Catholics mixed on E. It was well-known that the Protestant hard men – working-class criminals – were renowned for their levels of consumption of Es.

Going out was better there, because London is a collection of villages. Belfast has a specific centre so you know where the clubs are. Police didn't crack down on the clubs – they'd probably come along. Though they ended at 3–4 a.m. – not all-nighters like the English equivalent. The art college organised lots of events, with great DJs, some coming over from England.

I'm still into dance music. In Belfast everything was bootlegged – videos, music cassettes! I like dance music and rap, because it's a cultural thing, everyone can do it. I don't like indie stuff – I used to, but I've been there, it's not progressed at all. I suppose it doesn't have to, there will always be people at the same age I was (late school/college) who like listening to it, who don't mind having their mind set in that mould. I like plurability of culture.

## Daniel, 20, window dresser, Chatham

The rave scene is alive and kicking in Kent. I go to lots of huge one-off raves. The best are the ones they have from time to time at Lydd Airport. I went to one there last Saturday, in the aircraft hangar. They're really good – posters and artwork over the walls and lasers, with good, well-known DJs, playing mostly hardline techno. It's very much an E scene, though I don't usually drop one – I'm probably the only one who doesn't!

I've been going to them for a while – you hear about them by word of mouth, and have to get tickets in advance. Flyers are given out at clubs – there are some great clubs, like Warehouse II at Maidstone – or I pick them up at record shops.

People like to dress up and look good – I wear as bright colours as possible. I have got trainers – Dunlop Green Flag, they're a seventies-style plimsoll, though I don't wear trainers much of the time. I've got some seventies clothes – not many, I get what I like the look of.

I spend a lot of money on clothes – most of my wages – I like to look good. I buy most of my clothes from Next, and a designer shop in Maidstone. I don't spend a lot on my haircut – it's short (and blond). I had it long when most people did, but it's gone short now. You couldn't tell what I was into if you saw me going to work – I wear a shirt and tie to work, as a window-dresser in Maidstone and Lewisham.

I buy a few records, dance records mostly. I'm into techno, hardcore, and acid jazz. I haven't seen any mainstream bands for a long while. I get records I've heard on the radio. I listen to pirate stations; there are three or four different pirate stations around Kent – like Syndicate, which basically plays dance music. I don't listen to any regular stations.

This is my first job since leaving college (I did display). I like it, the work more than the company, but it's a step. I'd like to do display for a store in London, though that may mean leaving home – I'd have to think carefully about that. I live at home with my parents right now, which is better financially when you're not earning much, and I like the area. I travel to Maidstone and Lewisham to do the store windows at the moment. I wouldn't mind moving up to London – but not Lewisham! I'm not too fussed about leaving home right now.

There used to be a good bar scene round here. I used to go to the pub every Friday night, but the pub scene has died a bit. Also most of my best mates have moved away – they've gone to college or university elsewhere and left me. I go to the cinema a lot otherwise. I saw *Jurassic Park* – it was overhyped, I didn't like it, though I mostly see the big Hollywood movies – that's what we get here at the local cinema.

I haven't really travelled much. I went to Norwich recently to stay with a mate and we found some pretty good clubs up there, well perhaps it was 'cos it was new to me! I like doing that, checking out clubs elsewhere. I haven't really been on holiday abroad, as I don't get paid that well. I'm hoping to go to Spain this summer and sit in a bar – that appeals to me. Either with mates or with my girlfriend, it depends what happens. If I've still got a girlfriend, I'll go with her!

## Adam, 21, currently studying art in an east coast university in America

I wouldn't call myself a dealer, because although I bought and sold drugs for myself and other people, I never did it for money – for profit. I never saw it as a way of earning cash. I wanted to get hold of some, and if friends and others wanted them, then it was just as easy for me to buy a few at a time.

I'm not one of those people who deals for the kids in school! Yes, I was at school while taking E and acid, and buying stuff, but most of my buying and selling went on during school holidays, because that coincided with the time when I was going out a lot and doing most stuff myself. I can't go out and get out of my head every night. Once a week is enough for me.

I was 15 or 16 when I took my first E. I got into the music in about 1989. I missed 1988, sadly, but 1989 is vaguely respectable. I was really into the music – techno/house – and Ecstasy is part of that. You take Ecstasy purely for the sound! Obviously not everyone into the music is on it, but an integral part of taking Ecstasy is for the effects that the music has on you. You can really feel the bass, not just hear it, and that's the point. You can't feel it in the same way if you are straight.

The musicians and DJs who make the music are fully aware of the effects, or else it wouldn't be that way. It heightens the enjoyment, but more than that, you miss such a lot of the music if you don't take Ecstasy. Friends who've never taken E can't see what's so amazing about the music. You can't truly gel with techno if you have not had an E.

It's not a case of 'I'm going to a rave, so I'll take E'. You don't take one simply because it's the done thing, it's got absolutely nothing to do with peer pressure, it's purely because you want to hear the music as it is meant to sound.

If you were the sort of person who wasn't into drugs, you wouldn't feel obliged to take them just because you were at a rave. I feel really strongly about that. At raves, no one forces you to take Ecstasy, or any other drugs, that's a misconception that many people have about raves. If you were minded not to take drugs before you went, then you'd feel the same there.

I reckon about 100 per cent of people at the raves I went to were on E, but that was their decision, and it's simply because that's the best way to hear and dance to the music. The music is designed to go with Ecstasy.

Now I can listen to music when I'm straight and hear the little bits, and feel it as it should be, but it's only because I have heard it while on E.

I don't take Es any more. That's got something to do with change of lifestyle – I'm studying in America – and something to do with the change of quality of Ecstasy available. When I started, Es were really lovely, all the time. Even when I first came to America and went out in New York, I could get some good Es. But now, it's different. You can get just MDMA which is OK, but the Es are nasty, and it's the same in Britain. The things they (manufacturers) put into it are dodgy, there are no quality Es any more.

I only buy from people who've been recommended. It's the normal hype. Before I buy, someone I know will have bought a batch from them or will have tried one, if not I will try a half. I used to think you could bite an E and tell whether it was good stuff or not. But you can bite paracetamol and get a similar taste. I wouldn't buy more than 15 or 20 at one time unless I was sure of the quality. News travels fast. You know where the good Es are, sometimes it's from the same dealer, but not always. Someone who had a good supply one week wouldn't have a fortnight or maybe a week later. You have to beware of dealers. But we had a good network. Say of 100 friends of mine, at least 10 would be searching for Es.

I suppose I'm a dabbler. Just one night a week with a couple of Es was my preferred limit. I've mixed Ecstasy and acid a couple of times but it fires my head. I don't know the long-term effects it would have on me, but I could see a great dividing path in my brain, I'm sure I'd end up schizophrenic. It was a bad trip for me, I'm not ready for pure acid. I don't feel I've suffered at all from taking Ecstasy. I read all the research and reports I see about it, but it doesn't seem to have permanent effects – not taken the way I took it, anyway.

It's not hard to get drug supplies here, being English isn't a problem, especially as I know a lot about techno and house and, when I get talking about the music, they know I'm OK. But over here (America) it really is hard to get E any more, just pure MDMA, which I do a bit. Coke is the new thing here, and I'm scared of it.

There also isn't the same music scene here. There never was the same real rave culture, except a while back in California, though that was the LA homosexual scene, so it's very different. Raves in America are strictly 14-year-olds. Yes, I know it's the same in Britain now, but that's not how it was, there was always a lot of older people into raves in Britain (18–19–20 was the average age), but as it spread, the scene attracted younger people. That wasn't the case here. Having good drugs wouldn't help matters. People here, at least the people I meet and study with, take less drugs than people in Britain. Though almost everyone smokes a joint.

Now I just smoke grass, I've mellowed out. You have to, I'd die if I didn't mellow out. I couldn't keep going flat out for life! I was seriously beating myself for two and half, maybe three years, dropping Es or acid every week. You can't keep it up indefinitely, not if you want to do other things with your life. I try not to smoke too much, limiting it to the end of the night. I'm really straightening out. It's two in the afternoon and I'm not stoned, so that's a real improvement!

My listening habits have mellowed alongside. Yes, the drugs have to fit the music. I play more and more ambient music, not my white label breakbeat hardcore. I still hate vocals. At least the ambient stuff goes down well in America, you don't get many clubs playing Frankie Knuckles or O Bones; they're not ready for proper English-style techno. People here still ask for Madonna's 'Holiday'!

# J-Jay, 25, runs club Inner-vision, London

I'm out every night at the moment, I'm trying to hand out 44,000 flyers for our Christmas Eve happening. I don't like the word 'club', it implies something about the people, cliquey, closed – 'tribal gathering' is more appropriate.

I've been into music and DJing for seven or eight years. I went away, travelling to Athens and all round, doing DJing and stuff. In other countries I got recognition because I'm black and it was easy to work as a DJ. I don't do so much DJing now. There is just so much ego involved.

Most DJs now are so disgusting, they're only getting behind two turntables and playing sounds. They have this attitude, just because they play records, and they get irate if someone else is playing when it's their turn! I prefer making music, not so much music as in a beat, but a spiritual type of music. No one does it here. There's a great German DJ, Sven Vath, who makes spiritual music. It's something else. He's made records and DJs a lot, but he's far too expensive for our gatherings. Not that he isn't worth it, besides in the winter months he spends his time in Goa, from January until March, DJing and picking up sounds which he uses when he comes back home. I don't use bits of his records when I make music – no one should have the right to play around with this guy's work.

His music transcends everything, it's definitely years ahead. Even people who don't like it initially listen again and they can really get off on it. Each person is predisposed to a different type of music, but you can still get through to them. Few people listen to something and agree about it ... though some people's minds are limited and they can't see it. When you go to some events you can see the young people's minds are manipulated into the style of music they listen to, while the whole world's getting the music of the future.

I'm always learning. I like making instrumentals with a constant sharp, clear vitality, and a beat like a trance beat – ambient with a beat. Mix the two together.

I mix and play my own music. With DJing, if a DJ makes his own music then he's showing he's not just taking other people's ideas – he's creating his own picture. When I make records to play, I want it to sound like I'm making a picture, not just buying a load of records.

The authorities are scared of music, there is a power in it. That's why students have their music licences revoked, it all adds up. They don't want people to get together and play music, because of the message, attitude, whatever, behind it; music brings people together. The authorities want them to sit together in a quiet room. If you do that you just delay, put back the time they will come together and rise up. There were 35,000 people at Castle Morton – just through picking up flyers. They try to ban raves and gatherings, because they don't want people to get together. Tribes have been kicked out of clubs, but they'll come back, they'll surface somewhere else, find a way through.

Inner-vision has organised a few things. Our Christmas gathering is in Clerkenwell (Turnmills) but we've been involved in South London. We want to cover the whole of London – orbital London. When people see what we're doing, they want to be part of it. That's bit of a whole layer. Isn't it strange how young people have got influence over other people? Say 40–50 people are interested in something, if a large majority of them say party, so people all spread the word to 2000 people and more. It's a great organ. I was at a squat party months ago, that was amazing. That was all word of mouth. The vibes are still around.

## Jamie, 24, musician and DJ, London

I'm trying to get a record deal at the moment. I've been working on my music full-time making a demo tape, getting it down, so I can send it out to a few companies. It's kind of synthesiser, equaliser – dance music. Instrumental, I didn't sing on it, but I've got a singer who I work with.

I've been working in clubs and do some DJing. I'm kind

of known on the club circuit. I hosted at Kinky Gerlinky a couple of years ago, and got on the record decks to do some DJing. But I became a DJ to give me. the start to make records. It's an instrument. I like making records not playing them.

The music's really synthesised and different – it's noticeable. Pop more than dance, not really club music, despite the club background. Some of my friends work on underground club music, but I'd prefer mine to surface outside the clubs, it's slightly more commercial. We want to promote ourselves and go much further ... yes, all the way to the States! It's not pop as in Right Said Fred, they are too gimmicky, quite trashy – though I think they're great. Our music is more serious, but not like Simply Red. Influences are Yazoo – Alison Moyet, synthesised and dancy for their time, good songs too, serious pop. We're like them in that we're a guy and a woman. I met my singer in a club, we both write the songs, we work well together. We want to cultivate a strong image and play the part. I know she will do it too. We're going to make a video as soon as we've got our first song. The visual side is very important. I've been thinking about that already.

I'm used to acting a part, I've learnt tricks from the fashion world. I worked in fashion for a year, selling designer clothes at Way In in Harrods. I did it in the mid-eighties – the designer decade, when everyone, everywhere, was talking fashion, fashion, fashion. I also did a bit of fashion PR and had people from places like *Vogue* coming to borrow clothes. You help pick clothes to suit magazines. It gives you an idea on cultivating and knowing how to sell an image. Most of my friends are into fashion and went to St Martin's; one good friend is a designer, so I'm aware how important the right image is. Music is an image.

I was trying to do music while still working at the shop, and people would hear of it and come in and say you've got to get a group together. Just because they can see that you know about fashion, they think you can sell music through it. But it was a friend who was also doing music and trying to get a deal who really persuaded me. That was five years ago. It's been really coming together since I found the singer.

I still go clubbing a lot – Heaven, Maximus. There are one-off clubs, and friends run some, but Heaven seems to be the one that's always there, you know what you're getting, so you don't expect much. It's not as exciting as Kinky Gerlinky was, but then KG was only good once every couple of months, like sex. Heaven is consistently good, lots of people don't like it, they say it's boring, that it's never changed its interior. It is a bit of a dump, but as clubs come and go, it's stayed the course, and loads of others have come and gone. I know lots of people there – there are the people who live for it, they are always there, others hang around for a while until they go back to where they came from, and others settle down, get pizzas and stay in! I have got a boyfriend, but we haven't settled down – we both like going out.

You do have to turn some people away when you do the door, which I hate doing, it's cruel. All clubs have door policies. Close friends of people running the club come in – there's always a bunch of names who get in free. The Café de Paris was the first place I worked that I had problems like that. It was in Leicester Square so you got loads of passers-by, pissed people coming from the pubs at closing times, seeing a queue for a club and they didn't know it was. That's not the sort of person you want in the club. We didn't want men in suits, Essex lads or dollies in stiletto shoes. Drag queens get in automatically. Industria is in Hanover Square so you don't get people who just stumble across it, everyone who goes there is sussed. And if someone did wander in and wasn't spoiling it for everyone, I'd let them off. I never got trouble on the doors, and I had bouncers right by me to sort anything out.

Both clubs were really gay, with just a few straight people. Getting a mix is better, it's usually the same crowds at the clubs as well. I don't do so much door work now, bits and pieces, since the Café finished, which leaves me time to work on the record. Apart from clubs, what else do I do . . . go to see films. I like low-budget arty films, like films by John Waters and Warhol. I used to go to the Scala a lot before it shut down. I see more and more on video now.

I moved about more when I was young – I'm not from London, I was born in Scotland. I'd like to live abroad for a while – America: New York, San Francisco or Florida. But I haven't travelled abroad for while. I never went to Ibiza or Barcelona when people were going there clubbing, I was working full-time at that point.

## Michael Livingstone, 24, club runner, Brighton

I'm a club runner at the Reform in Brighton. My job is to get people into the door. It's basically about creating an environment . . . I took over Bubblegum Factory from Raj who'd set it up elsewhere, and moved its premises. He's still involved, he DJs on Fridays at the OO Baby as it's called now. It had been running for three to four years at various venues. I didn't create the club itself, but put it into a night-club in a larger venue. It was a sixties night, now it's acid jazz funk with the occasional sixties track from the likes of The Monkees thrown in – all very tasteful.

There's a big age range, 18–33, and all types, whereas before we got sixties diehards with Small Faces haircuts, flares and such things. Now it's a mixture of funk types and some into suede or cord jackets with 501s and a few students who probably have a Megadeath record at home.

A year and a half ago it was very cliquey and more or less 90 per cent sixties clothing, but it worked. It was a sixties night with no forward thinking, it didn't take into account the mass commercialism of the seventies or the hedonism of the eighties, it was there. Unfortunately a lot of the people moved away to London or whatever and it splintered off, and many other local clubs thought they'd make a sixties revival club which cheapened it. It lost its inspiration, bastardised it, and that was it. It's more mainstream, well, more of a club night now, not an expression of the sixties.

Saturday Giant is more New York garage/house. There are four areas, a bar, two dance floors and a seated area, jazz funk in the seated area.

You could say I worked my way up! I started collecting glasses at the Zap Club and worked my way up, through the rave culture. It's been an interesting period.

A lot of club runners try to take it personally. Most people's egos get in the way and they get greedy, for fame or money or both, which ruins a lot of the clubs. I think getting an atmosphere, the right vibes, and creating a space where people can enjoy themselves is more important. The club and rave scene in Brighton has been hit by zealous policing.

The main problem is police on a budget. The force don't want to have their police deployed on the streets later than a certain time. It makes it easier if they can say, 'All home at 3 p.m.!'

## Testcard, 21, art student, Brighton

I do lighting at clubs. Not as in wiring, but special effects. I'm into the music side of it – the experimental music scene. I usually do the lighting at the same club each week, and I'll do other one-off events.

I started doing the lights about three-and-a-half years ago when acid house was really big in Brighton. The first club my mate and I did, we were arrested for! Not a good start. It was a rave in an abandoned warehouse and it got raided. All the people on the door, doing the DJing or the lights got arrested and put in a cell for eight hours! It was a nightmare experience, but we weren't charged with anything.

I started touring abroad with bands doing lighting for their shows in Europe; Germany was pretty good at the time, it was for lots of hippie British bands. I wasn't into psychedelia, but initially I wanted to break into the scene and I liked the psychedelic images. It was a frustrating time for my partner Pete and I and we split up and started doing things on our own. Pete wanted to branch out and do London clubs and gigs, but I wanted to keep it low-key. I was working regularly. I stopped touring so much and got offered a job doing the lights at a Brighton club, someone just asked me to do it.

As far as my images are concerned, I really like using images from TV. I use stills from cinema films like *Liquid Sky*. I want the image to be now – not harping back to sixties psychedelia. It's like when I was doing lighting for The Bubblegum Factory, a sixties night, I made it colourful, I wanted it to feel more cybernetic, with slides and films and backdrops on the theme and loads of solar stuff. I want to create a whole atmosphere. I use smoke and beams and the images come through. No one tells me what to do, I just know what kind of club they have in mind. Anything goes. Whatever conjures up the right image. I've used nude films – I just think, will it have an effect on the club? I've used films of deep-sea fishing to give people the feeling that they were swimming around, and Martian landscapes. I've got sequences which I use with prisms that go in front of the slide projector which sweep you round so you get the feeling of movement.

I'm at art college so lighting and club work is for money. I also do nude modelling for drawing classes, which is a good source of money.

I like Brighton because it's free and easy. I've only been here for five years. Now things are starting to take off again, there are people running more in the way of different music venues and creating atmosphere. Some clubs are amazing.

There's a lot of pseudo-religious cult imagery in Brighton – they're starting a Church of the Sub Genius down here encouraging people to do abstract things, and the music is different too – they want to get more meaning into the music. It's like messing around with people's minds. That's really what doing visuals is; when you're projecting on huge screens and showing films on banks of

TVs you're hitting people with massive images. It's too huge for them to ignore, it goes in, even if it's subliminal and it's not static – I think that's the way of club visuals in the future.

# 9 Travellers

The villagers of Wellesbourne did not take kindly to having New Age travellers as neighbours, so when the vicar, Canon Norman Howes, mused that Jesus might have been one, they were perplexed.

Annoyed, even.

Matt Tapp, a spokesman for the Warwickshire police said: 'It's not a Christian view shared by shopkeepers who have had people peeing in their refrigerators.'

At their camp, the travellers were bemused. 'I have never compared myself to Jesus,' said Sean, 'but it's nice to see someone in the church on our side for a change.' (*Guardian*)

The 43,000 teenagers under 16 who run away every year in the UK (most of them 14–16) are mostly home within 48 hours. Only two per cent stay away longer than that. Most don't go far from home and are driven by hormonal upheaval, adolescent discontent or a desire to spread their wings.

Nevertheless, it has become alarmingly commonplace to find young people begging, sleeping in doorways, hanging out, looking rough. We are inured to it. It only becomes an issue when an important person draws attention to it. (*Guardian*)

## Neil, 23, NFA, Portugal

I've beome a bit of a farmer since I've been in Portugal. I went there at the end of March. I had a change of heart, left Britain and I've since been living on a commune in Portugal, learning all about organic farming. I didn't go with any money, we literally plough and plant and grow what we want. You get food and accommodation in return for helping out on the farm.

I'm used to not having anything – I've never had any money. Before I left Britain, I was doing a 'zine called *Dog*. It was all written by a bunch of dirty, smelly squatters, pasting bits together! All my Giros went into printing that.

I've spent years touring round and living in a bus. It

changes your perspective and how people see you. I have met some great people with good attitudes, and I've met with some bad reactions; police included. I have met some nice policemen! The problem is before they answer to their own conscience they have to answer to their superior officers. Also there's no better way to get promotion than by making arrests, so they develop an interesting way of getting signed confessions from people who haven't done anything wrong. When I did *Dog*, I got letters from prisoners, but many won't highlight their case or their traumas to the public for fear that they'll get extra punishment inside if they talk.

I'm not militant, but obviously if I believe in a cause I'll try and do my bit, rather than plodding along and ignoring it. That's when the police are out of order, like at the poll tax rallies. If you got anywhere near the boys in yellow [riot squad], you can see their attitudes at work, hitting out at people, just anyone. Even pregnant women were getting beaten up, just people caught up in the flow.

Squatting isn't vindictive. There are plenty of empty houses going to waste while people are living on the street. People who squat have nowhere else to live. It can also be putting facilities to use for a good purpose in a wider sense. One good example is a group who tried to convert an old mental hospital into a working gallery. A place for artists to gather, work and get encouragement. That's the sort of thing I'm interested in. It's not just squatting for somewhere to live and sleep, but also to help people realise their potential. There are not enough chances for young people to explore their creative skills. It's a desperate situation when people go into jobs out of frustration and all their creative talent has gone to waste. But it happens all the time. This scheme started well, the council gave it their blessing, but then went back on their word. That happens all the time too.

*Dog* is a kind of outlet for creative people to express themselves. I've been doing it a few years – probably the same length of time as *Club Dog* (Islington) has been around, though there's no link, except we're into the same scene, festivals and stuff. We didn't call ourselves after the club. Although it's my 'zine, there is no censorship, if someone wanted to contribute I'd let them, whatever their viewpoint. I suppose even if they'd written in with a fascist idea, I'd put it in and make them realise their misguided beliefs through what was around it. But that didn't happen as *Dog* attracted a different kind of people. I get sent a lot of stuff by people who read *Dog*, who feel it hits a chord, and what I put in will always tend to be my preferences. I suppose it's a delicate form of censorship if it comes down to it.

I believe in respect for all creatures, that's why I haven't become a fascist. Of course I have slipped up along the way, as have most humans, but I can still see a lot of potential out there, and that's what we can show. That's the attitude to the 'zine.

It started off when we were into bands and I wanted to blag my way in to see them. But I got bored of sucking up to bands, and wanted a way for people to share their ideas. I was pissed off at the appalling gap between bands and the audience. If you go to see bands, you watch them, then go home. The only interaction you have is if you buy a T-shirt. We should all be involved. If someone makes music, that doesn't make them God. I wanted to break down some of the barriers and develop a magazine that gives people a chance to have their say, to get involved. I knew so many talented artists and writers, and no one was sharing their art, because no one recognised it. There was no vehicle for them to get their work noticed, no way for them to show it. I believe that art is for all; that we should all share our talents.

There was no real structure to *Dog*. If I wanted some writing or drawings done for the 'zine, I couldn't persuade people to do something they didn't want to; it's mainly ideas that I throw out, and if I connect with people, it's good.

I couldn't ever tell anyone when *Dog* would be coming out. Deadlines are not for me. I did seven issues in two-and-a-half years. *Dog* 8 is now finished. It's been taken over by some mates while I'm away, and they're just as relaxed about deadlines and stuff as I am. Probably more so.

I don't want *Dog* to be classified as a particular thing, or to be boxed off, much of it includes a wide variety of ideas.

The music lingers on as a selling point, some people unfortunately won't look at a fanzine unless it's got bands in it. And it's read by a wide section of people. It's not got a cover price, people give donations, a token gesture of people giving for something they want. They don't always appreciate a fanzine if they get it for nothing.

It sells well at festivals. I go to lots in the summer. Glastonbury and the free festivals mostly. Reading isn't a festival. It's a money-making event for a big corporation. Even Glastonbury has lost its status as a festival for the people, it's become a money-spinner for the land-owner, and those people who have to pay lots for a stall pass on those prices when they sell things there. Even people with good interests are forced to charge far more for things. A real festival is about people sharing everything, not about making a profit. And at Glastonbury, there have been very few real people – Michael Eavis pays the police not to let in travellers ... the sewage travellers, as they call them. I hate that – New Age travellers!

I used to live in Glastonbury, and Cornwall, among other places, as a traveller, but both were really nice places, many of the people there had time for you. If you live outside of a city it makes you realise how unfriendly, how uncaring, cities are. It worked for me; countryside is where it's at. What I feel, is that there is life in fields. What drove me to that lifestyle? I have been through so many stages, idealistic to the point of being vegan, fed up with corruption and that sort of thing. It spreads through everything – the capitalist lifestyle scared me off. That's why I went to Portugal. I had the choice of staying here with quite a few of my friends and fighting the police, trying to bring attention to our plight. No one can see how it will change anything, it's a wasted life, I'm not happy fighting all the time.

A more positive example is living the way I do in Portugal. I'm self-sufficient, I don't take anything from the government. I couldn't do that in Britain. I had to go to them for dole cheques just to keep at subsistence level. I hate the idea of having to take something from a government I don't agree with. Everyone should have the right to work, or a certain standard of lifestyle; they don't help us to help ourselves. It's their fault that so many people are unemployed and they give out dole begrudgingly. I'm no longer signing on, so I don't owe them anything; I'm not compromising my ideals.

Where I live in Portugal, there are very young and old people; most of the young Portuguese people my age have moved away, others have come in to help with the land – Australians, Europeans, Malaysians. It's very mixed. At the moment I'm discovering all about growing things. You get great satisfaction from watching seeds turn into food. Most of the food feeds the people who live here; we sell left-over produce. It's an interesting time in Portugal. Portugal's desperately racing to catch up with the rest of Europe, and the mountain people have been left to do as they please. They don't get any help but, equally, they don't get any hassle. That's how it should be here.

Anyone can come to the commune to help in the garden. People come and go all year round, they stay for anything between two weeks and six months; it's not static. I've been here one of the longest. No, I haven't worked my way up the ladder, an interesting theory in a commune! There's no hierarchy in our little farm. Everyone lives in stone buildings and if more arrive, we can squeeze them in. I've met a lot of interesting people and found out a lot about life through them, many British, like a Scottish guy who left his family and came to find himself. Life is a wonderful range of opportunities and you can either go through it expanding your possibilities and contacts or narrowing it down. I like expanding.

I'm sure my background didn't predispose me to travelling. I did maths and physics A levels. Somehow I'd got the idea I was going to do electronic engineering. After two years of maths formulas I was confused – about what I wanted of myself. I did two weeks at art college, but three years of squatting and travelling was a far better education. Whenever I left London I realised how warm people could be. It's all down to space. No caged animal is a happy animal, and in London people are really on top of one another.

I was born and brought up in London (Pinner) but my parents were keen walkers, so we'd always be going off into the mountains. Kids love the countryside, they get a great buzz from being outside. That's why there are usually lots of happy children running around on sites, when there is a lot of safe space to play, and people to watch over them.

My first stint at travelling came when I left London with a friend and a tent one freezing cold day. We had to scrape the ice off the tent every morning. When we got to Glastonbury we decided to split. I was offered a room in a house at the end of a site. I stayed there until I was offered a trailer. Then I travelled with a guy in a dodgy old Telecom van. We saw a bit of the country then got bored, we never had enough money to buy petrol! We used to park on site. A lot of sites were like mini festivals. I was in a nice site up in the hills in Cornwall last March. We used to do a bit of daffodil picking for money. Seventeen of us worked in one stretch, it was like a day out, and you're getting on with the community, earning from them, then paying the money to the locals when you buy things.

There are lots of different sites. I always choose clean ones with no needles and lots of children with happy faces. That's children not just as in little people, but the child inside everyone who's enjoying life. I have seen sites which are like council estates, but it seems silly to me to leave the city, just to build one in the country. I've also done my fair share of squatting, because I had nowhere else to live. I don't go round looking for a suitable home, I just find an empty house and make it into a home. I miss my friends, but that's all. A few of my friends might join me next summer. I don't think anyone at home really knows what I do. I'm very busy here, I've a water tank and irrigation system to build, and lots of babies to deliver. Everyone seems to be pregnant at the moment!

## Sally, 23, Northern Ireland

People have the wrong view of travellers. In fact they think I'm a traveller and I'm not, just because I live in an old camper van – and because of the way I look. (I've got longish hair, wear jeans and shirts or T-shirts. What's strange about that?) I love old trucks and buses, old vehicles are so stylish, so beautiful, that's one of the reasons I choose to live in one. The others? A beautiful countrified setting – where else could I have my own detached dwelling? As a matter of fact, where else could I have my own dwelling? My experience of living before here was with my parents, which I got out of as soon as I could. Nothing wrong with my parents, they're great as folks go, but an individual can't live as he/she wants to under their parents' roof. Well, I found I couldn't. Or else I was holed up in some damp room, with no cooking facilities, paying a fortune, which I couldn't afford.

If I wasn't in the bus, I'd be on the streets. This is the most secure home I've ever had. Talking of security, because it is a permanent place – with a permanent address, albeit stationed on farmland and without a telephone – I can get post delivered and I am treated as a legal resident. I am a legal resident – we pay rent, a ground rent if you like – to the farmer who owns the land. We have OK relationships with him. I also have a job, not on the farm, but in a café. The only thing that separates me from any other citizen is that my home is not built of bricks and mortar.

You get all these people talking about filthy sites. They should visit this one, we've got bins! There aren't that many vans on the site though we have more in the summer, just visiting, passing through like, and of course a lot of people come to help on the farm in the summer months. That's how I found this place.

## Andy, 21, Faslane Peace Camp, Dunbartonshire

I came here in October 92. I've lived on the camp permanently for about a year. Before this, I'd always held firm beliefs on environmental issues and followed the peace movement. I'd joined a few rallies, but that's about it. I had a few friends who had come and stayed here and told me about it. I wanted to do something. I didn't live far from here, a couple of miles away in Dunbarton, so I personally didn't trek to get here, but we get people from all over the country, though there are more Scottish people coming up to help out when we have something happening, because they are more aware of the camp and its aims. Even so, the camp has been here for 12 years now and it's pretty well-known.

It's an important site because there's a submarine base and a nuclear site next to each other, a lot's going on there. There's all the nuclear issue and the effects of that on the environment – and the fact that the MOD have taken over such a lot of land and finance in the area which could otherwise go to a much better purpose.

We do various things to highlight the issues. A lot of the action depends on the weather, and what's happening at Faslane, but we're working on something day in, day out, keeping watch and notifying the public and other peace groups. When there's a convoy going out from the base, we inform everyone and organise something. Like when there's a warhead convoy ... We don't try to stop it but we organise protests, so that people realise what it means, and it brings our feelings home to the people working with it as well. It's one way to touch people's consciences.

We also inform Nuke Watch of developments – the national anti-nuclear campaign – who keep an eye on everything around the country. There are quite a lot of bases throughout Britain – militant establishments, not just anti-nuclear campaigns – and people go to and from them between Scotland and England. If there is a campaign, protest or activity we take it up, and help publicise it or whatever, and if we are planning a protest or campaign, they'll spread it around the network and keep people informed. We send out newsletters to local and national press, other groups and individuals. We have a huge list of individual people who support our cause.

As far as the media goes, a lot of the time newspapers are interested in what's going on generally. We'll always inform them of our actions. Recently Malcolm Rifkind [Defence Secretary] came to comment on the new Trident shotlift at the base. The media covered that, and our actions got some publicity, though we don't always get as big a coverage as we could. Sometimes it does work to our advantage, it depends. Some of the press are favourable, and will give us space. Some come up to the camp to report or mention our campaigns, it depends whether they're planning a large feature or short article.

A lot of folk leave the camp for short holidays, go to see their families. Everyone's free to come and go as they please. At the moment there are nine people living here permanently – that's very small compared to the masses that were here in the eighties. The number goes up depending on what we've got planned. We're not really worried about smaller numbers, I don't think it signifies a lack of interest in the peace movement. In the eighties, Faslane was one of the few camps around. Now there are quite a lot of peace organisations in Scotland and in Britain as a whole. CND was bigger and more publicised in the eighties than now, this just means the work of smaller groups is more important, keeping watch and spreading the word through the network. At Faslane we hear about things and try to get them in the public eye. We do approach the MOD and the base, though it's always the same – they won't deny anything, though they won't confirm it.

Faslane is a permanent camp, it's like a commune with everyone helping each other, and we all have a lot of beliefs in common. It's not all young people here, it's mixed, though the majority are quite young, just because young people are more inclined to think about peace issues and the future and want to do something actively to help. Also, they are less likely to have family commitments. As camps go, it's not like we've given up all home comforts. We all live in caravans with little stoves, and there's a communal caravan where we hold meetings and eat – we cook for each other. There's a generator there with hot and cold running water, it's just like a house.

When I first came – on 21 October 1992 – I came because the first Trident submarine was arriving, and came to help with that protest. I knew people staying here at the time and stayed with them. I moved in permanently and some others left. At one time I was sharing a caravan with eight people. When other people come, we try and cope with the influx, we'll always put people up. There were 20 people after the last weekend activity – weekend people. Scottish CND and National CND informed various groups about what we were doing, others got the newsletters and came to swell the numbers. Usually people come just for the activity, but some stay a short while.

It is frustrating that many people aren't aware of or in tune with what the peace movement is trying to do, like you couldn't go to a shopping centre and get everyone thinking about the issues. But the way I see it is that you have got to keep trying. Something has got to give eventually. We have to try, it's up to the individuals in the country, you can't just ignore it.

The problem is people think it has got nothing to do with them, but it has got everything to do with them. And they think, 'There's nothing I can do about it, I can't fight the Government, so I'll just accept it and hopefully nothing bad will come of it.' But that's a defeatist standpoint. We have to try and do something. So what we do is distribute information and keep the issues in the public eye so more people are aware and will try and throw their weight behind our campaign. Even if a lot of people don't join us physically they support in other ways. We have no funding – individually, some of the people at the camp can claim state benefit – but periodically the camp will get cheques from groups and individuals to help keep our pressure group going. The newsletters and mail-outs alone cost a significant amount. We're all giving our time voluntarily, we don't receive payments for any of our efforts and, at times, living here can be very stressful.

The local people have accepted the camp now, it's been here so long, and there aren't any hostile reactions from them. Back in the eighties there were, but not now. We're the longest running peace camp, since Greenham Common went. We do get a few odd incidents from sub-mariners and sailors – ships come into the base too. They'll go to Helensburgh for a booze-up and get rowdy, returning past our camp. The MOD go by regularly to keep a watch and occasionally you'll spot the odd person you've never seen before having a cup of tea and looking round and it sets you really on edge. Just by the look of them, you can tell they're not a genuine sympathiser. But we don't really get spies because we're quite open – people could just read the newsletters to find out what we're up to, unlike the MOD.

We don't have spies in the base, though there are ways of getting information. We don't try and make the people who work there feel guilty. A lot of folk just work there for the money, it's the biggest source of employment in Dunbartonshire – there's not a lot else. I personally am opposed to people working there, I feel it's wrong, but that's a matter for the individual, they have families to feed, bills to pay, and there's quite high unemployment in Scotland, as everywhere.

It's hard to tell how long I'll stay here – until the aims are complete. When I leave it will probably be to join another campaign. But there's a lot of work to be done here, it's a major environmental issue, a political issue and we've got to stand up for human rights.

### Colin, 23, squatter, London

Luckily we were on holiday when the Electricity Board raided the squats. There are three squats in a row here and we all had an electricity supply going. It's no different to living anywhere else – except you don't pay rent. It's clean, we've decorated it ... cats love it! It's the third squat in London I've lived in (all in the East End). You don't break in – you find a way in, often other people have broken in and squatted or whatever and you go in then. It's not illegal, just using space that would otherwise stay empty. My girlfriend's got a council flat in the area, but it's not as nice as this place (really) so she stays here most of the time.

Although we haven't got any hot water. You get used to cold baths or filling them up with the kettle.

People across the road don't bother us. Perhaps they were a bit dubious at first, but we've been here over a year and they can see we haven't had any wild parties or wrecked the place. What would you prefer, an empty row of houses opposite you or people living there?

I am trying to find work. I've had a couple of interviews and sent my portfolio out, but there's not much work for architects right now – not struggling newcomers, anyway. If I did get work, I don't think I'd move. Where to? I don't go out much – parties, I suppose. I can't really afford to. I don't smoke or drink.

## Sian, 19, Bath

If I'm not at festivals I hang out with mates at home, going to parties and stuff. Bath's very young and lively. I used to love surfing, and I'd spend most weekends at some beach with my mates – four of us camping out in a battered Beetle. Honest! We went to a Beetle bash once – a lot of surfers are into Beetles – I don't know why, and this bash was nowhere near the sea, it was on a race track near Reading, Santa Pod, I think. My geography's terrible – though it's getting better as I travel round more! It was cool, a bit like a rave, just loads of us camping out, with an outdoor cinema screen and sound system. Now I spend most of the summer at festivals. I've progressed to a camper van, there's more room, though it's still not mine, it belongs to the people who run the stall I make T-shirts for. It's like home from home.

## Suzy, 25, waitress, Brighton

I lived in London for years and worked (as a waitress) there, but I wanted to get out of the city. Brighton's like a town. It's lovely, there's a lot happening. It wasn't easy to find work, this is the second waitressing job I've had. I do get bored. Money isn't as good as London – especially the tips. Tourists in London tip a lot better. I trained as a designer, but I haven't ever had a job as one. I have tried to sell my stuff in other people's shops, but it wasn't worth the aggravation. I suppose my heart wasn't really in it, because I couldn't take all the knocks. Now, I just work to save up and go away. I've travelled round Asia/Thailand, I've been to Mexico and worked in Australia for six months. I'm saving up to go to Colombia and travel for a few months or maybe years! It does disorientate you, travelling. You come back and friends have settled down or got jobs. It's hard to keep track of everyone.

After Australia I thought I'd got it out of my system, but there's nothing to keep me here, so I may as well see as much as I can while I'm able to. It depends where you go and the tickets you get. I don't make too many hard and fast plans. Sometimes I'll meet someone who'll tell me where they've been or what they're doing so I'll go there. I'd rather stay in while I'm here and work hard doing evening shifts, then go away, so I haven't any social life here really.

The first time I went away I knew people in Australia to stay with, but this time I'm going alone. It doesn't worry me being female and travelling alone. If I thought like that I'd never get to see anything. I travelled round Asia on my own – though I met up with loads of people on the way. You do meet people on the way.

It's easy meeting people you like, but not so easy meeting people you can get on with for days or weeks on end, but you have to try, put yourself out a bit. It teaches you a lot about people and about yourself, it makes you far more accommodating. When I see some of my friends from college, they're so narrow. Yes, they've got careers which I haven't, and flats, but their lives are so limited and work gives them some kind of status or power. That's fine, but I'm glad I haven't missed out on what I've seen. And so many people say to me 'Aren't you lucky?' or 'I wish I could go with you.' Of course they could if they really wanted. Most of them could easily save up the money and rent out their flats, so they'd have something to come back to. There's nothing to prevent them from going away for several months, except they're too scared to leave their jobs and their stable lives.

# **10** Virtual Reality

Youngsters are turning into a generation of TV junkies, spending more than five hours a day in front of the screen.

Almost two-thirds of children have a TV set in their bedroom which they switch on as soon as they get home from school.

Viewing at weekends can increase to over seven hours, according to one of the biggest studies carried out into the habits of British youth. (*Daily Express*)

The belief that computer games can harm children's development was backed up today by a study which shows that those who play the most see themselves, and are seen by others, as bad-tempered and aggressive.

Girls and boys aged 12 and 13, who spent an average 13 hours a week on the games, which included Gameboys and Sonic the Hedgehog, had a sharper temper and got more frustrated than their friends who played less, psychologists revealed.

In the study of 120 children in Brighton aged 12 and 13, the psychologists found that the amount of computer games a girl played did not affect the amount she read, although boys who played a lot read far less than their counterparts who played just two to three hours a week. (*Evening Standard*)

A schoolboy computer hacker caused chaos when he dialled into a vital database at a Brussels-based centre for cancer research and treatment, a court heard yesterday.

The boy allegedly ran a rogue programme which generated 50,000 phone calls, and caused the computer system at the European Organisation for the Research and Treatment of Cancer to 'crash'. (*Guardian*)

## **Aran Phelan, 23, Virgin Games, London**

I used to do the customer support service which meant answering customers' questions when they rang in with problems with their games. So I had to know them all and be able to play them all right through the levels, as I spent my time telling people how to complete certain games. So I can honestly say I know how to get through every single Virgin game! I actually like playing games – even now – it's not just a job.

I work on the games before they are released to the general public. I have to test them all for faults and bugs and to see whether every game and stage is possible – especially for sophisticated games. If I felt there was something wrong or it could be improved in some way, I'd tell the producer who would go through to the programmer and he improves on it. It's a two-way thing, testing. Each game is really tested for four or five months' duration before release, though it depends on the scale of the game – some may just need one month, others six. I've played thousands of different games; I've been playing since I was 11 and I'm now 23 – still a young lad!

I've just moved to producer level so I help structure the games, working with the people who program them and the artists. I come up with characters, storylines, helping to produce original programs. You draw on people you know, and usual stereotypes, then expand on them. Some people like characters to be realistic, but most are exaggerated. You want them to be appealing.

At the moment we're doing dragon games based on the film of the life-story of Bruce Lee. We're using characters from the film and some extra characters, which requires research. It means watching an amazing amount of Bruce Lee and Kung Fu films with dodgy-looking characters. I've watched hundreds of Kung Fu films over the past few weeks, looking for ideas and plots.

We do buy the rights to film characters – most top-selling films license their characters to games, like with *Robo Cop V Terminator* on Sega. Characters from the two *Robo Cop* movies and the *Terminator* film actors were first pitted against each other in a comic, then the two were brought into video games. The programmers developed the characters from there.

We don't use the original film story, we develop a story around the characters. Though the story is important, usually when we're thinking up a new game, the story-board will be there from the beginning, plenty of beat 'em up, shoot 'em up.

It's an exciting time at the moment, we're really getting into multi-media stuff, so it's very interactive. Full motion videos which you can watch and interact with at the same time, that's what we're working on now – to be available in 1994. It's the next generation of video games.

It has the usual game, nice graphics, nice story, but it's not simply a totally formatted video with a formula game . . . the user has far more involvement. I'm sure it will take off. The price is very high but already coming down. Punters will have to swap their technology to take part. They'll need a machine for playing them – e.g. laser disc and a film CD . . . The game is run on CD not cartridge, so won't be compatible with old machines. People will buy a second lot of equipment or change their whole home system. The developments in video game technology will make the old consoles collectable – they are already. I'm on the look out for early consoles . . .

We're concentrating on films now. We're actively watching out for suitable new films being made. We buy extra footage at the end of filming, produced with the real actors and all shot by the film studios. They shoot the film in 3-D. Like *Demolition Man* with Wesley Snipes and Sylvester Stallone, we got them to film extra film at the end of the movie against a blue background so we could use footage for the game. That's what happens now – the link between the film and video game industries is close, it's not simply buying the video game rights after-wards – before they've shot it, we've actually already negotiated to put the film out as a video game with real characters, not just animation. We have the animation done by the same company too, so we even use the same animation studios and technicians as the film industry. It does make it more expensive to produce and the costs are passed on.

The storylines and the characters are the way they are because that's what people like playing.

I have heard about those religious video games which are intended to teach religious ideals – teach children to be caring through play. Yeah, sure it sounds a worthy idea, but how many will they sell? Ten? And those will be bought by Grandma. We'd never take on one of them unless it was a brilliant game. On the whole, we aren't looking for violent games, violence isn't absolutely necessary. In fact, my favourite – Super Mario Car – all about car races, isn't violent. They've got to have a lot of levels and interest.

Working with video games hasn't put me off playing them at home. It seems a real pain when I switch off here to go home and switch on again when I get there. But at home I play the whole range – not just Virgin games – and I'm actually playing rather than spotting errors and testing, so it's more relaxing when I'm playing for leisure. Though having said that, I often spot people's errors or games that aren't properly thought out and find myself criticising elements that don't really work when I'm playing other games!

Besides playing at work and at home, I do frequent arcades. I have to – it's part of the job! I watch what the other people are playing, which ones are popular, the games they've got and how the kids react to them. Some of the games go to arcades before research for the home market is finished on them. A lot of testing of new games from a lot of companies is completed in the arcades, just to see how they go down with the young kids. During holidays they all hang around the arcades and you can easily spot which are the popular games. During school days the owners are supposed to chuck children out.

Kids would love my job, yes. There are usually plenty of places going for people to test the games. But it's not a part-time job and not as easy as it sounds. People think it's easy. It may be easy to play some of the games, but you have to go through them all methodically, and give them an unlimited amount of plays. I can play through an entire game which could take about two hours, then play it four, five or six times a day. Most games are not linear, so you have the difficult stages and have to know how to get through from one level to the next to prove that it works, spot bugs and tell other people how to do it when they phone in tears. Yes, they do phone in tears . . .

I had one 40-odd-year-old guy phone in weeping. It was when I worked at another video game company before I came here. He'd got hold of a pre-release of a video game and couldn't crack the game. I hadn't finished it myself at that point and had to tell him that. His wife had threatened to divorce him if he didn't give up and stop getting frustrated, and I couldn't help! It's not always young kids who phone in, and it's not just kids who play the games. We send out forms with games asking age, sex and the games they liked, basic research, and that revealed an average age of 24 . . . we expected it to be 15–16. I suppose our players are 12 upwards. It depends on the style of the game – some attract younger, some older people – eight's probably the youngest user.

I first worked for a computer games company in Brighton doing something similar, testing games and working on the phones – the customer support part. It started as a two-week summer job. I had no training. I was at college studying law, hoping to go into that – but I think I found my niche here. I like playing games all day. Though honestly, there's more to it than that!

To get into the company, I had to prove I was more than good at games. I like playing games all day and being able to tell people over the phone how to get to the more difficult level or if they have technical problems or their machine won't accept something.

### Jem, 21, games buyer, Colchester

I'm not exactly a computer games addict but, yes, I do play at least one game every day of my life. I can't see what people get so fussed about. It's no different to watching television. In fact, the variety of couch potatoes who get stuck into games are at least using a little of their brains to stop getting kicked somewhere horrible by the onslaught of rivals, or to avoid some other dire fate. With television you're just watching a set and predictable plot numbly. It's also a good way to release stress, I think, because I'm switching off from the aggro of the day, though perhaps my girlfriend wouldn't agree when I get excited about 'a stupid game'! I know other people would say playing squash or something is a better way to work off stress, but I wouldn't play squash or any other game even if I wasn't into video games, and squash, or football even, can be just as aggressive or angst-ridden as one of the games. And that's aggression against other real people, not a character, isn't it?

I'm definitely not too old to be playing. I know people older than me into games, and who've just got into it, they're saying, 'Wow, I never realised it could be such fun.' So many people condemn it without trying it. You don't say that about TV programmes or football, do you? Who watches *Home and Away* or *Top of the Pops*? When you get to 20 you don't say, 'Right I'm too old for that now, better switch off.'

I started in 1983 with a little handset and video games you played on your TV screen. Very basic, driving a car and avoiding bends, playing tennis or shooting the opposition in a combat situation. They're far more imaginative now.

Of course, there are drawbacks. Expense is the major one. I'm sure there are some people who can get by with a few games, perfecting their skills and getting better scores, but once you've worked right through a game you want something different, so I do spend a lot on video games. I know my Christmas stocking will contain a couple. See, it makes me easy to buy for! Yes, there's always the worry that I've got them all! Other drawbacks – staying up well into the early hours because I'm really into one game, and ignoring my flatmates, girlfriend, whoever, if they happen to be around, but then if you saw my folks when they're watching *The Bill* or *The Larry Sanders Show*, you can't get a word out of them, and they look past you all the time, keeping their eyes fixed on the screen. It's all 'In a minute, love'. So, what's the difference? Yeah – they do sit several feet away from the TV and I'm right on top of my screen. But, they're lounging back, stuffing their faces through boredom, while I'm on the edge of my chair, munching peanuts to boost my nervous energy! I'm a panic peanut eater. The Panic Peanut Eaters – that's a good title for a club for video game addicts conducted via an on-line electronic noticeboard. I haven't really got switched into that yet, but it is appealing; I'd probably get really hooked if I did.

### Kas, 25, Norwich

I've got a six-year-old son and already he's well into computers. I don't like it, I don't mind so much if he uses it to create drawings and things, expand his artistic ability, but just playing games is mind-rotting. In fact it's worse than that. How can people say that playing violent video games on a regular basis has no effect on growing minds? It isn't even the violence but the 'me' attitude it reinforces, the winning aspect. It's teaching them, I must win over my opponent. There's no stretching yourself, all the games are set about beating the enemy, getting the upper hand. What kind of lesson is that? It's not like tennis or football when you're supposed to be taught to appreciate the other players' skill. In video games, you just want to kill them, it's very aggressive. How can you teach people to be good losers or praise others' abilities when they're constantly seeing that the rule of the game is to beat and to win by any means? I have played them, so I know how easy it is to fall into the trap, and I'm a grown man. There's no coincidence that they grew so popular during the eighties – it's that Maggie's mentality – all for yourself. I find it ironic. Computers are supposed to herald access to creativity to all (who can afford them), giving us all the tools to do artistic things, whether visual or making music, but what do we do? Sit inanely in front of them and try to shoot down the enemy.

## Jess, 16, North London

What do I spend most of my time on? Quasar – I like having a go at that, running round, shooting people! And when the guns talk to you, that's neat. But it's best when a lot of us play together. I know it's a game, but you do get the adrenalin going, creeping round trying to spot the other side and hit their HQ! It could be better, it would be great if there was interactive scenery, like virtual reality! At one time we went three times a week or so, trying to get better scores all the time. You lose points (and power) if people shoot you and get points if you hit others. We don't go so much now. I still go to games arcades occasionally, see what new games they've got, but I've got a Game Boy at home. My brother's got different video games to me so we trade time. I've had it a while. It's funny, when my folks bought it for me they reckoned I'd be bored with it within weeks. That was, what, over a year ago? I'm still at it, though I suppose I don't lock myself away for hours now. And dad plays a lot too, when he comes home from work, and there's nothing on telly. Mum ain't too keen, she's always busy, and hates the noise. No fun. I'm still at school right now. I don't know what will happen when I leave, go to college or something. I like engineering.

# **11** A Sporting Life

## Martin Smith, 19, footballer with Sunderland

I've been playing football since I was 4 or 5. I was always
kicking a ball. My dad used to play, until he was injured,
so he wants me to play for him! He didn't push us into it.
It was just always there.

I started going to see matches when I was about 6, I
suppose – Sunderland – me father took us. I played in local
teams with the boys and I got spotted. Scouts are sent out
to watch local sides in the local league. They asked me to
come in for a trial, and made me an offer. I joined the YTS
scheme – it's government-funded – a lot of young players
join similar schemes with football clubs for two years and
are offered a job or not at the end. But I only did it for a
year, because I was offered a contract for the first team.

While training you're in the Youth League – of 16–19-
year-olds either playing in the League for Sunderland or as
a reserve. I was in the youths for two seasons, in the third,
I went into the professional side.

The other Youth League players are behind us, they're
very happy for us, but wait until I have a bad 10 games!
I'm due to get a new contract soon – for three years, hopefully. It's always on contract to keep you playing well. I
love Sunderland and I want to keep playing for the team
for a while yet. I still watch a lot of football – I watch it
all the time – and watch for good players. Manchester
United are very good and Newcastle – but I don't play
with my mates or in local teams any more. You can't, you
get damaged! It's not malicious, it's the kicks, they're a bit
slow and legs come up!

We train every day and play the matches on the Saturday, but you get a day off. It's only from half past 10 to

2 p.m. every day, so I can't complain, it means I don't have to get up very early. It is very physical and hard work – running and that, you have to look after yourself – and that means watching what you eat and drink. You can't go out on the booze all the time. I still do go out with me mates though and to clubs. I went out last night, but I had today off, so I stayed in bed. What do I do in the afternoons? Sleep. Recover. If we went out to a club on a Friday on the booze, the manager would really have a go . . .

The coach does shout a lot, and the manager – that's how they get you to play well, having a go at you all the time. You know you'll get it if you don't keep up.

Football does change you, it makes you far calmer. I've calmed down a lot. You have to, you know the manager will have a go and you can't have a go back . . . and you can't just walk off. I'm calmer when I go out, as well.

I've kept all my old friends. None of them are sports players, but they're great, they stayed around and come to see me play. I love it. It's magic to know they're out there cheering for us. My girlfriend hates football – she never comes to see me play or asks about it!

Our fans are really good. They've stayed with us. We're not doing very well, and they'll come and see us play and cheer us on. We went to play Portsmouth and 1000 fans went down, too. They do travel to see us. They are well-behaved, you might get a few local lads being silly, but they are good, on the whole.

I have been recognised in the street, the odd fan has come up, and occasionally if I've been at a club or been for a drink, someone will know who you are and give you a free pint. It's a nice feeling.

If I wasn't a football player, I'd probably be on the dole. There isn't a lot of work round here. I didn't have any other career in mind, so I was lucky I fell into football. A lot of my mates are on the dole. You know it's a short-lived career, so as a young professional you have to try and make as much money as you can because there's only about 15 years in the game. But I haven't got plans for moving on, that's a long way off, and, no, I won't be making a daft pop song and going on *Top of the Pops*. The reason footballers go on to the stage and TV is because they can't stay in football forever but I really can't imagine myself doing that. I haven't thought about too far into the future. I'm so chuffed to be in Sunderland.

We're getting a new manager, as our old manager, Terry Butcher, just got sacked – because Sunderland aren't doing very well. We're at the bottom of the League – but there's not very many points in it. Mick Buxton is coming in instead. It's very worrying for me, because it was Terry Butcher who brought me into the team, and each manager has a different idea on players and tactics, and Buxton might not want me in. No, he shouldn't kick me out ... I hope. A change of manager does mean the players getting used to a whole new idea on how we should play and all that. We're always training new players – in the youth side, the 16–17-year-olds, but there are none coming up from there as yet.

Relaxation ... Apart from football and seeing mates, I go to see a lot of films with my girlfriend – and not ones about sport, usually the big ones.

## Malcolm Smith, 20, rock climber, Scotland

Rock climbing's not so much a living, it's a lifestyle. I'm 20 now and I've been climbing for five years. My dad's a climber and that's how I got into it, but I don't climb with him any more – I'm far better than he is! It wasn't because of a natural habitat in Scotland – there aren't many rock faces where I live, just south of Edinburgh. And I don't climb mountains, that's a totally different sport. What I'm into isn't about height, but difficulty. I usually choose short, ordinary pieces of rock which are apparently impossible to climb. I go out with a group of friends and climb crags. I prefer to find a short, difficult stretch, around the height that you can jump off, climb that, and then try to link to another problem and climb that, so I'm making a hard route.

I do it all the time, most days, though like all sports you have to have rest days. This time of year, the weather's too bad for outside climbing, you can't climb in the rain as the rocks are too slippery, so I'm hibernating – I'm in training. I train inside on a climbing wall. There are plenty of them springing up; climbing's becoming very popular. But I've got a wall in my bedroom! I built it myself, a 10 by 6 feet wall of plywood and fingerholds. I've had to move into a different bedroom as it's kind of taken over.

You can climb outside all year round if you go abroad, but that's very expensive. I've just come back from Majorca with a group of climbing friends. It was very dry over there. It was a holiday, but then all my holidays, my whole life, is geared around climbing. I've been climbing full-time for about two years – since I left school. You don't really make money from it, unless you're into competition climbing, but I get by, because of sponsors. I have sponsors who give me equipment – one will give you the ropes, another the boots. Some sponsors give you finance as well. In return, they know that I'll be seen in the gear and people will see me climbing well and so they'll more than likely go for that make when they buy new stuff.

But a lot of people don't get any sponsorship or financial help at all, and they climb full-time. A lot of my friends are like that, I don't know how they survive. Climbing takes up all their time, they're committed to it, so they don't do other work, and they have no money coming in. There's a limited amount of companies who can give sponsorship, and they're only going to give it to the best climbers.

My ambition is to be the best climber in the world. I'm getting there! It's based on who's climbed the hardest routes and I am one of only four who have ever climbed a certain grade climb. Climbers can find their own routes and cut them and climb them or use routes that have already been climbed. I climbed one that had already been spotted by another climber and he'd done it first, anyone can climb it, but it's too tricky for most, because the handholds are so small. You have to have very strong fingers. I have found a new climb which I'm working towards. I'm preparing it, and myself.

In climbing, a lot rests on trust. You don't have to have any witnesses, though in practice you'll always have some-one with you, and people know what you are capable of. Besides, you're doing it for yourself.

It's only other climbers that see you, because climbing isn't really a spectator sport, even at competitions. I have done some competitions, but competition climbing is very different.

Climbing matches are usually held indoors, and climbing an indoor wall and winning an event isn't the be all and end all of it for me. I prefer crags and climbing outside. I'd rather go on to the next stage in difficulty of an outdoor crag. The top British competition climber is Ian Vickers, who's excellent, but doesn't climb outside crags as well as me or other outside climbers. You're not usually good at both. There's a girl climber, Felicity Butler, who is good at competitions and outdoors.

Women are just as capable climbers as men – in France, many of the leading females are at least as good as the men, if not better. In a way, women have a strong advan-tage because they are usually lighter than men, and weight is very important, because you have to hold your body weight by your fingers. Many climbers go in for dieting, but I can't do that, it's too much like hard work. I eat a lot, I should eat less; I'm 10½ stone, which is quite a weight to carry up a rock!

I have changed my lifestyle totally to fit in with rock climbing. I drink hardly anything and get early nights – I'm almost a recluse! It's like any athlete, you have to work at it if you want to be good. My parents don't tell me to get a 'proper job', this is my work, and they understand, but then my father climbs.

If you want to climb in competitions, you have to join the British Mountaineering Council, which is why I joined it, but climbing is really a solitary sport, it's not about belonging to a local club. When I'm training I go off on my own – because you don't use ropes when climbing in-door walls. When I climb crags, I have to go with someone else so they can hold the rope. The rope isn't there to hang on to, or pull against, it's a safety device. It's a very safe sport. I don't ever feel scared, the adrenalin comes in trying to climb a tricky problem.

You can climb a crag anywhere, you just have to find them. Sheffield is the best place, it has a really big climbing scene, because it's got lots of steep, hard rock, which Scotland hasn't. There is a large indoor centre as well, in Sheffield, though that's just for training. There are lots of people who just climb there during the day because they've nothing else to do – it's become a very popular sport here in recent years. I don't know why that is. There has always been a lot more people into climbing on the Continent, and we're just catching up here. I suppose Europe has always had a more sporty base for its climbing, whereas in Britain it was based on a different route and moves – climbers went into British mountains with pick-axes and lots of clothes.

People have been going to France and picked up on the Continental style. Rock climbers wear as little as possible – cycling shorts, lightweight things. You get very hot so we put chalk on our hands, like tennis players, to stop our hands sweating, so we don't slip. When you're climbing, you don't think of anything else. I'm just totally into it, thinking where's the next hole, the next handhold. In competition climbing, I find it far harder to concentrate, you're aware there are spectators, so it's harder to give 100 per cent.

I don't worry about the future – unlike other athletes, climbers get better as you get older, they are generally better in their mid-30s, so I can expect to be better at 35!

## Dalvinder Sodhi, 25, rock climber/teacher, Shipton, Yorkshire

I started climbing about three years ago properly, though my first experience of climbing came at school. I was living in Coventry then, and the school used to do day trips to the Peak and Lake Districts. It was a big thing when you lived in the city to get out into the country. We just did walking, and then a teacher took us on a climb, more like a scramble. Then he took a small group of us rock climbing. We were all girls, the guys were interested in other sports. I didn't have another sport that I was into at that time. I found it frightening – I didn't enjoy it at all! I went again, though; another school teacher belonged to a climbing club and took us along. That was the taster, but it wasn't until I moved to Huddersfield to study that I decided to take up rock climbing. There was a sports centre with an indoor wall.

It wasn't expensive initially, all I bought was a pair of second-hand climbing boots and a second-hand harness. No rope, as you climbed up, then jumped and landed on a crash mat. I didn't get a rope for a while, as that's the most expensive piece of equipment; you can't buy them second-hand as you don't know their history. Really ropes should be changed every three to five years to ensure they're reliable and safe.

I met my boyfriend, Peter, while climbing at the centre. It's a good way to meet people as everyone's usually friendly, and at that time it wasn't usual to find a female by herself climbing. Even now, there are a lot more male climbers, though more women are coming into the sport.

Peter is one of the top climbers and very positive. 'Of course you can climb that grade,' he'll say, so it helped me try harder things and it meant we could go out climbing together. I've learnt a lot watching him. Also I was just climbing at the weekends, and although I knew people who climbed mid-week, I'd think 'that's a bit extreme'. That's normal for me now! Climbing mid-week is just like going swimming or typing on a weekday. Of course you can fit it in. Besides, climbing is very addictive, especially when you've only been doing it a short time.

There are two main sorts of outdoor climbing. Some people want a reputation for going straight on to the rock and climbing a hard rock straight off, the first time, without falling off. There are a lot of aspects involved, showing you can read the route correctly and make decisions about handholds as you're going along – is that a difficult handhold, should I use my left hand or right – because if you use the wrong hand you may have to twist to get to the next and come off. That's called onsighting.

Then there are other climbers who prefer getting a reputation for red pointing – climbing the hardest routes available. That involves more power – even for men. They do weights to keep the upper body strong, and usually have their own small climbing walls of steep chipboard with wooden holds. They go for tight angles and steep problems.

Women have got to be strong to climb. Though we have less muscles, we work weights and build them up. Before, it was thought that women wouldn't be able to achieve even an 8a grade. Now, people realise women can do that – many have. And in France, where they are very much ahead of us in climbing, women had mastered that as long ago as 1987 with no hassles. Opinion has changed.

I do both, red pointing and onsighting, though I really get most thrill out of onsighting. That's what I really want to be good at – I am good considering I've only been climbing for two to three years. I don't get so much satisfaction from red pointing as from finding a crag I've never climbed before and climbing it straight off, without having examined it first or even seen a photograph of it. The trouble is finding new rocks to climb that I haven't climbed before.

Where I live in Yorkshire, I'm ideally placed as there are a lot of local routes – Malum Cove and Winsley Crag – which people come from all over the country to climb. I know the routes and I've either done them or failed them so all I've left to do are the difficult ones which I have to attempt as red points. I have been the first female to red point a local route, but that's not what gives me the thrill. My passion is onsighting, which means I have to go to another area, to crags I don't know, and haven't seen, so I can climb without a head start.

The fact that you don't know how hard a route is going to be until you actually start climbing is part of the joy for me. They are pointed, which has mostly been done by men, as they are usually the ones who have found and climbed the route first, but the grades they are given can vary enormously. That's what I like, you don't know what the challenge will be. It can be graded as difficult, but you start climbing and complete it easily, whereas another graded the same proves much tougher going. That's often down to the build or the type of climber who attempted it first. Some have tiny cracks but clear handholds, which can be better for some climbers than those with big holes but steep angles, if they're more used to using the upper body, and not the feet.

A lot of climbers with a strong upper body can't balance the feet; they do weights to ensure they're strong enough to support their body as they climb, but they can be less agile with their feet, often gripping too hard as they're terrified of falling.

Also, if you do a sports route, the bolts were put in the rock by the first person who did the ascent, so you clip on to those bolts as you climb. Then if you do come off, you're only going to fall to the last bolt. I have hurt myself a couple of times, but not badly; it's a risk you take. The risk isn't death. When there have been fatal accidents it's been down to the ropework, not tying the knot correctly because they've been distracted or something. Top climbers do that, because you have to tie the same knot over and over again, and they're talking and thinking about other things while they do it. Or it happens when they're walking or abseiling down.

I do pay attention. Three years is quite a short time, and some people haven't led by then. The leader has responsibility for attaching rope to the chain and lowering it down for the seconder to climb up. If the seconder comes off he'll just dangle – if the rope's secure. It is a great responsibility. But I've always led, probably because my boyfriend is always saying, 'Come on, you lead.' A lot of women have done hard routes – red pointed tricky routes – but they won't lead. They should be encouraged more. I get a buzz out of being frightened. I know I won't die – I might knock my elbow or at worst break an arm or a leg if I'm unlucky.

People tend to climb in couples with one leading and one at the bottom feeding the rope. If there's a third person, they'd do nothing. But I try not to climb with my boyfriend all the time, because I get a lot out of climbing with other people. I mix higher and lower standards, though usually it's other men who are better than me.

I have got sponsorship recently, with a leading British harness-maker who supplies me with a harness and some money for equipment – which usually buys my rope! There are a lot of climbers who spend all their time climbing and have no money. They're just signing on the dole.

There are a few groups who rent a house together, all sign on, get housing benefit and income support and that's what they exist on so they can climb, and if they need to go to France or Germany to climb because the weather is better there, they'll go and camp.

A lot of climbers sign on. But that's not the sort of life I want to lead. I've done a degree and my teacher training. I want to climb, but I also want a reasonable standard of living. I want a car and a social life, to have meals out and visit other areas to climb. I don't see why I shouldn't be able to have both.

The way I get around it is by doing supply work in teaching. I cover when people are on maternity leave or sick. It's unpredictable – I don't know when or what I'll be teaching and what age group. I've been asked to do maths when I'm a science teacher. But generally I get a buzz from going into different schools. I didn't want to teach sports. At first I thought being a climbing instructor would be ideal, but I'd rather be climbing and I don't want it to be work.

Also, I don't see that this is a lifetime vocation, because I don't want to be seen on the rocks when I'm old and unfit ... I think the ideal body for climbing is similar to a gymnast's – light and strong. You get very light people, especially men when they're 17–18, and they're great climbers at 24–25 when they've built up their muscles, but by building up our muscles too much we're going to lose flexibility. The number one climbers are around my age. I'll probably have to find another sport to get into when I'm older!

I do competition climbs too and joined the British Mountaineering Council to get on the squad. They see how well you do in national events, how you're doing on rock and whether you've been training regularly. If you don't get in the British squad, you can still climb in competitions, but you have to pay for your own expenses, which can be prohibitive. My aim is to get good in competitions over the next few years and in hard routes on rock. I want to do both.

The sad thing about climbing is that a lot of sponsors of competitions are pulling out. Perhaps it's got a lot to do with lack of television coverage. I disagree when people say it's not a spectator sport. Whenever I'm climbing, passers-by will always stand and chat, ask thousands of questions and seem really interested, then watch you ascend. If more was made of it, then the public would really enjoy it. Channel 4 gives so much coverage to American football, a game we don't even play in this country, and there are loads of climbers, in competitions or just climbing for pleasure.

In the sports halls there are loads of climbers who just come along to try it out – and usually get hooked – and you're seeing more women too. I went to The Foundry in Sheffield, a large climbing centre recently, and saw two girls of 14 or 15 in a pair of boots, very casually, they'd gone in to climb together. They had a very casual attitude; it was great. It's not an expensive sport – most centres cost about £4 for a day ticket – you couldn't do many other sports all day for that amount.

I train all day Saturday and Sunday, one's a full day with weights, the other is a full day climbing. I have a rest day one day a week, say Monday, then I climb every other day, in the evenings if I'm working during the day. Usually it's in a centre, as that's where the training takes place. You can't really train on a crag because of the safety aspect.

# **12** Music: Young, Gifted and Slack

## Stuart Farnden, 25, singer, The Point of Departure, Kingston, Surrey

I wouldn't call myself a Mod ... though I suspect that other people might. The music's got a definite sixties influence. We pressed up 350 white labels of one of our songs, 'Magic Circles', just to test the waters, putting it out ourselves by mail order. Mark Radcliffe played it on Radio 1, and we had quite a bit of interest from record companies, but no big offers! We're hoping it will be properly released in the not too distant future, though I'd rather wait and get it right. We won't just accept anything. Meanwhile, a DJ in America – in Minneapolis – got wind of it and was very enthusiastic, giving it airplay in his state. Apparently, there's a big interest in the whole sixties scene over there. So we're putting out a second pressing in America through his label, a little label called Susstones.

I'm not tying myself down to the sixties and the retro thing. Obviously we're in it because we love it, but I'm not going to restrict myself. My image – that's not really for me to say – more outsiders. But I suppose anyone who goes home and listens to Traffic and the Beatles is going to look like they listen to it. I play a 1961 Gibson and a Rickenbacker so I wouldn't go into the studio looking like I was into metal.

Finding clothes is far easier for girls. They could just go into Top Shop and find something suitable, but it's not so easy for guys. I have had a couple of pairs of trousers tailored, but I usually just hunt around the shops. You can usually find something, like Levi cords with a great cut. I went shopping on Saturday and bought something second-hand – not second-hand so it looks like someone had worn it and rolled around the fields in it, but just old. You can find things if you look, shops buy old job lots and that sort of thing, like Kensington Market and that shop in Beak Street. It's usually London, there's nothing in Kingston. Some trendy shops are OK and come up with new designs of old clothes, but they're not quite right – too many pockets or some detail that isn't quite in keeping.

The band is my whole life – such a monastic existence! The band is mostly me, too. It's not really a band as such, I play everything bar the drums and I write with my pal Marc Jones, who produced 'Magic Circles' with me. Marc lives in Wimbledon. We're very similar, we used to be Mods, into the sixties a few years back and met at a few clubs. We drew up a masterplan for the band and we've moving up it, very slowly. We did everything – wrote, played, produced and even did the artwork for the record going out to America. The guy came back to us and said he'd do it all – the production and cover – but we wanted total control. The cover isn't very sixties-looking. It's a cross-over because I want people who work in Halfords or Woolworths to listen to it. Like the Suede covers – they've got a good typeface and look fun, but when you turn them over, you can see what they're into, and you play them and start digging them. And it's the same with The Jam: 'Start' had sixties influences, the single cover looked as though it could be anywhere but when you get into it, you realise where they are coming from.

Likewise, we've picked a plain typeface, the picture is sixties-style and from the lyrics you can see we're obviously not kaftan-wearers playing mini Moogs – like Lenny Kravitz. Actually you can excuse Lenny Kravitz for being so showbiz because he comes from America. It's just a pity that he's singing about such crap – no content, just pose value. It's not a pose for us and I think you can tell that from the lyrics.

Apart from the band, I had a part-time job in graphic design until six months ago, that's when I did the covers for the songs. We went in a couple of nights and got the photos sorted.

The white label did draw a lot of record interest, but we

felt we were received like Billy Fury – major labels had no confidence in us because we hadn't done any gigs and we had no fan base, so we were a big risk. 'How do we know what we can recoup from money we invest in you?' ... so we thought, 'Sod it, we won't wait around,' but the white labels were the only way we could prove commitment. Individuals were interested. Gary Crowley is a big fan and there's a guy at Creation who's been helping us find our way through American contacts, so things look promising.

Out of the initial 350 we had pressed, we sent some out, put an ad in *NME* and we've had to send cheques back. We're having some more pressed up now and a German magazine is giving away 2000 flexi copies of it with their magazine – they're doing it all. I do put a lot into it, but I could either sit in the front room and say, 'Is there any point to this, am I the only one who cares about this type of music?' or get on and do something myself.

I've never gigged with Point of Departure, though I've been in bands in the past and played just about every toilet in London. I don't really want to do it with this band. I don't want it to be two heavy metal bands and us ... I want the whole night to be structured around what we do, with DJs playing the right sound. We'd have to form a unit to gig, as we're not a band as such.

I wouldn't call myself and our music Mod. I was into it, then I was into acid jazz, but I've come out of that now. I liked the indie thing last year.

We've got lots of British influences. The Beatles 65–68 are a massive influence – as a lot of people must say. Other things we've been listening to are Neil Young, Cream in the early years, a bit of Tim Hardin. Nothing current – I wish that wasn't the case. Occasionally there's a single like Radiohead's 'Creep'. It was good, it had enough going for it and the singer wants to be a star and it shows! That's good. Other individual bands like Pulp are interesting, but there's going to be a whiplash against the seventies retro soon. (If I read another interview about Bobby Moore, I'll throw up.) Because a lot of people are precious about that old stuff and don't like to see it everywhere.

I would check out other bands if I liked them, but I rarely do. The last band I saw was St Etienne and that was at least six months ago.

The music I've been into is the tail end of the sixties – I know so much about that sort of music. The Beatles have almost become an obsession. I try to get studio out-takes and rare records, I'm almost anorak level about it – getting really excited if I can hear John Lennon cough.

I'm 25 – no one's young in bands any more. Big record companies want you to be on your second or third album by the time they sign you. When the Stones were signed up they were doing Chuck Berry covers and they were signed on the strength of that, then were given an environment where they could develop their own style and come up with material like 'Ruby Tuesday'. That doesn't happen any more.

We went into the studio and put down half an LP of songs and we've done some stuff with mellow acoustic guitars called Point of Departure Unplugged! So we've proved that we can show commitment. We've just got to find someone interested in us now.

## Sam Dean, 23, singer, Passion Fruit and Holy Bread

I don't like the idea of being tipped as the next big thing. Not that it's unflattering, but it implies that there is a succession of bands who make it – and that we will be short-lived, which we won't!

Passion Fruit and Holy Bread comes from a line in a Stone Roses record – 'She bangs the drum'. I suppose it does give off an idea that we were inspired by them, but we've been going for six years with that name and the Roses weren't at all famous back then.

When they became famous, I thought 'great', but now they've not delivered anything more. I think their second LP didn't deliver or build on the first. Is it such a good idea to be linked with them in any way now? Who knows? I don't know if they'd be annoyed that we borrowed from them ... or flattered. They should be flattered because that's how it was meant.

Our influences are varied. My father was into classical music, he played a lot around the house, and I like elements of that, the little movements you get in classical records, and I like a whole lot of other bands, but The Smiths and The Stone Roses are the ones people mention. I don't mind when people cite these as influences, because I like them, but when they say Suede ... I don't rate Suede at all, and they've had so much hype over here. Hype's not always a good thing. It's killed them for America; they'll never make it out there. I don't want to be the next Suede. I can see our music going on for years, irrespective of what else is happening alongside.

I've always wanted to make music, even before I went to art school, though that's where the band really came together. I was at art college with a guy called Dave, who was the original singer in the band, and Felix (the bass player). Felix comes from Lincoln. We went up for a visit to Lincoln and that's how we met up with Erik and Justin who lived there (and who now play drums and guitar/vocals respectively). It's kind of happened from there.

For the past few years, we've been practising and waiting for our time. We weren't good enough to 'go public'. Then in 1992 we were ready and the Suede thing happened. It shouldn't be that there is only one band who gets the hype at a time, but that's the way the press seem to want it. Really there should be a lot of bands together. Anyway, it just meant we put back our own launch, as it were.

We all came down to London in January 93. We now live in South or North London – not quite so far apart! I lived outside London (Surrey) with my folks before that. I gave up art college to concentrate on the band. It was a commitment we all made that the band would work. That we would evolve our musical style.

I wouldn't like Passion Fruit to be classed as indie music. I suppose we'd be tagged as mainstream indie – though I don't like tags, and I don't like indie because it has become one wide lump. I don't like to be pigeonholed. We could just as easily make a pop song – but we won't just yet. We wanted to have a record in our style first.

We played our first gig at the Dome in North London, where we met our manager, Neil. He came into our life about six months ago. Things kind of happened all at once. We sent a tape to a few press companies and told them of the gig. Excess couldn't send anyone down, so sent Neil who thought we were great and became our manager. Excess took on our press. We've now signed to London Records – our first EP, 'Jonah', came out in January, with three songs, 'Jonah Swallowed by a Big Fish', 'Arise' and 'Sky'; 'Crush' is likely to be the next single, and we're going to do the first LP in the summer, so it will probably be out in September.

There are rumours that the company will only do a very small pressing – like 2000 or so ... that's ludicrous. Though Elastica only put out 1500 but still entered the charts at 80. On the other hand, I'm a record fan and know the records will be deleted soon afterwards so they'll be collectable!

The songs on the EP are all old. I wrote them at least three years ago ... they're not new even if they sound sort of current. And we've got enough material for this LP in the summer – and another. Material has never been a problem. I write all the songs, music and words, though the band throws in bits when we're practising.

I play the piano and guitar. Because my dad was into classical music and could play and write music, he wanted me to learn something. I learned the piano. I suppose the influence is there. I was musically trained and could write all the parts down for each one of the band, but what's the point? I'll just show them what to play. Besides, it's flexible – if we want to add something or play around with something when we get together, that's fine, we're on the same wavelength. It's hard dealing with record companies and producers who hear some little side effect that you've put into a record and they say, 'Hey, that sounds good, let's repeat it a few times.' That's not the idea, I like finding an unusual sound in a record, it makes you want to play it over again.

Finding producers we like is hard. We were lucky for our demo, we had Barry Clempson who works with bands like Verve and Spiritualised and he just did it for free for the demo. Generally we just look and see what other bands' sounds we like.

I don't go and see other bands too much. There are so many bands that just knock about, and there are plenty of bad bands all over the country and their biggest ambition is to headline at the Falcon (in Camden). I wish they weren't around, it ruins it for us. You can see why A&R men get depressed.

Having said that, we've got our own label, Splendid Records, which is just for us, but we do get sent demos by lots of new bands and we give them a play. We will pass all good ones on to A&R guys who are likely to be interested. It's good to find new talent, and bands that could support us. At the moment there are some good new rap bands around.

I don't like the idea of doing an extensive tour – a string of dates would be better, because I don't fancy supporting other bands. We have supported a couple of good bands – Juliana Hatfield and Elastica. Juliana Hatfield was at Sheffield, Manchester, Bristol – so we've played big city centres and we got lots of press interest through it. But it's the public we want to reach.

That's why I don't think I'd like to play Reading or the other big festivals. There are too many bands and, unless you're headlining, it's not set up for you. It may be a showcase to the public but the public aren't seeing us at our best.

Good venues are hard to get – in fact, there aren't many good ones. I like the idea of playing the Town and Country (Forum) but not many venues are the right size and have the right atmosphere. I'm not into clubs . . . though can see our music going down well in the ambient room. What we'd like to do is find a few unusual venues, make it more of an event – someone's got to do it, why shouldn't it be us? We haven't really got a fan base, or know who our fans are as yet, though we recognise a few people at gigs – and I was recognised on the Tube the other day! I denied it was me.

None of us have jobs . . . and none of us have ever really had serious jobs. I worked in a hospital for a while, between college – never again. Justin was going to be a professional footballer and worked in a sports centre. Erik's the only one who's had a real job – and he got the sack, unfairly – he worked in a bowling alley. He's also worked in McDonald's! I haven't thought of any other career – I don't want to work. Music's not work! Though I put in heavy hours when we have to . . . We've spent the past six days in the studio and towards the end we hardly left it at all – we've had 35 hours without sleep.

I suppose art training is a very good thing, but I'm not good at art – I'd never make it as an artist. I also did animation which is good as I can visualise what we want to do on covers and videos, but I don't do them. Dave, who used to be the singer in the band, does that – he was the one I was at school and college with. He helped me out on the art side then – I probably went to art college because of him – and he's still helping me with the art now!

He left the band because he couldn't sing. I was playing guitar at the time. We did look for another singer, but couldn't find one. I was having singing lessons, which is good to stretch the voice, but I gave them up when I left college. I miss the lessons as they are good training for your voice, though they didn't teach me style or anything.

We aren't going to be on the EP cover. It's not that we're camera-shy, but why does it matter what we look like? It's the song that's important. Surely if people like the music and the video, what does it matter if they don't see us? The EP cover is having five clocks by the letters JONAH and you'll see just behind them, as if behind bars, a young girl taking Holy Communion. We want our video to be a bit like a cinema film, cinematographic – not like a video with us in it. We don't want to be in it all, which is going to take some convincing and persuading for the record company! I'd like to have just a beautiful film – not arty. Yes, I know it sounds arty.

But I love film – I go to see as much as possible, all types. Some arty – I've taped Derek Jarman's *Blue* to watch – but mainstream too. I saw *Reservoir Dogs* and *Man Bites Dog* – it was horrible, everyone was laughing at gruesome happenings which were sick, not funny. What's wrong with people?

As far as personal image goes, we don't put on a show – we perform but we don't dress differently on stage, or say, 'Let's dress up for the stage'. Like now we're wearing jeans and woolly jumpers because it's cold and we've been in a studio – not for an image! If a record company makes us have a stylist, as many do now, I wouldn't mind, just so long as I didn't have to wear anything I didn't want to. We do have definite ideas about the band, we know what we want and how we want to do it. Why should that be a problem? I think a lot of the press coverage has made me out to be arrogant, which I'm not, but I do believe in the band and I am sure that we'll be successful. Does that make me arrogant?

## Sonan Nayar, 23, singer, Carpe Diem, Birmingham

We're soul/rock, but we sing all original material – I write it myself. Music influences are really wide. Personally, I listen to everything – I like Lennie Kravitz, Jellyfish, Tracy Chapman, that sort of thing – but my writing style is going back to the old song-writing style: verse, chorus, break, rather than a few words over a groove. Like the Beatles and INXS, I want good melodies and strong choruses, they are the songs which stay around.

I used to write about deep political issues. That was in another band in the past when I was into reggae, and all the songs were about apartheid. I tried to make all the songs have meanings within meanings, and all the words had to sound too poetic. Now, I've learnt from listening to songs by bands like The Beatles that the most memorable songs have simple lyrics and a catchy tune! So I write about everyday things.

I have no difficulty writing songs, lyrics come easily. I've written hundreds of sets of lyrics. I've still got a lot to put to music. The only problem is I write more when I'm depressed, so the songs reflect that. I'm pretty depressed now as I got made redundant recently and I'm looking for work. In a way it's not a bad thing as it gives me time to concentrate on the band and we've got a lot happening with it at the moment. But it would be nice to have some money. I was managing a cinema in Birmingham until just before Christmas, but it was closed down – there's a huge complex which kind of took the trade away. It would have been nice to have broadened the use of the cinema and put on bands there, but it's owned by MGM and they weren't keen on that. I'm used to booking bands as I did that as events officer of the NUS when I was at college.

I did an HND in business, finance and marketing and then went in as a management trainee in a building society. I don't know why, I always wanted to work in music! It was a stop-gap, something to do while waiting for the band to take off. I've been looking for work in Birmingham and in Manchester where my girlfriend lives, we've got a flat there, so my options are open. I'd even consider moving to London. I think that's where the music connections are.

We've got a manager, he's young too, and works with a lot of Bhangra bands. He's currently negotiating a management deal for us with a large company to get financial backing and we've just been in the studio laying down tracks for a demo to send to record companies. We've got plenty of material.

I play a bit of guitar, enough to help me write the songs, but I don't play on stage. A guitar gets in the way when you're rolling around. The band help out with the music at practices. I have a tune in mind while writing, and I rely on them to help me get it right. It's great because they've all got their own influences. The bass player's very Level

42, the drummer's into guitar rock and the keyboard player can bring in some pop. It's good to have different viewpoints.

We're all male and all Asians, though the rest of the band have got English-sounding names because they're Christian Asian: Patrick Massih is the guitarist, his brother Marcus plays drums, and George Massih, a cousin I think, is on bass. The keyboard player is Gabriel Frank. Although we're Asian, we sing and perform in English, we don't play Bhangra or Hindi like many other local bands, which means we don't get bookings for Asian events. We go for the mainstream audience, like an average 'white' band!

The rest of the band are slightly younger than me – they're 20–21. I'm a couple of years older, and we met really through my brother's band. He's keyboard player in a large Bhangra band, Achanak. I used to go on the road with his band and our guitarist used to play guitar with him; we just got talking. At one point, we were all in another off-shoot band, but my brother got too busy; Achanak is a full-time commitment. Carpe Diem isn't Asian – it's Latin, and means 'Seize The Day'. It came from a Robin Williams film, *Dead Poets Society*, and we thought it sounded good.

We have played a few times in Birmingham, and just before Christmas we played two dates in East London, one at the Hackney Empire, for their Birthday Party, and the next night at Chats Palace supporting Cornershop. We went down really well, surprisingly, at Chats Palace, as Cornershop are completely different, much heavier. At Hackney Empire, we had the longest set, 40 minutes. We were first on, to warm up the crowd.

Both dates came about by us winning the East Quest – a nationwide competition to find a new British/Asian talent held at the Hackney Empire. I just saw it in an Asian newspaper. There were quite a few other bands, a lot of Hindi and Bhangra bands, and comedians and dancers. But we didn't get as much publicity from it as we'd have liked! That's what hopefully the professional management deal will mean – someone to organise photographs, and hopefully get a record deal . . .

## Zebby, 22, musician, writer, Rastafarian, South London

I get really upset when I go into clubs and hear the words to some of the records. They've got a great tune but the words are so full of disrespect. I write all my own songs – tunes and lyrics. I'm not really a singer, I say words really rather than sing. I want to make songs with a really good sound and beat that people will love and think, 'Hey, this is real' and dance away to, but songs that have really good words, with words from the Bible or just telling good things. Why should song lyrics be bad? It would be good to get people dancing along to songs with a good message.

Most of the time people dancing away in a club don't listen to the words anyway, so they'd get hooked on the music, love it and then hear the words afterwards. I want young people to realise you don't have to dance and listen to songs about guns, violence and anger.

One of my songs is called 'Bible Stories'. That's the one I'm really working on. I went to Jamaica and Ghana in 1991 for a holiday and I went down to where one of my favourite ragga musicians was playing at an open-air dance festival. I said I was from England and I had a song I wanted to do, so I sung it there. I was just saying 'Bible bible, bible, bible, bible stories', over a great tune and everyone loved it. That's how it should be. I did something similar in a club in Queens, New York, and it went down really well.

I've already made a single with Rostella, a reggae singer, in 1992, it was 'Voice – King Selassie I', which was played a lot on Kiss FM, especially in July – on Haile Selassie's day. It was on the Kristal Beach label. Over Christmas I'm going on tour with some DJs and Rostella, and we're doing PAs in clubs round the country – Birmingham, Manchester – and at various other northern clubs. A hectic schedule but I'm looking forward to that. I've done a bit of DJing and got a bit of work through that, but I prefer making music to DJing. I've got the equipment in my home, so I write songs and make music in the evenings and spare time.

I spend most of my time involved in music. Apart from making more music myself, I want to teach children to play music. Keyboards and other instruments. It's not just a vague idea, I'm working on it at the moment. Currently I do two adult education classes to get the English qualifications, and then I've applied to go to university to do a degree in music technology or music in film. That's a three- or four-year BA course, depending on which college I go to. I'm going to register with schools to run an after-school group to teach children of about eight years and up to play music.

A lot of children have to go to after-school play groups between the end of school and their parents finishing work. This will be enjoyable and they'll be learning something. Music is an important skill, but it's fun, it gives such pleasure, they'll love it. I'd like to do it from home, rather than in the school environment, so the place will have to be registered. I'm already designing and sorting out the equipment and props I'll need.

In the meantime, I've been writing some children's books, which tell a story about traditional African instruments and teach how to play them at the same time. They're almost finished. My two loves are children and music, and they fit perfectly together.

I don't feel I have time to waste doing nothing, so I'm always working, on my music or writing. Life's about experiencing new things. I've also done a short video course – which was full-time and grant-assisted for people who were on the dole in Wandsworth. That was good, and I met some lovely people. Small groups of us worked on a film from start to finish, though I was far more interested in writing the music for the films than anything else. But it's important that you get a picture and working knowledge of the whole process.

## Andy, 24, keyboard player with Senser, London

Glastonbury changed my life! I was born in Buckingham-shire and travelled round the country a lot because of my dad's work, so I lived in Liverpool, Blackpool, Manchester ... then in 1980 we settled in London. I did photography and art in the sixth form at school. I left and took every job imaginable. I worked in photography, then I sold pensions, stocks and shares, worked in every sort of shop, I sold fashion, worked in McDonald's ... I was trying to find out what I wanted to do! I was into music and started DJing at clubs and parties.

Then in 1987 I went to Glastonbury, for the first time. I went with a friend of mine. There was a travelling circus with performance artists, and bands playing there like The Levellers and Back To The Planet, the sort of bands that travelled round doing festivals and parties. I'd been DJing for a while and I got asked to DJ there because basically I was the only DJ about who was into that scene at the time. I was playing all sorts of stuff, like The Levellers and acid house, a lot of house music, even a bit of Pink Floyd – a huge spectrum. After that, I just travelled with the circus, DJing with them.

It was pretty rough and ready. I slept under a truck sometimes or with my sound system in a tent, but it was totally wild. They were really good times. It was all pretty casual, we'd just go to a field, put up the tents and let people know what was happening. There were hardly any hassles with the police, and there was always a great feeling.

Now you just can't do that. I could be wrong, but in a way I think it's probably because of the increase in festivals and tribes like Spiral Tribe and Bedlam. A few years ago it wasn't such a huge scene – the hippies had been doing festivals for years, but they were different, and the ravers are very different to the travellers. We were definitely a lot cleaner and more sussed, we'd bury the shit and clear away the rubbish. Ravers don't do that. Travellers clean up after themselves, they care about the countryside, that's part of the reason for being outside in the country. Ravers care more about the event. After a rave, you just see piles of toilet paper and stuff around the field.

I stayed travelling round with the circus for a while, going home in between. At that time I started living in squats and things. I've lived in a fair share of squats. I used to share one with Kirsty of Opus 3, she was on *Top of the Pops* at the time and having to deal with formal management meetings – but living in a squat! But it was a great place, it was in New Cross and everyone used to put on lots of parties there. I was DJing a lot and did a few clubs like The Limelight and The Wag Club. Very different audiences!

I like playing at travelling gigs because the crowd are the sort of people who are open-minded about the music they listen to. Whereas when you're just playing acid house, if you drop in a different record, the ravers tend to get a bit annoyed or disappointed; they prefer jungle music, or certain stuff they're into. I like to be open; I'll take along a collection and play what feels appropriate.

I started DJing with Spiral Tribe and then all of a sudden there were loads of similar DJs coming out of the woodwork, and some DJs had managers which was unheard of before then! The managers would go around getting the DJ's name about. I kind of got pushed out at that point! I joined Senser as a DJ and doing keyboards in 1992, I thought it was time for a change and liked the idea of playing with a live band. I still DJ now and again – at Mega Dog and a few parties in Deptford run by the Mega Dog crowd.

I miss DJing at the parties I used to do, because it was just me totally in control of what I was playing, but the festival/party scene is really changing. Last year there were a lot of things going on, but the scene got very bad with a lot of festivals being stopped and warehouse parties being busted by police. Loads of DJs got their record collections confiscated. It's getting difficult to get a party to happen, the police are just cracking down. That's why Senser are playing in a lot of clubs – like Mega Dog, because at least they go on.

I've never had my records confiscated but I've been at parties that have been busted, like one at a massive warehouse at Camberwell Bus Garage for 10,000–20,000 people. Just as the people were turning up, the police blocked it and stopped everyone going in.

That's happening to festivals. The police have got it in their mind to stamp them out. We've still been given offers to play at festivals and warehouse parties, but you never know if they will happen.

We played in Amsterdam on New Year's Eve which was a big bash and loads of people came over from England, but it was a very strange venue, the people who ran it were stopping English people coming in and they'd come all the way over from England! Those who'd bought tickets in advance were OK, but the organisers 'lost' the guest list, which affected a lot of people. I think most people managed to get in eventually. Amsterdam is lively, it's great to go to but a bit manic, a bit hard to handle. London's better, but that could be because I live here.

We've got a few big gigs lined up for this year – one at Aston Villa football club with Pop Will Eat Itself. We've done lots of large venues before, like Birmingham NEC and festivals, of course. We're supposed to be doing Glastonbury this year if it goes ahead. Michael Eavis (the land-owner) is supposed to be doing a film of it. That won't be the first film we've been in, we've just done some music for a film called *Shopping* – about ram raiding. It's got music by other bands like Credit to the Nation and it's been showing at the ICA.

Last year's Glastonbury was pretty phenomenal. We played the *NME* stage to thousands of people which was good but, better still, we played a small stage in an alternative event away from it all, off in the woods somewhere. Only about 400 people were there but the vibes were so good. That was more like the real festival.

# **13** All the Young Dudes: Mods, Scooter Boys

## Andrew, 25, Carlton, Nottingham

I'm not a Mod. I'm just into sixties fashion and music. All sixties – psychedelia, Mod, R&B, I like it all. I'm a bit old (25) to be into the Mod scene. I dress in sixties-type things, my haircut's a bit Modish – short – and I wear white Levi's and Ben Shermans. I've been through lots of phases. I grew my hair long, into a bob, the American side, with Chelsea boots and hipsters . . .

I used to run a club in Nottingham, The Cocktail Cabinet, and we played sixties music. There was no dress code, but people did dress up. The Mod scene has really all gone here, but they were replaced by the students who came to our dos. One girl captured it on video, filming one of our dos for her college project, but I never got to see it.

I'm getting another club together in late September, the Freak In – as opposed to the Freak Out. It will play lots of psychedelia: The Doors, late Rolling Stones and underground sixties stuff that hasn't been heard a lot.

Lots of my friends collect old records. We'll also play stuff by new sixties-inspired bands like The Stairs from Liverpool. They've got a record contract – signed to Go Discs. I've seen them play and we keep in touch by letter and things. They'll probably play at the new club. There are other new bands like The Mystreated and The Clique. The Mystreated are a new band into psychedelia and American garage, the Chelsea boots and longer hair look. I've seen them play at St John's Tavern in London (Archway). They're really into the sound and image. The Clique are more into the Mod image.

I've heard of techno Mods or whatever – the trendy clubbers into Mod image at the moment. I don't mind if people pick up on the look for a while. Mods did that.

Mods were always finding new images and what was in one week would be out the next. For a while there was a whole Mod-inspired scene in Manchester – the Hammond organs and guitars.

I've been a Mod since the 79 revivals but I've changed my image a lot. I get my clothes mostly from second-hand shops and jumble sales now. They're harder to find and they charge more for them now.

I've written a fanzine (*Summer In The City*) for six months. I was made redundant so I had time to do it. It's a hobby; I don't make much money from it. I worked as a carpet-fitter, nothing creative.

When I was working, I had clothes made at a tailor's. The first thing I ever had made was a pair of hipster trousers. I saw them in sixties films, hipster trousers with large belts that looked pretty cool, so I drew a pair and went into a tailor's and asked if they could make me a pair. They said someone had come in and asked for something similar before!

### Steve, 19, South London

I don't think there are constant revivals of Mod. Mod is very underground. If they tried to make it popular we'd go deeper underground. During that last revival (1979–83), dedicated Mods called themselves Stylists to disassociate themselves.

We're eighties–nineties Mods, so it's not a straight copy of sixties looks. I know it seems strange but there are trends. Last year it was the effeminate Mod style: tartan suits and Steve Marriott hairstyles. Now it's more dark navy suits and short hair. One week it will be open shirts, the next it will be ties. It changes – though we don't copy each other!

### Mark Raison, 25, Middlesex

When I go to work, or go shopping or whatever, I don't dress up as a Mod – I wear smart jeans, button-down shirt, plain socks – not white! When I'm casual, it's Puma trainers and casual Nikes and T-shirts. It's quite subtle. People couldn't probably tell I was a Mod unless they were one or had been one, then I suppose it's the hair and the little touches that you'd recognise. Most people don't know.

I've got short hair – it changes style to reflect what I'm wearing. It tends to be Mod rather than sixties stuff. It looks smart. If you're into psychedelia, you're going to wear the scarves and blow your hair – I've done that. But I've had it cut off now.

There are phases, though not as many and fast-changing as there were in the sixties. Original Mods used to spend a fortune on clothes. It's cheaper to be a Mod now … the clothes now last for longer – until you're bored with them, and we're getting them second-hand rather than the sixties guys who were having them made. I can't see myself ever getting bored with it.

All my clothes are second-hand, my shirts, jackets – nothing's new, it's all made in the sixties. I've got sixties suits, though I wouldn't wear them during the day. Some people are quite funny about their clothes, they won't let on where they get them! But I think that's probably more London.

Sixties garage style is popular too – which means longer hair. It changes, or really it varies, because although it changes a bit, people do tend to stick to their own style, not like it was in the sixties, when they changed from week to week.

When I first got into it, it was all soul; Motown stuff and obscure. Ray Charles … all black musicians and anyone white was frowned upon. Now it's virtually all British beat stuff, white musicians. I play all stuff, mixing both.

I got into it when I was at school, in 1981. My older brother was 20 and had a scooter and he talked about what he got up to. I was too young to go to a lot of the places. *Absolute Beginners* [the film of Colin McInnes' novel] came out at the end of 81, and there was Paul Weller with his curtain haircut, sunglasses and denim jeans. Now, Mods' thoughts on Paul Weller are split up – there's not one train of thought; a lot of people think he's cool; for others, it's old stuff only.

There are so many people calling themselves Mod, or who are just into the sixties or who only listen to music made between 1963 and 1966 – it's not like one movement. Paul Weller – I've got a lot of time for him – he's kept going and the influence is there, but he does what suits himself, not thinking, 'I'm meant to be like this.'

I don't restrict myself to anything. I play mainly old stuff from all parts of the sixties. I don't like the 1979 thing – The Chords and bands of that ilk. A lot of young people were really into The Chords, Secret Affair and The Jam – that's not really Mod . . .

There are lots of bands I like who aren't really Mod bands but they are bands that have a sixties feel. I've always been to see live bands and I'll always check out new ones.

There are not very many clubs that happen on a regular evening at set venues every week, people just don't go to them. Of course they'll moan about there being nothing to do, but they wouldn't support a club regularly. They'll attend the rallies. There's one that's really into the sixties and one that's across the board – sixties and Mods. There are two factions doing the rallies which is a good idea.

In the mid-eighties there were the National Scooter Rallies and most did go to those, but it was taken over by scooterists, who are really different to Mods. They're dirty, scruffy and into fighting. Mods wouldn't get involved. They have a totally different way of life. You'd get picked on or beaten up.

So they set up their own – the CCI – the Classic Club International, in 1985. We started doing our own rallies, which were much smaller and looked better – you had to look smart to join in – no jeans. Scooterists don't care about their image, they wear army greens and parkas, or not even that. They're not into the same music – just the scooters.

The Mods with scooters were the people with the mirrors, the authentic sixties scooters, but scooterists painted murals on theirs; there has always been lots of friction between the two.

It was all OK in the eighties for a while. Then another group started up because they didn't want The Jam and the new sounds being played – they were The Untouchables rallies.

I went to a rally in August in the Isle of Wight – they are still held on bank holidays. There was a lunch do from 12–5 p.m. then it was down the pub. We sat and talked and played records. In the evening there's a big do – where everyone dances. At one time there were loads of people, now there are about 400 – from all over the country. There aren't that many good clubs, which is why the rallies are so important. There aren't clubs for two reasons – a) there aren't that many Mods about and b) people wouldn't go all the time. This way there are four a year and you know everyone will try and make them.

Of the clubs, The Bubblegum Factory [now closed] in Brighton plays sixties psychedelia, soul and Paul Weller stuff on Fridays. That club's quite friendly, and last Christmas they put on a good do with Go-Go dancers. Most of the clubs come and go so quickly, you find out about them and they're gone.

The Dome in Archway have held Mod nights and the St John's Tavern – which is a traditional rocker's haunt but tends to put on sixties Mod nights. Bands like The Wilsons, The Revs and The Clique have played there. The Clique are the biggest current Mod band, really.

There are quite a few pockets of Mods, like in Essex, where my girlfriend lives and you'll find local pub nights with authentic sixties or smart sixties. The places come and go so quickly, so nowhere seems to stay. I DJ at a local pub in Uxbridge – it's not exclusively Mod. I wouldn't DJ at the real Mod dos, they'd laugh at some of the tracks I play! DJs at dos always play the same records. I like to mix in a few of my favourites from the sixties which aren't really Mod. I don't care!

I get my records second-hand – there's a good record shop in Soho, off Kingley Street. Lots of them stock/sell newsletters or hold leaflets for Mod clubs and events. Soho's not like it was in the sixties – nor like it was in the mid-eighties. There was a time when it was exciting, full of Mods going up and down Carnaby Street, coming to London. Carnaby Street is hideous now. It's got a couple of shops with clothes in. They're not Mod shops. There's the skinhead shop which has Mod fanzines. Skins shouldn't be anti-Mods – proper skins when they started liked bluebeat, reggae and ska and had smart suits and shirts. That was before the fascists in the bomber jackets came along in the seventies.

There was a time when Mod started to get popular among trendies – and some shops started selling 'Mod' clothes, like the Duffer of St George crowd, but that has died a bit. The look can't be bought off the peg – it requires a great deal of effort. You'd be able to tell proper Mods . . . not vaguely Mod. Real Mods don't try to be fashionable.

Most of the Mods that go out and about must have jobs. Well, I presume they have jobs to have the money to buy the clothes and records. I suppose a percentage of them haven't, but the people I know have. I'm a civil servant – not exactly glamorous, but I'm earning. You do need money, perhaps not for the clothes, though obviously they will cost you something, but the records; they're mostly old and they are becoming so scarce now so you have to pay hideous prices. You can pay £80 for a single and albums can be more. Some have been re-released or feature on compilations on CD, but a lot of Mods wouldn't play those – it's not authentic.

I'm into the music and the look, and the sixties films and books to an extent too. The roots of it all go back to before the sixties really – the Beat Generation. They were really Mods and they were in the fifties. Jazz with Jack Kerouac, William Burroughs and Ginsberg . . . but I don't know if lots of current Mods read those. I do a fanzine and I mention this in my fanzine sometimes, out of interest in the books and perhaps to educate the masses. They were around in 1955 – it goes back a lot further than people think.

Various shops sell the fanzine or I do at gigs, but mostly it sells by post. I go to see gigs and review them a few days later. I'll write about the things that capture my imagination while I'm out, things I see and hear. I don't listen to any radio. Occasionally if there's a sixties or Mod programme on TV I'll glance at it, but the records go on as soon as I'm up. I listen to music from the minute I get up to the minute I go to bed when I'm at home.

## Graham Scott, 23, Newcastle

I'm really into scooters, have been for years. I love them for the challenge, picking them up in a bad condition and doing them up. Currently I'm renovating a Corgi which is very rare. I was lucky as I got it from a classic restoration place and the dealers never had time to do it up themselves. They'd set it in red lead which has preserved it. I'm not at all an expert with scooters or mechanics, I just love doing it. I put ads in scooter mags for parts and information about the model, and you get corresponding to people too, you meet a lot of people through scooters. That's half the joy of it, hunting for particular books and reading the classic motorcycle magazines, tracking down the parts. I've got two other scooters, a Vespa and a Lambretta which I've done up, but I think I'm going to sell them now.

I was into the scooter scene in the early eighties – I was a young Mod, so I suppose I've been into the scene for 10 years. It has changed a lot over the years. I can't say if it's a good way or bad really, it's so different, it's dying out now. Back then, me and all my pals were into it, there were lots of bands and young people into the scene, now all my pals are out of it. But I keep it up. I still go to the rallies – not the national scooter rallies, just the local ones – on the bank holidays, which is like going boozing with other scooterists. They are usually one-nighters, a one-night disco, rather than the weekenders. I'm in a few different ones now, like the Vintage Motor Scooter Club which is for people with scooters over 25 years old – all the rare makes. I've been in that for seven years and I go to Lambretta Club of Great Britain rallies – the local one-day events.

I've changed a lot over the years. I'm in the Forces, living in a garrison and I'm married with a kid. My wife likes scooters, but she doesn't come to the rallies any more. I take my little boy, who's three, along now to look at all the scooters. At rallies they have competitions for showing your skill at riding and controlling a scooter, and a custom show day, so it's quite fun to watch.

Being in the Army means you can't go on about scooters, there aren't that many interested in them – there are a couple of guys here who know I'm into scooters, and I've met a couple of guys who used to be into Mod, but in the main, they're not the sort of people who'd share my interest. They're not accepting at all and could give you a hard time, so I keep it to myself. I share a garage with one of the guys here who is into old scooters, so he's seen the Corgi, but that's all.

I bought a 1961 Vespa and a 1961 Lambretta and both have been done up. They're not immaculate but look good and they took years to renovate, gathering parts and information.

I'm going to sell them now. I used to ride them a lot up until a few years ago. I don't feel I have to look the part to ride them; I haven't been into dressing the part for years! I've got a skinhead haircut because I'm in the Army. But it's the same at the rallies, you used to get loads of people in pilot jackets and combats and then it completely changed, you wear what you want, even at the National Rallies. The attitudes have changed in the last few years, probably because the scene has got so much smaller and they are changing to accommodate the people who still go to the rallies. It's dying out gradually. It's a weird mix now, and most people aren't into the music, just the vintage scooters. Some are people who have been into it since the sixties, old men who bought their scooters when they were young.

A lot of people think of classic scooters as Vespas and

Lambrettas, but there are many much older ones. Corgis have been around since 1950, they're far rarer. Even so, I'll probably have to sell the Vespa and Lambretta at a loss, because there aren't that many people who really want them. I haven't chucked away all my old clothes – they're in the loft somewhere. My records haven't been stored away – they're all under the stairs – because I still listen to the same music.

I started getting into the music in 1980. In 1979 there was the Mod thing with The Jam, The Specials and coming from where I do, it was Northern Soul as well as Motown, and I went to see that film *Quadrophenia* which was good. The scooter side developed from there. I was 11 or 12 at the time, but living in a small town in Scotland everyone clans together! I have met lots of friends through it.

Scooters are great for the social life that goes along with them. It's just a great way of making contact with other people, having a natter and a piss up. And when you put ads in scooter mags looking for parts or information, you always get lots of letters with people telling you about their scooters and inviting you to go and see them. Occasionally I meet up socially.

## Gav, 25, Co. Down, Northern Ireland

In 1978–9, the scootering scene in Northern Ireland was really big with large scooter rallies happening in most seaside towns. I was a young Mod and into bands like The Jam and scooters like Lambrettas (though I never had one then and I've still never got one!).

I've owned various Vespa scooters ever since. They are good fun, quite cheap and easy to run, and a good form of transport. I've had mainly PK 50s, 80s and 100 sports and PX 125s. The most recent one was written off by a car which didn't see it.

I restore about four a year, recently a Vespa PX for a friend and a PK 50. It was red when I got it, but it's now blue after hours of rubbing down and a re-spray. It still needs new indicators.

*Scootering* magazine and *Awol* are both full of stuff on clubs, dos, rallies, bikes and people, showing the scene is still alive. It's a good way of keeping in touch. Rallies are organised all over the North and South in summer. There are scooter clubs all over Northern Ireland, several in Belfast, and there's a Northern Ireland branch of the Motorcycle Action Group.

Most rallies are held in beautiful countryside and are full of people into bikes and scooters, so you get to travel, getting together for a laugh and a good time, you get to see what other people have done to their bikes, make new friends, get advice and bits, and show off your own immaculate bike or scooter.

Obviously I'm no longer a Mod, though the love of scooters lives on, and will always stay with me. And the rallies aren't the only gatherings I travel to.

I live in a bus, have dogs, a job (see what happens when you get a secure park-up!) and would like to start my own business, owning loads of scooters – and get a Lambretta.

I support the MAG (Motorcycle Action Group) who are fighting against anti-biker legislation springing up from Brussels, and I support travellers and ravers. Everyone deserves the right to travel and the right to congregate and party. If you agree, support your local MAG and help, because one day it might be your 'scene' getting the grief!

I listen to ska, punk, heavy metal, rave, soul – anything. It doesn't really matter what music you listen to or what 'scene' you're in, it's what you are that's important. My advice to everyone is to get a bike, get on it, and ride ...

# **14** Skins

Neo-Nazi 'Boneheads' dressed as Skinheads have been promoted by the media in such a way as to lead the general public to believe that all Skinheads are racist. This distorted view of SkinHeads must be challenged and the S.H.A.R.P. organisation will try through badges/ patches/and SHARP events to show that we are the majority and a true Skinheads is ANTI-RACIST ...
(*'SkinHeads Against Racial Prejudice' leaflet*)

### **Arfur, 21, editor of *Skinheads Don't Fear* fanzine, Wokingham, Berks**

I've just finished the third issue. We've got 30 regulars on subscription, but sold 150 of the first issue and 200 of the second through shops like Le Merc, Carnaby Street. I don't make a lot of money from it, but I just about break-even. I'm unemployed, though I get odd work on building sites. The magazine's for fun really, because there aren't any magazines writing about the bands I like to see and the things I'm interested in. And you never hear it on the radio or telly.

There aren't that many great skinhead bands around now. There was a bit of a revival in 88–89, but the ska scene is dead at the moment. Bad Manners are still going, and then there's 100 Men who came from Doncaster and moved to London, a kind of ska/reggae, and Oi bands Another Man's Poison and Pressure 28.

There are only a couple of skinheads around here. Best pub to hang out in right now is in London – The Blue Posts in Ganton Street, Soho, on a Saturday lunchtime, there are quite a few of us. We know each other. It's all word of mouth, there are no real places to hear about gigs and things. *The Skinhead Times* comes out irregularly so it's out of date. It's not his fault – I know the guy who does it, through writing to him – I know the problem, that's why I don't usually put events in.

I'm definitely into older-style clothes, brogues, original

193

Levis and Levi Sta-Prest. I buy them at second-hand shops, but there aren't that many good clothes left. It's a problem when you get old shirts and the collar wears through, but you can reverse them. I give them to the lady down the road. She does a great job. I've got some great mohair suits. If I go to somewhere decent, a soul do or reggae disco, I'll get suited up, but mostly it's brogues and Sta-Prest or jeans and boots. Not a lot of skinheads wear suits – just boots, jeans and braces, the media stereotype.

I was into it in 1981–82, but we were real kids and I can't say I was a 10-year-old skinhead. I liked Madness. The Specials had split up by the time I got into it. Then 1987–88 was when I got into it again properly. It was the image and the music. I was never really into punk or Mods, nothing else really appealed. Proper skinheads are into football, though there are no teams with a big skinhead following. I support Brentford.

I'm not into the politics. I don't vote. I live in a safe Conservative seat, so my one vote wouldn't change much. (I live with my parents.) The racial trouble you hear about is mostly not from skinheads. The areas where they (Asian people) live, Southall, Hounslow . . . there are hardly any skinheads.

I wouldn't go out and start on anybody, but you do get people who think, 'Look, he's a skinhead, he thinks he's hard, I'll go and have a pop at him.' I wouldn't start on anyone, but if someone starts I won't back down.

## Toast, 24, Ramsgate, Kent

All right. I've finished me tea – veggie burger, chips and egg. Right . . . Becoming a skin was a natural progression from being a rude boy. In 1979, there was a whole group of us who saw The Specials on *Top of the Pops*, and it coincided with that age when the ordinary school kid wants to change to be something. Mods had started here about 1980, but I didn't really want to be a Mod. I was probably listening to Pink Floyd before seeing The Specials on *Top of the Pops*!

Harringtons, DMs, Fred Perrys were the normal street fashion of the time, so that's how I started my skinhead collection. But there were three kinds of committed trends at school: the rude boys, casuals into Hawaiian shirts and New Romantics. Rude boy in Broadstairs was a general fashion, linked to the popularity of the music at the time – I wasn't alone. Madness were popular too, but they weren't liked as much as The Specials. While I was a rude boy, I always wanted to be a skin and looked up to the older skins. (I was only about 11.) Other bands I liked then were the Cockney Rejects and Sham 69 and I was listening to SKA 80 and Trojan LPs, and Tighten Up volumes one and two. I started collecting Trojan records and have a lot of bluebeat. You can't get hold of these records now. I buy them wherever and whenever I can . . .

They've started releasing compilations of old classics. I know people who won't touch anything if it's on CD, but the CD re-releases are all right, if you want to hear old music. It's not quite the same as tracking down the originals on vinyl though, is it?

Most of the rude boys and skins from that time have gone – they were more fashion victims, it seems, but for me it's a gut feeling inside. There are still a few going, but at that time the skins were huge. In the early eighties there were the Margate Skins and the Ramsgate and Broadstairs Skins – whole gangs – and we'd all go out. I was 15 at the time, a lot were 16–17 upwards, so I knew most of them.

At bank holidays, if there was any trouble anywhere, we'd all be there. Apollo's in Margate was a favourite haunt. It wasn't so much that we'd go looking for trouble, it was inevitable. The Ramsgate casuals would start and there were usually punch-ups. But more often it was more of a rumour than anything else, word got around, 'There's going to be a fight', and nothing ever happened!

I stayed into it right through. I'd travel around to see the bands I wanted to see and kept doing that. In 1990 I went on holiday to Torquay to see a band there, and I'd go to see bands at the Powerhaus, London, and Camden venues.

Because I was seeing bands and travelling round and still

interested in skins, I started up a skinzine, *Tighten Up* in 1989 – reviewing gigs and putting in tales sent in by people. I wanted to show the scene was still there and get people interested. I get a lot of people writing in. My wife Sue's a skinhead, she helps with the 'zine, she puts the pages together. She doesn't write anything – though she did the Laurel Aitken interview. When I'm working on *Tighten Up*, I get frantic and put it all together quickly. It could be better . . .

I done it really because this blood and honour thing was hijacking the skinhead faithful. The politics of that were obvious enough and drowning the skinhead image. I thought the more social, street kids should have their say, so I thought I'll do a 'zine and change things. A lot of the blood and honour thing were upstarts interested in their own ideas, not skinheads and music.

I print 500 – they all go. Sometimes more; they seem to go however many I print. I send some up North and sell others to readers by post, some through The Merc in Carnaby Street and other shops and at gigs. A guy in Germany handles about 120 and sells them there. There's a big skin thing out there. And a few organisations take it up . . . like in America.

The scene is bigger abroad, in Germany especially. The Potsdam Ska Festival in the summer attracted 2000 people – not all skins, but the large majority were. They didn't care about what the audience looked like, but some were into their image. A lot have bleached jeans with an eighties feel. You don't see that here now, though some of the blood and honour types wear them. There was one geezer with a black flight jacket, bleached army combats and high boots, he was German and had short hair; he looked like a fascist. We found out later he wasn't at all. We discovered they were Oi! but not fascists. Most fascists avoid gigs. It was a great time.

There was a Sharp – Skinheads Against Racial Prejudice – demo before the gig. Sharp is a good idea but it falls flat on its face. It campaigns here and in the States and it's needed because there's such a lot about racism now. I've run the Sharp logo in the skinzine. It aims to show the media that not all skins are racialist – each to their own, some are very left-wing.

Some people, not even skinheads, say Sharp have gone far enough. You can't be a skinhead if you've got dreadlocks or long hair, though you can like the music. And some Sharp followers say, 'We'll smash boneheads and get the blood and honour.'

The racist element are usually found at scooter rallies, and some bands are labelled blood and honour. It's all screwed up. They sound like the Rolling Stones in the seventies and some of it sounds more heavy metal. It's definitely not ska. In attitude, it's Oi! gone further. Some write saying 'Get the Asians out of the country and Jews' – they're all pathetic. I don't like the Nazi fascist element; it gets in the way.

I keep an eye out for everything to see what's going on – and look at different fanzines. I like to know what's happening among different skinheads all over – those that are left!

I'm more into Sta-Prest and Ben Shermans, though they are getting harder to find, especially in good condition now. A waste of time. Then there are the flight jackets you see on a lot of people now, though that's not strictly traditional. Mostly, I check out junk shops and charity shops whenever I go to a different area. Down here they've been cleaned out over the years. I went to Chatham and picked up some Permanent Press trousers recently. So you can be lucky. With shirts I try to get some original checked shirts, Ben Sherman, and Van Heusen, Brutus, and Levi mostly, though sometimes you can spot some lairy checks and patterns in other old sixties makes that weren't the main ones among original skinheads. Sometimes the pattern is just as important. Jaytex were OK but I've never seen a good pattern, and I don't like the big collars – 3-inch collars are as big as I'll go. I'm not really snobby about labels. If it's a good check, then a Woolworth's make – Winfield – would be fine. One of my mates got an old shirt in a Pound-stretcher shop, a great check, so he had the sleeves cut and a pleat put in; it looks spot on, you couldn't tell it was a cheapie one.

Some people are hung up about labels – I don't really care. Most of them are paying about £70 upwards for an original button-down. I'd rather pay £20–£25 for a good Ben Sherman, though mostly I spend a fiver! Boots are quite easy to get. There's a shop, Docklands, in London, that sells the boots and others around, and I'll also go to London to get the Levis – quite a few shops, like River Island, sell basic red-tab button-up 501 Levis.

The local band Intensified play in Folkestone, they attract anyone from students to scooterists – a really good mixture. There might not be that many skinhead bands at the moment but generally it's not a bad time musically. Because of the ragga thing happening, it's brought ska music into the open over the past two to three years. The likes of Shabba Ranks are nothing compared to the originals, but at least the music is getting a play, and more people are hearing and liking it.

It's not just the old ska records that are being repackaged, but the early album from The Specials has been re-released too. I haven't got it, but I imagine people buy it for nostalgia; they think 'It looks a pretty set so I'll buy it for the record collection', though lots will all have that already. So who's buying it?

We went to see The Specials and The Beat in Oxford. I told you I was prepared to travel to see bands. If I hear of new bands I will go and check them out. There aren't a lot of clubs or things happening on the ska scene here, now.

Mostly, Sue and me stay in and watch the TV. If I go out it would be to a gig. Most of my money revolves around gigs and the fanzine. I don't go to the pub drinking a lot now. I'm not a drinking person. I did! A skinhead is a pisshead, as they say. I used to get so drunk. Once we'd been to see one band at the Dublin Castle, Camden, and another at Camden Ballroom and we were so out of it. It had to be then that I met Mark Brennan, my hero. I don't know what I was saying, and straight after that Sue slipped . . . Were we embarrassed! I also head butted the drummer of The Loafers. It was a good night! I went to gigs once a month then, it was a great period; I was so excited as ska was picking up again – that was a couple of years ago.

Sue wears Levis usually, though right now she's pregnant ... There are not many maternity clothes for skinhead women! She sorts herself out. I got a suit second-hand for me and she chopped the trousers into a skirt for herself. She mostly wears suits and shirts and denim jackets. She won't wear loafers as we're both veggies and she won't wear leather. She wears DM shoes and non-leather DM boots. We're already collecting clothes for the baby – like little Levis and boots!

We both work. I'm in a dead-end job, spraying panels in a factory, Sue's a manager in a mental care home, but it's too violent. When she's had the baby, she'll try and do something more children-based. It's too stressful. She'll probably go and do a diploma in social welfare studies.

I can't imagine not ever being a skinhead, and not doing the skinzine. I suppose I'll keep it up until I get bored or run out of things to write about.

## Kev Gough, 22, Pressure 28, Oswestry, Salop

I woz running around like every other kid in the street with an Harrington on me back and a Specials badge on me lapel when two-tone was running cock-a-hoop round the country. When two-tone left the airwaves to make room for the next musical craze that never happened – well, nothing as significant as two-tone anyway – I was still into it, then a few years later came along the second wave – of Oi! bands. I was wearing the gear, but didn't have a crop. So I got one and jumped on the bandwagon.

I woz a bit green at the time due to being young. Anyway, 'skinheads rule' woz the call of the day – well, for me anyway. We still do of course ... Dress style usually differs from one end of the country to the other. It's probably not noticeable to an outsider, but you do notice differences from town to town: cut of hair length and jeans, for instance. Basically, though, Shermans, Levis, Doc is most standard dress, depends where I'm going for the night or if everything else is in the wash!

Dress is one of the factors that makes skinheads so unique. The crop, boots and braces are what make us famous. It's a working-class uniform, we wouldn't be skinheads without the gear.

I don't so much have favourite pubs and clubs, it's more getting down to it anywhere that will let you in. Which suits me down to the ground really, though, because half the places that won't let you in are crappy disco pubs anyway. I don't want to go out to a pub and have pop drivel blaring out of the speakers all night. Mind you, there are loads of loose women in them . . .

Are skinheads thugs? You get nutters everywhere in all youth cults, aggro often comes with the territory. But you are more likely to get glassed in the face in the local disco than in a pub with skinheads in there. You know what the press are like, skinhead trouble makes a better story than yer average punter having a ruck. We've never had any good press since day one and we still spread like wildfire through the football grounds of the seventies and eighties. I don't think it makes a difference what the press says, people believe what they wanna believe anyway. I'd prefer to be having a ruck than watching some shit documentary on the telly.

Skinheads have traditionally been anti-drugs. It's still the same nowadays as far as skinheads and drugs go – they don't mix, really. As for lager, ale etc., that's a different story.

Musicwise, at the moment there are quite a few good bands around: Another Man's Poison, great stuff, but I'm into The Specials (still), Cock Sparrer, 4 Skins, too many to list, the Business have just reformed so they should add force to the growing Oi!/punk scene.

I never listen to the radio, it only plays trendy music made by middle-class drop-outs spending mummy's money on fiddling round with synthesisers, cashing in on the mugs who are out for so-called fashion. Pressure 28, my band, is still going from strength to strength. We've just signed to Helen of Oi! Records for the next single and album and the album has got to be out before August. Since we did the demo, we've done two tracks for a compilation album on Hammer Records, then our debut single 'Get Ready' came out about in autumn 93 on Helen of Oi! Records. It's gone like hell and had blazing reviews. We recently recorded four tracks for the 'New Breed' CD on Step 1 Records which has just come out. We had a few problems in the studio, so it ain't come out how we wanted but what the hell, we'll make up for the bad reviews with the next single.

That's one of the problems, being limited with time in the studio. We're so fussy, we mess around trying to get the right sound and before we know it, we're running out of time and just have to band 'em off, and get completely the wrong sound. It doesn't half bug you when you hear the songs on vinyl/CD or whatever.

I don't think we'll ever crash into the charts. They would never let us for starters, we're skinheads, remember. Even if we ever did sell that many records, I think the figures of the sales would conveniently disappear or be quoted as quite a lot lower than they should be, etc. etc.

I live in hope, eh? I think I could get quite used to loads of money, living in complete luxury, never having to work again . . . a video and telly in my bedroom, slaves . . .

# 15 Bikers

Easter came early for patients at Maidstone Hospital when a fleet of kind-hearted bikers arrived laden with chocolate eggs.

About 50 members of the Kent group of the British Motorcyclists' Federation took part in the Easter egg run from Wrotham, through Meopham and the Medway Towns to the hospital in Hermitage Lane.

Patrick Gerrish, area representative for the Kent group which formed in January, said the run was the first in a series of events aimed at changing the public's perception of motorcyclists. (*Kent Messenger*)

## Taff, 24, North London

I'm a member of the 59 Club, which is in Hackney Road in London's East End. It was started as a youth club in 1962 by a rocking Rev., who rode a bike and wanted somewhere for young riders to go and to balance the image of bikers as wasters and delinquents. I've been a member for several years.

When it was started, bikes were the big youth thing, and the Rev. wanted to get away from the loutish image. I doubt if there's a member under 22 now! Bikes don't appeal to kids in the same way. More 17–18-year-olds drive cars, and if they were into speed, they'd opt for a souped-up Japanese bike, not a delicate old Triumph. Classic bikes are not the best thing for doing burn-ups on motorways now. You wouldn't want to – they're delicate and beautiful old machines. You've got to like the look of them.

We're not louts now. Bikers are all very different people, but we share a love of bikes. There are three distinct types. The seventies lot – who haven't just received the idea, they've probably been into it since the seventies, attracting a few on the way. They've got messy hair and wear cut-up jean jackets over their leathers and ride choppers. There are the Mad Max dispatch riders in matte black and full-face helmets on modern machines and then there are the rockers who love classic bikes.

Rockers wear leather jackets, jeans and T-shirts. Yes, it's classic like Marlon Brandon in *The Wild One* [seminal film of the fifties which was banned in Britain for 15 years] – but the look comes with the bike, we're not consciously stylish. In fact, there's something not quite stylish about bikers, probably the greasy jeans.

I suppose I am particular about what I wear, or really what I wouldn't wear. Just plain white T-shirts – rather than those with supposedly 'biker' logos – and checked shirts. Mmm, they're classic and pre-grunge! We're a conservative lot on the whole. And, I'd only wear an open-face helmet. Full-face helmets weren't around at the time the bikes came out.

Of course, there are changes over the years, more to do with outside influences. It's OK to wear cowboy boots instead of traditional motorbike ones – I do, if I'm not riding. Why wear heavy riding boots if they're not necessary? I don't get to ride my bikes (a Royal Enfield and a BSA) so much now. London traffic is so bad, even for bikes. I end up on the pushbike – it's quicker because you can take short cuts. No, I'm not too proud to go on the pushbike. Bikes are beautiful but they're not my whole life. I've recently gone back to college to study art after a period of doing odd jobs.

There are more yuppie classic bike-riders now. It goes in phases, there were a few years ago, and now again. It used to be a working-class cult, especially the early sixties café racer bikes, which were streamlined by the riders. It doesn't irritate me to see these trendy riders. I love old bikes, and the more people I see on them, the better. And it doesn't bother me if people wear the clothes 'cos they like the image and haven't got a bike. I love the image, too! Though there is an inverted snobbery among some bikers. In the late eighties, there was a great fuss made when someone put a 59 badge on a jacket for [singer] Terence Trent D'Arby. You can always tell a real rocker – look for the helmet, and the oily cuffs. Designer leather aren't well-made. They would never stand up to the rigours of riding.

## Caroline, 25, East London

Leathers are glamorous, but they are also showerproof and protect you if you fall off. You can't really wear lots of studs on a bike – or you would get really interesting scars if you crash. That's one way to tell whether a rocker is into the image or the bike! I don't mind the image copiers. If they admire the look, they'll show more respect to you on the road.

Girl bikers are often portrayed as the thing that sat on the back of the bike in those old (and not so old) road movies. There are bikers with long blonde tresses – I've got long blonde hair, and so has my friend Judy. But we ride our own bikes. I built my own Triumph Tiger 500. Though, I have to say, that now I've become a mum I don't ride so much!

Some of the biking fraternity outside town don't take us seriously, but classic bikers tend to be into the bikes, and want to see people riding them. They don't care if the riders are female, black or gay. It is an attractive, strong image – in fact I use it a lot in my work, screen-printing. A friend and I have been printing T-shirts and materials with biker images for a few years. Enfield, BSA logos and skull and crossbones. They sell. I don't think the images are menacing. I suppose little pistols aren't everyone's cup of tea, but I shouldn't think printing them or wearing them perpetuates an image of nasty rockers.

The bike is part of my identity, but without my bike I'm stuck. It gives me freedom.

## Tony, 22, trainee architect, Brighton

It's hard to imagine a time in the fifties and sixties when bikers were hated and if someone saw a youthful person on a bike they'd automatically think 'delinquent'! That's a word you don't hear much any more! Now, if people see me, either alone or with a group of us riding out, they give admiring looks. You see drivers looking at the bike from their cars. You wouldn't believe how many people come over and talk because of the bike, and usually it's older people. You can't say it's a threatening sight! Perhaps it's because they had a classic bike when they were young, or it brings back a bit of their past. It's like when some geezer says to his mate, 'Hey, George, look at that old thing' – they're not being insulting. I can understand, old bikes are beautiful, especially when I've been cleaning the chrome! Occasionally, you get a kid on a Suzuki or Yamaha, who spots you on the motorway or at traffic lights, and looks down his nose at you, before accelerating off. Who cares if his goes faster (well, yeah, him obviously!), speed isn't the point. I know what I'd rather be riding.

## Kevin, 22, Dorset

I ride a Harley. I bought it second-hand from a garage round here and did it up. It was in a bit of a state. A lot of us ride bikes, because we like the looks, but you have to ride something to get about here. There's no point waiting for a bus! Some of my mates have old bikes, some modern Japanese – but all second-hand. It's great riding round the lanes. We ride out to local country pubs. One of our regulars is an old pub in a village of three cottages or thereabouts! It's got a good games room – you can shoot pool, darts, a skittle alley – but it's just somewhere to go. Friendly; we know everyone. Yeah, it's funny, bikers in the same pub as families and tourists. You get them because they do pub grub and there's a restaurant at the back and garden for kids.

# **16** Essex Boys

## Cam, 19, Gants Hill

I am an Essex boy – although I've not always lived there, it's rubbed off. I've got the old Essex mentality – that is: anywhere, any place, any time!

There's some truth in it – the Essex lot, when they've had a drink, don't give a monkey's about what they do.

I'm half-Italian, half-Welsh. I have got just my dad here, but we don't talk – he lives in Wales. It's a personality clash; he's got a short temper, it's chaos in the house. He's the Italian half, very fiery, and very family-orientated. My mum passed away, so I was always under his feet. I've got no roots. I've got a lot of friends, and make friends quite easily, I'm always the Jack the Lad that makes everyone laugh.

It annoys me that I always have to move around. I've been in Chatham three weeks now as I've just started a course at college there so I haven't re-established myself yet. But I still go home to Chingford at the weekends. I lived at Aldgate East, then moved further east to Gants Hill, Ilford. See, I still move around; I get bored staying in one place. I haven't found anywhere that I'd like to live permanently yet.

I used to go to Italy twice a year – I'm one of these types who have to go on holiday, plus I've got a language. I can go and live the high life for a little bit and then come back to reality.

Going out is important. Where I am, we go to a place at Southend Pier, it was hardcore, now it's more garage. I used to be into hardcore raving. Six months ago, I used to be heavily into it but I had a bad experience, with E, and it took me off the road. I was naïve and wanted to experiment with everything. I'm not against people who deal with that, because I've done it myself, but then I've had a bad experience and been given something dodgy. I still like the sounds and I'll be the first one on the floor. The one-off events are usually the best.

A lot of people from around here go to London for a night out – and a lot of my mates I've met up with through the club scene, so they'd be travelling from other places anyway. The garage scene here is coming up now – and I can still dance without dropping an E. There were times when I wanted that extra bit of something to keep going all night and not sleep during the day, but it's not necessary.

I like to look good. Most people do on the garage scene. It was trainers/track suits at one time – now it's waistcoats, tight open tops, people dress up more. Faces alter and appearances alter from club to club – garage is more sophisticated, smart, not as in shirt and tie. A lot of the people who listen to hardcore got into garage, so it's not such a young crowd. A lot of people who used to be into the rave scene branched into hardcore, then branched into garage, so what happens next I don't know. I'd like to go to more festivals; I wanted to go to the weekender Glastonbury but didn't have the finance to get up there.

I'm at college studying spatial design and work in a wine bar on the weekends. I do get hassled in the wine bar. Like the other night, a bloke came in with his missus and she'd had a bit too much to drink and she got a bit friendly, so he didn't like it. I got a lot of abuse. A lot of that goes on. It's the long-haired treatment. A lot of blokes don't like guys with long hair. I've got a tattoo on my back, long hair and the old ear-ring, it doesn't go down well with a lot of guys. A lot of girls do like the rough look – a lot of guys, too!

Wine's not my own favourite tipple. We drink cider; it's £1 a pint. Snakesbite is too expensive – and a lot of pubs won't serve it, because it's lethal!

I do spend a lot of my time talking at college – that's the spatial bit of the design. Design-wise, I'm into simplicity, and a lot of my work uses simple designs, I like to use geometrical shapes. I do office design, houses, whereas my mate Phil would decide on the structure of the house, and then I'd design inside the house, that's where we interrelate. We could one day, if we both got enough people behind us, we could team up – call ourselves Essex Architects – with lots of secretaries, of course!

## Phil, 23, Basildon

That's the Essex code – been there, seen it, done it. I don't think Essex people are that different, it's just in a pub, people hear a dodgy accent and say, 'Where's that from?' So you say, 'The place where women are respected for their brains, a popular place . . .'

Essex people don't seem no different when you go there – it's when you take an Essex person out of their territory and put them somewhere else. If you're at a party and someone says, 'Where are you from?', if you say 'Essex', you have everyone round you. It always happens.

We have a real reputation behind us, so people think you've got to be that way, so you live up to it. Kent people aren't like it. At least it puts you on the map. People already have a stereotype of what that's like in a way. I mean, if you've got to say 'Southport', you're likely to get, 'Where's that?' and you'd have to explain, but when you sit in a pub, and say, 'I'm from Essex', people will say, 'Is it really like that?' and you can tell a few stories, and before you know it, you've got a crowd round you.

When I go out at home it depends what I want. If I want to bar-fly then I'd go to a pub, if I want night life I'll go to a club or often I'll go for a quiet drink. But there's a lot of fighting in Essex.

Everybody wants to compete and be seen as a bigger man than everybody else. There are certain places back home, that when you walk in, you keep your face to the ground – you don't have to do anything or say anything to get started on.

It's not just Essex, it's everywhere, but where you are you notice it more. When I go to Southampton, which I do occasionally, I don't see nothing of it, because I'm not there enough to see what's going down.

You have a fight with someone because they've picked on you and you beat him in a one-to-one, which is a rare thing now, then you'll be walking round the street a few days later and you'll be jumped by a crowd because you beat up another guy.

You can't ignore it, because it's always going on about you and the worst part of the problem is that the guys are getting younger and younger. Where I live, there's a 7–11 store. Now if I want to go in and buy cigarettes, I'll walk by and see who's over there first. Normally there's a crowd of 14- and 15-year-olds. Now if I see that crowd, I know who they are, I won't go in there ... not because I'm afraid, but because they want to prove themselves and pick on you, because you're big – I'm big ...

When I was 15, I was interested in girls, rugby and things like that. Now I know 14- and 15-year-olds who carry blades, deal in drugs ... back home you can buy grass, gange, shit like that off 12-year-olds. It's getting so much younger. Kids sit down and skin up in school.

It probably happens around other places too, but we don't notice it, because we're not so familiar with the area.

It used to be that you could have a fight, one-to-one. Now everyone carries blades and goes around in groups. I don't carry blades, but I think I'd rather draw blood than have a feud going on afterwards. If I had a fight with someone round here (in Kent), perish the thought, I would walk away and think no more about it. Back home (Essex), I know too many people, so if I had a fight with someone, even so many years younger, which I wouldn't want to do, but if I did, I know that a certain group would be tracking me down trying to get even.

Also, I know that where I come from, and probably where most people come from, the bulk of the trouble is caused by women. It is. I'll be walking down the local centre and someone will say, 'You're Phil, aren't you?

Sarah fancies you.' And you'll say, 'Who's Sarah?' They say: 'It doesn't matter. Sarah fancies you and I fancy her, so I'm going to have your arse.' Yes, that really happens. That's exactly how it works.

Everyone wants to be number one; they want to walk around and have everyone get out of their way. But most do nothing on their own, even the hard men don't say nothing until they've got boys and girls with them. He'll be the one to throw the first punch, then run to the back when the others steam in . . .

# 17 Sound-bites: From Pop Tarts to Tent Poles
## (Clothes, Clubs and Glastonbury)

Waiting for a bus outside a Kensington hotel one Saturday morning last month, I became aware of a weird squeaking noise, that crescendoed, building into a fierce scream. A squirrely teenage boy was leaving the hotel and climbing into a taxi, to the despairing yelps of 30 or so 14-year-old girls. One grumpily explained that this was Mark, hunkiest member of Britain's biggest teen band, Take That. (*Guardian*)

### Lisa M, 24, Surrey
(*Dress: flares, cropped top, low platform peep-toe shoes*)

I'm going to see Take That in Wembley this autumn. I don't call myself a teenybopper, but Mark is gorgeous! It's his fault, he shouldn't have a body like that. I'm going with Tina, my best friend at work (a department store in Ashford). It was her suggestion. Really! She couldn't get her boyfriend to go with her and he didn't think she'd find anyone else to go along! Tickets are expensive (about £20 depending on seats – we've got really good ones), then there's the travel. I know we'll be surrounded by babbling kids. My eight-year-old nephew wants to go! But it will be a laugh.

I'm really into dance music – Take That are more entertainment and fun. I used to go to lots of clubs (mostly travelling to London) and raves, in London, though I've been to one-offs as far away as Blackpool and Essex and a Sunday club in Berkshire, which is where I met my last boyfriend. We'd go clubbing at least once, usually twice a week and take lots of Es and acid. We used to go to Ibiza for clubbing holidays. I haven't been clubbing for a while, I feel a bit out of it. They've changed a lot in the past year but mostly my clubby friends have drifted apart from the scene. I usually go to friends' homes, or to pubs and bars now.

### Jo, 17, Take That fan, East Sussex (after Wembley gig)
(*Balloon pants, skinny-rib top*)

I was really disappointed. The girls screamed all the time. Yes, I suppose I should have thought they would, but what's the point of going, if you can't hear the band? I might as well stay at home, play records and stare at the pictures. I wouldn't have minded but they shouted for the wrong guy! They were going for Mark and he's gruesome. Well, I suppose he's all right, you know, but it's Robbie who's got the best body and moves so cute. I couldn't even see him properly as people got in the way. I would go and see them again, but preferably not Wembley, you feel so distant and just so insignificant, you know?

But I can't imagine them playing in a smaller place, really. I came with a group of mates – my friend's dad is going to pick us up from the station – it's a long way to come, but I really wanted to see them, and we had the day off and did a bit of Christmas shopping in London (West End) first, so it was like a big occasion. I think the excitement of waiting was half of it – we got the tickets ages ago, I didn't know what to expect – it's the first group I've ever seen play.

### Rachel, 23, Bristol
(*Braided hair, pierced nose, black skirt over black leggings, large maroon jumper*)

It's the only chance we get to see some bands live – best group playing over the weekend is Dodgy, but there aren't that many true faves this year. My real faves are The Levellers, Jane's Addiction (as was). Glastonbury's more of an event – we spend more time hanging around the tent or someone else's with a bunch of mates than checking out the bands. The tickets were so expensive, about £50, but it's a kind of holiday. We've been here since Thursday and won't leave until Monday. There's not much to do at home – local pub, friends' houses, so it's worth saving up for this.

## Sarah, 22, Bristol
(*Stripy bib and braces*)

I picked these up at the stalls [in the festival's shopping area]. I can't resist a chance to shop and I never take these off – big boots – they're essential if it rains [it didn't]. We came together but have met up with a whole bunch from all over. A couple of guys from Surrey and a Scottish girl and guy. It's really friendly, a brilliant atmosphere, especially at night. A lot of mates at home think, 'How could you go for that long without washing?' There are water taps, but they're a long way away from the tent, and loos – though the chaps have it easy as they use the bushes. When not at Glastonbury, I live near Bristol and work in a shop as a trainee buyer.

## Carl, 19, and brother Shaun, 20, Camberley, Surrey
(*Jeans, band T-shirt and long hair*)

We came last year, it was more ravey, with lots more parties on the site after the bands finished at 12 ... The Orb were brilliant last year. They're playing again this year. Best so far are Jamiroquai – got the crowd going. We haven't really got so much into the atmosphere this year. Usually days and nights merge with rounds of parties, crashing with mates or just staying awake. We went off-site to the local swimming pool today, did a few lengths and had a shower by the pool! It beats standing in the mud around the tap! Last year we didn't see water for the whole event – lucky we had our Wet Ones! At home, it's usually pubs, local club.

## Rick B, 24, Glasgow

*(Jeans – button-down Levi 501's – and plain, unlabelled grey T-shirt)*

I'm more into seeing bands. We've got some good live venues. Shops – really good shops in Glasgow selling Stussy, Chipie and labels. But they're so pretentious, like Ichi Ni San – good clothes but you've got to ring a bell to go in. A shop with a door policy!

Glasgow's really lively at the moment. Lots of bands playing locally, and other clubs, but the police have really cracked down on finishing times – it's all over by 2 a.m. Even clubs! It's supposed to cut down on violence, but everywhere's chucking out at the same time, so you get loads of people on the streets at the same time, all bored. A recipe for disaster. And they avidly check your bags and frisk you as some people have been known to sneak in knives and things.

## Ross, 22, Glasgow

*(Baggy denim overalls, stripy T-shirt, scarf tied round head)*

Glasgow's pretty brilliant – shops, clubs and things. The Tunnel (club) is good, even London DJs like Terry Farley come up, and the Sub Club, that's usually garage sounds, but it has different clubs on different nights. Techno's pretty strong up here too. Atlantis on Saturdays is well keen. But he's right [Rick] – it does all finish too early. It's back to a mate's for the party to continue – though not mine. I can't do that; I still live with my folks.

Some [clubs] are more dressy than others. There's nothing wrong with guys dressing up. OK, I might not look it now, but you should see my wardrobe! Diesel, Chipie . . . I get them all places. The Italian Centre's pretty hot. I'm not prepared to say how much I spend on clothes – a lot. It's important. I don't get out of it so much as I did, say a year or two ago . . . Now it's blow mostly.

## Dee, 18, Edinburgh

*(Ankle-length, loose, button-up black dress over Viv Westwood T-shirt, raffia platforms, short red hair with shorter fringe)*

Squid has to be the best right now. It's dressy, not hot and sweaty like too many clubs, and it looks right [the club incorporates a tropical fishtank]. It's at La Belle Angeles, OK, it's a bit posey – you do get the ones who stand on the balcony and peer down, but what's wrong with that? Lots of students hang out there. On Thursdays at the same club there's a ska night, rude boys and pseudo skinheads into the image – the Harringtons and short fringes, I mean, not the thug side! Gentle skinheads, if you like. You could say it's hip to like reggae here right now among a certain contingent . . .

I don't really listen to radio – tapes, usually, we make up takes of cool sounds for each other. I like ambient sounds, something a bit mellow, and acid jazz.

# 18 Sex, Love and Spermicide

There were no doubt sniggers in the House of Commons recently over a suggestion by Lady Olga Maitland MP that the Government should consider gagging the teenage Press, increasingly using sex to sell its produce to girls under the age of consent.

But is it over-reacting to get hot under the collar about the advice our school-girls are getting from their favourite magazines?

Not to anyone who has looked beyond the glossy covers. (*Mail on Sunday*)

Nearly half the people quizzed in a survey want the age of consent for gay sex raised to 99.

The Twin Network Pubscan Poll, which questioned pub goers throughout Britain, found only 17 per cent who thought the age of consent should be 16 or 18. One in 10 thought it should be 21. (*Daily Star*)

The Government seems to think that punishing the children of lone parents will stop the growth in their numbers – but it cannot explain how.

Most sensible people know that taking benefits from already-poor people will mean that their children will go hungry.

Cold, hunger, fear of the next utility bill – this is a way of life for most one-parent families.

At the end of October's Conservative Party Conference you could have been forgiven for thinking that teenage mums are the cause of all Government problems.

However, the vast majority of Britain's lone parents are mature, once-married men and women. (*Daily Mirror*)

## Cam, 19, Gants Hill

I'm a free liberal guy, man ... A lot of youngsters now have got no reason to get married. They don't need to just to have sex! No, it's not a lot of one-night stands. I've had long relationships. I've had a bad experience in the past (haven't we all?), and it does make you harder, bitter – not bitter ... it makes you wary ... What do I think about Aids? That's a bit heavy isn't it?

## Phil, 23, Basildon

Back in Essex, there is so much under-age sex. I know people who have had children and then a few weeks later gone on to collect their GCSE results. Loads of 15- and 16-year-olds are sexually active and have children. I know 16-year-old girls who have got their second on the way.

Sex is one thing, of course we all try to get it! But, see this ring, it was given to me by a girl who I loved and would have married if I'd been able to. She's gone to live abroad now ... Marriage is an option if you find that special person.

## Glen, Canterbury

My girlfriend's sister was only 16 when she had her baby. That's just how it is now.

## Andy, 25, miner, Nottingham

It sounds a cliché, but most people get married young and have kids young in this area – and on this estate there's a high rate of single young mums.

## Bobita, 22, shop assistant and voluntary worker, Medway Towns

I had an arranged marriage. We went on a holiday to India and while I was there they (my family) introduced me to my husband. I said no. I wanted to marry someone I met and loved. I'd been to college and studied hairdressing and wanted a career and to make my own life. But they persuaded me. He comes from a good family and business.

His father is the chief of the judiciary in his area at home, and my husband studied to be a lawyer. We had a big wedding and went to Kashmir on honeymoon.

We've got our own home and a little boy, but I'm not hairdressing at the moment – I cut my family's hair. I work in a local clothes shop. My little boy lives with my mum in the week because the nursery is too far away for me to take and collect him every day, I wouldn't be able to do it before and after work, especially as we haven't got a car. It is sad, and hopefully won't be for long. I'd love to have him here full-time. He calls me Jolly (my nickname) and my mum, Mum!

Although I'm married, have a home and a job, there are constraints on me. There always have been, even when I was at college. I was never allowed out in the evenings. Indian girls have no freedom. Not many Indian girls go out, they just aren't allowed out, during the daytime either. But they do. If they are at college, they make up excuses to go to day-time gigs.

There are special afternoon discos organised for the girls – and usually organised at times during the week when you'll be at college, so you'd have to bunk off to go. We all did. Or else we wouldn't have a social life. Many of them are secret and we find out by word of mouth, a DJ sets it up. There are bands and DJs – it's half-English half-Indian music. There isn't supposed to be any drink but I'm sure you could get it if you wanted it. Occasionally people would sneak to London for gigs. Some are advertised on flyers – a lot of parents can't read them!

My family are quite strict and adhere to the customs from their country. They think they are doing what's right for us, but they should relax. I'd let my son have more freedom – and a daughter, if I had one. My brothers have much more freedom. One's at university in London and stayed in digs for a year – I wouldn't have been allowed to go to college far away, if it meant staying in digs. I suppose as I'm female they were more worried about me, but also they have changed a bit over the years. When we were young, we weren't allowed out. After I got married, the started letting my brothers out. A lot of Indian girls try to study away from home, and choose a college at the other side of the country, to get some freedom. In a way they don't see our education as important as for the boys, as they assume we will get married and have a family, so what's the point? Usually most parents start looking for a husband for their daughter while she's in her last year at college. Of course we can still get a job, but the restrictions are there.

## Bobby, 19, Kent

As a male, we have more freedom to associate with who we like and marry who we like, but at the end of the day, it's all down to my parents, they have the last say. My sister had an arranged marriage, but I don't think that's typical of Indian people in Britain. It depends on different people, on how closely they follow customs.

Would I be more relaxed with my own children if I had them? Probably. Well, not a daughter. It's not safe out there, especially in the evenings. I don't know, it's hard to say, things may have changed a lot by then.

## Jamie, 24, London

Heaven – I know lots of people there – there are the people who live for it, they are always there, others hang around for a while until they go back to where they came from, and others settle down, get pizzas and stay in! I have got a boyfriend, but we haven't settled down – we both like going out.

I met him at a club. I was working at Industria, doing the door and guest list. He looked over. I didn't know him and asked, 'Who's that boy?' I'm known at Industria. Nothing happened. Then he came to the Café [de Paris]; I was working there too.

I worked on the switchboard of a rent boy agency. You know, people phone up for a boy, say the type they are looking for. It's mostly businessmen or tourists who find the number in the Yellow Pages and call up: 'I'm in London next week, can I have a blond boy, thank you.' . . . I never got to meet them, just made contact over the phone. I suppose all rent boys worry about Aids, but anyone who pays for sex is extremely cautious and there are things they will and won't do, like sucking people off. No punter would want to take a risk either. But it's the same everywhere, that's just the way it is. I have lost a couple of friends through Aids, you can't help but think about it.

## Jonathan, 22, London

How many boyfriends have I had? Oh, I don't know. How many hot dinners have I had? Multiply it by 10! I'm being flippant. I suppose I went through a spell of having lots of boyfriends. The more the merrier. Doesn't everyone, male and female? I've been with my current boyfriend for nine months, and it's still hot. I lived with one guy for 18 months, I thought that he was the one, you know. But he wasn't very faithful and I found out. It's a close-knit world. You can't betray a friend without someone finding out. Of course I was upset, devastated, but I got over it. Found someone else. I suppose most of us are looking for someone we can grow old with, it's human nature. It would be nice to have lots of admirers until the end of your days, but sometimes it feels so shallow. You need to know someone more deeply to take the relationship further. On the other hand, I do believe that sexually, you don't need to know someone very well at all, in fact at all, to have a great physical bond. Pure lust, yes, I suppose it is. I admit I've had my share of one-night stands – one-afternoon stands – no, I have had one fleeting moment in the park, but that was just curiosity. Now I like to share more than my body. You grow out of that stage.

Of course I worry about Aids. Doesn't everyone? Sex isn't just copulation, there are many ways of satisfying and giving pleasure without The Act, you know. Also, I have long-standing relationships with friends who I don't think sexually about at all. Well, not really – you can't help wondering! They are good friends – honest, and I've shared flats with groups of guys who have known me inside out – but not literally, if you know what I mean. It's like males saying they can't have a girl as a close friend. Obviously they can, unless they're really not bothered about who they sleep with, or so narrow-minded that all they think about is sex. Everyone can have friends they go to the cinema or for a pizza with, or just sit and have a coffee and a chat.

I meet my boyfriends at all sorts of places. I was introduced to my current friend at a party, that's generally how I get to know people, by introduction, at clubs, friends' homes. In a way, being gay can make it easier to approach someone, because you kind of have a mutual bond. I can definitely tell whether someone's gay or not. I think it's obvious. I can't say what it is, a way they look at me, quizzically perhaps? I don't know. I've never had sex with a woman (not unless she was a sex change and I didn't realise). Of course I kissed a few girls in my early years – puberty! I never really felt drawn to any in particular, though I have found several beautiful, but in the way I'd say Naomi Campbell's beautiful, but I don't want to leap on top of her. I think gay sex is more inventive. I don't really know, because I haven't stood and watched a straight couple at it for hours on end, but from my own experience and what I hear, friends chatting – gay and straight – and from what I imagine, and believe me I've got a very vivid imagination!

It's a shame there aren't more films with gay leads . . . in mainstream films; it's always the male and the woman, with the odd exception. I saw *The Crying Game*, I wasn't fussed. It made the transvestite out to be so different, and again it was a straight guy attracted to her, as if to emphasise it wasn't the norm. I suppose I should be used to it after all these years, but you can't help but feel angry. I suppose anger isn't the right word, who would I direct it at in particular? It would just be nice for gays to be accepted properly.

Yes, which brings me round to the proposed change of age for sex between consenting gay males [it was lowered from 21 to 18 on 21 February 1994] – I bet it won't be 16! The Government is full of narrow-minded hypocritical has-beens. Plenty of them are gay themselves, but some are so scared to come out into the open. That makes it worse on gay people because they are making it seem as if there is something to fear from being gay, when there's not at all. It should be accepted as part of your ordinary everyday life, as simple as who makes the coffee in the morning. That's what it is. Who helps wash the clothes and do the shopping in your home? Whether it's a male or a female, does it matter?

Don't they realise that if they stood up and were counted and showed no fear, then the lobby would be stronger all round, and the same goes for musicians and other people in the public eye. Anyway, I will be sad if the age isn't lowered to 16, but surprised, no. They [MPs] are so out of touch with everything else that's going on in the real world, how could they be in touch with the nation's sexual preferences? I've been a practising homosexual since before I was 21, most gay people don't wait until then. I wouldn't be surprised if it's because they want more ammunition against gays, they want to keep the idea of being a practising homosexual something that has to be done in secret, so that it reinforces the idea that it's perverse. They aren't forward-thinking enough to bring in equality.

### Lisa M, 24, Surrey

Sex before marriage? Doesn't everyone? Usually only if I'm in a long-term relationship, but I've never really had any one-night stands. I have been on the pill twice, both with boyfriends of two to three years. Now I've split from my boyfriend I'll probably stop taking it. I don't know, I suppose I'd have to use a Durex if I did want to sleep with anyone new – if I ever meet anyone I like! But it does make things more awkward and embarrassing, and it's not always the most comfortable situation, is it? When I first slept with my last boyfriend, I have to admit I didn't use any form of contraception, but I was lucky. You never know.

### Ken L, 21, West End shop assistant

Who do I find sexy? Sharon Stone – she's well cool. I saw her in *Basic Instinct* and I'll definitely see her new one, *Sliver*. I go to the cinema every week in the winter but less often in the summer. It depends on films around. I go to all the hot movies – anything by Quentin Tarantino. Curiosity really. You've got to see the main ones to know what everyone's going on about. I work so near all the cinemas, and there's not a lot else to do. I go with my girlfriend or a group of mates and Monday is a good night, 'cos a lot of cinemas do a reduction.

I do pay for my girlfriend. I think she expects me to. It's true, I'm sure there are plenty of women out there who look at a guy's clothes and his car before they even entertain the idea of going down the street with him. Yes, that's why guys are so hung up about the way they look, and the car they drive. How else can you shine? They're gonna see your cool shirt and neat hairstyle, long before they get a whiff of your personality, eh? And even so, if there's a choice between you and a guy who's going to spend wads on her, then who would she go for? I don't have a car! But I can drive. I work in town and get a Tube, and my mates drive me at night. I don't always go out with my girlfriend. We spend time with other friends. I don't usually take her to clubs, either, she might get in the way! You need a boy's night, to drink and have a laugh.

### Beth, 24, photographer's assistant, West London

I always say I would never sleep with anyone without using contraception. I'm not on the pill and don't automatically carry anything around with me. Well, now I do, but I'm in a relationship. It's good because it makes you think twice before sleeping with anyone. Not that there are a lot of hunks around anyway! But, I have slept with a couple of dodgy people in the past and not used anything, though I had known them for years and really liked them, which is why I suppose I did it. I used to always use a condom even in long-term relationships. I hate the idea of the pill, you know, changing your hormone balance and all that shit. Once I took the morning-after pill because I had unprotected sex with a boyfriend at a bad time of the month – you have to go to your family planning clinic to get it. Lately, I've started to use a honey cap because it's natural. You keep the cap in a jar of honey which is supposedly naturally antiseptic. It sounds nicer than a usual cap, and I bet the honey tastes nicer than chemical spermicides and pessaries you use with the ordinary cap! You can't get these from your usual family planning clinic, you have to get them privately.

I am 90 per cent – well, 80 per cent – monogamous. I have slept with a past boyfriend on a few occasions when I've been drunk or out of it at parties. (Coke is the only drug I've ever taken, apart from smoking dope.) Yes, I have to say that I'd hate to think my boyfriend slept with anyone else or even went out with other girls while seeing me. I know I'm wrong, but I never set out to be unfaithful, it just happened (I know, several times!) but it doesn't change the way I feel about my boyfriend. He doesn't know. He'd probably be upset and leave me if he found out. I think you can like more than one person at the same time. I like them in different ways, they are both completely different people, I'd obviously put my boyfriend first . . . I think.

### Claudia Cassalli, 19, glamour model

I've been modelling since I was about 17. I kind of got into modelling by accident. I went to the Valbonne Club in London, and entered a Daring Denim Show. This involved walking up and down on a catwalk and being interviewed. I didn't get anywhere, but it was fun, and after the show a photographer gave me his number. I went back to the club a few weeks later and was introduced to another photographer who'd seen me and he got me some work. That's the way I get a lot of work, through photographers and other models – we all help each other out.

I model under different names. People just ask you for a name and you say what comes into your head at the time, though sometimes I use my own name, it depends what the work is. I've been photographed for many well-known magazines, like *Penthouse* – I'm in the current issue of that [November 1993]. I do like to see and keep the pictures when they appear. My father goes in and gets them for me – I can't go into a newsagent and pick up *Penthouse*!

I started doing videos and some live shows, which are fun. At first you think you can't do that, especially as there can be a crowd around when you're working, but you get used to it and enjoy the work. I've done shoots for Electric Video, appearing in their *Asian Babes (3)* magazine – though I'm not Asian, I'm of Italian descent! And I've been on their live roadshow which was a right laugh. You have to dress up in classy clothes and meet businessmen like people from WH Smith's who sell the products. You just wander round looking the part and chat to reps from shops. Videos involve a little bit of acting, it's more moving around and following directions rather than just keeping quiet and looking sexy for the magazines. The first time was really hard and I felt nervous, but you get used to it.

I really want to be a singer and make a record. That's why I got into modelling. I did try to approach a couple of companies early on when I was still at school, but I didn't get anywhere. I think that by getting myself noticed as a model, it will make things easier. I've always wanted to be a singer. I left school early to concentrate on my career, and got turned down a lot. It just made me sit down and think, 'How do I get noticed?' Lots of people used to say to me that I should be a model – I was big-boobed at the time. I couldn't be a fashion model as I'm too short, just 5 feet 1 inch. Then I started to look into the business side of the 'career'.

I used to go to drama school – in fact, there were three drama schools fighting over me at one point, though I prefer dancing and singing to acting. I have auditioned for a few TV roles, as I'd like to do some television work – it would be great to be in something like *EastEnders* – but what I'd like most is to make a record. I've been told I've got a good voice, but it varies, it can be very high and strong. I used to have singing lessons when I was at drama school – practising lots of scales to keep it in control! It's a very powerful voice. I've been singing lots of Whitney lately, that's the style of music I like to sing. I have got two songs of my own, my music teacher at school wrote them for me. The next step is getting a new demo tape together to send out.

I don't think too much about the future. You see a lot of 26-year-old girls who have a great body but they've been on the sunbed too often and their skin is all wrinkled. If you take care of yourself, you can work for longer. I use fake tan – although I'm naturally tanned. I still need a bit of help occasionally – like when you shave your legs you get pale patches and that would show in the photographs – it would look strange to be brown with white legs! You really have to take care of yourself. I suppose I do a lot of sport – I work out at home, doing exercises with home videos. I don't do classes. I dance a lot too. I love dancing. I dance at home – we've got big mirrors in the house, so on my days off I dance, to reggae and dance music. It's great because I can try new stuff and work up a sweat. It's a great way to get the body into shape. And I love singing.

I suppose performing is in the family. My mum was an actress. She was supposed to be going to Italy to do a film but she was pregnant with my brother, which kind of spoiled her chances a bit. So she ended up looking after the family instead! I inherited her talent, so I'd like to do well for her. My father and mother are great, I wouldn't be able to do it if it wasn't for them. My father comes to shoots with me a lot, he's always carrying my baggage and chauffeuring me around, my brother sometimes takes me to and from jobs if he can. They're very supportive and encouraging, but it is a strict family. I don't go out a lot, though I don't like going to clubs anyway. You get all the weird people coming up and asking you out, I don't like that. I want to go out and be left alone. I meet a lot of people during the day so I don't need to meet people at night.

I haven't got a boyfriend, I'm not looking for one. I did have one for a while, but he didn't like me getting successful. He really didn't like me getting anywhere, so I pulled myself together and it finished. I feel much better not having to get dressed up for him, it's nice to be able to suit myself.

I have to dress up during the day when I'm going to photographers. I get bored with it. I have a huge wardrobe of clothes. I buy a lot myself – though there are outfits at shoots, I take along my own, too. I've got lots of lovely lingerie, I spend a lot on it, over £1000 last year. I keep it for work, I don't wander round the house in it. And I buy with shoots in mind – guys like a lot of lace, elegant stuff. Round the house it's leggings and tops, but I do get dressed up when I'm going shopping, in nice clothes and stuff. I have been recognised. I came out in *The Sun* last month and went into the local Tesco's with my mum and there were so many people staring. I didn't have any make-up on either. Modelling has given me a lot of exposure. A reporter from the local paper in Bishop's Stortford came and did a piece on the local girl made good, and modelling has made me feel more confident and more comfortable about myself. I do my own poses now rather than just being told what to do, which a good model will do. My other ambition, apart from making a record, is to do a calendar. I've always wanted to do a calendar . . .

## Raven, 25, ex-maîtresse, South London

My search for sexual identity led me across two continents – at least! I was born in Australia. SM was very interesting to me for a long time, even before I left Australia, although

Australians were never really into SM. There was no information about it at all. There isn't really even a stockings and suspenders culture. Out there it's suntan and small bikinis as sexy clothing.

The only thing I ever read about it, like everybody must have, was in *The Story of O*, the most easily available book – you could even get it in Australia. I didn't imagine myself as O or in any other role, but I was fascinated, and I really did think that if SM existed at all, if anyone was doing SM, anywhere in the world, it would really be like that, all secret societies. It would be so organised you'd never be involved in it. Then I saw *Cruising* and found the real side of it for me. I thought you had to be a gay man to get into it. There's far more of an SM culture in the gay scene, with such clear dress codes.

I went to America in my teens and came across it far more. I did go in search of it . . . There were the bars that I'd sort of seen in *Cruising*, it fascinated me but I did think that it wasn't the sort of thing that people I knew would do, or understand. I never had fantasies about what role I would take. I didn't really understand roles, that some people were dom and some sub. The O scene seemed historical, it didn't have anything to do with modern-day people.

I took odd jobs and, while working in a restaurant, a waitress friend said she was really into it. She said she'd been invited to an SM lesbian orgy – my head nearly blew off. I thought it can't be happening to anyone I know; let's go. But it was in Chicago, I was in Washington. We never went, but she said to me eventually, 'If you're really into it?' I said yes. 'Well what do you want to do?' and I said 'Everything!' So we did.

We were never really lovers, I didn't really know what I was meant to do or what she was going to do . . . but it worked out very satisfactorily. It was nothing really orgasmic, just a fascinating couple of hours. Perhaps it was because I didn't really feel for her and in any other circumstances we would never have been lovers. We did it all by roles. She said, 'Here, you put this on,' gave me a petticoat and a role to act out. And I was thinking, what's this got to do with it? Beat me up or let me beat you up! I can't pretend to be someone else.

But we really got into being these two other people. The bottle of Jack Daniels certainly helped. So there I was, role-playing my arse off, but it was much better than I expected. It blew my head off for a little while.

I am gay, then not, then bi ... it's more to do with the other person. If someone comes along and they're a good person to be with, you won't pass them up because they're the wrong sex, or wrong colour or too tall ... Back in Australia, I was not out, but I wasn't having any sex, so it's easier to label yourself gay.

When I came to Britain it all fell into place. It happened as soon as I moved to King's Cross. I started going to a pub at the end of the road called The Bell, religiously. I didn't know anyone. I started seeing all these dykes in black with sharp haircuts, big belts and whips. I couldn't believe it. I'd looked for it a million times, then moved in, went to the bar and saw it straightaway.

One night, at an event at the Scala, I went up to some girl with a big fuck off collar, all jewels and spikes. We spent the whole night finding her girlfriend, but she invited me to SM Dykes, at the Fallen Angel pub, a meeting group of like-minded dykes. I only went to one meeting. That night we went to a club at Heaven – The Sanctuary.

I'd read a bit more by then, and understood about roles, sub and doms. I really thought it was such an organised scene, I'd have to start off as a submissive and learn the tricks. I thought you went in at the bottom and worked your way up. So I'm all ready to get everyone a drink and be good, but then some girl came up and said, 'What can I get you to drink, mistress?'

And I said, 'I'm OK right now, thank you,' probably the best thing I could have said. But I thought, 'Oh, no, I haven't explained myself properly.'

And that was it, I never did get to be submissive. I became dominant by virtue of there being a great many submissive people, and I was happy as long as they were happy. I just got better at being dom – and took on clients to make a living!

Clothes-wise, I started with Marks and Spencer's underwear, stockings, suspenders, high court shoes and over the top a leather coat, which I wore religiously to clubs every week. Then I went shopping for clothes. I bought rubber 'cos it was the cheapest and the most far removed from what I was wearing at the time. I think shoes are still my favourite fetish item – I've got tons of pairs! And a large collection of whips, ball gags, and masks, including one beautiful leather full-head mask given to me by a client. One of my clients made whips for me, but generally they don't give gifts ... I'm being paid to do a job, that's the relationship. Other implements include a dog bowl and funnel and plastic children's sword – the sacrificial sword. I've got prototype stocks – people are always leaving prototypes in my playroom.

Apart from baby oil, I use pepper oil, which increases the flow of blood to the skin surface ... and it smells nice.

I've had 35–40 clients, some I see once a year, some once a month ... Mostly male. I've seen women and men together, but the only one time I've ever seen a woman by herself, it was excellent, really interesting. That was quite recent too, only last year.

I don't know why this should be so. Perhaps for some women, submissiveness isn't as easily accessible for them in that way – they can't dress it up and stop it when they've come. Perhaps it's too much part of their lives, they have to answer to someone such a lot in ordinary situations? Or perhaps there are many women doing it within relationships quite happily.

Many of my clients are in heterosexual relationships, and many tell their wives/lovers. Of course, some don't! I had one woman ring me up pretending she wanted to organise something as a birthday treat for a friend. I said it wasn't the kind of thing I'd take on as a surprise! It was a client's wife. The guy hadn't told her that he was into SM and she'd come across a pile of papers, outfits and my telephone number. Sometimes they tell me their wife won't understand, but I don't know how much their saying that is part of the thrill for them – I only get one side of the story!

In one case I've got the husband and wife to talk about it and they started doing SM between themselves! A kind of Relate/Marriage Guidance Council. At first I thought I'd learn a lot about psychology from it, but now I don't know. The thing is, you never know when they are play-acting and telling you the truth. They just tell you what they want you to know, to keep up the image they want you to have of them!

I don't do much SM personally for myself, and until recently I hadn't been doing any at all for about two years. Then I became dominant once more. It's like any hobby, once it becomes your work, the pleasure dies. I've gone off most of the clubs, except Submission. I go there because the music's good and I like dancing, plus I know I'll see lots of friends. I've made great friends through the SM scene.

But I've got a new girlfriend and she's into SM; we've put a lot of research into it and found some costumes that we really like. She's made it all new and fresh again. I've been saved – against my better judgement, I'm back into the scene. I am dom, yet again, but that's more to do with my size. I'm so much bigger than her.

She's the reason I'm giving up being a professional maîtresse. I don't want clients coming into the home I share with her. I'm getting rid of the dungeon. Though there will be some people I'll still see – I've been seeing them for years, they're part of my life.

I meet most of my clients through word of mouth, per-sonal recommendation is always the best. If you answer those small ads at the back of contact mags you can pay a lot of money just contacting them all, and how do you know who's good or not? I have to work a lot on trust and so far I've never been let down. They come to my home, and I don't even have their address and telephone number, or know their real name!

They're free to wander round my home. But none of

them have ever stolen anything. At first I used to be more careful and have a long chat first, I'd have a long correspondence with them and get to know them and what they wanted, but it hasn't worked out like that. But I've never been let down . . .

They usually tell me what they want, either before we meet, at the start, or it will come out in the course of proceedings. They've come for a purpose, so they'd be wasting their time and money otherwise. Especially if you think that's why they've come to a professional because it's likely to be something they can't do or are afraid to try out with their regular partner, if they've got one.

I've never once been asked to dress up like a schoolgirl! Yet if you read the *Sun* you'd think that was the favourite British kink. I've had some pretty bizarre requests involving all kinds of role-playing. I'm really pleased when people make them up for themselves, rather than picking one they've read about somewhere. The clients are really in control, it's directed, they know what they want, though if they want that factor disguised, that's cool. Orgasm is the object of the exercise. If they came in the first ten minutes I wouldn't have done my job properly, though they may come twice in an hour, it depends on what they want. I don't mind actually hurting someone. I don't want to sound flippant, but if they want pain, I'll administer it.

Aids – some people are incredibly misinformed, and they don't want to wear gags, though they can't catch it from them. All equipment can be sterilised after use and one does keep up hygienic standards . . .

I never lie about my life as a maîtresse, I've plenty of friends not into the scene, but I don't always tell everyone immediately because I had one experience which was sad, from someone I thought would be understanding about it. It didn't seem to be that weird, to me, not *that* weird. We don't talk any more.

# **19** Crime, Police and Trouble in the Cities

It is pretty hard these days to conjure up an image of a teenage boy who isn't either breaking into a car, abducting a younger child, robbing a granny, or sitting hunched over a hot games console, foaming at the mouth, in preparation for any of the above. When we talk about crime, violence and the current fear that our young people don't know right from wrong, we are almost always talking about boys. (*Guardian*)

Slowly, a new consensus is emerging between police who acknowledge the link between crime and unemployment and teachers who see little hope for their pupils, often black and doubly-disadvantaged when they leave school. Privately, senior officers are sometimes scathing about the Government's apparent indifference to the plight of the run-down inner city. 'We can find the money for all these glitzy redevelopments, but not the cash to give these kids decent training and the prospect of work,' says one.

'If it was New York or Chicago it would be difficult to crack ... but here it wouldn't take too much to pull it round.' (*Guardian*)

## Lee, 18, Clapton, London

It's like being in *Boyz 'n the Hood* [John Singleton's film about street violence in LA] man. Y'know, all those helicopters going over the area all the time. Did you see that film? They say it's to help find kids lost in the park or to help on special searches, but no way, kids don't get lost in the park at 10 o'clock every night, and there can't be incidents in Hackney every single night either! It's just the big brother syndrome. It's kind of threatening. You think, what are they watching, is it me?

The LA riots are very important, we have to learn from them. It's like the battered wives issue – I like using similes, I do it a lot, so I'll compare the LA riots to a battered wife. Think, after all the years of being battered when she's taken it and taken it, she suddenly can't take it any more and kills her husband. She's tiny, he's not, but little as she is, she overpowers him and kills him. Now think of the LA riots. There's been 400 years of black oppression, it's not just one lady, it's not even just one group or a nation of people, because the problem's not exclusive to South Central LA. That's a drop in the ocean. It's going to be worldwide.

What happened in the States is going to happen here, there's no question about it.

Some people don't see it or don't think about it, but evidence is getting stronger. Those fascist demonstrations lately with the BNP – some of the guys with shaven heads, tight jeans and boots, came through the station and gave me grief. When you see it first-hand it's frightening. But the worst thing is the police walk alongside them on the marches, almost like they're protecting them. But even if we go to a rap jam, just because it's 90 per cent black, there are police everywhere waiting. We'll go to our jam, have a good time, there'll be no trouble whatsoever, and we'll come out and see all these police. Is that fair? Imagine how it makes you feel.

American crimes are surfacing here, too. Everything that happens in the States follows here. It's like car-hijacking. That's something foreign to us, but it's happening here now. When did it start here? It's not necessary.

It worries me when I see all the kids involved in crime and the gangs, there's so much anger and bad feeling. Some kids do it for respect or because it's the norm for them, but it doesn't solve anything, it's negative. One of my poems is about gang warfare and a guy who's been told by a gang to hold up a shop. He does and shoots by accident what he thinks is a little boy who disturbs them. When he gets home that night he finds his parents crying because his sister went off to get something for them and was shot. It's not far-fetched. I depict gang violence, but not glorifying it, showing how wasteful it is, and how people involved just don't think about the consequences of their actions. But at the same time, people don't think about what causes kids to turn to gangs or drugs, no one's dealing with the issues underlying it all. It's what makes people do things that concerns me, there should be an alternative for them.

There are loads of gangs in South London. You can see the issues and the influences first-hand, just by looking around you, like that 19-year-old who'd committed thousands of offences. He's from the 28s, a local notorious gang.

## Bobita, 22, shop assistant and voluntary worker, Medway Towns

I really want to be a policewoman. I've investigated the possibilities already. I do voluntary work at the moment and in December I hope to start doing community work with the police force at Rochester. There aren't many Asian women police, and I think it would be interesting work. Rochester has been having a recruitment drive, so maybe that will be a possibility. It will mean a lot of training. I don't mind that, it will be a career, rather than a job. I know a lot of young people have a bad view of the police, especially around Chatham – but the reason is because lots of young people in Chatham are on drugs, that's why they hate the police – they feel that drugs should be legalised.

## Jonathan, 24, served six weeks on remand in Pentonville prison

I can't speak for a hardened criminal because my experience is quite different. I really elected to go to prison, rather than having anything hanging over me – I was given a three-month sentence (for non-payment of poll tax) and served six weeks.

I could have been sent to Brixton – a remand prison – but was happier to go to Pentonville. Brixton has a very bad atmosphere and there are a lot of drug offenders, whereas Pentonville is an old-fashioned Victorian prison – quite an interesting building – and has a good atmosphere.

It was an interesting time – not pleasant. I met a lot of contacts – I even got a job offer, which I had to turn down! The wardens are not like they are portrayed, most of them are good, bordering on social workers. They're happy to chat and take an interest in other people. They talk to everyone and know what's going on and they're full of stories.

When I went in I got loads of books and read a lot, I did a lot of research and wrote. I did a BBC French course while there. I had all the time in the world and I've never been in that position before. All your meals are cooked, your laundry done, you don't have to do any shopping. Your time is planned out for you very effectively, so it's the best possible environment to study. I was surprised that hardly anyone seemed to read – there is a library but it's rubbish. There are so few books there.

They do have classes there for practical subjects – computers, art classes – but for me that's a waste of time. I'd rather learn something I wanted to do. I'm a student so it was better for me to keep up my studies. As it is, it put me behind quite a lot, not just the actual sentence, but the court appearance and time leading up to it. And then there was the part-time job I was doing. I'm lucky there's no stigma attached to what I served time for, so it hasn't done me an awful lot of harm in the long-term. They'll give me work again when it comes up, because they were satisfied with the way I worked, but they needed someone to fill in my rounds – I was a bike courier.

Before I went in I was told it would be all petty criminals, but that's not true. There were all sorts – everyone waiting for their trial to come up goes on remand and some were accused of serious crimes. I had the chance of meeting one of the top drug dealers in the world – he was there at the same time. I didn't meet him, but got to know all about him from the wardens. There were burglars, drug offenders, some there for murder, and an arsonist. There were some very interesting people. One guy was there serving nine months for contempt of court. He was a journalist and argued with the judge. The thing about contempt of court is that it carries a sentence of up to two years, and it's totally decided on the whim of a judge. So if he takes a dislike to you, you can get a long time, and you're not entitled to trial by jury. It's very personal and very unfair, as it's got nothing to do with facts, just his opinion. You don't believe laws like that exist in this country.

The conditions were OK. The cells at Pentonville are traditional old cells – just like the ones in *Porridge* – and I shared with another inmate. The wardens came round at night to lock you in. It was immaculately clean, because there are people who have nothing else to do but clean all day. You do get jobs if you want them. There are many advantages to doing jobs – but I didn't want to waste my time, I wanted to use it to study. You can wear your own clothes when you're on remand, though I chose to wear uniform. Before I went in they said it would be better to wear a uniform, but I can't see any advantage really. The food is crap, of course. It's institute food. I am a veggie so I was better off than the meat-eaters, but the Muslims were better off still, so I should have said I was a vegetarian Muslim!

I did hear of a few violent incidents, but I didn't see any. I wasn't aware of a 'system' or prisoners being picked on – it's not at all like *Prisoner Cell Block H*! But there was a lot of dealing going on, and although I wouldn't say the wardens were involved, there was so much going on that they have to be aware of it. Someone came round every day to get your order in!

I treated it as an experience. It does change you. It's obviously made me wary of authority. I don't know if I'd be as ready to go to the police as I would before, it depends. But being on remand is different to being a convicted criminal, you are treated differently. Though at Pentonville remand prisoners are on a separate wing, I can't imagine the convicted prisoners are treated much differently. As a remand prisoner I was allowed a visitor every day, convicted criminals get one a week – there are minor differences.

Six weeks was enough. I used the time well. People who are long-term criminals and know what prison's like when they premeditate crime, and know they have a chance of going to prison, probably accept that as part of the risks. I don't think they use the time wisely. If I had to do three years I'd learn something useful in that time, and spend all my time on it. It's surprising how few people do that.

I suppose they just accept loss of liberty as par for the course and try to be more careful next time. It didn't seem to put them off at all – the people I spoke to. It's not a deterrent.

## Glen, Canterbury

A lot of fighting goes on in Sittingbourne – too many drugs ... There's a new night-club just opened up in Sitting-bourne, JJ's, yeah, and when you go there, you've got to keep your face in the glass. You look at someone and they think, 'What you looking at?' and they're gonna start. As soon as you get outside or get thrown outside by the bouncers, there's going to be trouble. And, it's not fist fights any more, one-to-one. It's knives ...

I deliver pizzas three nights a week. I got pulled over once by a copper on a routine check when I was on my moped delivering pizzas. There were three of them and one pulled me over and said, 'I'm looking for stolen cars.' I said, 'This is a moped, mate.'

He went: 'What's this box on the back?'

'It's what you put pizzas in ...'

'Where you off to now?'

'I'm going to deliver some.'

So I had to get off my bike, hand the three pizzas to the coppers to look at, one each, like. 'Oh, yes, so it is, sorry,' they said. So I said, 'Here mate, here's a menu each,' and handed them all one. They tend to leave me alone now.

## Cam, 19, Gants Hill

The worst cops are the young lot because they are trying
to prove themselves. Every night they have to set themselves standards, how many times they pull someone over;
they've got to look like they're pulling their weight or
whatever. Perhaps they get more money for doing it?

Where I am, Gants Hill, I got stopped four times in a
week – they thought I was doing house burglaries. The
thing that made me laugh was that I was wearing a shirt,
tie, good trousers as I'd just been to work in the wine bar
and I thought, do I look like a burglar?

My friend got stabbed in the back and the bloke who
done it got a fine, that's like a slap on the wrist, that was
all. Does that stop him doing it again? Nothing got done,
so the geezer took it into his own hands and it blew up into
the stage of gangs, getting really out of hand, it got to the
stage where shooters were actually brought out; really
heavy.

## Phil, Chatham, Kent and Basildon, Essex

The main problem around here is that locals don't like
students. They don't like it 'cos students get more perks
than the locals. Students ain't liked by the locals here, nor
the squaddies . . . there are plenty of squaddies here. They
see us walking down the street – when you're a student
you'll see others with purple Mohicans, ripped jeans, whatever, you don't think anything of it, but locals think
'weirdo students'. They don't like it. Guys from the local
barracks – Chatham Dock barracks – drink down Rochester, stagger out, pissed, 'I'm a big boy, come on, pretty lad,
let's see how far you go . . .'

I left home, came to go to college, cut all the ties and
forget all the trouble I'd had back at home. I thought
Chatham was a quiet place. And it was fine up until Easter
when we had trouble outside a pub with squaddies. The
police are never around when you need them, so they don't

help us. They hassle you instead, pick on you for insignificant things, they think you're a student, you're obviously into drugs and dodgy dealings. But honestly, here I've never had dealings with the police, but I never see them around, so they can't help if needed.

I think police hassle young people because they're bored, and they do judge a book by its cover, as the saying goes. They see someone walking along with long hair, and police think, 'Oh, trouble-maker, hippie, drugs' . . . things like that.

It makes them look like they're keeping themselves busy and they're on the ball if they stop people indiscriminately. I've known friends who had six or seven 'seven-day wonders' in one night. He's been pulled up for the third time and tells them he's already had a couple of officers stop him, but they still give him a ticket and tell him to bring everything down to the station . . . Now he keeps them for the week and hands them all over in bulk. The police all know him and the car and know it's registered, taxed and in order, but they still do it. Why?

I got pulled over, when I had a nice car, and it got searched through for drugs and what-have-you. But that was by older cops. They didn't like it because a 17-year-old was driving a big expensive car. They ask inane questions like 'Whose car is it?' 'It's actually a company car.' 'Does the company know you're driving it?'

Then I've come across really nice ones and I've chatted to them after they've stopped me wrongfully to search for drugs and I've said: 'I'm not being funny but you stop me and you know I haven't got drugs, so why don't you go round to where we all know the drugs are dealt – Pitsea and the market area, where they're all skinning up.' But they burble away, say they're following other leads. Everyone knows where the drugs are dealt but the police are scared to go there. You never see a policeman wandering round that area at night, 'cos they'll get mugged. Seriously. People do have a go at the police.

Like in Basildon town centre, all you ever see are security guards chasing after little kids who've nicked their walkie-talkies. The police have got such a bad reputation now, no one's afraid of police any more because they know they don't do anything. So most people take the law into their own hands, which is bad in many ways because they think they're sorting it out, but it only causes more trouble.

That's the worst part, but the police don't do anything. Well, not the way you want them to. They give someone a slap on the wrist while you're walking away with a cracked cheekbone after being attacked. You can see why some people have got no respect for the police force.

## Tony, 21, policeman, Dorset

I've been a regular for two-and-a-half years, a cadet for a year. When I was 16, I worked in a bank – and managed to stay there for six months. I didn't like that. After that I went to college to do A level history, and then left home in Cheshire when I was 17 to join the police force as a cadet in Dorset. I was one of ten out of 400 applicants who got in, so I suppose it is competitive. It was a big bluff, really! The idea is that you will go on to join the police force after cadet training, but you still have to sit the exams.

I suppose I thought it would be an interesting job rather than exciting – I wasn't swayed by TV cop programmes, though when I was a kid I suppose I was. It's pretty much as I thought it would be, except the paperwork. There is so much paperwork.

It's really on-the-job training. You do 15 weeks at training school, you spend 10 weeks going out with your tutor, then it's on the job. At the moment I'm stationed in Weymouth, and the biggest area of crime we have to deal with is public order offences – fights, drunkenness, that sort of thing, largely I suppose from young people – as in under 30. It doesn't worry me having to deal with people my own age or older. I look a lot older than my age, but I suppose it's strange apprehending people your own age. Especially when you get called to a domestic with parents whose kids are your age, that can be fun.

241

I don't really go out a lot on foot – there are not enough people to go round.

We find some people won't go out on Friday and Saturday (even Thursday) nights in town because of the groups of kids on the seafront. There's nothing wrong with them as individuals, but as groups they are threatening, and some weekends we get large influxes of people coming down, usually for stag nights. There's a lot of stag nights in Weymouth. They have a lot to drink and there's trouble.

Then there are bank holidays – 30 May is a big one, the two bank holidays around that time, there'll be a lot of trouble due to more people. It's difficult to know how you will react when you have to approach a large crowd of people during trouble, and you're out-numbered – our training prepares us for that. It's difficult to explain, somehow you just do it.

We work a five-week shift system – about 40 hours a week. That's a week of nights – 10 p.m.–7 a.m. followed by six days off, which is nice, then four 2 p.m.–midnights, then two days off, then three 7 a.m.–5 p.m. day shifts and two days off, then three 2 p.m.–midnights and two days off, then four earlies . . . it alternates lates and earlies. The changing shifts may be hard to get used to, but it's useful for travelling abroad.

Being in the police force does affect my social life. I tend not to go out in Weymouth. I'll go to the night-club complex in Poole, and places further afield. If it's busy, it's good because you won't get recognised. If I do see someone somewhere who I've had dealings with, or if I get recognised, then I'll leave. To them you're still a policeman even if you're off-duty. To me, if I'm off-duty, I'm off-duty, though I used to live at the back of the nick and it was difficult to get away from it. Now I've moved somewhere quiet so you can try to forget about work. But even so, if ever I'm in Weymouth I'll always watch my back.

Being in the police force doesn't bring you respect – perhaps from older people, but not from kids any more – so if you're recognised as a policeman off-duty you'll get hassle, and then if I'm out in Poole and not recognised you'll get people pitching fights with you. No, it's not that bad!

Weymouth is very busy. In incidents per officer it's the busiest area in the force [Dorset], probably because it's got 10 nightclubs for such a small town and a naval base, which can be a source of trouble. We get people from Bristol and other towns coming down for the festivals and races. We don't have any festivals at Weymouth but we are seconded to areas that need us, like Stonehenge, for public order standby.

My ideal day would be spending half of it catching up with paperwork, have an hour meal-time, then do a bit of patrol work, depending on whose car I was in. If it was the incident car they go out more often.

The sort of day-to-day crimes I deal with are burglaries, thefts from cars – we've had a spate of those – shoplifting, though there's not too much of that at the moment. Burglaries are my favourite, I suppose – especially if the suspect is still inside! It's the investigative side, if you're the arresting officer. I have had one or two dangerous incidents in Weymouth, at the time you don't think about it. If there's a report that they've got a gun, you wait for the arms squad to come, you wouldn't tackle them alone!

I'd like to be firearms-trained to know how to use arms if necessary, but I wouldn't like to carry them on the street. I think having the armed patrol cars is sufficient. We have got a helicopter, one, though it's stationed on a hill and always misty there so it can't go up. I suppose how frequently a force uses its helicopters and their importance in surveillance depends on how rich the force is. Some use them all the time. Dorset is poor, though we have brought in a computer system, but if we need special equipment, like a helicopter, we'd borrow from a nearby force.

I suppose the only way you could change that and improve the efficiency of the force is to cut back on one or two of the upper ranks that don't seem to do a lot. Another welcome change would be to reduce paperwork. The Met. have a good system; they just write pocket-book notes, civilians take down the rest. We have to go taking reports from everyone, checking the scene of the crime. Generally, with something like a burglary, we get the reports and stuff done within ten days then it all goes to Dorchester in their filing system. If new information comes up it can be retrieved from there. Sometimes there can be a lot going on at once, like in the summer when the 60,000 population swells to 250,000 and the thefts multiply. But it's the same in seaside towns all over. My mates and I go to Newquay in Cornwall to surf and you can see the same problems there. It makes you aware of what's going on.

I do keep fit. There was a sports programme for the force drawn up – we have to spend one hour every five weeks on sport! What kind of programme's that? Besides, I've never had that hour! But our squad is sporty, we play badminton and go to the gym, so that's what I do, and I like cycling and running. I did a marathon last year in Poole – and made it – but I won't be doing it this year. It's the same time as the Tall Ships Race so we're not allowed leave.

I surf, too. Last year I surfed all year round, but this year I bought a house and I've been doing that up, so it's taken my time. But I do surf when I can, I tag along with friends who go. I didn't do it before I came to Weymouth, it's living close to the sea. In Cheshire I'd never have thought about it. Now when I take my dog for a walk I'll head for the beach.

Other interests? Music-wise, the squad is really mixed in what we like. You can see it when you go to the bar. I had a 21st birthday bash a couple of weeks ago and the records people were asking for were so different. I'm happy listening to anything reasonably modern, but not heavy rave – unless I'm undercover at a rave party!

I went along with drugs squad officers, two of us went, just to see there was nothing illegal going on and check the use of drugs. We didn't have to do much really except enjoy ourselves, and I did. I knew it would be good. It was a laugh. I went to my mate's house and borrowed some of his clothes – he used to be into raves. You get a free ticket, which would be £15, and expenses. In situations like that, although you're enjoying yourself you do keep sober, but there's not usually drink at places like that, and I don't drink much anyway. I did when I was 16 and working in the bank! I drank a lot then, but not any more. The only time I drink is when I'm checking out licensing offences and then I get plastered. That's the idea, you have to keep drinking to see if he'll refuse you!

## Mark, 20, policeman, Bournemouth

I joined the force when I was 17, as a cadet. I left home in Hampshire to come here, as Dorset was the only force taking cadets. I've worked full-time as a police officer coming up to two years. I've always wanted to be a policeman since I was knee high to a grasshopper. Partly because I wanted to help solve crimes, partly because I like dealing with the public, and partly because it's a secure job. I know, I used to get the mickey taken out of me for being too mature for my age, but security is important to me. It is as exciting as I imagined it would be, though before you get out there you look through rose-tinted spectacles and think you're going to take on the whole world. You soon realise you're not in a position to do it! But you can help. Even if it's helping an old lady across the road or apprehending a robber who could have caused someone grief. That's another aspect I like – the diversity of the work. I never know what I'll be doing until I come on-duty.

We work the five-week Ottawa shift (borrowed from the Canadian police force) which means we get six days off in a row. Although you're totally unaware of what's been going on in the preceding six days when you come back, and things change very quickly in the police force, it means that you're rested and your body's working better. I think it's a great system. Though there are plans to change it, after Sheehan had his say – so we're a bit in limbo right now.

Generally, fitness pays dividends. I'm still in my first two years so fitness training is incorporated, but after that it's up to individuals. I run, jog and do weights. I feel they should make it compulsory within the next five years to give officers fitness tests at least every two to three years. We were all taught Tae Kwondo at training school as self-defence and we're supposed to keep that up, training regularly, but between the force and private life it doesn't leave many hours for that. I practise on my girlfriend!

The police force does encroach on your private life, you even have to get permission to get married. Nine times out of ten they won't refuse, but if it's someone who may bring the force into disrepute they will, like a known criminal, not that that would happen. I haven't applied but my fiancé's a traffic warden so she's already been vetted. Yes, I did meet her through work – that's another perk of the job!

Generally the force comes into your personal life as much or as little as you let it. There are those who switch off as soon as their 10-hour shift has finished, but I take it very seriously. I keep thinking about what I've done, whether I could have done it better or if I got a good result. It's personal in that I take pride in my job, and also I have aspirations on where I want to go, and then there's the service to the country. It sounds conceited but I do love to help others.

A lot of people help the public in their work. We're only part of it, but you feel it personally, when you sit with a victim of crime, even if it's an old lady who's lost her purse. To some people that's not a great hardship, but to her it's all she had. Sadly, there's not always the time to spend with victims that you want. Demands dictate where you should be. This has been highlighted recently – how can the police force give more support to those who are suffering? We don't have the time to do it. That's where the victim support agencies help out.

Dealing with crimes does colour your views on people. You become very cynical. When I joined, my brother said, 'I'll give you three or four years, then you'll be one of the most cynical people alive.' But we deal with the one per cent of the population who are nasty and we see them day in, day out, so we do become cynical, but they say 99 per cent of crime is committed by one per cent of the population. You have to remember that, but then if we don't have dealings with the rest of the 99 per cent, it's going to taint your view.

I don't think I'm particularly caring. I deal with people the way I would like to be treated by others. But sadly we don't get much respect from young people – for a 20-year-old to be saying it, that's bad. They don't respect the job we do or what we stand for. It also means they don't respect or care about other people or their property or old people. It all boils down to parents' conduct and attitudes and how the young people have been brought up.

I had a strict upbringing. I come from a military family, and we were taught to show respect to others, especially older people. We do have community beat officers who go round the schools trying to talk to young kids and get to know them, and we all try to do our bit generally, but it's hard when attitudes are against you.

And it's not just from those who commit crimes. When you see children walking the street at night, their distate for us is obvious. We even get four- and five-year-olds telling us to F off simply because we've got a uniform on! We're trained not to show anger or that it's upset us, but it's not very nice. If they don't respect us, who do they care about?

You can see that the attitude is having an effect. Crime in rural areas is on the increase. I know Bournemouth is urban, but it's not like a vast built-up city with all the associated problems. People think of Dorset as a sleepy old county with a pleasant atmosphere, but crime in rural areas is increasing far more than crime in urban areas, and it's not just from city-dwellers who come in to commit crimes, then escape.

Being a holiday area brings other problems. In the summer period the population increases by 50 per cent and assaults on students are rife, thefts from cars and theft of cars increase, though we have a lot of car thefts at the moment. There are definite trends in crime. Theft is probably one of the biggest areas of crimes here at the moment, from shops, cars, burglaries ... Violence goes up on Friday and Saturday nights when you get drunken yobs.

247

I don't really go out drinking myself. I was 17 when I joined the police force and I suppose I lived that side of my life in the first two years. I moved away from home and was free of my parents for the first time. I thought, 'Great', and got it out of my system. Now, I live with my fiancé and having a bottle of wine at home with her, or going to a restaurant, is my idea of a good time. Also, every Friday and Saturday seeing those drunken yobs makes you wary of what happens when you drink.

There's the other side too. When you're policing, you do run the risk of coming across people you dealt with a few weeks ago and I don't want to put my fiancé in a situation that could prove risky or unpleasant. You can imagine, if you were recognised – and you are, even without your uniform – they'd say, 'There's that copper who nicked me.'

Even if they are crooks, if I came across people outside work, I still would only speak to them how I would like to be spoken to and I hope that they would return the compliment. But the fact is, the criminal faction don't have the intelligence to do that, which means we risk danger in our personal life if we come across some of them.

I haven't done a lot of undercover work yet, as I haven't finished my probation period, but I have sometimes sat in stolen cars waiting, ready to make arrests. I'd really like to work with the CID or catch criminals with the specialist squads, but I have to get the foundation and thorough knowledge of the law first.

At the moment I go out with the mobile patrol – panda cars, answering 999 calls and so on. I haven't been in too much personal danger yet, though I've wrestled with a shoplifter and found he had a knife in his possession when we got back to the station, which he could have slipped into my back . . . Every time you go to a violent confrontation you are aware that there could be a knife, you have to accept that, though it's not acceptable.

In Bournemouth, as everywhere, there is a marked increase in the carrying of weapons – though not firearms, that's the big star crooks you see in the movies. But knives are carried by a lot of them and every time you go to a call you have to think, 'OK, there's a risk of assault and violent confrontation,' but we're there to protect the public, that's part of it.

Police pay is good and means it will attract new policemen, though I didn't join for the money. I love my job, I never wanted to do anything else. But the pay is a bonus! At 18 I was earning in excess of what most 18-year-olds were earning. At least it shows the police force are finding recognition, via pay, for the job they do. It's nice, especially as I'm taking on more responsibility – a fiancé and mortgage. And we are supposed to be responsible people, it means we can work hard and play hard – though nothing illegal.

If my friends were doing something illegal would I shop them? I find I have to face moral issues every day. We are taught to look at things differently, to separate ourselves from the situation. It's like while you are at training school, they put a chip in your head and programme your head to think differently. I wouldn't be doing my duty if I didn't, even if it was my son or daughter, though there are obvious approaches you'd take.

It would depend on the situation, too. If it was soft drugs – everyone experiments. Though not me! It's funny because I'm the youngest on the squad, I'm just 20, and people think I've taken drugs and I'm in the know because I'm young. I'm often thought the best person to deal with young people – get them on my side, know how to talk to them and so on. But I find young people don't want to talk to me, they think I'm a turncoat, because I'm 20 and wear a uniform.

I can't win, because some older people think I'm too young to be dealing with them. They think because I'm young I'm not capable, but if I wasn't capable of doing my job, I wouldn't have been sent there. It's very frustrating! I just laugh it off. When I'm 35 I hope I still look young!

I am ambitious. I don't know whether I'd like to move to a big city. I enjoy the type of policing I do here, but I do want to progress up the ladder and if it means leaving the area to do it, then I will. Due to the size of Dorset, it's a small force, so there are limited opportunities, but I could go somewhere with similar problems, like Hampshire, Devon, Cornwall ... which have also got larger towns like Portsmouth and Southampton.

I am proud of the uniform, because it's part of belonging to the police force. When I go on duty I'll make my shoes shinier than a 50p piece, so I'm proud in that way. The hat isn't very practical – it's the first thing that comes off in a fight, so it's not exactly protective. But our chief constable is getting us better equipment. We were the first force to use batons – extended batons as opposed to the old truncheons, and another piece of equipment that's proved effective is the quick cuff, which works on the nerves in the wrist, so with minimal effort people comply.

I don't think we should carry firearms, there's no need for it – yet. But sadly, I can see it happening within my service. It's going to happen. At the moment if we feel they're necessary we call the firearm team of specialists, but there'll come a day when that's not enough. And that will be a sad day for the British police force, because as soon as we start carrying them as a matter of course, then so will the criminals ...

# 20 Politics

A total 13.5 million people, or 24 per cent of the population, including 3.9 million children or 31 per cent of under-16s, are living on less than half the average income. This benchmark is the nearest thing to an official poverty line.

In 1979, numbers below the line were 5 million people, including 1.4 million children. (*Guardian*)

## Louise, 21, Kent

I don't listen to any politics. I blank myself off from politics. I can vote here as I have a British and a Tobago passport – Mum's British. I voted in Tobago because it was a desperate situation and we needed to get a certain politician in, to stop the devaluation of the American dollar and other stuff, but I'm not into politics.

I have my own views on how I think the world should be, in an ideal world, but it's too depressing as it is. I watched TV last night and heard about the IRA bombings, watching coffins being carried, it's so sad. People get numb, so it doesn't affect them, but it saddens me, so I cut myself off in my own little world. I don't like the world I'm living in. It's selfish but it's the only way I can get through it. I take my hat off to people who will go and rescue Bosnians, and do their bit to save the world, but I can't. Perhaps if I lived in Tobago, I'd be saving whales and dolphins, fighting for immunisation of children and better education, saying, 'Look at this wonderful country, such resources, let's use them.' You can't help but get involved in such a small place.

## Carmine, 19, Essex

If I was earning a lot of money I wouldn't want to part with it ... so I might start to think more politically; I would look at the policies behind the parties. Right now

I'm not interested in money, and if you haven't got any, you vote for the people who are going to help keep grants or who do more for people who haven't any money, and it's clear who that is.

### Anraj, 19, Kent

I study economics at college. I think I'd like to be a lawyer. You do take an interest in what's happening politically – at least on the economic side. What do I think of British politicians? Margaret Thatcher was a great Prime Minister, she had great policies – she gave us a boost in the economy. I'm not saying I like Conservatives, but you must admit she did have great policies. She privatised everything and made us some money which she ploughed into the economy. And it showed, there was a slight boom in the mid-eighties, wasn't there? It's just a pity she didn't invest it and get the interest on it! I know there's a recession now. Major hasn't got her style, he doesn't know what he's going on about.

### Arfur, 21, skinhead, unemployed, Wokingham, Berks

I'm not into the politics. I don't vote. I live in a safe Conservative seat, so my one vote wouldn't change much (I live with my parents). The racial trouble you hear about is mostly not from skinheads. The areas where they (Asian people) live, Southall, Hounslow . . . there are hardly any skinheads.

### Shelley, 17, Bromley

My family vote Conservative, so I suppose I will. They seem to be the party for people like my family. I haven't really looked into policies, but I have had arguments about it. My boyfriend gets really argumentative, he's a social worker and into socialist policies. He's always slagging off the Tories, and my parents for voting for them, but I don't agree with him. I think he's just got too many ideals, his ideas wouldn't work. I told him: 'I haven't done too badly out of them and they've been in most of my life. I shouldn't knock them.'

## Jamie, 21, Middlesex

London has changed politically in the past few years – the eighties were very different to the nineties. It's not as monetary or malicious – a lot of people have had the wind taken out of their sails. My college isn't very political. People at my college would think about homelessness and unemployment if they were directly affected – if their standard of living had slipped, parents made redundant or lost their homes – but people tend to need to be directly affected to take action.

For me, the most puzzling political question is who *is* it that votes Conservative? No one knows anyone who has voted Conservative – or who voted for Maggie Thatcher before, but they got in again, so who is it that votes for them? Either it's older people or the very young – or, as I suspect, the people who voted for them won't admit it! If they are denying it, why did they vote for them?

## Neil, 23, NFA, Portugal

I don't believe in politics or politicians, they are a figment of a bad imagination. I prefer to look at things on each separate issue that's relevant to our lives. A lot of the issues they concern themselves with are redudant to the lives of travellers and squatters. And they don't seem to take into account things that are relevant to us.

## Clara Barnes-Gutteridge, 15, Stirling

I'm too young to vote at the moment, but if I could, I'd vote Labour as I really hate what's happening to the country under the Conservatives. I know a lot of my friends aren't political; it is a pity if people don't think and care more about issues that affect them, but if they don't share my views on Labour or policies then I wouldn't ostracise my friends. Most of my family are on the left, but they don't try to influence me in that way, they just want me to read and question. If Mum mentions a news story that I haven't picked up on, she's incredulous, she'll say: 'How on earth could you have missed that?' when most people my age wouldn't have the faintest idea about it. It's like a constant pressure to know what's happening in the world.

A lot of my schoolfriends never listen to the news and don't care whether they vote. I find I'm probably being too judgemental about people. If they aren't interested and don't know what's happening, I wouldn't be as well disposed to them. Having said that, I'm not at all judgemental about looks. I have a rule whereby I try not to be particularly biased about people just because I wear weird clothes . . . it doesn't affect the way I see them.

### Jonathan, 18, Shipley

I will vote in the next election. I'm a middle-class Liberal – that's the way I've been brought up. I couldn't be right-wing but I'm not active in any left-wing politics. Besides, there would be no chance of a Labour candidate getting in here. It's a safe Tory seat, Sir Marcus Fox has held the seat for a very long time, so voting Liberal is more of a tactical vote. Liberals are more likely to get in.

I'm not terribly political. I've signed an animal rights petition and I'm anti-furs and I take an interest in things like that. I'm a vegetarian but not a complete one because I wear leathers, so I haven't given up things like cheese. I don't see the point when I do wear leathers. If there was an acceptable alternative then I would wear it. I get second-hand army boots rather than new, though they're still boots and made of dead cow!

## Iffy, 22, Wandsworth, South London

Politically, none of the parties seem to have grasped the issues or have our interests at heart. No one does anything constructive. I did vote in the last election – Labour – the best of bad options! But I know if they got in, it's doubtful that things would change. It wouldn't help matters to set up a new black party because there is a majority of white people in the country. Besides, politics isn't won on just one issue like racism.

What it needs is a black working party within the party in power to bring up and deal with the problems. Black issues need to be incorporated within general policy-making – in everything. It's like education. I didn't think, 'This doesn't mention black history so I won't listen', it's just that if something doesn't apply to you at all, it doesn't hold your interest so you don't take it in, or feel you want to learn it. There has got to be a better way of teaching.

There is already a group, Panthers UK, in this country trying to emulate the Black Panthers in the US, trying to get black kids motivated and interested in history and other things. It aims to take them off the streets and away from gangs. Groups like that are very much needed.

## Andy, 21, Faslane Peace Camp, Dunbartonshire

The problem is people think it has got nothing to do with them, but it has got everything to do with them. And they think, 'There's nothing I can do about it, I can't fight the Government, so I'll just accept it and hopefully nothing bad will come of it.' But that's a defeatist standpoint. We have to try and do something. So what we do at Faslane is distribute information and keep the issues in the public eye so more people are aware and will try and throw their weight behind our campaign. Even if a lot of people don't join us physically they support in other ways.

It's not all young people here, it's mixed, though the

majority are quite young, just because young people are more inclined to think about peace issues and the future and want to do something actively to help.

## Hannah, 22, treasurer, Youth Against Racism

I've been involved with YRA since it was first set up in October 1992. A Belgian organisation called Blockbuster who were fighting fascism held a meeting in Brussels, inviting young people from 11 different countries. Around 500 people attended from Britain. I was one of them. That was the first rally I'd attended though I was active. I was involved with the Youth Rights Campaign before that – which had a charter of 12 rights for young people we wanted to help achieve. One of the issues was racism, others included the right to a job, to a home, and health and safety issues caused by concern about the YTS schemes. That was how I heard about Blockbuster.

It was such a successful demonstration that a core of the British contingent decided to set up an organisation to fight racism over here. It was felt we needed a permanent organisation to raise public awareness – and to co-ordinate training and events. We want to combat fascism and the rise of the British National Party in Britain. It's not in the interests of young people to be racist and if blacks, whites . . . all races unite, then far more can be achieved for young people and we can fight the British National Party together. That's what we aim to show. And we've had a very good reception among young people.

We spend a lot of time going around schools, talking to students. Response from teachers varies. A lot of teachers invite us in to talk to assemblies, but we have had one or two more hostile responses. These have been from headteachers who don't want to bring the issues of racism to the surface, because they are worried about the backlash. When this happens, we realise that there's probably a problem at the school and we've leafleted outside anyway!

The response from the students is usually good. They are

all aware of the racism issues and want to help combat them. There is a minority of young people who are racist, and that's usually because they believe the lie that the reason a majority of people won't get a job or decent housing is because of over-immigration. Then it's hardly surprising given what you read in newspapers and the line taken by the Government. But that is only the minority of young people; we find that most young people are anti-racist.

We get people to set up groups, the idea being that unity is needed to confront the organised groups who are fascist. We help groups organise anti-racist activities, so they can present a strong image. People are more likely to hear of events like our national demo but that's a small part of our work. Generally, the YRA is involved with day-to-day work, publicising the issues, and helping to unite people against racism.

We have no funding, sadly, though we do have a membership and they help collect and raise money for our work and we get support from some trade union branches and community groups. People are generally sympathetic, but sympathetic people don't usually have a lot of money at their disposal!

There's also the album we put out at the end of 1993 – *By Any Means Necessary*. We are into profit on the numbers sold, though we haven't had any money yet. We will get it. The album featured Björk, Jamiroquai and other young up and coming musicians, many of whom sing about racism and associated issues. We did feature Fun-da-mental and Marksman who preach black nationalist ideals but they also say they are for unity. We hope to get more black acts on the next one. We'd like to work with a few Asian or black acts who have made a stand against racism and aren't hostile to what we are trying to do. They don't regard us as white liberals, but realise we are trying to do something positive and practical. We are standing up against racism. There's more shelf-life in this one, but we have a lot of material, so there will be another album.

Our headquarters is in Hackney, the reason being that we wanted somewhere quite central to London and someone in

Hackney was prepared to let us use this space. We seem to have a lot of supporters in the Hackney area.

Four of us work here full-time, though we are all volunteers. We get expenses – travel and so on – but that's it. We are all actively involved. There are groups around the country – but we needed a heart for the organisation to do a full-time job. Eventually we hope that we will become stronger and be able to pay people properly. Although the base is in London, it's a national groups with supporters all over the country. I'm originally from Wolverhampton – though I've lived here since I was 17 – and I know it's not just an issue that Londoners feel. In the past year, you can see how more young people are trying to do something, more are becoming aware of us. We have thousands of letters from people asking what they can do locally to help, and we have 40 different branches working in areas around the country. The furthest north is in Inverness and there's one in Cornwall. We even get them in cities where there isn't a large black or Asian population, no local British National Party and racism isn't an apparent issue; people are still interested.

Apart from leafleting and raising general awareness, the groups give practical support; if people are suffering racist harassment we do take it up. If neighbours are doing it we organise a vigil in the area, keeping watch and stopping people putting windows through or causing a nuisance. We produce leaflets to tell other people in the area why it is wrong and enlist their support to try and isolate the people who are causing the trouble. That happened in my area, Walthamstow. There was a family on a council estate suffering harassment, we kept a vigil and leafleted and identified the family carrying out the harassment. It was just one family responsible for most of it. That family were transferred from the estate. In that case we worked with every other group in the neighbourhood who would help.

Our membership is mixed and varies from area to area. For instance, in Walthamstow, the group is mostly Asian. Around the country there are more white people as a whole, but generally it's mixed and I'm pleased that so many want to be involved. We seem to be attracting more and more people and getting more letters of support all the time. That's what we want, more people and more groups.

I'm sure the reason more people are contacting us is because of what they can see happening in Europe. They don't want to see what's happening in Germany, happening here.

# 21 God, Sects and Spiritual Encounters

A young vandal struck with an uncanny sense of timing as minister Robin Boyes was telling his congregation: 'God's spirit is in even the most badly-behaved child.'

As Mr Boyes was addressing his flock, they heard the sound of a brick smashing through the rear window of their minister's old Ford Cortina, parked outside his Unitarian church in Stockton-on-Tees. Mr Boyes said today that he was standing by his faith in God's spirit, although he added: 'I would like to get my hands on the little so-and-so who did this.' (*Daily Mail*)

The Rev. Neil Whitehouse (leader of the Methodist Group in the Lesbian and Gay Christian Association) said more than 100 ministers were gay or lesbian but hundreds more were thought to be barred.

The Church of England has ruled against the ordination of practising homosexuals, arguing that their behaviour falls short of the Christian ideal.

The Rev. Paul Smith, a Methodist minister in Manchester and a member of an evangelical group, said Methodists had never knowingly ordained a practising homosexual and surveys indicated that they would not agree to do so now. 'It's quite contrary to the teachings of the New Testament.'

Paul Blackman, a lay preacher at Southport, Lancashire, said his chapel was withholding collection money from central funds in protest against 'a conspiracy to stifle proposals' by traditionalists. 'We are not just anti-gay, we are against all sexual activity prohibited by the Scriptures, including adultery,' he said. (*Guardian*)

## Zebby, 22, musician, writer, Rastafarian, South London

I was christened Josephine and brought up as Roman Catholic in Hackney for 18 years, and then I got into thinking about religion and Rastafarians. I read the Bible and decided that was a way of life that really suited me. I took the name Zebulum Zakeyah. Rastafarians call themselves after Jacob's 12 sons, and the name you take depends on the month you were born. I was born in September so my name was Zebulum.

Everybody has those names, it doesn't matter whether they are male or female. I took Zakeyah to make myself distinctive. My friends all call me Zebby, but my mum calls me Josephine ... 'That's what I christened you!' she tells me, otherwise she doesn't mind about it, it's nothing to do with her. I'm the only Rastafarian in the family.

It's really an easy, relaxed way of life; easy to follow and I feel very relaxed with it, which I didn't with Catholicism. I read the Bible and follow those codes. I don't go to a church, I read and think about it at home. There aren't strict regulations on what to eat and drink, it's down to common sense and health. You don't over-indulge or drink too much. Many Rastafarians don't eat meat or drink alcohol at all.

It's also about history, black history, my history – which the religion I was taught in school didn't cover. It's more personal for me.

I tend to dress traditionally, just a skirt and a T-shirt over the top, and hair-wrap. It's comfortable. When I was in Jamaica, I bought some traditional clothes in beautiful materials, which I wear on stage. I don't think much of those sisters who wear really short, tight clothes and dance expressively, as you see in some clubs. It doesn't do much for our image. It's not helping them get respect.

It's an easy religion to fit into your everyday life. I'm comfortable with it.

### Mark, 22, Dartford, Kent

I went to Mass every single Sunday, and we had a Mass at school on Thursdays – a Roman Catholic school in Kent. I even got to be an altar boy and I sang in the choir for weddings and some Sunday Masses for years – until my voice broke. It was just part of life, you had to go, I didn't question it. I kept on going, right up until my late teens, going to Midnight Mass at Christmas with my mates, after we'd been out for the night. All my family and school friends went. I stopped going a couple of years ago, when I was about 19 or 20. I just stopped going, when I was brave enough to stand up to my father. I was working, not at school. I was earning, giving the family money, so why shouldn't I do what I liked? Of course, they tried hard to get me and my brothers and sisters to keep going (I come from a family of five) but they realised their hold over me was going, although I was still living at home. They still went – and still do, and they still go straight from Mass to the pub with their mates, that's almost part of the ritual. Hypocritical, really, when they try to blame the fact that I've been in trouble for drinking and fighting on the fact that I don't go to Mass anymore! One of my brothers is married with children, and he doesn't take them to Mass – or go himself. Though he is planning to send them to an RC school. I'm just amazed that I went for so many years – though if you met my old man, you probably wouldn't be. My folks are sad characters, they can see that the faith here is dwindling, although they and their crowd still go each Sunday morning, but it's obvious it's not as strong, and it will get less important in this area as each generation comes up. They were both born in Ireland (Cork) and are planning to go back there when they retire. They feel it will be friendlier and happier because the whole community will go to Mass. I think they're in for a shock.

## Clara Barnes-Gutteridge, 15, Stirling

My mum's Jewish, my dad isn't – he's Church of England, and my mum doesn't follow the Jewish faith, so I haven't been brought up to follow it. There isn't a Jewish synagogue in Stirling, so I couldn't go to a local one if I wanted – though I could get a train to Glasgow!

When I was little I used to go to a lot of bar mitzvahs

and felt left out, not knowing what they were all talking about, but as I got older I read a bit and talked to people and discovered what it was all about, but I don't agree with it. I imagine people around me think of me as Jewish, but they probably aren't aware of the disagreements in beliefs – unless they talked to me about it.

I have Zionist grandparents. They're very strict in their beliefs and have high hopes of me following in their footsteps and going to Israel. I'm not going to. I don't agree with what they say. They're entitled to their opinions, but there are great arguments and discussions within the family. They think Israel can do no wrong and that Palestinians are the enemies.

I do listen out to hear about the Israeli/Palestinian struggles. I think it has made me more aware of the issues and I'm more likely to pay attention to the happenings; because I'm Jewish, I've an interest in the history. I see things in the news and listen to my parents. I read newspapers avidly – a wide range of them to get different viewpoints, including the *Jewish Chronicle* which our grandparents have subscribed us to! I may not agree with it, but I like to read what's happening, and know what's being said.

At one point I got into the history of Judaism and decided to learn Hebrew – at eight. I did try for a while, but there weren't any Israeli teachers in Stirling, so I never got far. I suppose knowing huge lists of words and phrases in another language would have been quite helpful but Israeli's not among the most useful of languages to learn.

Now, I'm an atheist. I find it impossible to believe in any religion. I have come across others, I went to state schools – most people in Stirling are Protestant – and they had assemblies and end-of-term services in churches, but I was never forced to go and pray and stuff like that. I never closed my eyes during prayers.

I think my mum violently rejected a lot of features of the Jewish religion and has taught me to question things. My dad's not religious anyway. I don't want to have to believe or do this or that – which is a feature of so many religions.

If I was going to follow any religion I'd probably become a Buddhist or something like that – I'd explore different beliefs. But I don't think I ever will.

My lack of belief does mean I don't celebrate Christmas. We don't have a tree or things but I do usually get presents. This year I didn't want one. Why should there be a present for me, if the country is celebrating the birth of someone I don't believe in? I know a lot of people don't believe and still accept presents, but I think it's hypocritical. So I asked my parents not to give me anything, and I didn't give anything except I did give my younger sister a present, and my parents got her a doll's house. She can make up her own mind when she's older. I decided I didn't want anything, so I didn't mind. I got my friends presents too, but I gave them as a token of friendship.

### James, 18, student, Bradford

We're forced to go to a religious assembly every morning. It's a Church of England school. Very few of the sixth form, if any, have any interest in a Christian assembly. Why should 17- and 18-year-olds be forced to go along to something they don't believe in? We haven't put forward any ideas about a replacement assembly, perhaps investigating other religions – it wouldn't be well received.

### Anthony, 22, motor mechanic, Hackney

I belong to The World Vision for Christ church which is based in East London. My local church is in Hackney. I've been going since I was five. I went with my mum as I was too young to be left at home. She still comes, but if she didn't I'd go on my own now. It's part of my life. I keep my social life and my church life separate, though we do so much that there's not a lot of time left. I'm quite involved.

Saturday night and Sunday night there's the service, on Tuesday there's a prayer meeting, Wednesday there's a special for kids, Thursday and Friday there are prayer meetings and Saturday daytime there's an 'Open air'. Those are great. We go to places like Ilford market or Stratford shopping centre and stand and sing and tell about the goodness of God. Today I've been giving out leaflets. You don't have to, but at the end of the day, it's worth it. You're doing a job, not keeping the word to yourself.

We all get involved in the church as well. I play drums. I used to do the sound and still help out there, but now I play the drums. Brother Chambers (who founded the church in 1969) knows a lot about music and he and his daughter Alberta taught me to play. They first asked me if I wanted to play the guitar, so that's what I learnt first. Now it's the drums. I can't really tell what the sound is like overall because I'm not in a vantage point for that as I'm right at the front. I've learnt a lot through the church.

During the service brothers and sisters are called up to say their story. It's like giving a testimony. That's interesting. Everyone comes from different walks of life and we have our own story to tell about how we found Jesus and what it's done for us.

It's made me more confident and happy. In fact it's really changed my life. Looking back now on when I was at school and the people I go around with – some are in jail, some doing this and that. That could have been me. It's transformed my life for the better.

I don't feel I could have helped to save them by introducing them to church, because usually it's a case whereby I left and went to a different school. I went to three schools in the area and when I caught up with them later, I'd see what had happened. But now I do encourage other people to come along to church. When Judgement Day comes they can't say, 'I wasn't invited, I didn't know'– they heard but they didn't come.

I haven't tried any other religions, I have found the one for me. I've been healed and I'm proud. It's for myself. I don't know your feelings on healing, but I have tasted what it's like and I'm proud. Healing is not just a feeling, it's something physical. When I was young I suffered from nosebleeds. Call it coincidence, but one time I had a feeling

and from then I was healed. It was during a conference –
a teaching in Gloucester that I went along to. They're held
periodically. It's not just London-based, we have ministers
in Birmingham, Bristol and other places. I know initially
they concentrated on poor inner city areas because there
the need is stronger, and they went to Birmingham at the
time of the Handsworth riots.

At 22 I'm not going because mummy says to go ... it's
good that people ask themselves that question and go because they want to. It's like when I worked for a company,
and we'd ask an apprentice to do this and that, they're
doing it because they have to, the attitude is completely
different to doing something because you want to.

We also have tent services on places like Clapham Common and Hackney Downs. It's a service in a tent and a lot
more people come along. That's the idea. People who
won't go into a church may go into a tent. It was at Hackney Downs that I made my dissertation. It was in 1981. I
just said to my mum: 'I want to accept Jesus Christ as Lord
and Saviour.' She took me to a counsellor to talk it
through. All you have to do is to say, 'Lord Jesus, I know
I am a sinner' – you've got to get that in the open, to admit
that you're a sinner. Then I repented and it was all uphill
– well, on an even keel!

Our aim is to spread the Gospel, and that's what I'm
helping to do.

## Sharon, 19, school monitor

I've been going to The World Vision for Christ church for
about five years. I had been going to another church
around the corner and got invited along to a service.
stayed. I kept telling my parents how good it was, but they
thought I was a bit strange or something, they didn't believe me. Eventually they could see I was serious and
they've come along several times. At school, my friends
were the same, wondering why I'd spend a lot of time going to church – I did talk about it with them. Unless the

266

come along, they're not really going to understand. I feel we're really privileged to have this church so near and be part of it. There's a lovely atmosphere, it's very friendly and everyone treats you just like family.

The church was kind of nomadic – having services in tents and hired premises, like a Methodist church, before they got this building (a Pentecostal church) about two years ago. Now it's got its own atmosphere. It's just a huge hut to look at, but it's full of atmosphere, and great feeling when the service is going on. Visitors remark on the fact that we don't need candles and elaborate decorations to create the feeling, it's through the people and the presence of Jesus. There's a very special feeling here.

The school is held here too – I'm a teacher there now – a monitor, we call it. There are eighteen full-time pupils, about half belong to members of the church. They start at four or five and the eldest is 13. We'd like to teach them all the way through their education but we'd need bigger premises. We don't teach the school curriculum – but we cover the same sort of subjects with a lot more time spent on religion. Regular schools only have to teach one hour a week's religious instruction – and only half has to be Christian education (about 22 hours a year), which we feel is far too little. This church – and Brother (Albert) Chambers, the founder – puts a great emphasis on teaching young children. We have specials for children in Hackney on Wednesday evening and Brixton on Mondays when parents from the areas are invited to bring along their children for an hour and listen to Bible stories and enjoy themselves. There's a need for more specials like that, when we can find the premises. The young children are the future and if they know right from wrong and learn to respect God and each other then they're far less likely to commit such awful crimes as you see around now.

## Toby, 24, East London

I'm a Buddhist. I go to India as often as I can and regularly for weekends away in Britain for teachings and yoga weekends. I've got quite a few friends who share my attitudes and I go with them. I arise very early, usually around five in the morning, and meditate for up to two hours. I do a lot of yoga and breathing exercises too. Lately, I've started working again – after a lengthy period of unemployment – so I meditate again after work for an hour to de-stress myself. It's very beneficial, makes you a far calmer, relaxed individual, and clears your head. It doesn't interfere with work at all. Most people wouldn't know about my beliefs. You can't tell from looking at me, can you? It's not something I go on about, though I'm not embarrassed by it at all. If people express an interest or the subject comes up in passing then I'll explain things.

It's certainly not a materialistic belief, far from it, and no, it doesn't bring you material rewards. I've spent most of my life living in squats, and now I've graduated to sharing a council flat with my girlfriend! I've always followed the path I've wanted to and been very clear about that. I've spent years studying, keeping the brain active, and I've taken all sorts of jobs to keep myself together. But I've spent years living on practically nothing. I'm used to it.

I care a great deal for my body, what goes into it is very important. My girlfriend thinks I'm a crank because I have periods of 'strange diets'. There's nothing strange about living on just rice and bananas for a while to purify yourself. I don't drink alcohol, nor coffee or ordinary tea – herbal tea, juices and water, usually. Generally I'm a vegan, but I watch carefully what ingredients go into food, so I cook everything myself – no packaged foods and I rarely eat out. There's usually nothing I can eat on the menu.

### Tommy, 24, Manchester

I can't do drugs any more. For years I had a great time going out clubbing to raves and parties and getting off my face. I took acid but mainly E ... we always did; everybody. Then I had a strange experience – a spiritual experience, and it totally freaked me. I know it was a sign. I'm convinced it was a kind of visitation and it was meant to set me thinking, about my life and the world – the universe. But the thoughts are just too big to handle.

I don't think I had the experience to go out and become a preacher, but just to tell my story to people and let them start thinking about things.

I think as you grow up in life you start learning, but doing drugs speeds up the process, they start you thinking, open doors. I know too much, the kind of things we wouldn't normally know until we are on our death-beds. I don't think my experience was anything to do with drugs – it certainly wasn't a trip or anything like that, which so many people are bound to say. I could have handled that.

When you do an E or acid, anything you see is there already – it's part of what you are, but you haven't thought in that way before. That's why I'm scared to take any more drugs. I think that they've unlocked too many doors in my brain already – I need to have the carpenters in and hammer a few back on! I think too much and can't help it.

It's size. Thinking about the enormity of the planet and the universe. You can never see the whole thing, you can't see how special it is. It's like a sheet with a hole in the middle – you can see the hole when it's small, but when it gets too big you can't see the hole. That's what the cosmos is – it's too big for us to see, but it's there. If you start thinking about it, ughh, you just can't grasp the enormity of it. And if you think about yourself, your head and the millions of thoughts inside. Your head is just one infinite space – full of thoughts. And that's within the cosmos – an infinite space – but there are millions of heads in this world – millions of infinite spaces going around. How can there be room for so many infinite spaces?

I've never been religious, I don't believe in God as in a man with a long white beard but as the universe, nature. A lot of people kind of have a mad idea that to die and go on from here is impossible, but life is too complex for that.

I think that our next step is becoming part of the cosmos – perhaps a star, or planet. It's like in life we are probably up to level five as adults. We have been sperm, embryo, baby, child, and obviously we can't remember being an embryo or baby, some people can't even remember being a child, so it's not unlikely that we don't remember what we were in a previous life. And we don't know what we're going on to, but it's all part of this cosmos, we've got more levels to go to – six, seven, eight, and one of them is bound to be becoming part of the cosmos.

I also think that things happen for a purpose, no matter how hard they seem or unfair. They are there to teach us, to make us grow and to make us better people. Like if our ego is getting too big, something will happen to knock us, to show us how insignificant we really are, like splitting up with your girlfriend or losing a job or something, it's to make you re-evaluate your life, and show you're not in control of everything.

## Janet, 22, student

Unusual things started happening to me when I was four or five. They're my earliest memories of ghosts and spirits. It never scared me, I didn't know any different or think it unusual. I could tell if a relative was around who had died, like my grandma, and pick up emotions. When my mum tucked me up in bed, someone would play games for me with shadows and make me laugh. My mum would come in to see why I was giggling and couldn't see anything. In the beginning I wasn't really aware of it all, the spirits didn't materialise, but things would happen and I'd get the blame. Rooms would be messed up, that sort of thing. Then my grandma died and I was very close to her. I had a dream that she took me off to the place where she was living. I told my mum and told her all the names of people that Gran had told me to mention, people I'd never heard of before. My mum went through old photos and showed me some of the people I'd named and I recognised them. I was nine.

It was a really confusing period because my mum kept telling me these things never really happened and wouldn't talk about it. But, as so many things happen in life, by chance there was a woman living a few doors down the road, Mrs Lily, who was a medium. She had told my mum she had a psychic child who needed help and said, 'When the time comes and you need help, let me know.' My mum had three children and thought she had got it all wrong and ignored her. But then, my mum had had powers herself but never did anything about them, so was probably keen to suppress it, but mediums can pick up on things like that.

When I was 12 I started getting images of people and incidents from 100 years ago, and then premonitions of disasters; I'd tell my family things and then they would happen. I have the most sceptical family in the world and they kept telling me not to tell people about it. They thought I was losing it. The premonitions got worse and then my mum said, 'It's time to see Mrs Lily!'

She was a medium and I just talked to her as a friend. She really helped me. Apparently adolescents go through a testing time with mischievous spirits. She explained that when people die their spirits have the same characters as they had in life, so there are spirits that are practical jokers. That was what was happening to me. They'd move things and tease me. Once I felt hands push me down the stairs but there was no one there; that was out of order because I could really have been hurt.

Things always happened to me in the same area of the house. It was a hard time for the family. My brother thought I was possessed and wanted to have me exorcised. Mum and Dad thought it was the house and were set to move. But spirits are everywhere, it's a knowledge, there are natural lines of energy crossing the earth, but where the lines cross there's a strong force and spirits can make themselves known.

Glastonbury has loads of lines crossing, which is why certain spiritual people are attracted to it, but it doesn't have to be on a special site, it can be in an ordinary semi-detached like ours; anywhere lines cross. It's hard for me to describe. Mrs Lily took me to a Spiritualist church and they helped to explain certain elements.

If a normal spirit is at peace with themselves then they don't do anything, but some feel they have been taken too soon or, if they had a sudden death, then they can be restless. Also they say everyone has guardian angels, not angels as such but people who look after them. I had so many questions to ask.

I've never really been into the Spiritualist church, and I don't go now, but I went there for reassurance at the time, to see there were other people who believed this as well; I wasn't the only person it was happening to. My brother had studied RE at school and he'd ask me what was my belief. All I could say was I know what I know. I have to believe what I see. He said it was a cross between Buddhism and Spiritualism. He stopped wanting to have me exorcised and was quite interested in what I did.

I've never really taken an interest in other religions. My mum and dad aren't religious, though we're C of E if anything. The Spiritualist church gave me a few answers but I've never felt part of it enough to go there regularly.

As I got older, 14, I was told it was time to make a choice. The raw energy was very strong and I had to be taught how to channel it – you have to train to use the power at that age when the energy is at its peak. You could either use it for faith healing, being a medium – even in beauty therapy the power is in your hands, there's a natural ability there. But I wanted to forget it, to be taught how to suppress it, I just wanted them to leave me alone.

I do now feel I have wasted a talent, and once a year I treat myself and go to see a clairvoyant. Not to tell me what's going to happen – I don't think any decent clairvoyant should tell you the future in certain terms. I feel that can have a bad effect on people, as they make things happen. I feel there are different paths you can take and whichever one you choose determines whether things will happen to you or not. But they can give ideas, and it's good when they tell you lots of things about yourself and the past. One clairvoyant did tell me I would go back to full-time education. That was two to three years before I decided to leave banking. I didn't believe her because I needed the money from work and just couldn't see it happening.

It wasn't the case where what she told me swayed what I did, as it was years before I changed course. I only thought about what she'd said after I'd enrolled. It's nice when that happens, you remember someone telling you something years later. I'm sure some are only in it for the money. It's like anything – there are good clairvoyants and bad ones.

I've left it too late now to train to use my powers, but for years all I wanted to do was clock it. I still get feelings. When I go to friends' houses and different places I pick up on things. I can feel they are there, in my own way I talk to people and help them but my power will never get to be strong.

Whenever I was at home things would still fly round the living room. Not chairs and furniture, but I'd be watching TV and I'd see things moving out of the corner of my eye. I'd turn around and a book would be moving across the table. My family kept challenging me, but my mum has seen it happen and even my sceptical dad. I'm like a catalyst, it's kind of like a video-tape replaying the same incident over and over again. I know it sounds a bit Star Trekky but that's the only way I can explain it.

It's like my dad's experience. He always stays up reading late into the night. We've got a cupboard outside which used to be the coal hole and my father's dad would always shovel the coal in there. One night while he was sitting there he heard the cupboard opening and coal being shovelled in. He went out and looked but there was no one there, although he could still hear the coal being shovelled. It's as if that was replaying.

We're just sharing the same space with the spirits, but they're in a different dimension, and I know that most spirits are as oblivious of me as I am of them.

It's only recently that my family will talk to me about it, as for years it was swept under the carpet, and most of my friends know nothing about it unless the subject came up and they believe in it.

When I moved to Bethnal Green with my brother, we were told the circumstances of it being a quick sale. A man in his early 30s had lived there and died of a brain haemorrhage. He'd been ill for years and had died while in Tokyo, not actually in the flat. My brother said: 'If you feel any bad atmosphere at all, let me know, we won't go ahead.' I didn't, it was really peaceful.

After living there a month, I woke up feeling there was a man by my bed. It was if he was saying, 'Who the hell are you?' I was sure he felt hostile towards me, that he'd come back to his home and found me there, and I worried that he felt he'd died too suddenly and was angry to find people in his flat.

I wanted to make peace so I went to Circle – part of the Spiritualist church where mediums and clairvoyants get together to talk and help each other. A couple of top mediums came round to the flat. They said that far from being angry he was content, that he'd never had a sister and felt he should look after me, that I was too young to have left home, and that's what he was doing. They told me all sorts of things about him and explained recent incidents I hadn't mentioned. For instance they said: 'When you saw him watching you whilst you were in the shower the other day, you didn't feel threatened, did you? Do you know why?' I replied, 'He's gay,' which they confirmed. I don't know why, but I've got a thing about gay ghosts. I always seem to get gay ghosts!

And they told me he was in the Royal Ballet, which made sense. I had bought lots of mirrors from Ikea, intending to put them around my room. As I was fitting them I felt I had to put them in two rows along one wall. When I finished my brother said the room looked like a ballet studio. Apparently my room was where he used to practise dancing. He's moved books from my bedroom into the kitchen, done little things to show he was there which I hadn't thought about before the mediums came over.

Mediums don't come in and put the candles on. There's nothing spooky about it, everything happens in broad daylight, not like it happens in films, though many of the myths do have some truth in them. The flickering light and semi-darkness myths start somewhere. Spirits need to harness energy, so that's why the electric light can grow dim, or the room goes cold because they're using the energy from the light or heat.

I've rarely been scared by my experiences, though it got very frustrating when I was young. I was told that if you wanted the spirits to go away, you simply told them to go, that was how to deal with the practical jokers. I got cocky and used to shout at them. I'd feel people giggling at me while I was watching television and I'd tell them to sod off. And also I never got to see any of them in a body form – that would be too hard to handle – usually it's just a feeling or essence of the person. Once when I was younger I felt I would like to see them, and when I got fed up with this person watching me from underneath the table, I said, 'Show yourself'. It takes a lot of energy for them to make an appearance and they have to use some of my energy to form an image of what they look like. It was weird, it was like particles of dust joining in the air, but I got scared and said 'No, go away,' and it did. There's no holding crosses up or anything like that.

I never equate my experiences with religion. I know there is life after this wherever it is and people who come back don't seem that distraught. For me God is the force of nature, the force of the universe. It's awe-inspiring. The knowledge I have is as much as I have ever needed. I don't take on board everything the Spiritualist church says, and I'm not an atheist, I have got enough belief.

I don't believe in heaven and hell but I have come across things that are unbelievably evil. I don't mean a person with a knife, but a force. I have been in a room where an evil feeling I got has made me want to jump out of the window.

It was in my family house, my grandma's own room – a granny flat over the garage. I've always felt it was a hot spot for energy, you get the feeling of the dead. I've always run past the door – it's totally irrational.

It's always been cold, you can see your breath there even

on a hot day, it's against nature. I was told I had to go in and confront it, so I plucked up the courage and went in. It was so horrible, I felt a spirit so evil I ran out screaming. No one likes it in there, the door's kept locked now and the room's used for storage.

# Addresses

Bugs and Drugs, PO Box BS99 960.

Dog, c/o 32 Hill Road, Pinner, Middlesex.

Girl Frenzy, BM Erica, London WC1N 3XX.

Ground Level, Slab-O-Concrete Distribution, 37 Blake Street, Sheffield S63 JQ.

Herb Garden, PO Box 66, Leeds LS2 7XH.

Invasion of the Sad Man Eating Mushrooms, John Overall, Darren Jones, PO Box 7, Upminster, Essex RM14 2RH.

Skinheads Don't Fear, c/o 26 Hawkins Way, Wokingham, Berks RG11 1UW.

Something Has Hit Me fanzine, c/o 44 Lawrence Drive, Ickenham, Middlesex UB10 8RW.

Summer In The City, Andrew Harris, c/o 117 Southdale Road, Carlton, Nottingham.

Tighten Up Skinzine, c/o 1 Shah Place, Ramsgate, Kent CT11 7QD.

Travellers of the New Age, John Harrison, Monolith Publications, PO Box 4, Syston, Leicestershire LE7 42D.

Conviction, PO Box 522, Sheffield S1 3FF.

Travellers Aid Trust, 41 Littledown View, Great Dunsford, Salisbury, Wilts.

British Romany Union, The Reservation, Hever Road, Edenbridge, Kent TN8 5DJ.

Positive Youth!, 618 Philbeach Gardens, London SW5 9EB, Tel: 071 373 7547.